WILD
HIGHLAND
MAGIC

KENDRA LEIGH CASTLE

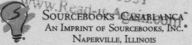

SOURCEBOOKS CASABLANCA™
AN IMPRINT OF SOURCEBOOKS, INC.®
NAPERVILLE, ILLINOIS

Published by Sourcebooks Casablanca, an imprint of Sourcebooks, Inc.
P.O. Box 4410, Naperville, Illinois 60567–4410
(630) 961–3900
FAX: (630) 961–2168
www.sourcebooks.com

Library of Congress Cataloging-in-Publication Data
Castle, Kendra Leigh.
 Wild highland magic / Kendra Leigh Castle.
   p. cm.
 1. Werewolves--Fiction. 2. Highlands (Scotland)--Fiction I. Title.
PS3603.A878W56 2009
813'.6--dc22

                          2008046863

      Printed and bound in the United States of America
           QW 10 9 8 7 6 5 4 3 2 1

For Madeleine, Connor, and Jack
You are my magic, and my heart

The Drakkyn Tribes of Coracin

The Dyadd Morgaine

A nomadic tribe of blood-drinking sorceresses descended directly from the Goddess Morgaine. Led by the *Dyana*, they roam the massive forests of the *Carith Noor* and are revered by the nonmagic inhabitants of their realm, the Orinn, for both their power and their beauty. Until the return of the arukhin tribe to the *Noor*, the Dyadd did not mate, and did not acknowledge the fathers of their children. Only one male has ever been born to a member of the tribe: Bastian *an* Morgaine, the brother of the current *Dyana*, Rowan *an* Morgaine.

The *Arukhin*

A tribe of forest-dwelling wolf shifters, once enslaved by a wicked dragon king, who long ago vanished from Coracin. Their descendants, the werewolves of the Earthly MacInnes Pack, were recently rediscovered in the remote Western Highlands of Scotland. Courageous and loyal, they have guarded the precious Stone of Destiny since the time of Saint Columba; that duty is now all the more urgent as the Stone was revealed to be the gateway between the realms of Earth and Coracin. The arukhin are the natural mates of the Dyadd Morgaine, and have re-formed a branch of the pack in Coracin alongside the sorceresses. The Earthly pack's Alpha is Duncan MacInnes. The Coracin tribe's Alpha is his younger son, Gabriel, who is mated to the *Dyana* Rowan.

The Athin

A tribe of powerful ice mages who once ruled the snowy Northern Plains. Legend has it that their High Mages could bend time and space to their will. Wiped out by a *daemon* plague, the isolated kingdom long ago fell silent, and there is no one left who can separate fact from fiction in the tales that have since sprung up about their gifts.

The Dragons

A tribe of dragon shape-shifters who vacillate between belligerent and terrifying, depending on which family, or House, is in power. Descended from the great god Drak, they inhabit the massive mountain fortress of Drak'ra Tesh in the impenetrable Black Mountains. Currently ruled by Kassius of the House of Arimnar, who won the right to rule after the death of one of the dragons' most feared kings, Mordred Andrakkar. Mordred's only son, Lucien, was captured by the *daemon* and vanished, and is now presumed dead. Mordred also was found to have fathered Rowan *an* Morgaine.

The *Daemon*

A fearsome tribe of flesh-eating sorcerers who inhabit the wastes of the Blighted Kingdom. Descended from Narr, god of night, they can't tolerate sunlight, excel at curses and torture, and prize pain above all else. The *daemon* are relatively weak, physically, but their skill at black magic has made them formidable opponents. Ruled by Cadmus for five hundred years, the longest rule of any *daemon* king. An exiled *daemon* and his Dyim lover created the Earthly vampires.

Prologue

Camp of the Dyadd Morgaine, Coracin

"BUT *WHY* MUST I GET UP, *AMA*?"

The boy rubbed his eyes as his mother gently lifted him from the warm, silken cushions on which he'd been so peacefully sleeping only moments before.

"*Sshhhhh*," Elara cautioned him, pressing a finger to her lips. The boy looked around the darkened tent that he shared with his sisters and heard the deep and heavy breathing that meant he and his mother were the only ones awake. Despite his fatigue, his curiosity began to be piqued. Though he never felt deprived of love, he was rarely singled out. Women held the power in his family, he knew.

But tonight, his mother seemed to want him for something. Just him, without his sisters. Pride and pleasure swelled in his small eight-year-old chest. Straightening to look into Elara's golden eyes, he gave a sharp nod. He caught just a flash of amusement in her gaze before she pressed a quick kiss to his forehead.

"Come, Bastian," she said softly, and with her humor already vanished, he saw the troubled crease between her eyes that was hardly ever there, except when Rowan had done something particularly bad. Like the time she'd singed off the ends of Reya's hair. Bastian grinned at the memory. He loved Rowan almost as much as he loved his mother. And his troublesome sister was excellent cover for getting into less-noticeable mischief of his own.

His grin faded quickly as Elara turned to lead him from the tent, moving with the grace of a goddess despite the belly swollen with what Bastian was certain would be yet another sister to run him ragged. He had been told that there would be no more boys; that there had never been a boy born to the *Dyana an Morgaine* but him. Sometimes that made him feel special.

More often it made him feel lonely.

Elara lifted the flap of the tent, and the two of them emerged into the moonlit quiet of the camp, with its dozens of high-peaked tents adorned with pennants that flapped lazily in the warm night breeze. She turned to look back at him only once, and the sorrow that flickered across her lovely face, just for an instant, gave Bastian pause. Maybe he didn't want to be the special one tonight. Maybe his *Ama* could pick a sister for whatever she was doing instead. After all, there were four of those and only one of him. And Lari had thrown mud at him earlier.

He opened his mouth to suggest a replacement, but his mother was moving away again, the fabric of her night robe shimmering like a ghostly beacon. Bastian shivered in his thin tunic, though the night was not cold, and ran on skinny legs to catch up. He was having *the feeling* again, the one he sometimes got before something really bad, or really good, was about to happen. It crackled all around him, like the sparks Rowan sometimes gave off when she was mad, prickling across his skin and making the tiny hairs on the back of his neck stand up.

He had felt this way the morning before his cousin

Marisin had drowned in the river. But he'd also felt it the first time he'd found one of the secret magic places, the ones no one could get to but him. The wonderful and the terrible, though no one else seemed to be able to sense either coming.

Somehow, he thought tonight might contain a bit of both.

Instead of heading for the Great Tent, which was Elara's domain, his mother surprised him by heading for the edge of camp where the striped *hershas* that pulled their wagons slept peacefully in the long grass. The two of them made no sound as they walked on bare feet toward the trees ringing the clearing that was the Dyadd's current home. Soon they would depart for another part of the endless forests of the *Carith Noor*, in the bright whirl of color and sound that was an integral part of who they were. It was their way. This Bastian knew and accepted. But sometimes, he wondered what it would be like to just... stay.

As the tents fell behind them, Bastian realized that he and his mother were not alone after all. Just at the place where the Silverwood trees burst from the ground, monoliths that stretched upward until they seemed to scrape the sky itself, stood a lone figure that looked more animal than man, covered in pale fur and hunched as though ready to pounce. Bastian's pace slowed, his feet beginning to drag as a sick dread coiled in the pit of his stomach.

Was his task something to do with this creature?

Elara, for her part, did not slow until she reached the odd beast, and only that kept Bastian moving. He refused to act a coward in front of his mother, whom he was fairly certain ruled the world—and not always benevolently. As he got closer, though, the fear eased considerably when the beast straightened. Bastian could see then that it was not really a beast at all, but a man dressed in a cloak of heavy furs who seemed to be relying on a gnarled staff for support.

The strange visitor was not truly young, Bastian saw, but neither was he extremely old. He had light hair and pale eyes, much like himself, and a face that bespoke both pain and nobility. His hair was clipped short, as was his beard, and his garments, though odd for the *Noor*, were obviously of rich fabric. He could be a king, Bastian thought with sudden interest. He had never met one of those. He could be a wizard or a dragon, beings that interested the boy even more. Still, he had no idea why it was so important that only *he* come tonight.

Then those pale blue eyes connected with his own, and the knowledge slammed into Bastian with a force that nearly brought him to his knees.

This is my father.

And right on the heels of that came a sick certainty: *my father is dying.*

Bastian stopped short, feeling as though all the air was being squeezed from his lungs. He had no idea what to do. His gaze darted, panicky, between the two people who had created him. Elara watched him intently, her fine features giving away nothing of her thoughts, though some inscrutable, intense feeling poured from her in waves that rippled toward Bastian through the darkness. And the man… his *father*… looked at him with a naked longing that both frightened and thrilled him.

This had been his dearest wish, his most closely

held secret. Though Bastian loved his family—mother, sisters, cousins—with all his heart, he had dreamed of the return of the only one who might understand the things he could tell no one. The only person who might be like him. He had wanted, so badly wanted, to know his father.

Yet now that it was finally happening, Bastian's heart constricted painfully. For Elara to have allowed this, when no *Dyana* acknowledged the fathers of her children, simply living and loving freely without attachment to any one man... and to see with his own eyes that the man he had dreamed of meeting would soon leave this world for the Higher Kingdoms...

Bastian's eyes welled with hurt and childish tears. And though he was ashamed at the display, feeling far too like his overemotional sisters, nothing could banish them.

The hard lines of the man's face softened. He beckoned gently.

"Come," he said, his voice deep and warm, though edged with strain. "Come to me, boy. I would speak with you."

Though his legs seemed locked at the knee at first, a faint but encouraging nod from his mother finally got Bastian moving. He straightened as well as he could, wanting to show his father that, despite his tears, he could carry himself like a man, like a warrior, and closed the distance between them. When he was only a step away, Bastian stopped and looked up.

"This is Adryn," Elara said, her voice soft and comforting music. She shared a quick and meaningful glance with the man before continuing. "He's..."

"My father," Bastian finished, scrubbing an arm across his eyes to wipe away the hated, yet thankfully finished, tears. "Yes. I know."

Adryn, who seemed almost as tall as the Silverwood trees compared with him, smiled. For a moment, all hint of illness vanished, and Bastian could see the man he must once have been. Powerful. Keenly intelligent. And somehow deeply, deeply sad.

"Smart boy. Though I would have expected no different." To Bastian's surprise, Adryn reached down and ruffled his unruly mop of pale blond hair affectionately. Then he crouched, with obvious effort, to speak to Bastian eye to eye. "Had I known about you, my boy, I would have come for you long ago, tradition be damned." The look he now threw at Elara was sharp, though it again softened as it returned to Bastian. "You are my only heir, you know. The last of our kind."

Worry and elation warred within him. Of course he wouldn't go away with this man. But maybe, if it were just for a short while, a visit might not be so bad. After all, this was his father. "You've come to take me with you?" Bastian asked, not liking the way Elara's lips thinned at his words.

"Of course not," she said, frowning at Adryn. "He is of the Dyadd, boy or no, and with his people he stays. I asked you to come because you might help him understand some things, Adryn. And because, quite honestly, I had heard your time was short. Tell him what you must, instead of filling his head with things that will never be."

She paused. "I had hoped this would never be necessary. But I didn't feel I had a choice. He is," Elara murmured, looking wistfully at Bastian for a moment before returning her attention to Adryn, "very much like you."

Her words stung him, though Bastian could see that Elara hadn't meant it as an insult. Not really. But it clearly wasn't a similarity that made her happy, either. And once again, the loneliness he carried with him always, that feeling of an impenetrable barrier between himself and the rest of his world, crashed down around him and left him in isolation. Bastian dropped his eyes.

Only to lift them again in surprise when a rough hand slipped beneath his chin, urging his eyes back up to a weary but kindly face. The sympathy he saw there was instantly soothing.

"Like me, eh? Well, you and I need to have a talk then. Man-to-man." He looked to Elara, who nodded.

"I'll leave you to it, then. But I warn you, Adryn. I expect my son returned to me shortly. Nothing good will come of provoking me." Elara stroked a loving hand down Bastian's cheek before turning to go. "All will be well, sweet. Listen to your father. Learn what you can. And then come back to me. Where you belong."

With a final, inscrutable look at Adryn, Elara was gone, gliding quickly away until she had vanished, as though she'd been nothing more than a spirit conjured by some trick of the moonlight.

Alone with the man who had fathered him, Bastian was suddenly shy. His mother, larger than life, had been a comforting shield. Part of him wanted to run after her, but he forced himself to stand firm. Whoever, whatever, this Adryn was, Elara had not feared him. So neither would he.

Adryn gazed after Elara until she was out of sight and then looked down at Bastian. Again, Bastian had the impression of deep and ancient sorrow before the man's lips lifted into a gentle smile.

"She always did insist upon being in charge. That was one of the many things that drew me to her. But even if she could have, I don't think she ever would have truly belonged to me." He sighed. "Well, you're young to understand that yet. Come. Let's go for a walk, you and me. There are things that must be said, and as Elara mentioned, my time is short."

Bastian nodded. Adryn straightened, his bearing becoming regal even though Bastian noticed that he still leaned heavily on the gnarled staff, comprised of whorls of some pale and unidentifiable wood, that he carried. Though Adryn's legs were long, the pace he set was slow, and the two of them ambled into the deeper darkness of the trees. Bastian could feel his father collecting his thoughts, determining how best to begin. So he was silent, watching tiny points of light flash and flicker in the distance as the wood sprites went about their business.

At length, Adryn spoke.

"First, I want you to know that I am sorry. The path ahead of you would have been difficult enough had you been properly trained. I meant it when I said I would have taken you if I had known you existed." He looked down at Bastian, pale eyes gleaming in the shadows. "The power we have is easier to bear when one is not so alone. Though we are always, in our way, alone. As I have been." He paused. "As you will be."

The words rippled through Bastian like ice, and he

shivered, though the night was warm. "I'm not alone," he protested. "I have *Ama*, my sisters. An entire tribe."

Adryn raised an eyebrow. "Yes, you do. For now." At his words, a cold breeze slipped around the two of them, shoving back the warm air as it coiled around them with a sinister slither. Bastian's heartbeat quickened, and the relative comfort he had felt with his father evaporated, only to be replaced by the first prickles of fear.

Fear… and for the first time in the forest of his home, the feeling of being watched by something darker than the shadows. Something that wished him ill. Something hungry.

If Adryn sensed it too, he gave no indication. He only continued quietly. "But do they understand you?" he pressed, and Bastian could see from his look that Adryn already knew what Bastian had always felt: that as much as he loved them, no, his family did not truly understand him. Not at all.

"Have you shared some of your more interesting talents with them?" Adryn stopped walking and turned to face Bastian. "Do they know where you go when they think you're off hiding? The worlds you have seen? The things that you sense, that you feel in here"—he fisted his hand and pressed it into his chest—"that none of them can? Do they know what you can do with water…?"

"Stop! Stop it!" cried Bastian, backing away, feeling as though the trees were closing in around him. "I'm not like you! I don't know what you are, or what you've brought with you, but I can't do anything! *I'm not like you!*"

Moving with speed Bastian wouldn't have thought possible for one so obviously ailing, Adryn lunged forward, grabbed him by the shoulders, and dropped to one knee, his face inches from Bastian's own. His weathered face was grim, and his eyes burned with feverish urgency.

Bastian tried to struggle, but the man's grip was unbreakable. Still, when he spoke, there was no anger. There was only terrible sadness in his voice, and love.

"Yes you can, my boy. We both know you can do those things, and a great deal more. And though I wish it were otherwise, with all my heart, yes you are. You are like me. You are the last of us, the great ice mages of the Drakkyn who once ruled the lands of the north and have now fallen to ruin. I have come to give you our legacy. And in so doing, I must also pass to you our curse, in the hopes that you will break it. That," he said, his mouth tightening, "or that you will let it die with you."

Bastian began to shake, again thinking of his mother, wishing desperately that she would sense his terror and come to take him away from all of this, to banish this man and whatever horrors he brought with him from the *Carith Noor* for all time.

"Please," he begged, hardly caring that his voice came out in a whimper. For all the time he spent trying to be a man, right now, he felt very much like the young child he was. "Please, let me go home. I don't want to hear any more." And somewhere close by, hidden by the trees, something gave a cruel, gurgling chuckle. This time, Adryn looked in that direction, and Bastian knew it was not his imagination.

Adryn gave him one hard shake, focusing on him once again. "You *must* hear it, or you won't even live to fight it. We are the last of the Guardians of the *Athin*, those who built their kingdom of ice and snow to rival all the jewels of Coracin. Now that land lies empty and in ruin, its people gone. Our magic is almost at an end, like so many of the Drakkyn who have destroyed one another over the centuries. And after tonight... there will be only you."

Bastian's throat worked furiously, but no words would come. At last, he managed only fragments of questions. "How? Why?"

The lines in Adryn's face seemed to deepen. "A curse, visited upon my father's grandfather by a *daemon* who had demanded that our houses, our kingdoms, unite. He wanted the High Mage's sister for his own to seal this pact. There was, in fact, some suspicion that this sister might return some of his feelings, though loving a wretched creature such as that is barely thinkable. But in any case, the High Mage himself, my great-grandfather, would have none of it. He told this *daemon*, Cadmus by name, that he would never let such darkness befoul the light of the *Athin*."

Bastian swallowed hard. He had heard of the *daemon*, of course. They were invoked to scare all the children of the *Noor*, Dyadd and nonmagic Orinn alike. But he had never seen one, thank the Goddess, and had sometimes wondered if they weren't just made-up creatures. Pale, hairless beings who walked like men but ate the flesh of other Drakkyn with their hideous teeth, who shunned the sunlight and wielded all the wickedest powers of *Narr*, god of night, who had fathered them in the days when gods and goddesses walked this realm.

To be told that they were real, and responsible for the ruination of one half of his heritage, was nothing short of horrifying.

"Cadmus, in his rage, cursed the *Athin* with a plague that, over time, killed them all. All but my family. *Our* family." Adryn seemed to sag suddenly, all the energy rushing from him at once. When he spoke again, his voice was reedy and thin. "As a special punishment to the High Mage, he cursed my great-grandfather and all his line ever after with a *narial*. It has passed through four generations so far, destroying them all… including me. I can no longer walk with it. So tonight, my poor, unfortunate son, I have come to pass it to you."

"I don't want it," Bastian moaned, the world tilting oddly in his vision. "I don't want a… a whatever-it-is. I want to go home…"

"It is a *narial*," Adryn said. "A soul eater. It will follow you through life, feeding on your emotions, sapping your strength, and isolating you from the things that would sustain you. Happiness, hope, joy… it will steal these things from you until your soul goes dark from despair. It will stalk you each night when darkness falls, draining you slowly until you would gladly offer yourself to it, just to end the misery.

"And had I not told you, when I died, it would have made short work of you without you even understanding what it was, or why it had come. I can't help you hone your powers, which I'm sure are considerable. Those, you must struggle with as best you can. But at least, this way, I can offer you some hope. Or at least some time, though I sometimes wish I'd had less of it."

Bastian's mind reeled, paralyzing the rest of his body. The night had started with such excitement, and now he wished he had hidden from his mother. Maybe then this wouldn't have happened, and whatever awful thing a soul eater turned out to be would have simply moved on and left him alone, no matter what his father said.

"There must be a way to make it go away," Bastian insisted. "Something you haven't tried. I don't know what I can do."

Adryn closed his eyes for a moment, as though wracked by a wave of fresh pain. Just when Bastian thought that he wouldn't answer him, though, his father spoke in a voice that was tight with strain.

"Our family has searched far and wide for knowledge of the shadow-who-walks. And in all of those travels, only a handful of information has been gleaned."

Adryn opened his eyes to look at him, and in them Bastian saw what bleak years of having all happiness denied him could do to a man. It shook him to his core, to think that this might be his future.

"The *narial* is pure darkness, the antithesis of light. It hates and fears all that is bright, all that is beautiful and pure. Its every instinct is for the destruction of such things. All I have learned tells me that to pull it into the light is to destroy it utterly. But though there are tales of great Drakkyn who managed such a thing in the distant past, we never found any evidence of how, or whether it was anything more than legend. A *daemon* could lift the curse, certainly. But they would only torment you with the possibility of freedom. And in any case, Cadmus must not know you exist."

Bastian could only stare, horrified. He was being left to deal with a creature that no one knew how to defeat? Given a task that a great tribe of mages could not accomplish? *He*, the odd and untrained only son of the Dyadd? Bastian's thoughts were a jumble of anger, resentment, and fear. He might be young, but he knew he was being robbed of his future as his father spoke.

"Stay with me, Father," he pleaded. "Or let me go with you. We'll find a way together…"

At the sound of Bastian calling him "father," Adryn smiled with genuine pleasure. "I wish there were time for us, my son," he said, giving Bastian's hair a final, affectionate ruffle. "But I'm weary, sick in a way that I hope you will never have to understand. No, my time has come. And you are strong, so strong, I feel it.

"Let the power flow through you, and you'll do just fine. You'll learn. And with luck, the blood of the Goddess running through your veins will help you be more than I have been. Stronger than I have been. But you must learn to be alone, Bastian *an* Morgaine. You must guard your emotions and give the *daemon* shadow little to feed on, little to inflame it. It will wound you any chance it gets, so don't give it an excuse."

Adryn's eyes went far off for a moment, the lines in his face deepening. Beyond in the darkness, not far from where they stood, a hideous sound reminded Bastian of a hungry animal licking its drooling maw, knowing it was about to feast.

When his father continued, his voice was soft, but his tone was grave. "One final thing, and it is of the utmost importance. For the love of all the Higher Kingdom, do not give your heart to another while the shadow still follows you. Love is the most powerful emotion there is, stronger even than hate. The *narial* lives to destroy it and will stop at nothing to take it from you, should you be so unwise as to allow yourself to feel it. The pain afterward, believe me, will be your undoing. Love, above all else, will destroy you."

Adryn shook his head slowly, looking as though he understood this intimately. "No. Better that you never fall in love, never take a mate. Never father a child. Because then, if nothing else, the curse will die with you without taking one more innocent life."

Bastian's voice sounded very young and very unsteady to his own ears when he spoke.

"I don't want you to go." Then a thought occurred to him, startling him because it was so obvious. "Father, maybe *Ama* could help! She has such strong magic. Maybe *Ama*…"

"You will not speak to your mother of this," Adryn said sharply, cutting him off. "She doesn't know. No one must know. The shadow follows you, but it will gladly attack anyone who strikes at it. Telling Elara would only endanger her and all the Dyadd. She thinks I'm dying of the same disease that killed the rest of my people, and that's best."

"But then why did she send for you?" Bastian asked, confused.

Adryn rose, looking down at Bastian with affection. "Because she knows more than you think she does about your abilities. And she also knows that you feel separate from the rest of them, that you're different from them. You may have the fangs and a bit of the blood magic, Bastian, and as I said, that may help your cause, though I don't know… but you are no Dyim. You are *Athin*. And as the last in a great line of High Mages, I expect that you will protect this tribe to your last breath."

He sighed, seeming to stoop under the weight of his burden, murmuring to himself, "But how does one protect anything from a shadow?" Then Adryn shook his head. "Perhaps, with the grace of the gods and goddesses, you will have better luck than I at solving that puzzle. None of the oracles I've consulted gave me any hope. Seek them when you are old enough to make the journey on your own… perhaps they can help you more than they did me."

Adryn's eyes cleared, and he shocked Bastian by drawing him into a quick, hard hug. "Take care of her, of the Dyadd," he said gruffly. "Never speak of the *narial* to another soul. It cannot walk in the light, so every day shall be your own. But at nightfall, you must be always on your guard. Bear the burden like the man I know you will be. And guard your heart, my son. Cadmus, king of the *daemon*, may sit on his throne for a thousand years more. I would have those years be empty of the pleasure of watching any more die from his wretched curse."

Adryn released him then, and the two walked in silence back to the clearing where the rest of the Dyadd slept, unsuspecting, in their tents. Bastian moved in a daze. He felt as though he had left the camp a child and returned, though he still looked outwardly like a boy of eight, teetering on the edge of being a man. Again, he wished that this were all a dream from which he would wake in the morning. But he knew he was going to have to accept that even in the morning light, his life had changed. His future had changed, and possibly been cut short, by something that had taken greater men than him. And after tonight, he would never see his father again. At least, not in this life.

Adryn stopped just short of where the *hershas* still slept, their great striped backs moving gently with each breath. All was peaceful here. But in the forest, something now walked that would change that, Bastian knew. At least for himself. And possibly for the rest of his life.

"May the Drak keep you, my son," Adryn said when Bastian turned to look at him. "The Drak, the Goddess Morgaine, and all the brightest lights of the Higher Kingdom. Whatever happens, know that I will be watching you. And that I am proud."

Bastian looked at him, feeling the weight of expectation heavy on his shoulders, and nodded. "Good-bye, Father," he said softly. "I'll try my best to stop this. I'll try."

"I know you will, Bastian." Adryn considered for a moment, then pressed the long white staff he carried into Bastian's hands. It stood taller than he did, Bastian thought, and his hands warmed instantly from the power he felt coursing through the wood.

"Go on to your mother now. And good-bye."

With a final, gentle smile, Adryn turned back toward the forest, which had gone black as pitch. Bastain backed slowly away, watching his father square his shoulders, take a deep breath, and then start away from him, walking bravely into some unknown fate. Suddenly, he stopped, though he didn't turn.

"Go to your mother, Bastian. You don't need to see this. Go." Then, as the air began to thicken with a malice that Bastian had never felt the like of, Adryn roared it. "*Go!*"

Bastian turned and fled in blind terror, careening through the camp without a thought to where he was going, staff clutched lengthwise to his chest. All he knew was that he must get away, must not see whatever might crawl from the darkness to devour his father whole. He saw nothing, heard nothing as he raced away. A gift, he would later realize.

And suddenly, like a dream, the Great Tent loomed before him, its billowing gold silk shining even in the absence of light. Bastian hurtled through the entrance, then toward the dais at the far end of the room where his mother reclined on a bed of pillows, reading from a small, embossed journal. At his entrance she looked up, a smile of pleasure on her face. That quickly turned to concern, however, as she got a good look at his terror and at the staff that he carried.

There could be no doubt about the finality of Adryn's visit.

Silently, Elara opened her arms to him, and Bastian quickly dropped the staff into the pillows before collapsing gratefully against her, not even minding the irritable kick from the belly he rested against.

"What's wrong, sweet?" she asked softly, stroking his hair and rocking, rocking. "Did he scare you? I warned him… I'm sorry, so sorry, Bastian. Tell me what's wrong, and I'll make it better. I swear I will."

Yes, he was scared, Bastian thought. But not of his father. And for the first time in his life, he realized that he was not going to be able to let his mother make it better. Because she couldn't. He was on his own.

"No," Bastian said softly as he rested his head on her chest. "No, he didn't scare me. I just… he's sick… dying… I won't ever see him again." His stammering lapsed then into quiet misery.

Elara sighed. "No. But I hope he has helped you understand something of yourself, Bastian. You're special, singular among us. Still, though, you are Dyadd.

Dyadd, above all. And nothing will ever change that."
Her voice hardened, and Bastian wondered just how
much Elara suspected about Adryn's affliction. But she
would never speak of it, he was sure. It was not her way.
But neither was defeat, he thought. And that gave him
some comfort.

"I love you, *Ama*," he whispered, clinging to
his mother as his exhausted body sought the refuge
of sleep.

"I love you, Bastian."

From a loving mother's hands came the magic she
knew he most needed: that of healing oblivion.

It was the last he had for a very long time.

Chapter 1

THE DUNGEONS STANK OF DEATH.

Bastian *an* Morgaine crouched low as he made his way along the dank corridors far beneath the Blighted Kingdom. Faint cries echoed in the distance, somewhere far beyond the small circles of light cast by the torches that lined the walls. Cries… and the sharp cracks of a whip.

The sound only served to bolster his determination to get what he sought and get out as fast as possible. And luck, it seemed, was on his side. Despite the distant noise, there was not a single twisted soul to be seen. Just a bit more luck, and it would remain that way until he reached his destination. The *daemon* did not take kindly to intruders.

Daemon. His lip curled at the mere thought of the word. The wretched creatures that dwelled in the desert of the Blighted Kingdom slept in daylight, much like the dark companion he'd been afflicted with for so many years now. But there were the zealots among them, those whose devotion to destruction and pain kept them going long past the hour when all others had lain down to rest. And he wasn't foolish enough to think that the one he had come for would be unguarded.

Bastian slid in and out of shadow, his pale blond hair glimmering when it caught the firelight, the gentle fall of his feet upon the dusty floor making no sound. And of course, the one time it might have been useful, the tortured voice that had so often filled his mind for many months now was silent. Still, he scented smoke and incense. He was close.

The bastard had better not be dead.

A low moan sounded just ahead, emanating from the dark recesses of a large, arched cell set into the wall, its inhabitant prevented from escape by thick metal bars that ran from top to bottom. There were no locks on such cells, Bastian knew, his heart thudding dully in his chest as he prepared to make his move. He saw no visible way of entering or exiting. And it was certain that the bars, if touched, would draw blood.

There was little the *daemon* loved more than blood.

Bastian inhaled deeply, filling his lungs with the acrid air to draw what little strength he could from it. He reached inward for the cold power pulsing at the center of his being and said a silent prayer to the Goddess Morgaine, mother of his people, that it would be enough. He had never tried to break a *daemon* spell before.

Just a curse. And thus far, his luck with that had been less than inspiring.

Bastian clenched his jaw as he thought of the thing visited upon his father's people, and then himself, by the creatures through whose kingdom he now crept. The *narial*, the shadow-who-walked. He had searched far and wide for an oracle who could help him, living only a half life for all these years. Everyone he loved moved on without him, not realizing that as long as he walked among them, so, too, did death.

Then he had found Aleuthra, the ancient, by the frigid waters of the Rythian Sea. And everything had changed.

He only wished her instructions had been less difficult to carry out. Or at least that they had required the assistance of one whose company was more palatable.

Still, he couldn't imagine that even Lucien, after a year of unspeakable torment, would deny him. He just hoped that the silence of the past few days didn't mean that Lucien's mind had finally been broken. If it had been, or if the man himself was hopelessly close to death, then Bastian knew that this year would likely be his last. And it was already half gone.

The groan sounded again, and this time, from the shadows beyond the cell, there was an angry hiss in response.

"Silence, dragon! I'm trying to sleep! I've never heard such whining, and from a creature I'd been told was so mighty. It's been days since you were bled. Shut up, for the love of *Narr*!"

Bastian paused, watching from a pool of blackness. There was a moment of silence from the cell, and then a choking cough that went on long enough that Bastian half expected to hear a death rattle at the end of it. Instead, once the coughing had subsided, a voice so thin and weak that it was barely recognizable drifted to his ears.

"Then just kill me and be done with it, you son of a whore. I'll shut up if I'm dead."

Bastian smirked, darkly amused by the prisoner's defiant tone. Lucien Andrakkar might be on his last legs, but he was still a son of a bitch. He should have expected no less from the shape-shifting sorcerer who had hunted him and Rowan across worlds before being taken by the *daemon* on the battlefield. It was bound to be less funny once they got out of here.

If they got out of here.

There was a low growl, more animal than man, and a figure stalked slowly into view. Bastian bared his teeth instinctively. The *daemon* was tall and slim, like all of his kind, with a build that was deceptively willowy. His skin was white, without a single hair to mar it, and Bastian knew that if the creature turned, he would see the red eyes and sharp teeth that marked the *daemon* tribe. With his back turned, however, clad simply in a gray tunic and leggings, the *daemon* could almost pass for a man. Almost.

This one, angry and half-awake, wasn't trying to pass for anything right now. And Bastian could only hope that he didn't take Lucien up on his offer.

"Damn you, dragon," the *daemon* snarled. "Don't tempt me. It is beyond comprehension that you continue to spout off with that wretched mouth when all it has ever earned you is punishment."

"Perhaps I grow bored with your punishment," Lucien returned, the weary tone in a voice once rich and full doing little to disguise the undercurrent of steel there. "My body is destroyed anyway, Dorgin. I can't even properly be called a dragon anymore. My ability to shift is long gone. Just kill me and do what you will with the useless carcass left behind. You're not the only one who is tired."

Dorgin turned just enough that Bastian could see the ugly speculation on his face. He bit back a groan. Leave it to Lucien Andrakkar to ruin even his own rescue.

A long and pointed tongue snaked from between Dorgin's blood red lips, licking them as he regarded his prisoner. *Hungry, of course*, Bastian thought. *Doing as he was commanded, but still hungry.*

The daemon *were always hungry.*

"I'm under orders, Andrakkar. Death is to be denied you at any cost. But perhaps I can bring you enough pain to take you under, to bring you respite from this place, just for a while. Shall I hurt you, dragon? Shall I make you scream until the darkness comes for you?"

Bastian had heard enough. It was now or never. And thankfully, surprise was on his side.

He dredged up all of his power in a wrenching wave, despite the fact that doing so was bound to leave him dangerously drained in his already weakened state. He had no choice; he would have but one chance to take out the *daemon*. Their command of dark magic was beyond any other Drakkyn tribe's understanding, and though their bodies were fragile, their power was anything but.

Surprise was crucial. One chance was all he would get.

Dorgin's head snapped around as he sensed the gathering magic, feral red eyes meeting Bastian's cold blue ones for a split second before a bolt of pure white erupted from each of Bastian's fingers and slammed into the *daemon*. Dorgin screamed in agony as the frigid blast of energy hit him dead-on—and with such force that the creature was lifted off the ground and slammed against the far wall as though he were nothing more than a rag doll. The shriek stopped abruptly when his head hit hard stone, and the lifeless body dropped in a heap to the floor.

Bastian emerged quickly from the shadows, fighting off the gathering fatigue that he knew would require hours of sleep to remedy. Soon, it would overwhelm him, forcing him to rest whether he wanted to or not. So time, as he well knew, was incredibly precious. If only it were over now… but that had been the easy part.

Fortunately, screams were so commonplace in the dungeons that he doubted anyone awake would even have batted an eye at the sound. But now he had to actually get Lucien out of a magically reinforced cell. And he had yet to understand exactly how such a thing worked. Hopefully, the dragon had a few ideas on that. It was a welcome shock that, judging by his responses to his *daemon* captor, a year of torture didn't seem to have stolen Lucien's wits.

But it had stolen almost everything else, Bastian realized with a sinking feeling as he looked for the first time into the cell and saw what had become of the sleek and dangerous Lucien Andrakkar, once a prince among the dragons. And for the first time since he had begun plotting this rescue, Bastian felt the dark bloom of fear unfurl its blackened petals within his chest. Perhaps he'd been fooling himself after all; maybe there really was no hope.

A man, or the remains of a man, lay curled into a fetal position in the middle of the floor of a small and barren space, no bed in evidence on which he might have rested. Naked, he was rail thin, his skin so pale that it was almost translucent. Bastian stared in horror, able to see almost every separate bone outlined sharply against what looked like paper-thin skin. The man's face was hidden in his hands, but what Bastian remembered as a sleek crop of ebony hair had grown into a dirty, matted thatch. This, though, was not what made Bastian question whether this trip had even been worth it, whether it might not just be more merciful to put the dragon out of his misery himself.

It was the blood that did that.

Bastian felt his gorge rise as he saw what had been done, sickened now that only moments ago he'd been thinking about the possibility of bartering this wretched creature back to the *daemon*. Now he understood the wordless shrieks of pain that sometimes seeped into his consciousness from the man who had turned out to be Rowan's kin, her half brother, trapped here in this forsaken place.

It was a wonder that Lucien Andrakkar was still drawing breath, Bastian thought, because his ability to heal himself had obviously been lost long ago, one of the last stages of weakness before death. And yet he was alive, barely. *How?* Bastian could see no part of his body that hadn't been abused, sliced into, gnawed on. Long slashes from repeated whippings crisscrossed his back and his legs, some of the wounds trickling blood even as he watched. And then there were the bites…

As though he sensed other eyes upon him, Lucien slowly, and with excruciating effort, raised his head to look at Bastian. His handsome face was gaunt, his cheeks sunken. But his eyes, at least, were just as Bastian remembered. Twin violet flames, still bright with a keen and dangerous intelligence. That, and an unbelievable amount of pain.

"You." He said it flatly, with no inflection to give Bastian a clue as to what he was thinking.

Bastian gave a curt nod. "Me."

Lucien spoke haltingly, carefully, but his speech was still slightly slurred. "If you've come to finish me off, I'm afraid I'll have to direct you to take your fun elsewhere. I've developed a surprisingly high tolerance for torture. Though you can kill me if you like… in fact, I rather wish you would."

Bastian shook his head. "No such luck, Lucien. I've come to collect you. If you can tell me how to open the door to your cage, that is."

Lucien surprised him by baring his teeth at him. *So much for gratitude.*

"Come to… as though I should be thrilled to place myself at the mercy of the Dyadd!" He snarled, eyes burning with impotent fury. "Tell me, Dyim, since you despise me and my kind as much as the rest, why is it so accursedly hard to just get someone to put me out of my misery?"

Taken aback by the vitriol, Bastian frowned. This was the last thing he needed right now. He was impatient to be gone while he could still use his power to escape. As he thought that, the world tried to go fuzzy, just for a moment, before he concentrated and managed to focus again and keep his head above the dark and beckoning waters of oblivion. But for how long, he didn't know. And damn him, Lucien stared as though he expected an answer.

Bastian threw up his hands with a frustrated sigh. "Humans call it karma. The universe repaying you for your deeds. None of them like it either. Now come on, Lucien. Tell me how to get in."

There was a baleful glare as Lucien lowered his head and turned away. "Go away, Dyim. I've paid for my transgressions a thousand times over in this place, so go happily. But go."

"No."

"Yes."

"No."

Lucien growled, and it was a decidedly dragon-ish sound. "I'm not interested in being your good deed, Dyim!"

Footsteps sounded in the distance, someone approaching. And whether or not they suspected that all was not right in the dungeons, if they got this far, there would be no hiding the fact. Exasperated, Bastian crossed his arms over his chest and stepped as close as he dared to the bars.

"Damn it, Lucien! Would you feel better if I told you this has nothing to do with pity for you, and everything to do with desperately needing you to help me do something you will doubtless *not* want to help with?"

There was a long pause as Lucien thought, and the footsteps grew steadily closer.

"Maybe."

"Tell me how to get you out, or your torture is going to stay the same old, same old, Andrakkar. If they haven't let you die yet, they're not going to."

Bastian gritted his teeth as again Lucien made him wait, lying on the floor immobile, as though dead. He might have actually thought death had claimed the dragon, had he not been able to see Lucien breathing. As the seconds dragged out, and the rhythmic fall of the footsteps drew ever closer, Bastian fought the urge to embark on a full-fledged tirade against the mulish prisoner. Was going with him really as painful as being tortured to death? It was infuriating, and more than a little insulting. Perhaps, Bastian considered, Lucien's mind hadn't been unscathed after all.

Finally, however, when Bastian was certain that the approaching *daemon* would come into view at any moment, Lucien saw fit to answer.

"Dorgin… that would be the charming creature you disposed of… always touched the center bar, right on the small symbol engraved there, and recited an incantation."

Bastian let out a huge breath as Lucien gave him the words, ones that had doubtless been seared into his memory forever. He moved quickly to repeat them as he touched the small mark etched into the metal, a serpentine shape coiled around an inverted cross. His fingertips burned at the contact, but it was at least bearable. And sure enough, after his repetition of the words Lucien gave him, the bars vanished into black smoke.

Thank the Goddess, he thought, his growing lethargy making his limbs heavy. Bastian rushed in and crouched beside Lucien long enough to scoop him up, wrinkling his nose as the stench hit him. Bathing obviously was not part of the regimen here.

Lucien had been starved to the point where he seemed to weigh no more than a small child, and despite his fatigue, Bastian lifted his wasted form easily. For his part, Lucien didn't try to resist, though his tone, when he spoke, was withering despite the weakness of his voice.

"My hero."

"Oh, shut up."

There was a sudden shout as the approaching *daemon* realized that something was wrong. Whether he saw the gaping hole where the bars to the cell should be or simply heard an unfamiliar voice, Bastian wasn't sure, but the measured footfalls instantly became a dead run. Taking a deep breath, he braced himself for one final bit of magic. They had to go now, before he was spotted. He had no interest in being hunted by the *daemon* on top of everything else.

One soul-sucking pursuer was enough.

"Hang on," he whispered. "We're leaving." Lucien simply rolled weary violet eyes up to look at him.

"And where are we going?"

Bastian tried not to wince at the thought of what he had planned. It went against everything he was, to betray the goodwill of those who trusted him. But Coracin was not an option, not for this. He needed solitude and privacy to try and nurse the ornery dragon back to health, things that were in short supply in the Dyadd's camp. And he couldn't risk staying in his own realm with the *daemon* doubtless searching for their escaped prize.

So he had laid his plans, imperfect though they were, and hoped he could resolve the brewing disaster that had been his life for so many years now before he was discovered. He was not prepared to die on principle, and it had never been in his nature to give in without a fight. Still, he didn't think this was the time or place to reveal to Lucien where they were heading. He doubted the dragon would appreciate, despite everything, that Bastian was taking him right into the lion's den. Or more accurately, the Wolves'.

"I'm taking you somewhere safe," Bastian finally said.

"Ah. Pity we won't get out of here alive, then," Lucien sighed, closing his eyes. "You haven't begun to see the worst of what they can do. They'll never let us get aboveground."

Despite the situation, Bastian smirked and gave a soft snort of laughter. Lucien opened one eye warily.

"Sorry, what part of that was funny?"

Bastian simply shook his head. The entire situation was ludicrous. How was he ever going to get this dragon, much less any purebred dragon, to allow him to drink its blood so that he could have the strength to destroy the shadow that stalked him? *"Willingly given,"* the oracle had said. And she'd been very adamant. *"You'll need it full strength, and as you well know, negativity mars the blood in strange ways."*

He sighed. *Strange ways, indeed.* But Lucien, the only dragon to whom he had any connection, was his only hope. He pictured his destination and gathered his remaining strength, allowing the magic within him to envelop them both, rendering them at once immaterial as air… and pushing open an unseen door into another realm.

Bastian only hoped he was doing the right thing. The MacInnes Pack had become like family, and he had no desire to break their trust. But who would think to go poking around a tiny cottage in the middle of nowhere? Who would even bother?

The shout rose to an angry scream as the *daemon* rocketed toward the cell, the very ground beneath Bastian's feet beginning to tremble with the force of the dark creature's fury. But it no longer mattered.

In a flash of white light, Bastian and Lucien were gone.

Chapter 2

"HEY, CAT. DID YOU NOTICE THE WAY THE AIR smells up here?"

Catriona MacInnes turned to give her younger sister a look. Since it was Poppy, she had a pretty fair idea of where this was going.

"Yeah, I saw the cows back there, Poppy. Thrilling."

Poppy rolled her eyes. She huffed one of the shocking-pink strands woven through her curly brown hair out of her face while Skye giggled at Cat's deadpan remark. Cat couldn't help but smile back. The way they were acting, her sisters seemed more like they were eight and ten instead of twenty-two and twenty-four.

Family vacations, she thought. *Guaranteed to turn grown women back into children in the blink of an eye.*

"No, genius," Poppy sighed, doing her best to look put-upon. "Not the cows. I mean the actual air! It smells like... like..."

Cat raised her eyebrows and tilted her head. "Air?" she supplied, a slow grin spreading over her face as Poppy nodded vigorously.

"Exactly! No stinky smog. No pesticides. Just grass and trees and moss and... yeah, there's definitely some cow." Poppy paused, scenting the air again. Her nose wasn't nearly as keen as Cat's, but she still did far better than the average human. Cat waited for her to finish, having picked up on the interesting fragrance as soon as they'd driven into the Scottish Highlands.

Couldn't have been able to levitate things, she thought, watching Poppy concentrate. *Or even read minds once in a while. No, Catriona, on top of the ability to turn into a giant dog, you have also been granted the ability to pick out, at a great distance, such olfactory delicacies as—*

"Sheep!" Poppy cried triumphantly.

"That's what you get when you don't shower," Skye muttered with a wicked grin.

Cat sighed, shifting her weight from one foot to the other and folding her arms across her chest. Normally, she would have been inclined to play with her sisters, who were obviously excited to be on vacation. But she'd been smashed in the backseat between Poppy and Skye all day, forced to listen to her father's copy of *Rubber Soul* until she wanted to throw herself through the windshield and hungry because, as usual, she'd overslept through breakfast. Currently, her patience was at absolute zero.

This trip was going to be worth it, or she was damn well going to kill somebody.

"If you two start poking one another again, I'm going to have to send you to your rooms," Cat informed Poppy and Skye.

"Hey," Skye replied, her eyes alight and her index finger suspiciously close to Poppy's arm. "Remember the time you locked Poppy in the hallway in nothing but her towel when we went to the Grand Canyon, and she got even by throwing all of your underwear in the pool?"

Poppy grinned widely. "Mom threatened to turn us into pack mules, remember?"

Cat laughed, her mood lightening despite herself. It really had been too long since she'd gotten away with her sisters. She hoped this time they could keep a lid on their inclination for getting into trouble. Although, as she looked at the women who had always been her partners in crime and recalled exactly how all their other vacations had gone, she wasn't sure how much hope she should hold out for that.

Not that this vacation wouldn't be fun, even if things did go as usual.

Picking up Cat's thoughts, as she often did, Skye considered the large wooden doors.

"They're probably going to hate us, huh?" she asked, her gray eyes narrowed skeptically.

"Oh, of course not," Cat assured her, brushing a long, silken lock of hair back behind her ear. But as she looked up at the grand, imposing facade of the manor house where her Birkenstocked, tie-dye loving father apparently had grown up, she muttered, "They might think we're white trash, but I don't think they'll hate us."

Skye snorted with laughter as their father knocked at the door once again, looking as though he was worried that no one would answer, leaving them all standing on the front steps until they went away.

"Dad, are you *sure* they know we're coming?" Cat asked, turning to scan the grounds, which rolled away from them in a rich shade of green she hadn't even known existed. Well-manicured lawns gave way to thick, inviting forest not far from where they stood. But there wasn't a soul to be seen.

Cat had a sudden vision of a group of relatives huddled behind a window, snickering at her family's consternation and waiting for them to give up and go away.

Frederick MacInnes gave her a surly frown, planting balled fists on his hips. "Of course I'm sure. I spoke with Duncan just last night. The pack gathering starts in two days' time, so we're only a wee bit early. He assured me it wasn't a problem."

"I think the problem is the forty years you didn't speak before that," Poppy muttered under her breath, low enough so that only her sisters could hear. Cat shot her a warning look, but inwardly, she was inclined to agree. She reached up to toy with the chunk of raw amethyst that glittered at her neck, willing it to do its job and calm her nerves. It helped a little, as her mother had insisted it would when she'd given it to Cat a few days ago. And thank God *one* of her parents was comfortable enough in her own skin to help out with a little magic now and then. It was just too bad, Cat thought, that she'd inherited a lot more werewolf than witch. Maybe if her abilities were more balanced, she could actually be of some help here.

Years of training, and she still couldn't divine for crap, but give her a full moon and she could wolf out better than Michael J. Fox had in that stupid *Teen Wolf* movie. She'd quit thinking of that as an educational video when her attempt to try out for junior high volleyball in Wolf form had resulted in a massive school lockdown and an invasion by cops armed with tranquilizer guns.

Total humiliation. Still, the memory made her grin. That was the day she'd discovered she was as graceful and fast in Wolf form as she was clumsy in her human one. She probably would have kicked ass at volleyball after all. Too bad fur wasn't an acceptable uniform alternative.

Just like it was too bad that her werewolf father hadn't shared her excitement about the discovery, Cat thought, her smile fading. Even after all this time, the man just didn't seem to want to deal with what he was and what his children were. That, more than anything, had caused her parents' divorce nineteen years ago. She knew that now. Still, she loved him. They all did, even her mother. But she didn't understand him, or any of this.

Hopefully, being here would help her figure it out.

It was crazy how much more alive she felt just standing here in the place her father's people had come from. The Scottish Highlands had always seemed like a mysterious, magical dream of a place to her. Cat breathed deeply, feeling unfamiliar but welcome energy shimmer through her body. She couldn't wait to explore this place. Something about it called to her and felt, strangely, like home.

A quick glance at her father, however, told her that not everyone in their little group was reaping the same benefits from being here.

He looks awful, Cat thought as she sneaked another look at him, distracted from her sisters' continuing good-natured reminiscing (now about the time Poppy had called animal control on Cat and Skye during a trip to a psychic fair in Philadelphia) by the sight of her obviously ailing father. He had always been the picture of health, but over the last few months, he'd looked more haggard each time she'd gone to see him, his stocky frame too thin and his complexion more gray than ruddy. The three of them—she, Poppy, and Skye—had discussed it at length, and they'd had to agree: something was seriously wrong. The kicker, however, had been the invitation to the annual MacInnes Pack gathering in the Highlands of Scotland.

Probably because up until two weeks ago, Cat, like her sisters, had completely bought the standard line that her father was an orphan. Oh, and that werewolves were freaks of nature. At least Freddie had genuinely seemed to want his daughters to come with him, Cat decided, taking note of the way he shifted anxiously from one foot to another as he waited. That was new. Though he could've handled the way he'd presented it to them a little better... as usual.

She taught first graders who were better at expressing themselves, she thought with a twist of her lips.

"Coming, hang on... coming..." A faint voice from within the massive house finally echoed to them, and Freddie turned to his daughters, his expression serious.

"Now remember what I told you, girls," he said, his voice soft but gruff and still holding a fair amount of Scottish brogue. "This is a big place, and you've barely been out of the city. I know you're adults, but you're also my daughters, and I don't want you running wild around here. The woods are off-limits at night, or you'll answer to me."

He looked around them, eyes wide as he took in what little they could see of the massive estate, shaking his head in awe. "Christ, it's even bigger than I'd remembered. Dangerous enough for a well-trained werewolf..." Freddie trailed off, looking away into the trees that surrounded the manor house, all part of the endless green of the breathtaking scenery that comprised this part of the Western Highlands.

"Sure, Dad. We all know how inept we are," Cat bit out, irritated at being treated like a child, and even more at the reminder of how lax her education had been in the fur-and-fangs department. It had taken her quite a few years to figure out how things worked… and amazingly, the police had only been involved a handful of times.

Cat frowned. Her father, lost in thought, didn't even seem to hear her.

The man was a complete waste of sarcasm.

"Smile, will you? You look like you're about to bite, and someone's coming!" Poppy's stage whisper drew her out of the brooding thoughts she normally took pains to avoid. Cat quirked a small smile in her sister's direction to placate her. She was going to have to hang on tight to her sense of humor to get through all of this… with any luck, it hadn't gotten lost along with Poppy's luggage. There was just so much to digest, and Cat knew, from the looks of this place, that she hadn't seen the half of it yet.

Being able to laugh at the weirdness was bound to help. It always had before.

Footsteps approached loudly from behind the door, and Cat fought the urge to fidget. She was a people person, always had been, which was fortunate since it made up for the fact that she was often falling into things: doors, furniture, other people, you name it. The first graders she taught in California liked her enough, at least judging by the sweet collection of handmade gifts and glowing letters from parents she'd accumulated over the past few years. But kids and humans were one thing. She didn't have a clue how she was going to do with werewolves.

Then the doors swung open, and all Cat could think was, *Make that* really big *werewolves.*

Everyone froze—the bedraggled crowd on the steps and the larger-than-life Alpha of the MacInnes Pack—taking drawn-out seconds to size one another up. Cat shifted her eyes quickly to her family, taking in her father's Grateful Dead T-shirt and Poppy's brand-new pink highlights (not to mention one of her stylin' Goth dog collars) and wondering what sort of a picture they presented. A quick glance at Skye, who gave her a pained look and shook her head slightly, confirmed it.

Oh God, they really are going to hate us.

Cat stared, amazed. Her father had always seemed so big to her, but her uncle was nothing short of huge. Well over six feet tall, with a massive chest and arms that looked like they could crush a normal man, Duncan MacInnes was every inch Cat's idea of a rugged Highlander. She knew he was around sixty, but he looked at least a decade younger, sharp featured and handsome with short silver hair and a close-clipped beard. He was dressed simply in battered jeans and a plain T-shirt in kelly green. And he couldn't have been more opposite of what she'd expected. She slid her eyes to her father, who seemed somehow diminished in the shadow of his vital brother.

Are these two seriously related?

"Welcome to *Iargail*, all of you," Duncan finally said, forcing a broad smile that didn't quite touch his eyes. Then his gaze slid to his brother, and whether because of Freddie's sickly appearance or just the memory of whatever had caused their rift so long ago, their host seemed to falter.

"Freddie, long time no... ah, good to have you..." He trailed off, his uncertainty over how to handle this creasing his brow and winning him Cat's sympathy in an instant. Duncan looked like he was torn between hugging and punching his long-estranged brother, which was a sentiment she understood intimately.

Scant details had been given about why her father had left this place, but knowing him, the original fight had probably had something to do with his chronic aversion to responsibility. She loved him, but helping her sisters through the baggage associated with being were-wolves—while he was nowhere to be found for advice or comfort—had long ago taken care of any romantic illusions she might have had about her father. Frederick MacInnes wasn't a bad man. But she was stronger than ten of him put together.

She'd had to be.

Between her dad fidgeting and Duncan glowering, it looked like she was going to get to be the designated grown-up today. Again.

"Hi, Uncle Duncan. I'm Catriona. It's nice to meet you."

Duncan's eyes, the same shade of iridescent gold as her own, shifted to her immediately. Cat was relieved to see them warm considerably at her introduction. His large and calloused hand swallowed up her own slender one as he shook it, and his smile was obviously relieved. Cat couldn't help but return it. He might be incredibly big and intimidating, but the smile went a long way toward setting her at ease. After all, anyone with so many laugh lines around his eyes couldn't be all bad.

"Well, it's nice to meet you, too, Catriona," he said

in a wonderfully thick burr that Cat had decided, just in the last twenty-four hours, was her favorite accent in the world. "Your name's as pretty as you are, though I wouldn't expect any less. You're a MacInnes, after all. Good-looking lot if there ever was one." His smile widened. "Even with fur."

Cat laughed, feeling a strange little thrill at being lumped in with the rest of the MacInneses, a group Duncan was obviously proud of. She'd never been much of a joiner… she'd spent too many years worried that if she made herself too visible, she'd be found out. She still had nightmares about the parents of her students running her out of town with torches and pitchforks. But the prospect of belonging to an actual pack, of being accepted by others just as she was, was way above and beyond French club or the dreaded volleyball team. This was important. And she hoped very much that they would all be as welcome as Duncan said.

Duncan released Cat's hand, looked at the other girls, and finally, almost reluctantly, turned his attention back to their father.

"Well, Freddie," he said, voice little more than a growl. "Are you going to introduce me to the rest of your family, or am I going to have to do it myself?"

Cat watched her father tentatively step forward, unconsciously wringing her hands as she watched the two men size one another up, wondering nervously whether the outcome would be a battle or a handshake. It was so odd, seeing them face-to-face. She could at least see the family resemblance now, though Duncan's physique looked chiseled from stone whereas Freddie had gotten soft in the midsection over the years.

She would also bet money that no one had ever told one of Duncan's kids that their dad looked like David Crosby.

But brothers… yeah, she could see it. Cat found herself holding her breath, hoping that whatever had happened to break their relationship could stay in the past for the duration of this trip. And that healing this breach would make her father well. She'd jumped at the chance to discover more of herself, yes. But she'd come here just as much for him. He'd seemed to want their company so badly. It was both wonderful and worrisome.

She only let herself breathe when Freddie's mouth slowly curved into a wide smile. He grabbed Duncan's hand and wrapped the other meaty paw around his brother's back to pull him into a one-armed hug.

"Duncan," he said softly, with a tenderness in his voice that she rarely heard. "I've missed you, brother."

Duncan's eyes widened for a split second in surprise before going suspiciously shiny, but Cat couldn't get a good look beyond that because the two men were slapping one another's backs hard enough to knock the wind out of a normal person.

"Missed you too, Fred. 'Course I have."

"It's good to be home, Duncan," Freddie said, drawing back to look at his brother's face and chuckling. "Christ, you've gotten old."

The reply was an inelegant snort. "And you've gotten old and fat." Duncan grinned, though, and Freddie gave a loud, booming laugh that made Cat's breath catch in her throat. It was the sound of her favorite childhood memories, before her parents had split and everything started to go to hell beneath every full moon. It was a sound she heard all too rarely these days.

"Been far too long," Freddie said when the laughter had subsided, a wistful tone creeping into his voice.

"Well," replied Duncan, dropping his eyes to the ground and stepping away, his smile becoming strained. "Well. Better late than never, Fred. Better late than never."

Freddie gave Duncan one last clap on the shoulder, looking as though he was struggling with what to say. Finally, he managed, "About when I left…"

But that topic, it seemed, was off-limits for now. Cat didn't miss the way Duncan's jaw tightened right before he cut Freddie off.

"Time enough for that later," Duncan interrupted, waving his hand dismissively. "It's waited this long, after all." There was an unmistakable hint of bitterness in the wonderfully rich voice, and Cat wondered again what could have happened between the brothers to cause a forty-year estrangement. Duncan, however, wasn't going to give her time to ponder it.

"So," her uncle said, settling his hands on his hips and puffing out his chest, looking a bit like a general surveying his troops. "It seems I am going to have to introduce myself, after all." He then turned his attention to her sisters, doing his best to charm each of them as he got their names and shook their hands in turn.

"Poppy! I'd never thought of wearing a collar, myself, but it does look lovely on you."

"Skye, eh? Not a Mary or a Jane in the bunch, is there?"

Cat had to hand it to her uncle: he was good. The

man teased, complimented, winked, and smiled his way into both her and her sisters' good graces in very short order. When that was done, he eyed the trunk of the rental car, which they hadn't quite been able to close properly because of the luggage. Or more specifically, because of the large suitcase of shoes that the girls had been prepared to mutiny over if it had not been allowed to come.

"Hmm. Well, let's get you all, ah, situated, then," Duncan said, still staring at the overstuffed little car with extreme apprehension. "Go on inside, and your dad and I will get the bags. Go on, make yourselves at home. We'll be right along."

The three of them filed into the entry hall and lapsed into wondering silence. It was, Cat decided, like stepping from one time into another. Like visiting a museum, but better, because people actually lived here.

Her people.

"God, this is cool," she murmured.

Light poured in the front windows to reflect off the grandly curved marble staircase and illuminate the high ceiling, which was painted with a mural depicting fantastic creatures romping beneath a rising moon. Art, mostly paintings of rustic scenes from a hundred years ago that looked old and very expensive, covered the walls. An array of antique knickknacks in bright bursts of color winked and peeked at the sisters from gleaming cherrywood tables and shelves all around them. It was like wandering into Mr. Darcy's Pemberley, Cat thought, thoroughly enchanted as she craned her neck to take in everything.

Iargail. Twilight, her father had told her it

meant. And the seat of the MacInnes Pack since time immemorial.

Poppy gave a low whistle. "We need to make friends with this branch of the family, obviously."

Cat grinned. "No problem. And if Colin Firth actually lives here, I'm never leaving."

Skye quirked an eyebrow at her, tucking thick and wavy ash-brown hair behind her ears. "Only if you win in the steel-cage death match I have planned for just such an eventuality."

Cat put up her fists playfully. "Okay. But I'll really hate having to kill you."

Duncan and Freddie joined them then, grappling with the suitcases. Cat felt a momentary twinge of guilt when she saw that the suitcase of shoes appeared to be causing the most trouble, possibly because the numerous high heels within had deformed its shape and made the handle tough to grab. Plus, from what she remembered, the suitcase was really freaking heavy. Fortunately, it didn't appear to be bothering Duncan, who was lugging it.

"Why did you all pack so many rocks?" Duncan asked, eyes crinkling. "Plenty of those here already. Come on, then, let's head upstairs and I'll show you…"

Cat let Duncan's good-natured ramble fade into the background as she took another look around, in awe of the beauty of this place. Rich werewolf relatives, she thought with a smile. Who would have thought? Her nerves were rapidly being replaced by a keen interest in her surroundings, which she knew she was going to have to watch out for. Her tendency to throw caution to the wind in favor of exploration of the new had gotten her in trouble more than once. Still, she'd felt a connection right away with her big, gregarious uncle. Tomorrow or the next day, she had every intention of cornering him with the list of questions she'd been drawing up since her first Change. This place made her want to know all there was to know about her Wolf half so badly that she ached.

Maybe the knowledge in this place could heal them all.

Cat turned her head toward the back of the house, eyes sweeping the room casually as she thought, but not looking anywhere in particular. A flash of movement at the corner of her eye drew her gaze instantly to a tall, rangy figure that had just emerged from a doorway. He had stopped dead to stare at the lot of them, looking as though he had just taken a wrong turn and regretted it deeply.

Of course, *she* didn't regret it at all, Cat thought, craning her neck to get a better look. How could she? Masculine perfection didn't cross her path often. And this particular specimen had a beauty that had nothing to do with femininity and everything to do with looking like a battle-hardened fallen angel. If he was a cousin, she was seriously going to cry.

Yum, she thought, staring unabashedly.

Fallen angel. Yeah, that was about right. He looked like he could tempt a saint to sin. Her eyes swept over him from head to toe, appreciatively wandering over a body she suspected would be, minus clothing, right out of an Emporio Armani underwear ad. Tall and broad shouldered, with pale blond hair that was mussed into short spikes, the stranger could have been chiseled from marble. His worn jeans and rumpled blue button-down, which was rolled carelessly to the elbows, couldn't disguise the fact that he was lean and muscular, with a bearing that was more like a soldier than a lazy vacationer. Sharp and angular features were almost ridiculously perfect, the only hint of softness being a shapely mouth that, right now, looked disinclined to smile. *Especially* right now, Cat thought as she watched his frown deepen. He looked puzzled and, if she wasn't mistaken, irritated.

On him, irritated looked very hot. Though Cat was betting that even extreme nausea on that face would send most women into a frenzy of lust. She had to admit, she'd be no exception.

Cat sighed, grinning when she heard the answering exhalations of her sisters. Well, she decided, this should give them something to talk about while they were here. A resident stud muffin would provide a welcome distraction from their usual problems, and anyway, there was nothing Cat liked better than dishing with Poppy and Skye about men.

Too bad guys with faces like this one's (not, she silently amended, that she'd ever seen a face quite as gorgeous as his) usually demanded a healthy amount of worship, at least in Cat's experience. He'd probably be so busy working out or doing his hair that they'd never see him anyway. Such a shame, Cat thought. It would have been fun to look, even if she'd sworn off worshipping at the altar of pretty men after her disastrous almost-engagement. This one already looked like escape was on his mind.

Of course, knowing her family like she did, Cat couldn't really blame him.

"I'm sorry," the angel said to Duncan, inclining his head slightly. His voice was soft and sensual, the accent mostly American with a little something exotic, something unidentifiable, thrown in. "I didn't mean to interrupt, Duncan. I never know when you've got guests coming in." He gave Freddie a strained smile. "Enjoy your stay here."

He turned to go, but Duncan's bellow stopped him in his tracks. Cat watched the stranger's shoulders bunch defensively a split second before her uncle's shout, as though he knew what was coming. She had to smile. Apparently, he was right.

"Nonsense," Duncan insisted, a mulish glint coming into his eyes that Cat fully appreciated. "You're not interrupting anything! And you're not skittering away that easily, either. I said I wouldn't bother you out at the cottage, and I haven't, but we're not there now, are we? So come over here and be sociable for a change, Bastian. I'd like you to meet my brother and his family. They're in for the summer gathering, of course."

Bastian stayed right where he was, looking as though someone had just slapped him. "Gathering? That's next month, isn't it?"

Duncan exhaled loudly through his nose, not bothering to hide his annoyance. "No, it's *now*. Well, two days from now, on Friday. And it lasts for a week... Christ, Bastian, we've been over this! This lot is a bit early, but by tomorrow, this place will be overrun with MacInneses!"

Bastian went quickly from looking flummoxed to looking completely horrified. Something told Cat that however many MacInneses might show up, this guy was definitely not one of them. Which, considering that lapping him up with a spoon sounded heavenly, was probably a good thing.

"But… but I was positive it was later… you mean to tell me that there's going to be some… some epic campout here? *Now?*"

Duncan's eyes narrowed to slits, his voice dropping to barely more than a growl, and Cat suddenly understood why this man was Pack Alpha. He might be friendly, but he could also beat someone to death with their own bloodied limbs if he felt like it. And this Bastian looked like he might be in danger of crossing that line soon.

"An epic campout that you're going to help manage, Bastian *an* Morgaine, as promised. You'd no doubt have seen it coming if you ever came out of that cottage, instead of skulking about like a certain type of creature you don't like being compared to. Though I'm not sure if you even come out at night anymore."

Cat didn't miss the flash of temper that flitted briefly across the stranger's beautiful features, and she had to hold in an amused snort. Both of these guys were huge, so it would be interesting to see whether youth or experience won the battle brewing between them. Though she hoped no one broke any of the antiques before she had the chance to really admire them.

Bastian surprised her, though, with the speed at which he collected himself. He straightened, took a deep breath, and walked over to her uncle, shaking his head. When Bastian spoke, his tone was sincerely contrite. Maybe he wasn't such a jerk after all.

"Sorry, Duncan. Of course I'll be helping. I just lost track of time, I guess." He laughed, sounding more tired than amused. "You must be rubbing off on me. I'm becoming an awful grouch."

"Hmm," was Duncan's only reply. He looked as though he wanted to say more, but Cat guessed he didn't want a huge scene in front of guests he didn't know. She slid her eyes to her sisters, who looked to be thinking the same thing as she was: *too bad*. The situation was just getting interesting.

Bastian's eyes roved briefly over the group as he approached them, his gait a self-assured, if somewhat reluctant, saunter. Then, as though pulled back by some invisible force, his gaze returned to her.

In the instant those ice-blue eyes met hers, Cat forgot to breathe.

Oh. My.

A strange, electric tingling sensation shivered through her, making the tiny hairs on the back of her neck and arms stand on end as Bastian *an* Morgaine focused his complete attention on her. His eyes locked with hers, fathomless blue lit with a faint spark of light as she looked into them. Time seemed to slow, grinding almost to a halt, as her body began to awaken to sensation in a way that it never had. Every separate pulse of her heart, each faint breath of air that wafted on the currents from the open windows, was suddenly a revelation. Cat's eyes widened. She didn't want to move a muscle, unsure of what was happening to her but positive that she didn't want it to end.

One single, shallow breath and Cat was enveloped by the cool, clean scent of him, like a winter breeze off the ocean. There was something so achingly familiar about it, though that was impossible. And quickly, she felt an inner shift from bliss to beast that was exhilarating and terrifying. Her Wolf senses, normally kept tightly under wraps, expanded with a vengeance, intensifying her sight and sense of smell until the Wolf that resided deep within had raised its shaggy head and was snapping at the end of its tether. Teeth sharpened before she could make it stop. The tips of her nails lengthened into points that dug into her palms. As time sped back up, all she saw, all she felt, was the man looking back at her, to the point where each time her heart beat, she heard an echo she was sure must be his own.

Cat's pupils dilated as her hunter's instinct kicked in, threatening to turn her from woman to animal and leaving her reeling. She had wanted men before. But this wasn't just want. That she could handle. This was pure, unadulterated need, coupled with something so alien that she couldn't even put a name to it. The feeling threatened to overwhelm her before she could get a handle on it.

I know you, she thought dazedly. *I don't know how, but I know you…*

Without warning, Bastian looked quickly away. In that single instant, her strange and fragile connection to him was ripped from her, leaving Cat dizzy and faintly ill. She blinked rapidly, trying to reorient herself, while the world around her resumed its normal pace as though nothing had happened. Her sisters continued whispering to one another and giggling, and Freddie and Duncan stood waiting as Bastian approached them, his gait as steady and assured as it had been moments before.

He reached Duncan's side, shaking hands with her father and making small talk as though he was oblivious to everything that had just passed between them. Which raised the unpleasant possibility that he might be. Not to mention that she was, in that case, probably losing her mind.

Cat drew in a shuddering breath as silently as she could, glancing around at her family and seeing nothing to indicate they'd noticed the brief, intense moment she'd shared with the stranger. She swallowed hard, trying to collect herself and wondering whether he'd felt even a hint of what she had. Wondering what the hell she'd felt in the first place. Hoping she didn't just melt into a puddle right there. Or get all hairy.

She looked down at her hands, and saw nothing but her own golden skin and the French manicure she'd gotten on Monday. No fur, no claws. So that was something, at least.

Still, she was hardly comfortable celebrating just yet. Because he was, she thought with a sinking feeling as Duncan dragged him over, even more amazing close-up. For once in her life, she didn't have a single clue what to say, except to herself.

Down, girl.

"Girls, I'd like you to meet Bastian *an* Morgaine. He's a guest here for the next little while, and my son Gabriel's brother-in-law." Though he still looked somewhat disgruntled, Duncan dropped a sly wink at Cat. "He's terrible company, really, though you've probably guessed that. Maybe one of you can pry him out of the woods and remind him what day it is once in a while."

Bastian raised one pale brow to give Duncan a withering look before shaking hands with Poppy and then Skye, murmuring his hellos. He managed a pleasant smile. He also pointedly avoided her gaze, Cat noticed with a prick of irritation that managed to slice neatly through the drooling lust. Make her head fuzzy and then ignore her, would he? Well, they'd just see about that.

"This is Poppy and Skye," Duncan was saying. Both her sisters had big, dopey grins on their faces, she noted, and gritted her teeth. Which led to the discovery that smiling was out, because her teeth were still quite a bit sharper than they should have been.

"And I'm Catriona. But everyone calls me Cat," she forced out, trying to banish the violently erotic thoughts cascading through her brain like a waterfall by being proactive. She stuck out her hand, though for a moment she wasn't sure whether he'd actually take it. But he did, though his jaw tightened a little as palm met palm and heat shimmered deliciously up her arm. Cat heard herself inhale sharply and then forced herself to focus on something other than the wonderful feel of his skin.

Unfortunately, the first "something" that came to mind was his mouth, which she was absolutely certain would feel even better.

"Cat," he said, the sound of her name spoken in that rough voice scraping pleasantly across her nerves. "Nice to meet you." He shifted his attention immediately to Duncan, dropping her hand like it had become a hot poker and taking a quick step back. "Well, I'll leave you all to catch up with one another. I've got a few things I have to do." Then he turned on his heel and loped off so quickly he was almost running, leaving Cat startled at the abruptness of his departure and Duncan with a disgruntled expression on his face.

"Something is wrong with that boy," Duncan

muttered under his breath. He didn't seem particularly perturbed, though, just irritated. So maybe this was what passed for normal behavior with the beautiful, bizarre Bastian. And that probably should worry her more than it did, but she was definitely in the throes of... well, *something*, anyway.

Cat closed her eyes and tried to re-center herself. She'd dealt with all kinds of weird crap in her life, but apart from actually turning into a Wolf, this little incident took the cake. She felt like she'd just been plowed into by a tornado. Why the hell did she feel so deflated now that he'd left the room? He'd acted like she was some sort of leper. She wouldn't have been shocked if he'd pulled out hand sanitizer after he dropped her hand.

She should *not* still want to have sex with someone like that. Had to be the jet lag. Or out-of-whack hormones. Or needing to eat.

Because she totally still wanted to. Except worse than before.

Unable to process the whole bizarre encounter so quickly, Cat's head began to throb. Duncan, beside her, sighed irritably.

"Well. That, in a nutshell, was Bastian. Feel free to ignore him or annoy him at your leisure while you're here." Duncan shrugged, picked up the suitcases he'd set down, and directed everyone to follow him upstairs.

With considerable effort, Cat got moving, though she was unable to get involved in her sisters' conversation (which, from what she could gather, was about how Bastian's butt had looked on his way out the door). Her head was killing her. As she trudged up the staircase, she felt the fatigue from two days of traveling, not to mention the aftermath of her intense meeting with Bastian, settle on her like a warm and heavy coat. Her eyelids drooped. Beside her, Skye yawned loudly, and Cat patted her on the shoulder. At least she wasn't the only one.

"Sounds like a good nap is in order for everyone." Duncan chuckled. "I guessed as much. You've had a long trip. But we'll have a fine dinner for you when you wake up this evening. Our Harriet's a brilliant cook, so look forward to it. She's making the meat pies and hotchpotch as we speak."

"Meat pies?" asked Poppy, eyebrows raised.

"Hotchpotch?" Cat queried, hoping it wasn't anything with a head in it. She was nervous enough about eating haggis, which her father had told her (with discernible glee) was non-negotiable.

Duncan smiled kindly at her. "You'll love it. On my honor."

She probably would, Cat decided, unable to help but trust her uncle's earnest face. And after her first adventure in Scottish cuisine (provided a few aspirin and some sleep did what they were supposed to), she planned on taking a good look around. Maybe try to bump into Duncan's reticent guest again and strike up a conversation in earnest... hopefully without any drool on her part this time, though she knew there were no guarantees. She had no idea what had passed between them, but one thing she was certain of: she wanted, no, *needed* to see him again, and as soon as possible.

Well, she thought with another lusty yawn, that shouldn't be too difficult. They were stuck on the same estate in the middle of nowhere for the better part of two weeks. They'd be seeing plenty of one another. Dogged determination, after all, was one of her finest qualities.

He could run, but he couldn't hide forever.

Bastian an *Morgaine*, she thought, a sleepy smile curving her lips. Then, as an afterthought, *I wonder what kind of last name that is, anyway?*

"Damn!"

Bastian slammed into the small cottage in the woods he was currently calling home, allowing the pent-up anger and frustration over Duncan's revelation out now that he could. He strode into the tiny living area, shoved his fingers into his hair, and pulled with a growl of wordless fury. He should have known, should have remembered. But these last few weeks had been like a slow-moving nightmare, something outside the realm of time and space. This pack gathering couldn't be coming at a worse time. Malcolm usually handled everything, and with him gone, Bastian was, in a word, screwed.

His sister Rowan was right, he decided. Humans had excellent words for awful situations.

A weak cough drew his attention to the door, slightly ajar, of one of the two small bedrooms. Bastian let his arms drop to his sides. He felt like falling into one of the plump plaid chairs and just staying there until something happened.

Until the dragon decided to live or die, or until the *narial* simply claimed its prey, and his soul, at least, was free. He hated that he was beginning to think like that. But it was hard not to, when he'd just been blindsided by longings better left buried and now coursing like madness through his blood.

Catriona. Call her Cat. Bastian pressed the heels of his hands against his eyes, trying to push it all back, but he saw only her in the darkness. She might be a werewolf like the rest of the MacInnes Pack, but unlike her big, muscular cousins, her body was long and lithe, her curves gentle and small so as not to interrupt such graceful felinity of form. She was tall for a woman, though she only came up to his shoulders, and had a long, sleek waterfall of hair that was the color of rich sable. Her face, he recalled, savoring the image despite himself, was beautifully angular, with her sharp little nose and long, heavily lashed eyes, as well as a generous mouth that looked made to smile. And ideal to kiss.

The way she'd looked at him, that brief but intense blaze of connection when their eyes had met, had utterly floored him. It was as though all of the moments he'd had to turn from in his life—attraction, lust, and even just the initial spark of being drawn to a beautiful woman—had been condensed into that bright flash of what had passed between him and Catriona MacInnes. He had wanted her so badly in that instant that it had been all he could do not to march over to her, toss her over his shoulder, and head out the door.

Which was impossible, of course. But that didn't change the fact that she was here. For a week, if not more. And that he would undoubtedly see her again.

I really, really don't need this right now. Bastian blew out a breath and removed his hands. He was going to have to get it together. He wasn't in any position to be entertaining pretty fantasies. His main priority, for the time being, was the destruction of his curse… and somehow saving the man languishing behind the door he now faced. Besides, if Duncan, or any of the others, for that matter, discovered who he was harboring here, he doubted Catriona would look at him with anything but disgust… right before he was ordered out of *Iargail* permanently.

Duncan had welcomed him as a guest because of his talent for working with the Stone and because Malcolm was often with the Dyadd since the birth of Bastian's niece, so Duncan enjoyed both the company and the help. Bastian was afraid he hadn't been much company lately. But if he didn't want to arouse even more suspicion than he already had, he was going to have to bite the bullet and be a genuine help for this gathering.

Whether or not he wanted to have rough, wild sex with Duncan's niece every time he saw her. Which, given his usual luck, was bound to be frequently.

Bastian gave himself a moment to tuck his thoughts away, not wanting to telegraph his frustration to his houseguest. The Goddess knew that Lucien Andrakkar needed all the bolstering he could get. And probably, he was beginning to realize, more than he was capable of providing.

The *daemon* had done far more damage than he'd thought. And it wasn't as though Lucien had been such a treat to begin with anyway. Bastian was banking on some sense of gratitude, or at least obligation, to prompt Lucien to give him the blood he needed. But as time went by, he still had no idea whether the man was even capable of operating at that level. Of course, if he never recovered, the point was moot. And that thought, as always, was the one that got Bastian to put one foot in front of the other.

He moved to the door, opening it just a bit wider to peer in, not wanting to disturb Lucien if, as so often, he was still asleep. Apparently not, though, as a now-familiar voice, deep but painfully thin, reached his ears.

"I can feel you gloating from here. I'm not dead yet."

Bastian pursed his lips and pushed the door open the rest of the way, cocking his head to regard the pale figure who lay in the small wooden bed. Several blankets were piled on top of him, despite the fact that it was the edge of summer.

"I wasn't sure," Bastian said, eschewing kindness because it didn't work anyway. "You still look like a gnawed-on carcass."

Lucien narrowed his eyes, which were glittering violet against his pallid skin. "I blame the quality of care." He started to say more but was wracked by one of the violent bouts of coughing that always left Bastian wondering whether the dragon would still be breathing when he stopped. Lucien curled into himself as his lungs spasmed over and over, tense and shuddering, clutching his midsection as though he was afraid this fit might finally break him in two.

Bastian could only watch, feeling even more helpless than he had the day before. It had been just over a month since he had brought the dragon here from the hellish dungeons of the Blighted Kingdom, and though most of the obvious wounds had healed, there was no way around the truth (though the Goddess knew he had tried to find one): Lucien Andrakkar was dying. And Bastian knew nothing that could stop it. Still, he couldn't bring himself to give up trying, despite the abuse of the thank-less dragon. He'd pinned all of his meager hopes on a restored Lucien. Bastian couldn't bring himself to give up, even now.

But then, he thought ruefully, he'd always been inor-dinately stubborn.

So he did as he had become accustomed to doing, went to the nightstand and poured water from a blue ceramic pitcher into the glass that stood beside it. Silently, he waited for the wracking cough to subside, looking on grimly as the dragon at last wiped an arm across his mouth. Bastian didn't miss the fact that when Lucien pulled his arm away, his white cotton shirtsleeve was stained with blood. Useless, weakened, bitter blood.

"You want help?" Bastian asked, indicating the water. Lucien's answer was to give him a foul look, struggle up until he was half-raised, and snatch the glass from his hand. After another fulminating glare, Lucien drank greedily.

"Well," Bastian said, rolling his eyes to the ceiling, "nice to see you're feeling well enough to be your usual charming self today."

Lucien drained the glass, shoved it back at Bastian, and collapsed back onto the pillows, exhausted. "I could say the same," he replied, and then cleared his throat with a wince before continuing, "considering your entrance. What happened? Some mangy MacInnes finally discover you were harboring the enemy?"

Bastian felt himself clenching his jaw. He was justi-fied in all of this, he felt. His life was at stake, and in his present condition, Lucien Andrakkar was no threat to anyone. But it still pained him to have the situation painted in such stark terms. *Betrayal.* It went against everything he was. And yet… that truth didn't change what he had done.

Somehow, he managed to keep his tone light when he answered.

"No, if that had happened, your head would already have been carried out on a pike. There's a… a minor situation, though. We'll have to be particularly careful." When Lucien just raised one quizzical ebony brow, Bastian sighed and elaborated. "Two days from now marks the start of the annual family reunion."

Lucien closed his eyes, his expression pained, and gave a growl more ferocious than what Bastian had thought he was still capable of.

"This entire place, crawling with wretched furballs?" he snarled. "If I had the strength, I'd kill you now, Dyim, I swear it."

Bastian just shook his head. He'd heard this many times, and worse. "That would serve neither of us, Lucien. Our fates are entwined now."

"Because of you. Because you refused to let me die in peace," Lucien snapped, baring teeth that had begun to sharpen into points as his anger rose. Bastian glared at him, feeling his own temper rise in return. They might share a half sister, but that was all they had in common. Such close quarters, particularly under the circumstances, were doing neither of them any favors.

"You were not in peace, I might remind you," Bastian snapped back. "And the *daemon* were not about to let you die. You might have lived years more."

"Better that than being forced into the debt of some foul, half-breed sorcerer." Beads of sweat began to pop out on Lucien's pale brow, and he panted with the force with which he tossed the words at Bastian. For once, Bastian found he didn't care. He felt his blood chill, for him always a bad sign, and felt the ice gather in his veins, ready to be used. Perhaps it would be better if he just killed the dragon now. Killed him and took what time he had left before the *narial* claimed him.

Only the thinnest tether kept Bastian from violence.

"I can always take you back," he growled, and satisfaction flooded him when fear, unmistakable, flickered in Lucien's eyes. The dragon's foul temper, Bastian had noticed, often got ahead of his mouth. Just now, he was tired of humoring it.

"You… you need me. My blood," Lucien sputtered.

"You're right, unfortunately," Bastian returned flatly. "But you're just as easily used as a bargaining chip. And having an actual *daemon* remove the curse would save me the fight I'll still have on my hands, should you miraculously develop a sense of honor. Now if you'll excuse me… I've got better things to do than hover over your sickbed. Either live or die, Lucien, but for the Goddess's sake, quit lingering. It's getting old."

Bastian turned on his heel and stalked out of the room, the sound of Lucien's venomous hiss following him into the living room. He kept on walking—out the door, across the small clearing in which the cottage sat, and into the soothing half-light of the woods where the only sound was the rustling of the leaves in a gentle breeze. As he walked, his long stride eating up the distance, Bastian felt his anger leaving him. It ebbed out slowly, clearing his head.

Clearing, but for the vision, seemingly seared into his

mind, of Catriona MacInnes. And since it calmed him even more than the woods, he allowed the picture of her to linger in his mind for now. He envisioned her as she would be this evening, sitting at Duncan's table and sampling some of Harriet's hearty fare, a dinner to which he'd been invited but declined even before he'd known guests would be attending. He imagined the sound of Cat's laughter as she listened to one of Duncan's tales with interest. Her bright golden eyes. The toss of her head. The curve of her neck. The long, slim line of her waist.

Dangerous. All of his better judgment screamed it at him. Bastian knew, without a doubt, that was correct. To lose focus now would mean his death. It had just been so long since he'd had anything but his teeth in a woman. His mistake, his problem... but he knew with a searing certainty that Catriona MacInnes wanted him as well. Though he suspected it might be more than simple want.

Bastian shuddered as a sudden chill swept through him. *All the more reason to stay far, far away.*

Movement in the woods behind him momentarily derailed his thoughts. Bastian looked around, going deadly still. The tiny hairs along his arms and the back of his neck prickled as even the lush green silence of the Highland woods grew suddenly ominous.

But it's daylight... the shadow only walks at night... it's daylight...

It came at him without warning, a dark mass materializing a split second before slamming into him, *through* him, and taking Bastian immediately to his knees. He gave a harsh grunt as he landed, the force of the impact forcing the wind from his lungs. Paralyzing him.

Bastian struggled to draw in air, helpless as he realized that his strength had left him as the *narial* had torn through him. It was all he could do to lift his head, a final show of defiance before the death blow. This had to be it, he knew. If it was strong enough to attack him while the sun shone, able to risk its own annihilation in the light because of its fierce hunger for him, he was out of time. Bastian wished futilely that he'd spent his final days in pleasure, if all of his efforts to stop this had been for naught anyway.

He could not fight it. He wasn't ready. But he would be damned if he didn't die like a man.

So he waited, looking defiantly ahead as his lungs began to work again, as sweet air flooded his system and set him coughing almost as fiercely as Lucien. But as the minutes passed, nothing happened. There was only his steadying breath in the silence.

Bastian tentatively got to his feet when he was sure they would hold him, exhausted from even that one blow… and bewildered. The *narial* had hurt him before, when he'd been foolish enough to give it a chance. Each attack had drained power from him that he seemed unable to ever fully recover. But never had it been so blatant. Why was it not finishing the job it had long been about, when it was so obviously ready to finish this on its own terms?

As though the shadow had heard Bastian's thoughts, a moaning growl that smacked of anticipation sounded from somewhere behind him, deep in the trees. Then, one word in a voice that seemed to slither from the deepest pits of darkness in the Blighted Kingdom: "*Soon.*"

As quickly as it had come, the oppressive feeling in

the area lightened, and birds resumed their merry songs. By now he knew better than to search for the *narial*. For whatever reason, it had decided to toy with him just a while longer. He remembered what he had said to Lucien about the *daemon* allowing him to live for years in agony rather than letting the dragon die. He had meant it as a threat, a reminder that he could return Lucien to a place where life was unimaginable torture, where death was a prize always dangled just out of reach.

No one knew how perilously close he was these days to feeling exactly the same way. To feeling just as he was sure his father had—right before he'd walked willingly into the jaws of the beast. Then Cat's face rose once more in his mind, unbidden.

There are still things worth fighting for, whispered a voice in his mind, sounding uncannily like Adryn's voice from all those years ago. *Don't stop yet, my son. Not yet.*

Bastian took a deep breath, straightened, despite the ache that always came after the shadow had stolen a bit more of him, and staggered forward. He needed peace and rest, and the chance to regroup once again. The house was out, and he had no desire to stay in the woods, where there were so many places for a shadow to hide, even now. There was really only one place to go.

Weary, but not yet defeated, Bastian turned toward the one thing that had always given him solace. He went to the water.

Chapter 3

CAT LEANED AGAINST THE WINDOWSILL, LOOKING out over the moonlit gardens and trying to be content with what had been both a much-needed nap and a delicious dinner. The bed behind her was cloud soft, and Cousin Harriet, who'd turned out to be a plump sweetheart of a woman, was one hell of a cook, exactly as advertised. The meat pies had been small, warm, thin-crusted pieces of heaven, as far as she was concerned. And the oddly named hotchpotch was a savory soup that had earned itself a place on her mental list of favorite comfort foods. Normally, a dinner like that would have been enough to sate her and put her right back to sleep, but tonight Cat was having no such luck.

She was way too eager to start exploring. And contentment and she had never gotten along very well anyway.

Sighing loudly, Cat threaded her fingers together and arched her back, stretching out muscles still tired and sore from traveling so far.

"Screw it, I'm going to bed whether I like it or not," she informed no one in particular. Poppy and Skye were in the rooms on either side of her, and she supposed she could have wandered into either one if she'd felt like talking. But she'd been unsettled all evening, and it was no mystery why. She looked out the window again, wondering where he was, what he was doing. Whether he could possibly be thinking about her.

Cat frowned. Probably not. He hadn't shown up for dinner, which Duncan had grumbled about. Though dinner had been an interesting enough affair, with discussion about the hotbed of supernatural issues *Iargail* had apparently become during the past couple of years. It still blew her mind, and she probably *was* going to have to sleep on some of what she'd been told. Magic stones, otherworldly ancestors, ornery dragons… it was like being dropped into something Tolkien might have written. And even though she herself was a creature that most people didn't believe in, the whole Drakkyn story was hard to swallow all at once. She'd believe it, she supposed, when she saw it. Which it sounded like she was going to in the next few days.

There was a soft scratch at the door, and Cat smiled. *Someone* was in the mood for conversation. The faint scent of cinnamon, as familiar to her as if it were her own, told her who her visitor was before she even poked her head in.

"Hey, you," Cat said as Poppy padded in, her curly hair piled on top of her head in a messy bun. Her pajamas, a tank top and baggy cotton pants, were black but covered in skulls as pink as the streaks in Poppy's hair. The studded collar, however, appeared to have been put away for the night.

"Hey. Mind if I sit?"

Cat raised an eyebrow. "Does it matter?"

Poppy grinned, amber eyes twinkling. "No."

Cat swept her arm to indicate the plump armchairs flanking the darkened fireplace. "Then by all means."

Poppy looked at the chairs, wrinkled her nose, and hopped onto the bed instead, getting comfortable and sitting cross-legged. Cat snorted with laughter and then joined her.

"We're going to be eighty-year-old women having gossip sessions on the bed someday." She chuckled, secretly glad that her baby sister still came to her when she needed to talk. Even though there were only four years between them, Cat felt like she'd done a lot of the "mom stuff" for her sister for as long as she could remember. Cat felt lucky that Poppy still treated her like a sister and shared secrets accordingly. Sometimes containing more information than she might have wanted, but it was hard to be picky.

"God, I hope so," Poppy sighed, wiggling her toes. "Men are fabulous, but they stink at gossip. Besides," she continued with a sly look, "they have better uses in the bedroom."

"Mmm. I think I remember something about that. And you're not supposed to know, since you're obviously staying a virgin until you get married." Cat flopped down, propped herself on an elbow, and listened to her sister's bubbling laugh.

Despite the semi-Goth thing Poppy stubbornly refused to outgrow, she couldn't help but look like a naughty fairy, with her delicate build and fine, pointed features. It drove her sister nuts, almost as much as it drove men nuts, Cat thought. Though Poppy had been too busy being her lovably conflicted and angst-ridden self to pay much attention to the latter. It was going to take an interesting sort of man to catch Poppy, Cat often thought. She just hoped that "interesting" didn't end up also encompassing "kind of freaky," but there were no guarantees.

"Yeah, whatever makes you feel better," Poppy said.

"So, what's up?" Cat asked, willing to listen even though the desire to keep brooding continued to tug at her. Which was dumb, she told herself. She could moon over Bastian all night if she felt like it, and she wouldn't get any further than she was right now.

"Can't go to sleep yet," Poppy replied. "My brain won't shut off."

"Or your mouth, as usual," Cat remarked, earning a swat on the arm. "But yeah, I know what you mean. Two weeks ago I was reading *JoJo the Friendly Frog* to a bunch of first graders. Tonight I'm sitting in the ancestral home of a pack of werewolves." She shook her head, feeling the strange reality of it begin to sink in, just a little. "Even though I guess I'm technically part of that pack, it's a lot to take in."

"No kidding," Poppy breathed, leaning forward. "And the whole thing about the Stone of Destiny? The gateway to another world?" She frowned. "How can you look so *calm*? This is kind of major, Cat. Our ancestors were from another universe and you're, like, thinking about what color to paint your toenails."

Cat stuck her tongue out, earning her another smile, before answering. "Shows how much you know," Cat said evenly. "I finished thinking about that two minutes after you walked in. I'm on to other things."

Poppy stared at her for a long moment, eyes narrowed slightly, obviously considering. Cat crossed her eyes at her, hoping to get her to quit… Poppy's brief bouts of intensity could unnerve a meditating yogi… but Poppy wasn't deterred. Finally, just when Cat had decided to start poking her, Poppy's lips curved into a knowing grin.

"Oh. You're thinking about *him*, huh? I should have known. I thought flames were going to start shooting out of your ears earlier."

"Him who?" Cat asked, slightly unnerved. Poppy could occasionally pull thoughts like that out of thin air if she tried hard enough. She wasn't sure if her sister was just bright and perceptive, or if a little something else was going on there, too. God knew they had a strange enough genetic mix, what with the witch-werewolf combo, but Poppy, while happy to discuss it in the abstract, tended to clam up about her own particular gifts. She was still, Cat knew, trying to become comfortable in her own skin. Or skins, depending on how one wanted to look at it.

Weren't they all?

"Tall, blond, and smoking hot *him*," Poppy replied, looking extremely pleased with herself. "And I'm right! I can tell. You've got good taste, Cat. I'll give you that. Okay, I'll tell Skye you've got dibs. It's about time you met somebody interesting."

"I don't have... I mean, you don't have to," Cat sputtered, finally resorting to protesting, "I go out with interesting guys!"

Poppy's skeptical "uh-huh, sure" expression was more eloquent than any words, not that Cat really wanted to get into that debate right now. Because her sister was totally, annoyingly right. She did, technically, go out with guys from time to time. But not that often. And they could definitely not be considered interesting by anyone except possibly those who liked researching the modern-day link between human men and Neanderthals. Todd, on whom she had happily wasted two years, had seemed to be the exception.

Her mistake. At least their relationship had gone down in flames worthy of a bad made-for-television movie. The memory of her broken engagement, now less raw after seven months, *was* funny in a sick sort of way.

But she hadn't had a date—or, God help her, sex—since shortly after Todd had gone bye-bye. It wouldn't hurt her to at least think about trying for one, the other, or both, with a guy who inspired the kind of lust in her that just about made her hair stand on end. Even if he did appear to be antisocial and a little odd. After all, gregarious and guy-next-door hadn't worked out so well. Cat slid her hands over her face in defeat.

"Okay," she muttered. "I've got dibs on the hot, weird guy. Thanks."

Poppy patted her on the back. "No problem. What are sisters for? I would have wrestled you for him, but I don't think I've ever seen you look like you wanted to jump a guy in public, so I'm being magnanimous."

Cat separated her fingers enough to peer back at her sister, her stomach sinking a little. "I was that obvious?"

"Only to the ones who know you best." She turned her gaze to the moonlight spilling through the window. "Lucky. You deserve it, after the ass-tastic mess that was Todd. But I'd like to meet my own Drakkyn. Maybe I should slink through that stone and find a hot dragon or something."

Cat rose to a sitting position, rearranging herself next to Poppy and frowning. "Lucky nothing. He took off fast enough. With my luck he's gay or something. And he's not a Drakkyn, is he?"

Poppy tipped her chin down and gave her a look that plainly said *duh*. "He's Duncan's son's brother-in-law. Did you not get the part of the conversation where he mentioned that our cousin Gabriel happens to be married to some kind of dragon sorceress?"

"Um," Cat said, feeling as though she'd just gone down the rabbit hole in order to have this conversation. "Yeah, kind of."

Poppy rolled her eyes. "Wow. You do have it bad. Aren't you supposed to be the astute one? And he's not gay. He was into you."

"Hence the running, obviously. My beauty is both legendary and deadly." Cat shoved at Poppy playfully, but inwardly she was busy trying to digest the new angle on Bastian. The Drakkyn. What did that make him, exactly? A dragon? A sorcerer? The boogeyman? She pressed her fingers to her temples.

"I think my head hurts. Again."

"It's just so cool," Poppy sighed. "Other werewolves, *finally*. Men who won't freak out about a little fur. Real magic everywhere."

Cat eyed her. "If only the men weren't so... related."

Poppy wrinkled her nose. "Yeah. Bummer. Maybe Mr. Hot-and-Weird has friends."

Cat thought back to earlier, about how cool and aloof he'd seemed. "Somehow," she said slowly, "I doubt it."

The door opened again, and Skye peeked around the corner, her gray eyes alight with mischief and a conspiratorial grin on her pretty face.

"Uh-oh." Cat laughed, glad for the distraction.

She wasn't sure she wanted to think too deeply about Bastian the Freakishly Magnetic tonight. Or at least, she didn't feel like discussing her thoughts on that. "I sense a disturbance in the force."

"Oh, look"—Poppy smirked—"An entire person created from deranged midichlorians. Beware, young padawan. Beware the funky side of the force."

Skye bounced the rest of the way in, shutting the door behind her and joining her sisters on the bed.

"Okay," she said. "I'm going out. Who's with me?"

Cat had to laugh at Skye's bravado. Everyone who met her thought she was quiet (and in some cases, mute). This bubbly, mischievous person in front of her, not at all quiet, was the girl Cat wished everyone could see, the one who dreamed up interesting and potentially dangerous adventures. But as yet, Skye seemed to hide her fun side from everyone but the ones she loved best. Considering how reserved she tended to be around the universe at large, only a small group got to know the real deal.

Cat knew Skye had her reasons. She had a suspicion it was because Skye had gotten a healthy dose of the Sight. At least their mother, Mariana, said Skye had. Being around hordes of people still got her wires a little crossed and freaked her out because blocking and filtering thoughts wasn't easy. But Cat didn't poke at her. Skye talked about her gifts when she needed to—just not that often.

Cat sometimes felt guilty for taking up a lot of the time Skye wasn't talking with werewolf-related bitching. But at least her sisters always seemed entertained, and she didn't have many outlets for venting.

"Hmm. Sounds like trouble. I'm in." Cat looked to the remaining holdout. "Poppy?"

"If Dad finds out, he's going to kick our asses," Poppy replied, looking thoughtful.

"Meaning?"

Poppy's grin was pure evil. "Meaning 'Hell yes, I'm in.' This beats running around the park dodging criminals and horny teenagers any day. Clothing off, ladies. Let's go howling."

Pajamas flew through the air, cluttering the floor where they landed as the sisters disrobed quickly. Cat barely spared the other two a glance, completely unselfconscious. They'd been through far too much to be shy about it. Awkward adolescence had taught them all that clothes and shape-shifting simply did not work together. And heading out to amuse themselves at the full moon, even at the stupid park, was worth the momentary embarrassment of shedding clothing.

Besides, who were they ever going to tell about the cute little birthmark on Skye's butt? Apart from her future husband, that was.

Cat raised her arms above her head and stretched, closing her eyes and letting the Wolf within rise to the surface. She felt the Change begin, and as there always was when the moon was nearly full, she felt a glorious sense of relief as her human skin began to give way to her animal one. Bone changed form as the skin rippled and shifted over it, and Cat dropped to the floor with a satisfied sigh that ended on a throaty growl.

Claws and muzzle lengthened, teeth sharpened, and fur sprouted as the Change sped up, nearing completion. Cat waited, letting her body do what it had been made to, until the burning sensation that always accompanied the process subsided and she could give her Wolf form a good, satisfying (and as Poppy liked to point out, dog-like) shake.

She gave the air a testing sniff as she waited for her sisters to finish, pleased at the scents that filled her senses. There was a lovely earthy-mossy smell (Duncan, she guessed), something plummy and sweet (Harriet), the scent of leaves and wood smoke (her father), and other, fainter undertones that had been left by other Wolves some time ago. And wound through it all was the scent of the Highlands—oak and ocean, heather and earth, and even more that was wild and wonderful and nameless but for the place it emanated from.

A short bark drew her attention. Cat turned her head to see her sisters: Poppy, a beautiful russet Wolf as lithe in this form as in her human one, and Skye with a beautiful silver coat that matched her eyes. Neither was as large as she was, or as powerful in this skin, but they'd decided long ago that neither had gotten as full a dose of the werewolf gene as she had. Poppy and Skye did just fine as Wolves. But, Cat thought with a burst of pride, neither wore this skin quite as easily as she did. She might not be able to shoot sparks from her fingertips, but when she shifted, she was as swift and silent as a shadow, able to become part of the night itself.

Not that she'd ever rubbed that in or anything.

Cat barked in reply to her sisters... *ready!...* and then trotted to the door to nudge it open. She paused in the doorway, ears pricked, scenting the air for any sign of their father. When she was sure he was nowhere near, Cat led the way, thrilling at the thought that moving about *Iargail* as a Wolf was just as commonplace as walking around as a human.

Down hallways, around corners, and finally down a back set of stairs that had once been used for servants, Cat and her sisters padded without seeing another soul. Cat was certain there would be a door back here somewhere, and bounding out the front door just seemed like asking for trouble. But at the base of the stairs, claws clicking on hardwood, Cat paused, uncertain of which way to check first.

The voice took her completely by surprise.

"Ah, girls! Glad you're up and about!"

Duncan appeared through the doorway of what seemed to be the kitchen without so much as a sound or even a whiff of his presence. From the pleased gleam in his eye, that had obviously been his intention. Cat looked at her sisters and then at her uncle, uncertain how to act or whether this was truly okay. She wasn't in the habit of wandering around houses like this; none of them were.

Duncan, however, seemed perfectly at ease. "Beautiful night for a run. I don't blame you. Bit tired myself, or I'd join you, but I'm trying to rest up for the circus that's coming in tomorrow." He looked them over appraisingly, eyes lingering on Cat with glittering approval, and then nodded, satisfied. "Knew you'd be a good-looking lot. Plenty of Alpha blood in there. Of course, there was bound to be... can't just wish it away, thank God..."

Duncan trailed off, frowning to himself, and Cat wondered if he was thinking of her father. But after a moment, he snapped back and inclined his head in the direction they were already heading with a warm smile.

"Door to the terrace is just back that way. Can't miss it. Enjoy the night, girls, and the grounds… you're MacInneses, after all. This place belongs to you as much as it does to me."

Impulsively, Cat padded to her uncle and gave his hand a friendly nudge. The small gesture seemed to please him, as he laughed and gave her flank a good-natured swat.

"Oh, go on now, you. Have fun, and stay the hell away from my sheep."

With yips of joy, Cat and her sisters bounded through the house, out the door, and into the June night. As soon as they were outdoors, they picked up speed, loping through the grass and heading for the sheltering darkness of the woods. Cat could feel something begin to thrum through her, a white light that filled her veins with song. An ancient song, buried deep underground, that her blood and heart knew even if her conscious mind did not.

Is that… the Stone?

But then the moon, hanging almost full in a sky brilliant with stars, was calling, blotting out all else. Cat raced into the trees, Poppy and Skye close at her heels. Finally, and for the first time, she could run free.

And it was time to play.

An hour later, Cat was totally, completely, and blissfully alone.

She felt a little bad about giving her sisters the

slip, but ten rounds of hide-and-go-seek was more than enough for her. She needed time to center herself in this place, to familiarize herself with the scents and sounds that permeated this little corner of the Highlands. More, she just wanted a few minutes to breathe without the warm but all-consuming whirlwind that was her sisters' company.

She slid through the trees, a fleet-footed shadow. Something about *Iargail* appealed to her like no other place had, making it seem like home even though she had never been here before.

Cat had spent years trying to live a life as human as possible. That was what her father had wanted, and even her mother, to a certain extent. Best to blend in, to treat her gifts as a small part of who she was, instead of as the dominant part of her nature.

She'd done fairly well, she thought, making it through college with a minimum of harrowing incidents. (Choosing a fairly rural campus had helped.) She even enjoyed teaching. But try as she might, she couldn't help but feel that her Wolf half kept her grounded in her life, instead of just being background noise that was better ignored. She channeled what she'd come to think of as her wolfish playfulness to herd and manage her adorable and sometimes unruly first graders. And her focus was so much better as the moon waxed toward fullness, though taking the occasional nighttime run in her more graceful form did wonders to clear out her mental clutter any day of the month.

What would it be like to live here? Cat wondered. To have all of that simply accepted, even encouraged? She could only begin to imagine. But ever since setting foot outside of the car, she'd felt a strange sensation she couldn't quite identify creeping up on her and taking hold, growing ever stronger.

It was only now that she recognized what it was: peace.

A sudden, cool breeze toyed with her fur as it passed, and Cat stopped midstride. The faint whiff of a crisp, clean scent, at once familiar and deliciously unknown, blew through her like a burst of strange magic. Even now, having only smelled it once, she'd know it anywhere.

Bastian.

Then, right on the heels of that: *Damn it, what* is *it with me and this guy?*

Cat took a deep breath, trying to clear her head. When that didn't work, she shook it. It was as if someone had popped a balloon full of sparkly heart confetti in her head the moment she became aware of his close proximity. Her sense of inner peace evaporated instantly, leaving her uncertain and quivering. Lust and other strange, messy emotions were making a complete muck of her insides, loosing what felt like deranged butterflies in her stomach. The sensation was fabulous and almost as frightening. Was this okay? Was it even normal?

Her sisters would have been a safer bet. But since her every animal instinct was straining against "safe," Cat headed for Bastian *an* Morgaine, despite the protestations of her rapidly weakening common sense.

The butterflies might be deranged, but they were determined little suckers.

Cat raced through the underbrush, her focus completely on tracking the source of that wonderful, captivating scent. Small, warm-blooded animals scattered as she passed, but Cat paid no attention. She was consumed utterly with finding it... finding *him*. About five minutes later, her concentration was rewarded when she saw the glimmer of water through the dense trees.

That, and as she emerged into the moonlight, the man standing with his back to her, staring out at the waves of the loch.

Cat stared, unsure whether to make herself known. She wasn't in the correct form to have a conversation, but part of her wanted to let him see her this way. She might not be the world's most skilled werewolf—being singular in her own little family, she had no real way of knowing how she stacked up—but she had always considered her animal form beautiful. It was sleek and strong.

Not a bad way to have Bastian think of her, if she could get him to think of her at all.

The alternative, of course, was to stop thinking about him. But even now, presented with nothing but his back, Cat felt the same strange and irresistible pull toward him that she had earlier. Her head lowered, and she was barely aware that she was crouching in the shadows, jet-black fur becoming one with the darkness as the instinct to take down her prey drove her movements.

It was a moment before she realized he wasn't simply standing there. His hands were making small, deft movements in a continuous rhythm, almost as though he was conducting an unseen orchestra and commanding the players to crescendo and then decrescendo. She took a tentative step forward, trying to see what exactly Bastian was doing, and then another. When the waters of the loch came more clearly into view, her eyes widened in shock.

With every rise and fall of Bastian's hands, the water rose and fell, turning one section of the otherwise still loch into a glimmering, moonlit ballet of waves and fountains, impossibly perfect arcs and swirling sprays that defied any explanation but one: Bastian was playing the waters as adeptly as any virtuoso musician played his instrument.

Cat watched, less concerned with silence as she grew engrossed with the strange and beautiful show. She felt as though she was intruding on something terribly private, and yet she couldn't look away. There was something incredibly soothing about the dancing waters, and she felt her rapid heartbeat slowing along with her breathing as she watched.

She was so engrossed that she nearly jumped out of her skin when Bastian suddenly froze and spoke, dropping his hands to his sides and letting the waters go still. If she'd felt like an intruder before, Bastian's words only confirmed that she was.

"Leave me alone. For the love of the Goddess, give me peace tonight, creature. Wasn't the piece of me you got earlier enough?"

His voice was harsh, and something in his tone bespoke bone-deep weariness. Cat stayed where she was, frozen, torn between guilt at having disturbed him and anger at being addressed this way when she'd met him for all of five minutes. She'd taken a piece of him? He made it sound as though she'd torn into him, purposely and maliciously, instead of just shaking his hand.

At least now she had her answer about whether

he'd shared that intense moment back at the house with her.

The fur on the back of neck began to rise with her ire.

"Damn it, shadow," Bastian snarled, whipping his head around to glare at her. "The way things are going, you'll have me soon enough. Why can't you just let me…"

The way his voice died in his throat should have told her he'd mistaken her for someone else, but it was too late for Cat's wounded pride. All she saw was the fury written plain across his face when he turned, his eyes glowing blue in the moonlight, lips pulled back to reveal incisors that were long and deadly. He looked amazing. And his disgust was so strong that she could smell it.

A searing punch of lust was no balm for her feelings. Cat bared her teeth. Bastian *an* Morgaine didn't have to like her. But she'd be damned if she'd let him treat her like this.

The Change came swiftly, as it always did when Cat was gripped by strong emotion. With a threatening growl, she leaped into the air as a Wolf and, with effortless grace, landed directly before Bastian as a woman.

A very, very pissed-off woman.

It was at least gratifying to see the way his mouth dropped open as she straightened, shaking her long hair back over her shoulders and facing him, hands on hips, wearing nothing but righteous anger.

"If you have anything else to say to me," she snapped, "I'd prefer you do it to my face."

Bastian's eyes moved incredulously down the length of her and back up again, his gaze sparking a traitorous heat on every inch of skin it touched. She had to force herself to concentrate on the words that had infuriated her to this point, even as her nipples hardened in reaction to both the cool night air and Bastian's thorough inspection of her naked form.

Cat simply raised an eyebrow, waiting for a reply and feeling more than a little smug. He might be an irritable, antisocial pain in the ass, but he wasn't immune to the fact that she looked pretty damned good without her clothes on. It wasn't fighting fair, she supposed, but all things considered, Cat had no qualms about using that to shut Bastian up.

And sure enough, his anger seemed to evaporate completely. Right along with his powers of speech.

Cat watched his Adam's apple bob as he swallowed, hard.

"Catriona?" His voice was little more than a ragged whisper, and the shock she heard in it was the first indication that all was not quite as it seemed.

"Oh, it's not just 'creature' now, huh?" She glared up at him, daring him to provoke her further. But he didn't seem inclined to do much except stare at her in awe.

"I," he stammered, "I'm sorry… I didn't realize it was you. I just assumed… that is…"

Cat pursed her lips. He really did look shocked. Just-about-knocked-on-his-ass shocked. She began to wonder if she'd been a little rash in the way she'd reacted. Not that she could do anything about it now. Getting into a naked argument with someone was hard to do over.

Besides, she wasn't buying his act completely.

"Whatever you assumed, I don't appreciate being bitched at for doing something I'm allowed to do and for being somewhere I have every right to be," she said flatly, poking one long finger into his chest.

Naturally it was rock hard, Cat thought, annoyed. And naturally even that tiny bit of skin-to-skin contact had her hormones singing the "Hallelujah Chorus." She gritted her teeth. *I am going to hold it together*, she thought.

Bastian stared down at her finger, looking like he didn't know where he was anymore.

When he glanced back up at her, he still looked confused, but there was heat there as well. Lust formed a leaden ball in her lower belly, but Cat fought to ignore it. She had no intention of letting bygones be bygones and having make-up sex with a perfect stranger.

Not yet, anyway.

"Cat," he tried again. "Honestly, I had no idea it was you. I…" Bastian trailed off, closed his eyes as though he was in pain and ran his fingers through his hair, obviously agitated. "You're, um, not wearing any clothes."

She raised her eyebrows, trying not to laugh. Apparently, the Dyadd, or whatever he was, didn't find being naked in the great outdoors as refreshing as werewolves did.

"Thanks, Captain Obvious. I had no idea."

He opened one eye, still wincing. "Is this really necessary? I swear to you, I would never have said those things had I known it was you. Okay?" He waited a beat, and Cat merely cocked her head at him, interested in what he was going to say next. She hadn't sparred with a guy in a long time, and never under circumstances anything like this. She'd almost forgotten how entertaining it could be. Besides, Bastian deserved every ounce of discomfort he got, considering he'd treated her like she had the plague earlier.

He exhaled loudly through his nose. "Aren't you going to turn back into a Wolf now? I said I was sorry."

Cat pretended to think. "Hmm. No, I don't think you did."

Both eyes opened again, this time to pin her with a disgruntled glare. "I'm *sorry*. There. Now, please, for the love of the Goddess and all that is blessed, put on some… some fur or something!"

Now she did smile. The man standing in front of her, beginning to sport what looked like a blush, was nothing like the ice prince who'd barely given her and her family the time of day earlier. She'd wanted him, but she hadn't liked him much. The discovery of an actual personality, complete with rather charming embarrassment, gave her a small thrill.

Sadly for him, she was nowhere near done playing with him. They were alone, and for better or worse, she now had his undivided attention. Wasting it was absolutely out of the question.

Frowning, Cat held out her arms and then looked down at her bare skin, illuminated in the moonlight. "God, Bastian," she said, feigning indignance. "Is it really that bad?"

His gaze followed her own before he fixed his eyes on some distant point above her head and uttered a strangled groan, along with a muttered response.

"Sorry, what did you say?" she asked sweetly. "I didn't catch that."

"I said, you know damn well it isn't," Bastian replied. A muscle at the corner of his eye twitched. Cat kept her expression neutral, but the animal lust she was trying to hold at bay was slowly tying her insides into knots, even as she allowed herself a moment to gloat. Whatever else Bastian *an* Morgaine was, he most certainly was not as cold as he'd seemed.

And maybe he wasn't so oblivious to her after all.

Bastian stared at the trees over Cat's shoulder—her bare, creamy, delectable shoulder—and wondered if he'd done something to warrant extra punishment by the Goddess. He could think of no other explanation for why, when he was already nearing the end of his rope, he should find himself standing here having this ridiculous conversation with a stunning, naked woman.

Out of the corner of his eye, he saw Cat's slow, seductive smile and went as hard as rock. *Make that a stunning, naked, and completely evil woman.* Something told him she was enjoying this.

"So if you weren't talking to me, then who *were* you talking to?" she asked, sounding genuinely curious. He gritted his teeth. This was his own fault, he knew. He'd let his exhaustion get the better of him and hadn't been as cautious as he should have. All he'd heard was the snap of a twig. The silence that had followed was so like the *narial* that he had simply assumed the damned shadow had come back to torment him a little more.

Now he was being tormented in an entirely different way. And he didn't have a clue how he was supposed to answer questions when Cat continued to stand there not wearing anything.

"No one," he growled.

"Oh, right," Cat said. "You actually expect me to believe…"

He raised his eyes to the indifferent night sky, saying a silent prayer for patience. "I can't have this conversation if you're not going to get dressed."

Cat stopped short, and he heard the laughter in her voice when she replied. "Well, I can't have this conversation if I shift back into a Wolf. But if you've got a fig leaf handy, we can compromise."

He had to look directly at her then, and her glowing golden eyes were dancing with mischief. Despite himself, Bastian felt his heart stumble in his chest. There wasn't an inch of her that wasn't perfect, her long, lean form draped in nothing but moonlight. Her breasts were high and made just to fit a man's hand, her legs long and shapely beneath the slight flare of her hips. He didn't want to notice. He shouldn't want to notice. But how the hell could he not notice?

By the Goddess, he thought, breathing deeply and catching an enticing whiff of her scent, all night-blooming flowers and magic, *she's beautiful*. And every second he spent in her presence was making it more and more likely that he was going to do something incredibly stupid. He needed to get the hell out of there.

As soon as he could figure out how to make his legs work again. Right now they felt cemented to this very spot.

"Hey, wait," Cat said in the low, musical voice that he was sure he'd hear in his sleep tonight, barely suppressing a giggle and apparently oblivious to her intoxicating effect on him. "I have another idea."

She obviously had no intention of letting him be. So on a wave of mounting sexual frustration, Bastian gave in. If nothing else, that almost guaranteed she'd run off and leave him in peace.

"So do I," he said. In one fluid motion, he grabbed her long, slim waist, pulled her to him, and crushed his mouth against hers in a kiss meant to send her running far, far away from the pervert in the woods.

Too late, Bastian realized he hadn't factored in what Cat's naked body pressed against him would do to him. Or to her, for that matter.

She tasted like moonlight, strong and pure and ripe with possibility and magic. And she'd been waiting for him to make the move. That was Bastian's last coherent thought before Cat opened her mouth for him, her hot little tongue teasing out the need that had been lurking beneath the surface since he'd first seen her. And as for need, Cat's soft and broken sigh indicated she had plenty of her own. He could feel it thrumming beneath her skin like an electrical current. Everything in Bastian rose and responded to it before he could shut it down. He was caught helplessly in her thrall as she fitted every seductive curve precisely against him.

Bad idea, warned some semi-coherent voice in the back of his mind. But for the love of the Goddess, it had been so long since he'd allowed himself to feel need like this. And he was painfully, achingly aware of the dark curls at the apex of Cat's thighs that pressed tightly against the hard length of him, turning him to living stone and making him throb. As though she knew it, Cat gave a long, low moan rife with pleasure and rolled her hips against his, trying to get closer.

Bastian deepened the kiss, his blood heating to a near boil with arousal. He nipped, bit, and licked at her full lips, breath beginning to catch in his throat as Cat responded in kind. He wanted to taste all of her,

to explore with his mouth the topography of the body
matched so perfectly to his own. He dropped his hands
to the sharp juts of her hip bones and squeezed to still
her restless motions, making sure she could feel how
ready he was to drive into her, how badly he needed
what she tormented him with.

In return, she slid her hands up his chest, fingers
splayed as though she wanted to touch as much of
him at once as she could. The thin fabric of his shirt
gathered beneath her palms, and Bastian had a sudden,
mad urge to just tear it off, to be rid of the last scrap
of a barrier between them. He continued to plunder her
mouth, reveling in the surprising sweetness of it while
he let his hands roam over warm and velvet-soft bare
skin. He felt her arch into his touch, seeking more, and
felt the last shred of his reason going up in flames. He'd
had women over the long and solitary years, but he'd
always managed to hold himself apart. To be cold, so
there could be no pain for either party.

But as he slid his hand up to cup one small, perfect
breast, he was on fire for the first time in his life.

He broke the kiss, reveling in Cat's breathless gasp,
in the way her honey-gold eyes glowed with fierce need.
There was more, though, so much more that he wanted.
He would show her...

Bastian slid his tongue down the side of her neck to
lick at the pulse beating wildly at the base of her throat.
Cat's fingers wound in his hair, holding him to her,
urging him on with her ragged breaths. He kissed a path
to the side of her neck and heard an approving growl
as she tipped her head to the side to allow him better
access. And he felt the old bloodlust rise in him, the

need to take what she offered so that his own essence would retain its power. Or what power was left.

The same bloodlust… and yet somehow different. There was an urgency to drink from Cat that had never been present with anyone else. He felt her slide one long leg up to hook around his waist, opening for him, ready for him.

"Catriona," he breathed against her, both a command and a plea. He was dizzy with need, almost desperate to join with her. Bastian nuzzled into her neck, feeling his incisors lengthening, sharpening.

One simple word from her, barely a whisper, decided for him.

"Please."

When he sank his teeth in, it was like tasting paradise. Cat jerked against him, her breath a sharp gasp even as her hands fisted in his hair and she held him against her. Bastian closed his eyes, riding a wave of sheer bliss like he'd never known as the dark, rich wine of her blood flooded both his mouth and his senses. He drank deeply, pulled down into a darkness that was nothing but Catriona… her heartbeat, her breathing, everything changing time to match his. Slowly, Bastian became aware of thoughts and emotions flickering faintly at the edge of his mind that were not his own.

Want you, need you, shouldn't be doing this, God it feels so good to have his teeth in me, I can't believe he's biting me oh, please, need you inside me, Bastian…

That should have stopped him, should have terrified him that he was forging a connection with her. But he was drowning, drowning, until there was nothing but the two of them. Bastian tore his mouth from her neck and claimed Cat's lips in a bruising kiss that had nothing to do with romance and everything to do with sheer, raw possession.

Her nails turned to claws as they raked down his back, slicing neatly through the fabric and biting into his skin. When she nipped his lip, she drew blood. Cat ran her tongue over the tiny wound, still coiling herself around him. When she spoke, Bastian heard her voice... but it was also the voice of the beast that resided within her.

"*Now*," she demanded. "*Right now.*"

He could be inside her in seconds. But before Bastian could move a muscle, two things happened simultaneously. First was the unmistakable sensation of Cat's teeth sinking into the tender flesh between his neck and shoulder, provoking a sensory implosion that rendered him temporarily paralyzed, pleasure rocketing through every single nerve ending.

In that instant, his sweetest dream and his worst nightmare became reality.

Oh, no, no, for the love of the Goddess, no...

But she was completing what he had foolishly begun, binding them permanently, unbreakably, marking his flesh as he had marked hers. Doing what her *arukhin* instincts told her she must. And he'd known, he should have known...

Her essence slammed through him like a wave, nearly taking him to his knees. Pieces of her memory flashed in his mind, like flipping through an old family photo album at high speed. Her babyhood. A ballet recital. Christmas. Love for her family, her sisters. But there were also darker images... fights and divorce. Helplessness and the moon. Fear. A cage. Confusion. Loneliness.

He finally understood, but too late: She had no idea what she had just done.

But something else did, something that had been watching in the darkness with both revulsion and horrific glee.

Bastian had only seconds once the hair on the back of his neck began to rise and he heard the faint sound, like the mewlings of a rabid, deranged animal, rising from the woods. It was a familiar sound, but the hunger in it tonight sent a chill like ice down his spine. It had been deprived for many years now of much sustenance. He'd gotten good at moderating his emotions. But tonight, he had foolishly let his guard down. And the *narial* sensed a feast.

Cat raised her head, her eyes clearing an instant before the shadow oozed through the trees and came for them, came for them both. Desperate, he did the only thing he could: he grabbed Cat by the shoulders, picked her up, and shoved her away from him with all the strength he had... the strength her blood had given him. He barely heard her startled, pained cry as she hit the ground. All he saw, all he heard, was the utter blackness, punctuated only by a pair of burning red eyes that materialized out of the shadows of the forest and enveloped him, tearing at him and dragging him under.

Stealing another little bit of his soul.

With a groan, Bastian gave in to the darkness and fell to the ground unconscious, Cat's tortured shriek ringing in his ears.

Chapter 4

"No!"

Cat sprawled on the ground where Bastian had thrown her, watching helplessly as a black mass slithered from the shadows of the trees and materialized into a hulking figure that looked only vaguely human. It slid over the ground like a ghost, two arms rising from it. Long, hooked fingers reached for Bastian. But instead of grasping him, the thing's hands sank *into* him as Cat stared in horror. And for Cat, that was when the agony started.

She felt as though her own heart had been grabbed and was now being slowly squeezed, each painful throb bringing it ever closer to simply bursting. And God, it burned…

She gagged, eyes rolling back in her head as the shadow thing slid slowly through Bastian, making a vile noise as though it was smacking its lips with pleasure. She heard Bastian groan, but as the shadow passed through him, a misery darker than she'd ever experienced rolled through her, threatening to suffocate her. Every heartbreak, every disappointment she'd ever experienced, multiplied a thousandfold to expand inside her, creating a despair so pervasive it seemed to settle into her very bones. And she couldn't breathe, couldn't move. It felt like the very essence of herself was under attack, and as it was pulled and twisted, it was screaming.

She was screaming.

Cat writhed, lungs almost bursting before she could draw one blessed, shuddering breath. She nearly choked on the cool air that flooded her lungs, but despite the spasm of coughing, Cat managed another breath, and another, drinking the air greedily. She rubbed at her chest, trying to soothe the strange ache that had settled there. At least the excruciating pain had gone. Cat coughed again weakly, her body shaking and freezing cold. Fear and confusion consumed her as her thoughts began to make sense again. What the hell had just happened? For the first time in her life, Cat had felt like she was dying. And the hideous, faceless thing that had come from the trees hadn't even touched her. It had only touched Bastian.

Bastian.

Cat pushed herself up onto her side, having to work hard because her limbs were strangely lethargic, and looked to where the shadow had slid slowly through Bastian like water. Her stomach was painfully knotted as her eyes darted over the area, taking in moonlit grass, trees, and the now-peaceful water. But there was no longer any shadow, and the malice she'd felt crackling in the night air had dissipated, vanishing like the shadow creature, without a trace.

Now there was only a still June night and Bastian's crumpled form lying motionless on the ground where he had fallen.

Her heart caught in her throat. She stared at him, willing him to move. But there was nothing, not even evidence of a single breath. Everything about him— from his broad shoulders to his hand, cupped loosely and thrown at an angle from his body—was utterly motionless.

The shaking intensified, and nausea coiled in her stomach.

He was dead. He had to be.

A low, keening moan reached Cat's ears. It was a full minute before she realized the sound was coming from her. She put her hand to her mouth, willing the dreadful noise to end, but she didn't seem to have any control over it. The ache in her chest intensified again as she thought of the moments right before all hell had broken loose. He would have made love to her, she knew. She'd felt it in every fiber of her being, had wanted him desperately, especially after the shockingly erotic experience of having been bitten by him. She knew she shouldn't have bitten him back. That was the one rule, though of course never fully explained, that her father had given the girls: *never bite a human.* She knew her bite could kill. But Bastian wasn't human. He was Drakkyn. And with every instinct screaming at her to mark him as he had her, to complete the circle, it had seemed natural and right to give in.

What had happened when she had, though, had gone beyond even her wildest imaginings.

Cat tried to rise, staggered and fell, and finally scrambled on all fours to where Bastian lay. He faced away from her and was still, so still. She was afraid to turn him, afraid of seeing death on his beautiful face. But she forced herself to reach out a trembling hand and lay it on his neck, feeling for a pulse she was sure no longer was there.

His skin was still warm to the touch, and even that

small bit of contact flooded Cat with a strange sort of comfort. Her heart welled with strong emotion as her mind reached for his, willing him to hear her in whatever dark place he had been taken. She didn't know whether he could hear her, but reaching out this way felt right. Maybe he would at least feel the emotion that was behind it, much of which she hadn't begun to sort through herself.

Need you. Stay with me. Please…

It made no sense to her, but it was true. Her entire universe had shifted in some fundamental way tonight. She didn't know why or how, but it was all to do with the man who lay before her. She had seen into him, into his memory, and had tasted his blood. And she still felt him running through her veins.

Cat jumped. Beneath her fingers, she felt the tiniest flutter, then another, and another, growing slowly stronger. A pulse. Life.

She exhaled on a relieved sob, not bothering to wipe away the two tears that escaped to run down her cheeks. In truth, she barely noticed them. All she knew was that Bastian was still alive. And for whatever reason, that meant everything.

Cat moved clumsily to turn Bastian onto his back, cursing herself for trembling like a leaf. His face was drawn, terribly pale, and smudged with dirt. But when his eyes opened to look at her, pinning her with intense blue, they were crystal clear with lucidity. She ran her hands over his cheeks, over his chest, and through his hair, trying to reassure herself that he was, in fact, still with her, knowing she must look half mad and not really caring.

"Cat," Bastian grated out, in a voice almost as faint as the light breeze that still drifted through the night air. He licked his lips, winced when he swallowed, and then continued only slightly more strongly.

"I need to get home. Can you help me?"

Cat nodded. "I... I can," she stammered breathlessly. "I can go get help. I can get Duncan. Duncan can carry you…"

But Bastian was shaking his head vehemently, his frown thunderous, and Cat trailed off, not understanding. "No," he insisted, his voice weak but firm. "You… you can't tell anyone… about this. Too dangerous. No. Just you." He looked up at her, beseeching. "Please, Cat. Just you."

The things she had seen when she'd bitten him rose to the surface of her mind, unbidden: a boy beloved but apart, hiding, alone, and terrified of something that lurked in the shadows when no one was around. Something that could destroy him. Destroy everything.

"But what was it?"

"Mine."

One word, full of unfathomable pain. And somehow, it didn't ring quite true. Hadn't she felt as though she was being torn apart, too? For now, Cat knew she was going to have to accept his answer as enough. There was no time for all of her questions. She needed to get Bastian somewhere safe… if anywhere was safe.

"Okay," she said quietly, nodding, and was immediately rewarded with Bastian's palpable relief. "I'm going to need a little help, though. I'm strong, but you're pretty big."

"I'll help you," he assured her. "Here, give me your hands, I need to sit up first."

Somehow, Cat managed to accommodate all the pushing and pulling needed for Bastian to rise. It was a struggle, but Bastian sat up, then kneeled, and finally gained his feet using Cat to steady himself. Cat panted softly, taking all the weight he had to give and allowing him to lean heavily on her once he was all the way up. The physical work helped dull the knife edge of her worry when she saw how drained he was. His pupils were doing strange things, and Cat had a sudden, terrible premonition that he was going to fall back to the ground, and that this time, he wouldn't be getting up.

But he didn't fall. He just turned his head to look at her.

"My cottage is this way. I need to sleep, and at some point I won't be able to stop myself from giving in to it. We'll have to move as quickly as you can, okay?"

She nodded. "Are you going to make it?"

Bastian gave her a small, rueful smile. "I certainly hope so. I've made it this far. It'd hardly be fair to lose now."

She had a feeling he was talking about more than just gaining his feet, but she let it go for now. "Which way?" she asked.

"This way," he replied, taking a shaky step toward the woods with her support. Cat stopped dead, though, staring nervously at the darkened forest.

"But won't it... is it going to come back?" she asked, feeling for the first time like she might be in danger from a creature more powerful than herself.

"I don't think so," Bastian rasped. "I think it's had

its fill and gone off to gloat for tonight." Amazingly, he laughed, though it was a hollow, bitter sound. "It doesn't seem to want to kill me just yet."

She wasn't reassured, but there was no way she was leaving him out here either. Cat took a deep breath and took as much of Bastian's weight as she could. Together they stagger-stepped into the trees.

As they made their way slowly forward, Cat barely noticed the underbrush that crunched beneath her toughened bare feet before they emerged on a cleared and moonlit path through the trees.

A bird of prey shrieked in the distance, setting her shattered nerves even more on edge and focusing all of Cat's attention on getting Bastian home as fast as she could manage. Every sound, every flicker of movement caught out of the corner of her eye seemed sinister and dangerous. Their footsteps seemed abnormally loud, making them an easy mark for anything trying to track them, and Cat found herself breaking out in a cold sweat as they trudged onward. The trip seemed to take forever, though in reality it wasn't long before they reached the clearing where the little crofter's cottage sat, squat and charming even in the darkness. The windows were aglow with cheery, welcoming light.

"Almost there," Bastian growled. More to himself than her, Cat thought. But she found her tension easing a little in the warm circle cast by the cottage. It was good that they'd arrived there when they had, because she could feel Bastian getting heavier, his shoulders beginning to sag against her.

"Come on," she urged him, beginning to pant beneath the added weight. But they made it, though she was beginning to falter, and the arm wrapped around his waist was beginning to ache from holding him so tightly. Thank God she was a werewolf, Cat thought. She could bear a lot more weight than a human woman her size, but she was reaching her limits. It was all she could do to get him through the door. She got only a quick glimpse of a small, cozy living area as she rushed them through it and into his bedroom. There appeared to be one other bedroom, but that door was firmly shut. The intense concentration that hauling Bastian to bed took didn't prevent Cat from noticing that the smell in the cottage was very odd. A little like incense, though she couldn't imagine why that would be. Bastian didn't seem at all like the potheads she'd known in college who burned the stuff all the time.

She made it into a simple room furnished with only a bed, a low dresser, and a small wardrobe. With an unladylike grunt, dumped Bastian onto the smallest double bed she'd ever seen. His large frame took up almost all of it. At least he fit, Cat decided, if only barely. She looked down at him, hesitating only a split second, and then slid off his sandals.

"I'm not going to take advantage of you," she informed him as she went to work on his jeans. "I'm just trying to get you comfortable."

"Hmm. Can't be comfortable. You're still naked," Bastian replied, his words slurred with exhaustion. Cat just shook her head. Maybe the attack had done something to his brain. Then again, most men acted impaired anyway, in her experience.

"I think we have bigger problems, but thanks for the update."

Cat unbuttoned his shirt, trying not to let her hands linger overlong on the sculpted muscles of his chest, which was dusted with hair as blond as the hair on his head. Bastian appeared to be mostly asleep already, as trusting as a child as she tended to him. At least his color was coming back, she saw. With his perfect features in repose, there was no evidence of any toll taken on him except, on close inspection, some fine lines of strain around his eyes.

Angelic, Cat thought, shaking her head ruefully. A man shouldn't be allowed to look so icily perfect at all times, especially because she was sure she had pine needles in her hair, dirt on her knees, and smudges in various other places all over her person. At least he hadn't been paying much attention, she supposed.

Cat was pulling the quilt over him when she caught sight of the bite mark, flame red and unmistakable, on his shoulder. Guilt flooded her, though she didn't know why. That wasn't the worst he'd gotten tonight, and her intentions and the shadow's had been entirely different. She figured her own bite mark was still plenty visible, too. That was one of the odd things about being a were-wolf. She healed incredibly quickly, except when the wound was inflicted by another werewolf (in her case, always one of her sisters). Then it could take weeks to heal and almost always left a scar. Considering that werewolves were, according to Duncan, actually an ancient Drakkyn race, she thought it likely that Bastian had the same quirk.

Which meant they were both sporting the supernatural equivalent of a hickey.

Though God knew Bastian had more pressing issues.

"How do you feel? What do I need to do?" she asked, trying to keep her voice even. She couldn't see a single injury besides the one she'd inflicted. But that didn't mean he didn't have anything wrong internally.

"I'll be fine."

Cat's eyes widened. "Are you kidding me? Bastian, you just got attacked by…"

"I know," he said wearily. "It's happened before, and I've managed. You'll just have to trust me, Cat. I'm not going to die just yet."

She didn't like the sound of that at all.

"If that thing is wandering around out here, Duncan needs to know. It could hurt someone else."

"It won't unless someone intentionally gets in its way. I told you. It's mine."

She paused, debating, and then plunged ahead. "It hurt me."

The horror in his eyes was almost too much to bear.

"Did it come after you?" he demanded, his voice suddenly stronger, urgent. "Cat, please, I need to know what happened… did you go to it, or did it come to you?"

"Neither," she admitted, and Bastian's obvious puzzlement mirrored her own. "I don't know why, but I could… I could feel it, when it attacked you. Just like I was the one being hurt." She shuddered at the memory. "It was like being torn apart from the inside. I couldn't move. I could barely…"

"Breathe," Bastian finished for her, and Cat saw that understanding had joined horror in his expression. Somehow, he knew what had happened. She needed to know, as well. She just wasn't sure she wanted to.

"What happened out there, Bastian?" she asked softly. "To you? To us?"

The lines of strain around his eyes deepened again as he closed them, wincing against some lingering pain she couldn't begin to imagine.

"Not tonight. Tomorrow," he rasped. Tired of resisting the urge, Cat smoothed his tousled hair back from his brow, marveling again at the silken softness of the strands as they slid through her fingers. Each hair gleamed like pale fire against her golden skin.

"Tomorrow?" she asked, nervous about returning to the woods with that *thing* out there, and even more concerned that Bastian seemed suddenly resigned to some miserable fate while she was still completely clueless about what that terrible fate might be.

"I swear it," he returned, turning his head into her touch and then stiffening and turning away as he realized what he was doing. Cat sighed, seeing hints of the remote stranger from the manor house earlier. That was no one she wanted to see again, having glimpsed how much more there was to Bastian beneath that indifferent surface.

"I'll stay with you," Cat offered, knowing even before the words had left her mouth that he would refuse. For whatever reason, Bastian made every effort to hold himself aloof. And she thought she might have glimpsed that reason tonight.

"No. You should go back," he said softly, proving her right as his voice faded. "I just need rest and some time to recover. I'll be all right by morning. Then I'll come up to the house, and we can talk about… everything."

She frowned at him, though with his eyes closed,

he couldn't see her irritation. She'd never seen a man who needed looking after more than this one, and of course he'd rather languish out here alone in the spooky forest than let her help him. She was insulted despite the situation.

"What do you think I'm going to do, crawl all over you?" Cat asked. "I'll sleep in the other bedroom."

"I… that's… not a good idea," Bastian murmured. And incredibly, another voice drifted from behind the closed door to join the discussion.

"I disagree. I'm sure I could keep your friend entertained."

Her mouth dropped open. "Who the hell is *that*?" Because she was quite sure that everyone thought he was staying out here alone.

She didn't miss the daggers Bastian glared in the direction of the phantom voice before he looked back at her.

"Please, Cat," he pleaded. "I know it looks bad, but I would never do anything to hurt the MacInneses. At least trust me on that." His eyes blurred and began to close. "Damn. I don't have time to explain tonight, Cat. Just please, before you jump to any conclusions, give me a chance. Please…" His eyes closed before he could finish his sentence. Cat watched him, utterly torn. But in the end, she went with the impression of him she couldn't shake, despite how little she knew of him. If nothing else, Bastian *an* Morgaine was an honorable man. Strange and full of secrets, but honorable.

"I won't tell Duncan… at least for now. But we're going to have that talk bright and early," Cat murmured, tucking the blanket beneath his chin.

He surprised her by answering, though his voice was so soft she could barely make out what he said.

"I know," he replied, eyes closing as he turned his face into the pillow. Then Bastian's silence, coupled with his deepened breathing, told her that sleep had finally claimed him. She sighed, not liking the dark smudges that had appeared beneath his eyes. Even more disturbing, however, was the way her heart seemed to fill up every time she looked at him. Feeling this way made no sense, not when she barely knew him. Even when she'd been engaged, the feelings she'd had for Todd hadn't been this intense. Ever.

None of which changed the fact that there was something really, seriously wrong with Bastian *an* Morgaine. All of which she knew she ought to tell her uncle immediately. And none of which she was going to, not right now.

Leave it to her to get lost and turn her entire life upside down.

Cat ran her fingers back through her hair, pushing it out of her face, and considered her options. The urge to stay was overwhelming, but she didn't have any clothes. Besides, though they were used to her heading off on her own, her sisters were bound to raise the alarm if she didn't come back. The last thing she wanted right now was a search party combing the woods for her. That would just add embarrassment to the mountain of anxiety she was already dealing with.

Plus, considering the creature that they'd encountered in the woods, she didn't really want to deal tonight with whatever Bastian had hiding in the spare bedroom. So she would go now and come back early if he didn't show up as promised. And then, she hoped, she would get some answers.

Unable to help herself, Cat pressed a quick kiss to his lips, which were worryingly cool. Then she padded quietly out of the room, giving the closed bedroom door a wide berth. That voice had sounded human, but she seriously doubted that whoever it belonged to was. She paused at the front door, not wanting to go back out with the thing that had hurt her without even touching her and that had taken a powerful man like Bastian down without a sound. But she had no choice.

So she opened the door into the night, stepped outside, and Changed, letting flesh give way to fur and claw. With a single backward glance, she raced into the night.

But she couldn't shake the feeling that when she left, she was leaving a part of her heart behind.

Chapter 5

The Blighted Kingdom

THE SCREAMS OF THE DAMNED ECHOED THROUGHOUT the dungeons of the Blighted Kingdom, rising and falling in the *daemon*'s favorite sort of musical abomination. The crack of the whip, the faint *whoosh, whoosh* of the deadly pendulum, and the creak of the rack all kept time in the freakish symphony, depending on where in the extensive warren of chambers and cages one stood, and who one sought. Each *daemon* had his own favorite method of inflicting torment, and while most were not actively employed as dungeon masters, torture was well known to be a great reliever of stress. The favored of the court were granted access… and Jagrin had, until recently, been considered most favored of all.

That was how Grelag knew where to find the *daemon* he was lucky enough to serve. He had never seen a creature so consumed with fury as when Lord Jagrin had received the news of the dragon's escape. And King Cadmus, just as furious, had seen fit to take small payment for his troubles out of his loyal lord's hide.

Grelag had been sure that Jagrin would eventually slink away to exact payment in kind on some other trapped soul here in the pits. He was certainly nowhere to be found above. And sure enough, before long, down a dark and narrow corridor, Grelag heard not the rack, nor the whip, but the whispering slash of claws rending flesh.

Relief flooded him. *There.* It could be no other. The claws were Jagrin's way, and the Orinn scum who were sometimes foolish enough to hunt the sun-fearing Drakkyn had whispered his cruelty into legend. Grelag assumed that Jagrin had decided to visit one of these dirty, stupid villagers, so easy to catch with their lack of magic. Oddly, though, there were no screams.

The young *daemon* scurried down the corridor, his simple, gray leather tunic flapping quietly around his legs. The heavy wooden door at the end stood slightly ajar, and Grelag slipped around it, careful to be absolutely silent. He knew how his master hated to be disturbed when he was working.

In a small, dirt-walled room with a low ceiling, lit by a single smoking torch, Jagrin stood with his back to him, naked to the waist. Grelag could just see the body levitating before the *daemon* lord... or rather, what had once been a body. Now, it was a bloody mess, barely recognizable. And still, Jagrin tore at it, arms rising and falling rhythmically as claws found purchase and rent flesh in two. Flesh which, Grelag was certain, was at this point quite dead. Though he would not have wanted to be Jagrin's victim.

The *daemon* lord had been down here two full days.

There was no sound in the small chamber except the soft grunts and growls as Jagrin destroyed what was left of the carcass. Grelag hung back, reluctant to summon his lord out of his violence-induced haze. But King Cadmus had been most explicit in his instructions. And however afraid he was of Jagrin, one of the most powerful *daemon* in all the Blighted Kingdom, Grelag was far more afraid of the king. He had ruled for five hundred years, longer than any other, and his cruelty and cunning, they said, had kept him unnaturally young.

Perhaps that was true, for Grelag had never seen a being more vicious than Cadmus. It was awe inspiring. He would do well to take a page from that book and not cower before Lord Jagrin.

"M-my lord?" Grelag winced at the sound of his own voice, which was barely a squeak. Clearing his throat softly, he tried again.

"My lord."

Jagrin's voice, when he answered, was little more than a feral growl.

"This had better be good, boy, or you shall replace this useless hunk of meat."

Grelag swallowed hard but pressed on. He had no choice.

"My lord, the king requests your presence in the great hall."

Jagrin paused, one arm suspended, blood dripping from lengthened black claws. "And?"

"And... and what, my lord?" Grelag stammered, edging closer to the door. He was well aware of the volatility of Lord Jagrin's nature since he had returned to the Blighted Kingdom with the dragon. Being in such an enclosed space with all of that anger and near-ecstatic bloodlust was setting off all the alarms built into Grelag's carefully honed sense of self-preservation. Just one thing he had gained quickly from being Lord Jagrin's page.

Jagrin turned then, and despite the fact that Grelag sometimes dreamed of being a lord with access to the dungeons himself one day, the sight took him aback. The *daemon* lord's white, hairless skin was painted almost completely red, covered with crisscrossing streaks and spatters of blood. His long, pointed teeth were bared in a snarl, and eyes as red as the blood glowed with fierce light. He had been waiting, Grelag realized, for this summoning. And Jagrin wanted to know whether he needed to prepare for a hunt… or his own death. After all, the dragon had been his responsibility.

The dragon who had vanished without a trace over a fortnight ago, leaving not a single hint to where he had gone or how he had accomplished what no other had ever managed: escape.

Grelag exhaled quickly. On this score, at least, he could set the lord's mind at ease. "Some new information has come to light regarding the… the, ah, disappearance of the prisoner. His highness seemed quite pleased and is adamant that you come quickly so that he might discuss it with you."

Jagrin's demeanor changed immediately from feral nightmare to cultured member of the high court. "Of course. Just give me a moment to clean up."

The corpse fell to the floor with a dull thud, instantly forgotten. However, Jagrin attended to his own appearance with great care. Murmuring several words, he passed long, pale hands before him, and as he did, the blood vanished into the still cavern air. In moments, there wasn't a remaining droplet of blood to be seen on Jagrin. He held out his arms to examine them, and with a satisfied nod, calmly lifted his own simple gray tunic from where it lay crumpled on the floor in the corner and pulled it on.

"Now then," he said, his snarl gone soft and cultured, "let's go."

The great hall was alight with the red glow of torches, the tan stone of the walls left mostly unadorned but for carefully placed spikes, upon which were mounted the skulls of the vanquished and the very unfortunate. The floor on this level was purposely covered in sand. From it sprung stone chairs and tables, many occupied by various *daemon* courtiers engaged in deep, intense discussions. Beneath it, there were secret doors that could be sprung at the king's pleasure to unleash one of his prized beasts or to allow an offending party to join the beasts in the chambers hidden below.

It was considered great entertainment when Cadmus chose to leave the trapdoor open after using it to send someone beneath. There were times when the screams had been reported to have been heard for miles across the barren desert.

As Jagrin approached the imposing *daemon* who sat on a simple stone throne at the head of the hall, he couldn't help but wonder whether he'd been summoned under false pretenses, his hopes raised just to facilitate such a show for everyone else. That would have been just like Cadmus, whom he respected and feared in equal measure. He hated him a bit, too, of course... but that was to be expected. No *daemon* enjoyed taking orders. And Cadmus truly loved to give them.

That he gave them well, and prudently, was only a slight consolation.

"Ah, my lord Jagrin," said Cadmus, his voice resonating throughout the large room and drawing the attention of all who attended him, despite the fact that he always spoke quietly. "I've been waiting for you. I trust you return to us from the dungeons feeling… better?"

Jagrin stopped several feet before the slightly raised platform upon which the throne sat and bowed deeply. He wasn't fooled by Cadmus's mild tone; he knew full well that the king was annoyed to have been kept waiting while Grelag searched for him, though he did breathe a little easier at having walked all the way across the room without having fallen into a hole. He shifted slightly, showing no outward reaction to the continuing dull ache of the lash marks that went deep into his back, though the pain still sometimes crescendoed until it was nauseating.

He'd needed the two days in the pits. As for remorse, he felt none.

"Sorry to have kept you waiting, your highness," Jagrin said. "The boy serves me well, but he's slower than most."

"Hmm," was all Cadmus said, resting his chin on his hand. His eyes, such a deep red that they were almost black, watched Jagrin unblinkingly. His tunic and leggings, unlike all the other *daemon*, were of black leather, and around his neck, on a thin gold chain that dangled to midchest, he wore a single clear stone in the shape of a tear. A reminder, Jagrin knew. Just like the smaller throne that sat beside Cadmus, empty.

Evidence of love, coming from any other of his kind, would have disgusted Jagrin. But it was hard to find fault with the way his king had handled the situation.

Cadmus might have been foolish enough to love once, but he'd ensured it would never happen again.

Not with any of that particular tribe of Drakkyn, at any rate.

"What do you require of me, your highness?" Jagrin asked, folding his hands calmly before him.

"I wish to share something with you," Cadmus replied. "Come, and sit beside me, my faithful lord. There is a matter of great importance to discuss." He gestured to a small, backless chair that was adorned with a single plump cushion and had been positioned beside the throne for whomever had the king's ear. A place of honor. Jagrin had held it many times before and was pleased to think he hadn't lost the privilege after all. Quickly, he moved to Cadmus's side and sank onto the cushion. Around them, the low sounds of conversation resumed, though plenty of curious looks were leveled in their direction.

Jagrin supposed his brethren wondered why they'd been deprived of their entertainment for the evening. His mouth curved in a mirthless smile. Perhaps one of them would become the entertainment instead. He still had power here after all, it seemed.

"It's about the dragon," Cadmus said, watching him closely.

"Yes, your highness."

Cadmus smirked. "Don't pretend you don't care, Jagrin. We both have an interest in the Andrakkar's blood, which, as you know, is quite potent, even if it hasn't quite lived up to its potential for us... yet."

"Well do I know it, your highness," Jagrin replied softly, recalling the jolts of pure power he'd felt while drinking a goblet full of Lucien Andrakkar's blood. There was so much strength there. But no matter what they tried, his *daemon* brethren had not yet found a way to convert that potential into what they all sought: a way to walk in the light without burning, and more, the ability to shift forms. If they could do that, they would no longer be bound by the limitations of their weak bodies.

They were already children of the gods. With the power of Lucien's blood, they would be gods in their own right. Or would have been, if they'd only had more time. But even if Lucien hadn't done the impossible, Jagrin thought, there was no guarantee that he would have lived long enough to endure much more. Between the regular bloodlettings and the discipline he often invited with his sharp tongue, the dragon wouldn't have lasted much longer.

He'd been dying at last, finally infected with the sickness that extended periods of torture in the pits brought on. All the signs had been there.

Yet another reason why his escape still made no sense.

Cadmus relaxed into his throne, angling his body toward Jagrin. "I believe I know how Lucien Andrakkar escaped us."

Jagrin sucked in a breath. He'd spent these last weeks scouring Coracin for any scrap of information and had come up empty-handed. He'd assumed that if he could find nothing, then there was nothing to be found. His reputation in such matters was impeccable. But it seemed his shame was not yet at an end. Anger and embarrassment welled up within him. Still, he kept his expression impassive. He would not show weakness before his king.

"How, your highness?"

Cadmus smiled, showing dagger-sharp teeth. "I can see you're surprised, Jagrin. And indeed, I doubt anyone but myself would have thought of it. A benefit of having ruled for five hundred years. None of the rest of you would even remember... but I"—he shook his head—"I cannot forget."

Jagrin frowned, confused. "Your highness?"

"You know, of course, about my beloved Reynelle," Cadmus began, and Jagrin had to fight back a cringe at the use of the word *beloved*. It was unnatural for a *daemon* to have such feelings. Fortunately, though, Cadmus continued without expecting a reply.

Cadmus's ruby eyes went far-off. "It was so long ago, but I still remember her face so clearly. I never dreamed she would return my affection, of course. I was shocked that I had any feeling for her to begin with. But she and I began to meet in secret... so easy, with the *Athin* so convinced of their dominion over the Northern plains. Our power, combined with theirs, would have made a grand alliance. We could have had all of Coracin at our feet. But her damned brother would have none of it, locking Reynelle away where even I couldn't reach her."

"So you destroyed them all," Jagrin said with a nod. This was the only part of the tale of which he wholeheartedly approved. "A fitting punishment. And cursing the ruling line with one of the *narial* was an inspired touch, your highness. But I'm sure it devoured the last of them and returned to the deepest recesses of the pits years ago. A *narial's* hunger is never denied for long, and everyone knows they only grow stronger the longer they're forced to stalk one person without sustenance." He cocked his head, puzzled. "But I don't know what this has to do with the dragon."

Jagrin knew he'd said the wrong thing when Cadmus's eyes narrowed with a dangerous flash. "You doubt me, Lord Jagrin? You, who couldn't even keep a dying dragon in a dungeon from which no one has ever escaped?"

Jagrin felt his skin grow cold, and the cuts from Cadmus's whip began to burn. "Of course not, your highness. Forgive me. I may not understand, but I've learned never to doubt your instincts." *By the blackest gods, how tired he was of pandering.*

Cadmus considered him for a moment, and Jagrin barely concealed his sigh of relief when the king continued talking as though Jagrin had never made the ill-advised comment.

"I was up late into the morning, thinking about what Lorgan said he saw right before he discovered the dragon's cell empty."

Jagrin nodded. "A flash of light. And there were two voices speaking."

"Exactly. Then, as I often do, I thought of Reynelle, and what her brother did to keep her from me. And suddenly I knew."

This was a part of the story Jagrin hadn't heard. "What did he do? I always assumed he locked her away and placed a spell on her so that you couldn't find her."

"No. There is no place on Coracin I would not have found her, no spell that could have kept me from her."

Cadmus's voice lowered to a growl as he remembered. "But the *Athin* rulers had a rare gift, one that has never again been seen in our realm. It did not deter the *narial*, of course. Once you have been cursed with one, it is bound to your soul. But Reynelle was poisoned against me and then taken somewhere far beyond my reach. For the rulers of the *Athin*, apart from just being masters of water and ice, could also leap from world to world in the blink of an eye." He looked directly at Jagrin. "Or a flash of light."

Jagrin stared at Cadmus, aghast. *World jumpers?* He had heard of such things, of course, in the context of legend. But he had no idea such things were possible. True, his kind had a connection to the Earthly realm, sister to their own, but it was tenuous at best. And passage between any two worlds, to his knowledge, had to be facilitated by the stones that the gods had left behind.

If there was one who could do such things, the implications were staggering.

"Do you… do you think that one of the *Athin* lives?" Jagrin asked, stunned. "Have they managed to break the curse?"

Cadmus smiled again, a terrible thing. "Yes. And no. I have spoken to the shadows, and there is one among them who has not yet returned."

Jagrin shuddered at the thought of descending to the level of the pits where the *narial* dwelled. As a *daemon* he cherished the blackness, yes… but though his powers gave him dominion over the soul-eating shadows, the creatures made his skin crawl. He never completely trusted that they wouldn't turn on him before he could use his abilities to stop them.

"But even if this is so," Jagrin said, "even if one remains, the *Athin* dwelled far from the Black Mountains of the dragons. Far from everyone! Stealing Lucien would make no sense…"

Cadmus's smile widened. "It would seem not to, on the surface. But in fact, something has bothered me since the night when the dragons battled the Dyadd Morgaine. The night you brought Lucien Andrakkar to me. The description of the one who shouldn't exist, the male Dyim, and his power."

Jagrin thought back, though it wasn't a night he cared to revisit. The Andrakkar had promised him an *arukhin* slave in return for his help in procuring the Dyim witch he coveted. Had sworn a blood oath, in fact. And broken it. The fight that had ensued in the dark of the woods of the *Carith Noor* had involved a being who should not exist, a fair-haired, blue-eyed man who could cast icy death from his fingertips. A male Dyim, when there had never been one.

Then Jagrin remembered it, the humiliating loss of a half-dead *arukhin* to a man who had come to rescue it in a blinding flash of light, so bright he and others had been burned by it. So bright he had never been able to make out a face. And everything clicked into place at once.

"The Dyim," Jagrin said hoarsely, stunned. "The male Dyim. He is half *Athin*."

"Indeed," Cadmus said, sounding pleased. "The very last of them, no doubt stalked by the *narial* that will have killed all others of his line. I can't imagine how hungry the shadow must be by now, how great the need to finish its duty and return to the deepest reaches of the pits. The Dyim must be quite strong. A function, I suppose, of the blood of Morgaine also running through his veins."

Jagrin sat shaking his head. "Amazing. How many years has it been?"

"Oh, two hundred, at least," Cadmus replied. "I assumed the curse was long over by now. Though it is gratifying, I must say, to know that the line is still being punished. Not that it will return Reynelle to me, but still. Fitting. The plague with which I afflicted the rest of that tribe was far too easy a way for the ruling family to die." His lips curled. "As though the other tribes are superior to the *daemon*. As though we are dirt beneath their feet, when we could destroy them all with a wave of the hand."

"He is a strange one, this Dyim," Jagrin said. "To help the dragon who once hunted his sister so ardently. I know the lengths to which Lucien went. He risked all."

"And lost all," Cadmus added. "But really, the Dyim's behavior is not so strange. He is a blood-drinker, like the rest of the Dyadd. And there are only two ways to destroy a *narial*, neither of which are realistic for most. One is, of course, to bring the shadow into the light, no easy task. The other…"

Jagrin laughed, stunned by the Dyim's audacity as he realized what he was after. "He thinks to drink the blood of the dragon and fight. But," he said, his eyes flicking to Cadmus, "the blood would have to be at full strength and totally pure, freely given." He laughed again, his mood lightening by the second. "They are enemies, these two. And no dragon would willingly give his blood to anyone. What can he be thinking?"

"He's obviously desperate," replied Cadmus. "You

and I have known the power of dragon blood, even weakened and taken under duress. Who can blame him for trying? But he'll fail, and miserably. That dragon was near death. Nothing can save him now, after how long he spent in the pits." A noise escaped him that sounded almost like a purr, completely self-satisfied. "It pleases me greatly to think of how desperate this half-breed *Athin* must be. How he must, more and more often, think of just giving up. That as more and more of his soul is torn away, he longs for death."

"And so he keeps the dying dragon and hopes for a miracle." Jagrin imagined it, amused despite the anguish he'd endured over this. "He is a fool, your highness. He will die, right along with the dragon."

"Of course," Cadmus said. "But it's not enough. Not nearly."

Jagrin saw the bloodlust in his king's eyes, and felt his own rise in response. "What do you have in mind?"

"He is the last," Cadmus replied, leaning forward slightly, his eyes alight. "The last of a tribe I swore to destroy. And now, he has insulted the *daemon*, stealing from us what is ours. I wish to see him die, Jagrin. More, I wish to look into his eyes as he dies and see the light of the *Athin* vanish forever. It is my right."

"So it is," agreed Jagrin, though he was less interested in final justice than he was in exacting payment for the humiliation and pain the Dyim had caused him. "Do we destroy the Dyadd, then, as you did the *Athin*?"

"That would please me," Cadmus growled. "But no. The Goddess Morgaine watches over her people yet. And the *Dyana* Rowan is a dragon halfling, beloved by her people and more terrifying in her anger than any who have come before her. Too, she has the support of the returned *arukhin*, who have proven to be formidable in their own right. It is not a battle I think it wise to engage. Not now."

"Then what do you propose?"

"Suffering, of course," Cadmus said, his voice like a caress. "Singular, beautiful suffering for the last ice mage. A fitting, final payment for my beautiful Reynelle. But first… I will need your help, old friend. You are the greatest hunter among the *daemon*. I would ask no other."

Jagrin stared, surprised at the compliment and the endearment. But then, he supposed the two of them *were* friends, of a sort. They'd certainly known one another a very, very long time.

"Anything you need, your highness," he said solemnly. "I will do all I can."

Cadmus laid a long, slender white hand on his arm, and Jagrin could feel the dark magic coursing through him. His mouth began to water in anticipation of all the glorious pain that was to come. He had never forgotten the burns he'd endured at the hands of the faceless sorcerer who had taken his *arukhin* prize. Nor would the lash marks he bore because of his actions soon heal. Now, he and his king would make the Dyim pay.

"Find him," said Cadmus, his smile hungry. "Find both of them. The rest will be my pleasure."

Chapter 6

CAT AWOKE IN A TANGLE OF LIMBS THAT DIDN'T SEEM to belong to her, with a finger in her ear and a knee uncomfortably wedged into her stomach. She opened one eye and groggily surveyed the scene on her bed, wincing a little at the cheery morning light. Inches from her face was a pile of brown curly hair threaded through with pink. As she looked at it, it snored softly. From behind her came a sleepy sigh, and the finger jabbed harder into her ear.

Oh yeah. Sisters.

"Ugh," Cat groaned. The only response she got was another snore.

Slowly, the memories of the night before returned. She'd talked with Poppy and Skye into the wee hours, until they'd all fallen asleep curled together like a pile of puppies. It had, Cat reflected as she tried to wiggle away from the knee with zero luck, been both comforting and comfortable at the time.

Now, not so much.

Still, they'd all needed it. Her sisters had been almost as shaken up as she was when she'd gotten back, waiting silent and somber in her room.

"We went looking for you," Skye had said, gray eyes enormous in her pale face. "But we found Dad instead." She'd looked to Poppy, who looked more unsettled than Cat had ever seen her.

"What happened? What did he say?" Cat had demanded, both worried and frightened. Poppy's reply hadn't done anything to make that better.

"Nothing. Not to us, anyway. He didn't see us." Poppy had sighed, looking more worried about their father than Cat had seen her in a long time; usually she just was angry. The anger, somehow, had been less troubling.

"He looked so lost and alone, Cat," Skye had added, her gray eyes stormy. "Except… Poppy and I aren't sure he *was* alone. There was such strange whispering. And the funniest smell. But I just don't *know*, and that's the worst. How can we help him if we don't have any clue what's going on?"

That was exactly what Cat was wrestling with, though now she seemed to have a double dose of it. So she had given comfort as well as taken it. And she'd shared a small part of what had happened to her because she'd desperately needed to, just to try and make some sense of it. Cat knew that she could trust Poppy and Skye implicitly; they wouldn't breathe a word to Duncan. But still, she hadn't been able to tell all of it. The kiss, that stunning, drowning kiss, she'd kept to herself.

That and the bite. It wasn't like her to hold things back, but for whatever reason, what had passed between her and Bastian felt intensely private. She wasn't ready to share it. Especially not when she didn't understand it.

Some vacation, Cat thought. It had certainly started off with a bang.

She was plenty worried about her father this morning. But even in sleep, her thoughts had been consumed with Bastian. She needed to see him, to be with him. To make sure he hadn't vanished into thin air during the night…

or worse. She hoped he would be here to talk to her bright and early as promised. She'd wing it from there.

She suddenly realized that the sun peeking through the slit in the curtains was awfully bright. She shot a glance at the softly ticking alarm clock on the night-stand: 10 a.m. Her eyes widened. *God, he could be here already!*

Cat sat up quickly, dislodging Skye's finger from her ear and scooting away from Poppy's sharp knee. She tossed the covers off, eliciting groans from her sisters as she slid down the middle of the bed to land on the floor.

"The hell?" Poppy grunted.

"Cooooold," Skye complained, curling into a little ball.

"Seriously," Cat replied, rolling her eyes as she grabbed fistfuls of the white eyelet comforter and tossed it over the two of them so that not even their heads were visible. "Go back to sleep. You're not done yet."

She moved quickly once her feet hit the floor, digging through the open suitcase propped against the wall. She didn't usually shoot for "beautiful" on such short notice, but she could at least not look like something from *Night of the Living Dead*. Cat tossed sweats, several T-shirts, and an old pair of shorts on the floor behind her before settling on her favorite pair of jeans and a hunter green tank top that she'd been told brought out the color of her eyes. Her pajamas sailed into the rapidly growing pile on the floor as she dressed quickly.

Cat debated the practicality of a pair of heels, but remembering the acres of grass was enough for common sense to win out. In the end, she shoved her feet into her ancient Birkenstocks and decided just to be thankful that her pedicure was at least new. She clomped quickly into the bathroom connecting her room and Skye's to brush her teeth and do something with her sleep-snarled hair. That was one of the good things about having pin-straight hair, she decided as she began to drag a brush through the long fall of deep-brown silk. There wasn't much a decent brushing couldn't fix.

Considering how exhausting last night had been, Cat's first look in the mirror startled her. Instead of seeing the pale, sleepy wraith she'd expected, she looked somehow more alive, more vital than she did even on her best days. Her eyes shone like sun-kissed honey, while her cheeks were faintly flushed. And her skin, she noted, running one hand down her cheek in near shock, was just about *glowing*.

Apart from being the most gorgeous man she'd ever laid eyes on, Bastian was also apparently the world's most effective beauty treatment. As though anyone would need an extra reason to hang all over him, she thought wonderingly. She was stunned that he wasn't completely covered by clinging women at all times.

As the hair on the back of her neck began to rise at the thought, she was also very glad that he wasn't. If there was going to be bloodshed at this gathering, she didn't want to be the responsible party.

When Cat emerged from the bathroom, Poppy was sitting up looking blearily at her.

"Where are you going?"

Cat considered her options and then decided she didn't have time to argue with her younger sister about any of them. "Out."

"Oh." Poppy swung her legs over the side of the bed,

stretched languorously, and yawned. Then, frowning, she touched one black-painted fingernail to the corner of her mouth. "Ew. Drooled."

"Gross." Cat wrinkled her nose.

Poppy grinned unrepentantly. "Yep. Also, I'm coming."

A muffled voice beneath the covers chimed in immediately. "Me too. I'm getting up. Almost. In a second. Hang on…"

"Um, you don't have to get up right now," Cat offered, even as her sisters began to do just that.

Skye sat up and tipped her head to the side, eyebrows raised above smoky gray eyes. "We wanted to meet the relatives coming in today, right? Hard to do that if you go and we stay here. And anyway," she continued, a wicked smile blossoming, "I want to see you work your seductive powers on Mr. Hot-and-Weird again, since I missed the show last night."

Cat could only roll her eyes back into her head and groan loudly. "Are you *both* going to start calling him that?"

"I still think we could help him remove some of the weird," Poppy grumbled. "What good is being born with powers if we never get to use them to help out? And by the way, not to be a complete bummer, but I'm not sure how cool I am with you snuggling up to some guy who gets chased through the woods by his own personal boogeyman, Cat. Understand where I'm coming from on that, okay?"

"I do understand, Poppy," Cat replied. "But you need to understand where I'm coming from too… Bastian expressly said this was his problem, and that anyone who messed with it would be in danger… but only if they messed with it." She looked away, afraid the guilt of her lie would show brightly in her eyes. "Which is why I was *not* supposed to tell you."

Poppy fixed her with a stubborn glare. "Relax, Cat. We know our limitations. But if I feel as though I can do something useful for a change, I'll at least give it a shot. Fair warning."

"Fair enough," Cat said, knowing well enough to be scared of the mulish expression on her sister's face. This compromise was the best she was going to get, so she would have to take it.

Cat shook her head helplessly, watching Poppy get up to rummage through her things while Skye nearly fell out of bed and then skulked into the bathroom. Cat knew exactly what Poppy meant about making herself useful and was surprised she'd offered. Surprised and touched. Poppy's perfectionism was well known to the family, and though she was willing to work on her abilities in private or with her mother and sisters, she very rarely used her gifts on or around anyone else. She didn't like to screw up, and she really didn't like to be *seen* screwing up.

And, since magic was hardly a science, screwups tended to happen. A lot.

Cat was intimately acquainted with that fact.

Cat sighed and crossed her arms over her chest. She knew she might as well accept the company and get on with it, because she was getting it whether she wanted it or not. And really, if Poppy and Skye were willing to use their magic to help out, it would be stupid *not* to bring them.

Cat watched them move around the room in what looked like slo-mo. "Fine. Just hurry up, okay?"

She wasn't sure how much good the admonition would do; Skye, in particular, was a notorious primper when it came to her hair. Some of their teenage fights over the bathroom had been legendary. But to their credit, neither sister took more time than she had, and about ten minutes later, the three of them headed out. Poppy, Cat noted with wry amusement, had managed to wear all black once again, even though they were *her* clothes and she didn't remember packing any plain black shirts.

The upstairs was completely deserted, every door shut, not a soul around except themselves as they made their way quickly to the back stairs. Cat thought wistfully of the excitement they'd all felt the night before when they'd taken the same route. Now, there was only tension and worry. And she knew it wasn't just her. They descended quickly, their footfalls the only sound in the strange silence of the manor house. Poppy frowned at her watch.

"It's after ten. Wasn't everyone supposed to be coming in today?"

Cat didn't have an explanation, and there was enough on her mind without worrying about the lack of company. *Iargail* was a big place. No one had mentioned what time the MacInneses would start arriving, anyway, so she didn't find the silence all that odd.

"Count your blessings," Cat said. The three of them trooped down a hallway, past the same series of elegantly appointed but notably empty rooms they'd seen the night before, and through the double doors that opened onto the circular stone terrace. Skye was first out, jerking to a halt so suddenly that Cat and Poppy nearly toppled over one another as they emerged into the bright sunlight.

"Oh my God," she said.

Cat could only stand there, open-mouthed, and stare at the sea of tents and people that seemed to have materialized overnight, covering the rolling lawn so that *Iargail* now looked as though it was about to host a rock festival instead of just a family reunion. Dozens of white peaks had sprung up, as well as a ratty old camper that looked as though its glory days were long behind it. Mingling around the tents were scores of people, laughing, chatting, or just wandering around. With the unmistakable resemblance most bore to one another, there could be no doubt: the MacInnes Pack had arrived. In a crowd like this, she had no idea where to begin to look for Bastian.

What had been Cat's fondest wish for two weeks was now her worst nightmare.

Shit.

Somewhere in the boisterous crowd, a fiddle burst into a merry jig to delighted cries and the sounds of rhythmic clapping. Cat realized, all at once, that most of the men were wearing kilts. The plaid was striking—a deep green crossed with bright blue and shot through with thin bands of yellow and red. But to see it worn by so many was positively overwhelming. And she had to wonder…

"Do you think they're wearing them the right way and going commando?" Poppy whispered, putting Cat's thoughts into words and making Skye giggle at the thought of a huge crowd of men without underwear.

"I hope it isn't windy while we're here," Cat murmured, shaking her head. "I don't think my heart could take it." No doubt visualizing what would happen in a gale-force wind, Poppy laughed right along with Skye.

"Girls!" cried a booming, jovial voice, a welcome distraction from Cat's speculation. She turned her head to watch her uncle approaching, striding through the crowd like the king of the castle and wearing a grin that plainly said he was in his element and delighted to see them. He wore the MacInnes plaid as well, and Cat was again struck by the fact that the man was in his early sixties. He barely looked fifty. Whatever gene had facilitated that, she hoped like hell she'd gotten it.

The biggest surprise, however, was striding right along beside him.

"Dad?" asked Cat, laughing incredulously. Freddie MacInnes had apparently brought his own traditional Highland clothing to the gathering and not mentioned it, because he was dressed just like his brother. He looked somehow healthier and more vibrant in the kilt and crisp white shirt than he ever had in his purple Jimi Hendrix T-shirt.

Until he got closer, that was, and Cat could see that his smile was a little too forced, a little too strained. And that it didn't quite reach his tired, reddened eyes.

Where were you last night, Dad? she thought.

Cat noticed her sisters sharing an uneasy glance and knew she wasn't the only one concerned.

"Morning, girls. Though I was beginning to wonder whether it would be afternoon before we saw you," Duncan said with a wink at Cat. "How was your run last night? I thought of going out to join you, but I woke up in the damned recliner about three this morning." He chuckled. "It's hell getting old."

Cat stiffened and shot a quick look at her father. As she'd feared, his smile had faded away at Duncan's words. He was now glaring at her. The oldest. The one, as he'd once told her in a rare moment of candor, who was responsible for keeping her sisters safe.

But what was he afraid of?

Poppy quickly sought to turn the subject. "So when did everyone show up, anyway? Seems like we missed the party."

"Ah, no, no," Duncan replied with a dismissive wave of his hand. "Takes everyone a while to get set up, and we're missing a few people yet. Gideon and Carly flew in last night, so they'll be driving out from Edinburgh later today. You'll enjoy them, I think. Carly's a sweetheart, and she's much better natured since the morning sickness stopped. And then the whole Dyadd's coming in tomorrow night. Rowan's promised us quite a show, so you won't want to miss that. I was telling your father..."

He turned to where Freddie had been but trailed off, frowning, when he found his brother had disappeared. Cat felt her stomach begin to knot. He'd vanished as soon as Duncan had turned his head, taking off at top speed into the crowd, but not before raking his daughters with a look that contained more fury than she'd ever seen in him. Her father was a noted screwup, but Cat had always thought of him as fairly docile.

That enraged look, so unlike him, had scared her.

"Hm," muttered Duncan, oblivious to what had just happened. "Well, he was just here, anyway."

"Shame," Poppy said flatly and then turned the subject before Duncan could do more than raise his eyebrows at her tone. "So what's on the schedule for today? Looks like a party to me, even if it is a day early."

"The gathering has pretty well started," Duncan agreed, and Cat breathed a silent sigh of relief that he seemed to have been diverted by the question. She just hoped he didn't look at Skye too closely. She had gone very pale.

"The games won't start until tomorrow, though," Duncan continued. "For instance, we'll have a weight-throwing competition right over…"

A loud cheer went up at the far end of the crowd then, roughly in the place Duncan had begun to gesture. All of their heads turned in that direction, and Duncan's smile was suddenly strained as they watched what appeared to be half a tree go sailing through the air in the distance.

"Speaking of seeing things," he said through clenched teeth, "have any of you seen Bastian skulking around here? I'd like to have a few words with him about all the help he was supposed to be in corralling this lot."

"I saw him," Cat volunteered. "Last night. Um, just in passing. He mentioned not feeling well… that could be why he isn't here yet." She could see she hadn't managed to diffuse much of Duncan's obvious irritation, but she supposed every little bit helped.

"Hmph," Duncan snorted as yet another tree went flying, to more raucous cheering. "I'm not feeling very well myself, watching my forest be uprooted for caber-tossing practice. I can't be everywhere at once. The lad's capable of exuding authority when he wants to. And his ability to fry people's asses doesn't hurt, either."

He shook his head, wearing a thunderous frown. "He asked to come stay for a bit to work some things out for himself, and I figured it would be good for him to get a break from all of those sisters for a change. Now he never comes out; I haven't a clue when or if he plans to leave; and worst of all, I'm stuck with minimal help and four hundred werewolves who've come for a party. That's what I get for my bloody soft heart," he snarled.

"What's caber tossing?" Poppy asked, completely distracted.

"We see who can throw the pine tree the farthest," Duncan replied. "The actual game is tomorrow."

"But... they're not throwing pine trees," Skye said, frowning as what looked more like an oak, leaves and all, caught some air. When Duncan simply glared at her, understanding dawned. "Oh."

"If you need something done, we can try," Cat offered, even though her heart was sinking more with every minute that passed with no sign of Bastian. Not only was he blowing her off, but he was letting down Duncan, whom she liked very much. Had he lied to her? Taken off? Or worse, died? She was rapidly approaching the point where banging on his door and yelling at him became an appealing option.

If he had been one of her students, he would so totally be at the Desk of Disgrace for a week. *Minimum.*

"Well, that's quite sweet of you," Duncan said, and though his tone was appreciative, Cat noticed that his eyes were sizing them up as though he was examining potential slave labor. "We've got quite a contingent of the pack cooking up a storm, but it would be good to have you three try and keep it from becoming a feeding frenzy..."

Duncan's voice trailed off as his eyes dropped to study something on her shirt. Cat silently cursed herself for having gotten dressed so quickly. She was probably wearing something totally stained. But that wouldn't explain the way Duncan's voice, when he found it again, had changed in an instant from warm to potentially violent.

"What is that?" he asked softly.

"What is what?" she asked, confused, glancing down at her shirt and seeing nothing. Then she saw where his flashing eyes were riveted, and she understood. He wasn't staring at her shirt at all.

She'd forgotten to cover up the supernatural hickey.

Cat's stomach dropped, and she quickly dragged her hair forward to cover the bruised puncture wounds on the side of her neck. She felt as though she'd been warped back to high school, accosted by her disapproving mother over some very obvious kissing-related whisker burn after a hot date. Though Mariana had never looked like she was about to go nuclear over it.

"Where is he?" Duncan growled.

"Who?" Skye asked, looking nervously between her sister and her uncle.

"It's not his fault," Cat began, and watched Duncan's eyes flash angrily.

"The hell it isn't! I've let him stay here, skulking about the grounds at all hours. I've trusted him and made a friend of him, even though he's odder than most of the Dyadd, which is saying something. And he repays me by sinking his teeth into my niece the first night she's here! Taking full advantage of the fact that you haven't had any experience with his lot and their blood-swilling ways, of course…"

Poppy looked at Cat, startled. "He bit you?"

She could only wince. "Well…"

"He sure as hell did," Duncan interrupted her, eyes going a shade of yellow that wasn't exactly reassuring. "I can't see why he looks down his nose at vampires when he acts just like them!"

"He didn't take advantage of me," Cat insisted, beginning to bristle at the way Duncan was so ready to blame Bastian for something in which she'd been a willing participant.

"You don't need to defend him, Catriona," Duncan thundered, ignoring her. "They're all far too pretty and far too used to having whomever they like. He could have stayed away. I suppose he was waiting for the first moment you were alone…"

"Um, Uncle Duncan, isn't your son's wife one of 'them'?" Skye asked softly, pointing out something Duncan appeared to have forgotten in the heat of the moment. He didn't much like being reminded of it, from the look on his face.

"Well, that's… that's different!" It didn't make any sense, but Skye shrank back and found something interesting in the distance to study anyway. Cat didn't blame her. She was torn between being touched at Duncan's concern and being pissed that he'd gone from zero to complete meltdown over the situation in the blink of an eye.

"I'll be having a word with him," Duncan snarled, wagging his finger for emphasis. "Don't you worry, sweet. He won't be after you again once I'm done with him."

"Why didn't you tell us that he bit you?" Poppy demanded, apparently stuck on that point. Cat gave her a withering glare before turning it on Duncan. He was definitely pushing her toward "pissed."

"I don't *want* you to have a word with him!" she snapped, her head spinning from the argument. "And he didn't take advantage of me! I was fine with it!"

"Seriously?" asked Skye, looking intrigued.

Duncan, seeming to realize he might have reacted too strongly, tried a new tack and patted Cat's arm sympathetically. That backfired miserably, as Cat felt her own temper begin to hit critical mass.

"Now don't get upset, dear," he said kindly. "You couldn't have been expected to defend yourself. You've never met a Drakkyn before, and a tricky lot they can be if you're not used to them."

"I can't freaking *believe* you didn't tell us he bit you," Poppy muttered darkly, glaring from beneath sooty lashes. *Great*, Cat thought. *Just great.* Poppy had joined Duncan in being angry about the sordid details of her nonexistent love life. But Poppy was just mad that she hadn't gotten the details, while her uncle was mad that the details were at all sordid. She couldn't win.

Wistfully, Cat glanced at Skye, who had somehow managed to sidle several feet away without anyone noticing and looked prepared to take flight. God, she wished she could bolt right about now. It was one of those times when being one of the X-Men would have been a lot more helpful than being a plain old werewolf.

Duncan gave Cat a knowing glance. "She didn't tell you because it was that bad, Poppy. Give your sister the benefit of the doubt."

That was it. Oblivious to the fact that heads had already begun to turn curiously in their direction, she balled her hands into fists and let out a short, infuriated screech that finally stunned her companions into silence.

"Goddammit, would you all listen to me? Yes, Poppy, okay? Yes. Bastian bit me. And it was hot and fabulous and you know what? I didn't really feel like I needed to share that with you! And you know what else?" She turned away from her gaping sister and rounded on Duncan, who had begun to look extremely uncomfortable on top of the anger. Well, she thought angrily, if he wanted to get into her evening with Bastian, then he was going to get adjectives like the ones she'd used.

"I didn't need to defend myself! I didn't want to defend myself! Because I'm an adult woman who occasionally likes to…"

"Now, just hang on a second," Duncan interjected, a look of horror on his face as he put his hands up, as though he could ward off whatever comment Cat was about to make.

Cat crossed her arms over her chest, tossed her hair, and glared defiantly up at her uncle. "No, you hang on. I may not have had the training that the rest of the MacInneses have, but that doesn't make me naive or stupid or defenseless. Far from it. And if you're going to bitch Bastian out, you might as well bitch me out, too, because I also bit *him*!"

The statement had popped out without one iota of thought, but she couldn't take it back.

Even though she really, really wished she could.

Poppy, Skye, and Duncan all gaped at her in unison, their mouths dropping open in such perfect time that it looked like they'd synchronized it beforehand. It would have been funny if Duncan hadn't also looked so stricken.

So much for her triumphant last word, Cat thought, suddenly feeling a little sick. She was reminded of the day, back in college, when she'd taught almost the full lesson for the class where she was assisting before realizing her fly was down. In front of *everyone*.

"You did *what*?" Duncan asked hoarsely.

"Oh, Cat, you know Dad always said we're not supposed to," Skye said, eyes wide.

"Well, yeah," Cat stammered, searching for some sort of defense. "But it's… um… we just got carried away, you know, and… Jesus, Skye, don't look at me that way! He's some kind of sorcerer! Dad just said not to bite *humans*! And Bastian was fine—it's no big deal. I don't think it's any of anyone's business, honestly!"

She sounded a lot more nonchalant than she felt. Because while it was true that Bastian hadn't seemed hurt by the bite, it had actually felt like a *very* big deal. And Duncan's stricken expression only confirmed that.

"Do you have the slightest clue what you've done, lass?" he asked. "Could you really not know what you've done?"

He wasn't angry anymore, Cat saw. Now he looked like she'd just killed someone.

The anger had been preferable.

She glanced at her sisters, who, though solemn, each shook their heads at her questioning look. So she turned back to Duncan reluctantly, not really wanting to hear what he was going to say next. Maybe she *had* hurt Bastian. Maybe she'd contributed. But why hadn't he said anything? Then again, things had gotten crazy awfully fast last night…

"Uncle Duncan?" she asked, suddenly feeling very young and very out of her depth. And more worryingly, a little dizzy. "Did I hurt him?"

Her uncle spoke through a clenched jaw. "Not as badly as I'm going to hurt your father. How could he not have told you?"

A strange, foreboding chill slipped down her spine, making her shiver. "Told me what? Are you sure I didn't kill him?"

She fully expected more yelling or a solemn, terrible acknowledgment that, yes, she had sentenced Bastian *an* Morgaine to die. But instead Duncan just sighed, scrubbing a hand through his hair and appearing to be at a complete loss. Finally he said, "No, lass. You, ah… you've mated with him."

Cat stared, waiting for the punch line. Poppy giggled nervously. "She didn't say she did *that*. Did you, Cat?"

Cat frowned. "No, I… no, Uncle Duncan, we didn't. Um, do that, I mean." God, how had she ended up in this conversation again? Skye, however, seemed to have realized something she and Poppy didn't. Understanding flooded her face, closely followed by sympathy.

"Oh. *Oh*," she murmured. "Oh, Cat."

"What? What the hell did I do?" Cat demanded, beginning to be a little frightened.

Duncan reached out and placed a hand on her shoulder, and Cat wasn't sure whether it was to steady himself or her. It was better than the patting, but not by much, considering the circumstances.

"You and Bastian are mated now, Cat," he said slowly,

looking in her eyes so the news would sink in. "The bite of the werewolf is permanently binding. It's why we don't normally bite humans... most of them can't handle the Change. My own sweet Laura couldn't. It seems to work differently with other Drakkyn, though. No," Duncan said, "I'm sure Bastian will be fine. He's just, ah... yours now. Forever." His smile looked pained.

Permanently. Forever. The words echoed in her ears as the world tilted strangely beneath her feet and her head felt suddenly separate from the rest of her body. She'd be damned if she'd faint, though. She'd work through this like she did everything else. Who needed getting to know one another and dating? It could be worse. Bastian was gorgeous and interesting. Not to mention semivampiric. And disturbingly secretive. And dying of some freakish curse. It was nothing to faint over.

"Holy shit," she heard Poppy say. "Which one of us gets to kill Dad for not mentioning this mating thing?"

"Do you think we should welcome Bastian to the family?" Skye asked.

"Cat?" That was Duncan. "You don't look very well..."

And with that, she hit the ground.

Chapter 7

BASTIAN WOKE TO THE SOUND OF DRUMS.

At least, that's what his exhausted mind insisted the sound was. But as he slowly dragged himself into consciousness, the drumsticks sounded more like fists. And the drums, he became increasingly sure, were none other than his front door.

"Bastian? You in there?"

Sort of, he thought. It depended on the definition of "there." He seemed to be in one piece, but he felt as though he'd been run over about a dozen times by a Mack truck. And that was the easier part to deal with. His patchy memories from the previous night, not to mention his throbbing shoulder, made it impossible to ignore the fact that some very important things in his life had now changed. Permanently.

And his and Cat's biology didn't give a damn whether that had been a bad idea.

"Open up, Bastian. It's Poppy MacInnes, Cat's sister? Hello-oo?"

Her sister. Fantastic. He had sisters. When they banded together on anything involving him, it had always boded very, very ill. What was this one doing here? Had Cat sent her? Had she shown up on her own? He remembered then that he'd promised to talk this morning to Cat about his issues—which appeared to be increasing in number by the moment. But it couldn't be that late. His eyes wandered to the alarm clock, and he sighed.

Oh, yes it could.

Bastian scrubbed a hand over his face, trying to block out the banging at the door, and hoped that once he woke up fully he'd be able to figure out what to do. No scenario that he'd envisioned was anything like this.

He now had a mate. The cursed Dyim hiding a dragon in the middle of an estate of werewolves had gotten himself a mate. Unwittingly, to be sure. But he hadn't exactly been pushing her away. In fact, from what he remembered, he'd decided that kissing beautiful, naked women in the moonlight was an exceptionally safe pastime for him. Especially when his father had mentioned something about need, about *love*, destroying him.

Not that he loved Catriona MacInnes. He didn't think. Yet.

Bastian groaned and considered burying himself beneath the covers for the rest of his wretched life, however short that turned out to be. *Stupid*, he thought, shoving his head under his pillow. He'd been stupid to spend any time with her, knowing how attracted he was. And utterly insane to have kissed her. Among other things.

What the hell had possessed him to drink from her? He'd always taken care to make what blood drinking he needed to keep his strength up distant and anonymous. The women had been strangers, and it hadn't been difficult for him to keep it that way. But Cat was different. He'd known it.

For the first time in his life, he hadn't been able to help himself.

Bastian could still taste her blood on his tongue, dark

and sweet and alive with the power of the moon. He had never had anything like it, an elixir so heady that he'd found himself almost drunk on it. And even now he could feel her running through his veins.

Of course, that was what happened when you drank a woman's blood and then allowed her to bind herself to you forever in return. There was a certain closeness about that, right?

A closeness that seemed to extend to the pain the *narial* inflicted on him. No wonder his father had warned him. But it was too late to undo it. How he was going to keep himself safe—and so keep her safe—would have to become a main priority. Just as soon as he figured out how the hell to do it.

The knocking continued. "Bastian, open the damned door. I can hear you shuffling around in there. Look, I know what happened last night. So does Skye." There was a pause. "And so does Duncan."

Duncan? Bastian pulled the pillow off his head and lay there, staring at a crack in the ceiling. If Duncan had seen the bite marks, he'd be dead before the *narial* had another chance. He considered the old Alpha a friend, but somehow he doubted that taking blood from his beautiful and inexperienced niece was going to go over well. And by the Goddess, from the flashes of her past he'd seen during their bonding, "inexperienced" didn't even begin to cover the disservice her father had done her. Her bravery was a wonder; thanks only to that and her stubborn, inquisitive nature, she'd learned to manage her physical abilities. But Cat had had no way of knowing the rules or of understanding the very essence of what she was.

And now, for her trouble, she'd saddled herself with him. It couldn't possibly work.

Just like it couldn't possibly be undone.

The theme of his entire existence to date, all the way back to his conception, appeared to be impossible situations. It was making him very, very tired.

Bastian buried himself back beneath the pillow, wondering whether Cat would be relieved that their union was probably going to be a short one.

The click of the lock surprised him, but the voice that spoke immediately afterward had Bastian tumbling out of bed and running for the front door, despite the angry protestations of every muscle in his abused body.

"Oh, how lovely. A stray," said Lucien, his deep voice dripping with derision. "I don't suppose it occurred to you that some people might not answer the door because they were *asleep*."

Bastian realized he wasn't wearing anything a split second before he emerged into the living area. Panicked, he yanked open a drawer, pulled on the top pair of boxer shorts, and careened back out of the room as Lucien continued to upbraid their uninvited guest.

I'm dead, Bastian thought. He was glad to find that even though he was sore, he appeared to have recovered well enough from last night. Looking like the wrath of Drak would not help in this encounter. He was certain that Poppy had brought someone who would recognize the dragon who had caused so much trouble. Like Duncan, who had probably already decided to kill him, and who would now make it excruciatingly painful. Silently, he cursed his captive. Of all the days for Lucien to finally get out of bed and wander around, why did it have to be today? All he'd managed in the rest of the time he'd been there had been quick and tottering trips to the bathroom. Now, at the worst possible time, Lucien Andrakkar had decided to start accosting people who knocked at the door. Granted, it *had* been more like pounding, but still.

When Bastian emerged into the tiny living room, all he could see was his sickly houseguest taking up the doorway and clutching the doorframe for support as he lectured the interloper. At least Lucien was wearing a robe, Bastian thought. He wasn't at all sure how his only wearing underwear was about to be received.

There was a clipped reply, not really decipherable but definitely expletive-laden, to something particularly obnoxious Lucien had said. And the dragon, damn him, chuckled.

"I'm not sure that's even anatomically possible," he said, his voice sounding more like his old silken purr than it had since Bastian had rescued him. "But you're welcome to try, if you're brave enough to get anywhere near me, little girl. After all, I *am*…"

"Half out of your head with cold medication," Bastian interrupted, shoving his way in beside Lucien and earning a fulminating glare in return. He was hard-pressed to care, considering that it sounded like the dragon had decided to tell anyone exactly what he was. He would never understand Lucien. The determination to cause him trouble at his own expense was both frustrating and mind-boggling.

"I don't know what you're talking about," Lucien said flatly.

"Come on, you know how grouchy you get when

you're sick, ah… *cousin*." Maybe that would work. It had to work. But the way Lucien's lip curled was not at all promising.

Hoping the dragon would at least shut up so he could change the subject, Bastian turned his attention to the visitor on his doorstep and realized immediately that his boxers had been a poor wardrobe choice. He also realized that he was being visited by the MacInnes sister with the pink highlights and the face of an impish faerie. The one who looked like she might bite if crossed. No Duncan to be seen, at least, but the perplexed, distracted expression on Poppy's lovely face made it impossible to feel the least bit relieved. It was Lucien's fault, naturally. He sent one last death look in the dragon's direction before addressing his guest.

"So. Poppy. I… I wasn't expecting to see anyone this morning," he managed, unable to keep from looking to the trees for any sign that a massive black Wolf was lying in wait for him. And he couldn't keep from asking, "Duncan didn't come with you, did he?"

Poppy raised her honey-colored eyes from a quick, stunned appraisal of his naked torso and arched one dark brow. "No. Did you know that you have glow-in-the-dark bananas on your underwear?" she asked him. Bastian looked down and saw that she was right. Of all the days to grab the birthday gift that the always-charming MacInnes brothers had given him…

"Jesus, she really did bite you, didn't she?" Poppy murmured, catching sight of the bite wound at his shoulder with wide eyes. "Way to embrace the heritage. Damn."

"What bite?" Lucien snorted. "Bastian, you idiot, what did you... *oh*." An unkind smile curved his lips as he craned his head around and saw what Bastian was quite sure was an egregious bite mark. "Was this what the company was about last night? Well. That's what you get for playing with wolves. I'd rather be dead than shackled and chained to an *arukhin* for the rest of my life, myself, but I'm sure the two of you... no, wait, the *three* of you," he amended with a knowing smirk at Bastian, "will be very happy together."

Poppy glared at Lucien, who looked as though he was enjoying himself.

"Since you look like something the cat dragged in, no self-respecting Wolf would have you. I don't think you need to worry about it."

Lucien raised his eyebrows, feigning surprise. "Oh? Did I miss something? Have your kind suddenly developed self-respect?"

Bastian cringed as Poppy's mouth dropped open, right before her hands balled into fists and she bared teeth that were suddenly very sharp. So much for Lucien shutting his mouth, he thought wearily. If things continued going this well, he'd be burying the dragon's shredded carcass in the woods before noon.

Poppy's gleaming eyes shot to Bastian. "You said 'cousin.' How closely is this asshole related to you?" she asked.

"Not very," he replied. "Why?"

"Because I want to know how badly I can hurt him without upsetting you."

Lucien's deep chuckle told Bastian it was time to defuse this before he had to pull Poppy's teeth out of Lucien's throat. Stepping neatly between them, he looked first at Poppy.

"Since he doesn't have enough brains to apologize at present, I'm going to have to do it for my cousin, Poppy. No one likes him much, but I'm afraid I can't let you kill him. Even if he does deserve it."

He turned to Lucien. "Now go back to bed before I *throw* your ass there."

With a sniff and one final, condescending look at them, Lucien turned away, his gait unsteady as he began to make his way back to his room. "Typical. I'll just… leave you… to your scintillating conversation," he informed them, his speech halting with the exertion even as he gave an imperious little backward wave.

I hate you, Bastian thought, gritting his teeth.

Poppy watched Lucien go, her skepticism written clearly across her face. "Do all of your cousins blow smoke out of their noses when they're being jerks?"

"Not exactly," he allowed, not missing the surreptitious glance Poppy again stole at his ridiculous boxers. "Look, do you think you could wait a minute while I put on some clothes?"

"Um, sure," Poppy said, still watching Lucien's retreating form. Then she shook her head, as if to clear it. "Look, I hate to barge in like this, but you really need to come back with me. There's a little issue with Cat."

"What is it? What's the matter?" His anger at Lucien evaporated in the face of his concern for Cat and the certainty that he'd somehow harmed her just by touching her. "Is she all right?"

"Well, she managed to pass out in front of the entire

pack," she said, her gaze pointed. "Something to do with some blood loss, I think. Among other things."

Guilt twisted in his stomach. "Is she hurt? Has she woken up?" *Had he taken too much blood?* Bastian couldn't believe he'd done that to her. He'd wanted to taste her so badly that he'd let it steam roll his common sense entirely. It would have been one thing if he'd been the only one who stood to get hurt. But he wasn't.

"She's groggy," Poppy replied, and he didn't miss the faintly accusatory gleam in her eyes. "Somebody brought her some juice, and Duncan moved her someplace quiet. But she's asking for you." She looked away and muttered, "Seems like you might have a few things to discuss anyway."

"Drak's blood," Bastian growled, cursing himself for having created this untenable situation. He just hoped Cat was truly all right. "Of course I'll come. Just, ah…" He shoved a hand into his hair and tugged, trying to force himself to be all there and as alert as he needed to be. "Just hang on. I'll need to throw some clothes on." He started left, then right, bumped into a chair, and then pressed the heels of his palms against his eyes and growled again, frustrated.

Poppy watched him with curiosity. "Honest to God, you look like Cat before she's had her coffee in the morning. It's a match made in heaven after all."

He removed his hands to glare at her, but she was looking past him. Her smile evaporated.

"Crap. Move it." She shoved past Bastian with a sudden burst of supernatural speed before he even registered what she was doing. When he turned, he immediately saw why: Lucien had stopped in the middle of the room and gone sheet white, his eyes rolling back in his head as he started to crumple to the floor.

Poppy reached him just in time to soften the fall. She was not quite strong enough to stop it, but she managed to slow Lucien's descent by supporting his tall, lean form with her own small one.

"Damn it," Bastian muttered, rushing in behind her to help get Lucien safely on the floor. Leave it to Lucien to go down this time in such grand fashion. He would doubtless be pleased about that when he woke up. *If* he woke up. Lucien's breathing was shallow, his lips faintly blue. He looked as bad, in fact, as he had the night Bastian had brought him out of the dungeons. Bastian crouched down at Poppy's side as she checked for a pulse. Lucien seemed to have one, but that was all the good that could be said of it.

Lucien, you damned fool, Bastian thought, torn between worry and anger. Lucien was far too weak to be out of bed, and yet he'd managed to drag himself to the door just to be obstinate. Had even, in fact, managed to appear less than deathly ill for a few minutes before collapsing completely. He had to admire the strength of will, even though the dragon never seemed to use it for anything good.

He watched Poppy lay one small hand against Lucien's cheek, and the concern inherent in the gesture surprised him. Granted, she didn't seem to know this was a dragon, her natural enemy. But Lucien had been his usual rude self for the few minutes she'd known him so far.

"What *is* he?" she asked, so softly that Bastian wasn't sure the question was even directed at him.

He considered his options and finally decided on a bit of the truth. "Dying," he said. That seemed to satisfy her for the moment. Poppy nodded.

"Dying," she agreed, and placed a hand on either side of Lucien's face. "Dying slowly, like something's been eating away at him for a long time," she murmured. Bastian stared as the places her skin made contact with Lucien's began to glow with a warm, pulsing white light. Her eyes dropped shut, and she frowned, concentrating.

"I've never felt anything like this," she murmured, her voice taking on an edge. "There's so much pain… I can't tell whether it's all from the sickness. But there's definitely something…"

Bastian watched her, utterly dumbfounded. He had never, in all his years in Coracin, encountered an actual healer. There were both Drakkyn and Orinn who were skilled with medicines and remedies, of course. But though there were stories about ancients who could harness their energy to heal, these healers were either incredibly well hidden or had been gone a very long time.

"You can heal him?" he asked hoarsely, mind racing with possibilities. If Poppy could heal Lucien, he was that much closer to winning the battle. To freedom.

After so many fruitless years and so many setbacks, he had learned not to get his hopes up. But as he watched Cat's sister, as he actually *felt* the healing energies flowing from her, all of his long-buried hopes surfaced and began to rise. Poppy said nothing at first. She opened her eyes and withdrew her hands, looking at Lucien with such a mixture of pity and sympathy that

Bastian felt like he was intruding on something private. He did not have her gift; he didn't know what she'd felt or seen. He began to wonder whether she had even heard him, but after a moment, she turned her gaze back to him.

"I think I can help him," she said. "But I need to know everything you can tell me about his illness. Because this is like nothing I've ever seen. And he sure as hell is not human." She paused, her eyes narrowing. "I don't think he's your cousin, either."

When Bastian answered, he gave her the truth with no reservations. He doubted Poppy would help him without it, and he wasn't going to turn his nose up at a gift of fate.

"This is Lucien Andrakkar," Bastian said, and as he'd feared, understanding flashed in her eyes almost immediately.

"Andrakkar... not the dragon. The dragon who hunted your sister all over creation? The one with the psycho father who wanted to steal the Stone?" When he nodded, she looked less angry than simply amazed.

"Are you *trying* to get my uncle to kill you?"

"No. I'm trying to lift a curse that's been passed through, and killed, four generations of my family." He sighed and looked ruefully at Lucien's obstinately still face. "I'm followed, always, by a shadowy beast from the bowels of the Blighted Kingdom, a minion of the tribe of the *daemon*, and I need dragon blood to have even a chance at drawing it out and defeating it." His jaw tightened. "Though the dragon blood must be freely given. If I could just knock him out and bite him, I'd have a much easier time."

"Freely given," Poppy repeated, looking from Lucien to Bastian. "From this guy? Are you nuts?"

"More like desperate," he admitted ruefully. "I rescued Lucien from the dungeons of the *daemon* kingdom, on the off chance he might feel indebted." At Poppy's snort, he smiled thinly. "Yeah, I know. But I told you: desperate. This thing feeds off me, ripping away at the parts of my soul it hasn't managed to smother yet. My father eventually sacrificed himself to it just to make it stop.

"An oracle told me I might have a chance of defeating the shadow if I drank the blood of a willing dragon. I know you don't have any experience with them, but believe me when I tell you that dragons barely tolerate one another most of the time, much less some begging outsider. So I decided my one chance might be Lucien. He and my sister Rowan share a bloodline... he had to have some possibility of redemption, right?"

Poppy looked down at Lucien, her skepticism obvious. "In theory."

"But he'd been tortured for close to a year and was, *is*, incredibly weak. At first I thought he'd get better if he just rested. All Drakkyn self-heal, you know, not just werewolves. But he can't even do that anymore. He should, by all rights, be dead now." He considered the dragon, who he swore had a surly expression on his face despite being unconscious.

"Probably too damn mean," Poppy offered. "Happens all the time with humans."

He'd actually considered that. "You may have a point there."

"Torture." Poppy shuddered. "That explains some of

what I felt in him. They really messed him up and obviously infected him with something to boot."

At her words, Bastian felt the first sympathy for Lucien he'd had since he'd found him, bleeding and naked, in the dungeons. He had deserved punishment for his misguided violence. But he still suspected that Lucien had, at the end, allowed himself to be taken by the *daemon* instead of Gabriel, a shockingly noble action. He wasn't half the tyrant that his father had been. Whatever he thought of the dragon's personality, Lucien hadn't deserved to be broken the way he had been.

"Messed him up," Bastian murmured. "That's a way to describe it, yeah."

She looked as though she wanted to ask more, but at that moment, Lucien moaned softly and half opened his eyes, which were a dull and dusky violet.

Poppy blew out a breath. "Well, that's one small step, anyway."

"You did that?" She'd only had her hands on him for a minute, maybe. But as Bastian looked more closely, he could see that Lucien's breathing had eased and that the bluish tint was gone from his lips. He still looked like the wrath of Drak, but he no longer looked like he was about to die.

Poppy shrugged, and Bastian could see she wasn't comfortable talking about her gift. Which was a shame, because he was deeply curious about the way such healing magic worked.

"He wanted to wake up. I just helped it along."

"Can you make him well?"

"I can't make any promises, Bastian. Animals, I'm good with. People, not quite so much." She looked away, troubled. "Not that I get to practice much. Zapping people freaks them out."

"But you'll try," he said, adding a sense of urgency to what was essentially a question. Poppy's tentative nod lessened the weight on his shoulders instantly.

"I'll give it a shot. But it could take days. And I have to be able to do things my…"

"What are you still doing here?" The voice was soft and weak but unmistakably Lucien's.

Poppy looked down at him, her tone dry when she informed him, "This is your lucky day, Lucien. I'm going to be baby-sitting you."

He looked vaguely surprised. "It was you?" he asked cryptically. Poppy seemed to understand. She nodded, her expression guarded. Probably, Bastian figured, steeling herself for another nasty retort.

Instead there was a long pause. Bastian watched them, the dragon and the Gothic pixie, sizing one another up. Finally, when Lucien replied, it was with the two words Bastian hadn't been sure the dragon was capable of even speaking, much less understanding.

"Thank you," he sighed, closing his eyes.

"You're welcome," she replied, looking a little surprised herself. Then she shifted her attention to Bastian.

"Help me get him in the room before you go?"

Bastian sighed. "This feels familiar," he muttered, getting his arms beneath Lucien's wasted form and picking him up easily. He carried him back into the bedroom, Poppy trailing closely behind.

"I really can't promise you anything, Bastian. I'm no expert. He's probably going to die anyway." Poppy moved quickly and efficiently as she talked, stripping Lucien of his robe without batting an eye at his nudity before pulling the sheets over him and getting him settled. Bastian only caught the slightest pause in her movements when she saw the multitude of scars, some nearly white, others still angry looking, that marred Lucien's torso.

Bastian raised his eyebrows. "I'm glad you're thinking positively about this."

She shot him a dirty look that reminded him of Cat when she was angry. It surprised him that the memory of Cat yelling at him was still so appealing. "All I'm doing is warning you. And if Duncan finds out you've got a dragon out here, once Duncan kills you, I will personally kill you all over again."

He snorted, amused. He couldn't help it. "You're a very violent little person, aren't you?"

Poppy smirked. "You have no idea. Now go." She shooed him with her hands. "Duncan and Cat are waiting for you in the Chamber of Secrets or wherever they keep the Stone of Destiny."

"I'm going." Even though he would rather have Cat to himself. He didn't relish the thought of having Duncan's famous temper trained on him. Not today, at any rate, when he felt so ill equipped to fend it off.

He ducked out of the room, heading into his own bedroom to pull on a pair of faded blue jeans and a white T-shirt. His energy returned as he quickly went about his business, which was a blessing, but he had no idea how he was going to explain himself to Cat. Or, for that matter, to get Duncan to allow him to keep his head. He at least hoped that the rest of the MacInneses hadn't managed to destroy the property yet... Malcolm had told him a few hair-raising stories before traipsing off to Coracin without a care.

Moments later he found himself stopped short in the threshold, watching Poppy smooth a hand over Lucien's brow and wondering at the quick shift in her attitude toward the surly dragon. The tenderness in her expression surprised him deeply. Almost as deeply as watching Lucien turn his head, ever so slightly, into her touch.

She jumped a little when Bastian spoke. "I can't thank you enough for helping him, Poppy. Really. You don't know either of us; I've given you no reason to trust my judgment; and Lucien is... well, you saw how he is. It's not just the illness. I owe you more than I can repay for just trying. You have a rare gift."

Poppy flushed and flashed an embarrassed smile. "Don't thank me yet. I accidentally exploded a wounded frog once. I got a little carried away with the healing."

Bastian suddenly had a vision of coming back to a scene of total carnage and one apologetic witch. He had to force himself to continue breathing normally. Poppy, however, laughed.

"Don't worry. I don't think this one could be over-healed right now. Oh, which reminds me! I was thinking this couldn't hurt..." She trailed off as she hurried around the side of the bed, rushing up to him and grabbing his hands. At first touch, Bastian could feel the latent power in her, thrumming like a live wire, and he knew what she was about. He tried to pull his hands away, but her grip proved surprisingly strong.

"You really don't need to do this," he said, tugging.

He'd never liked having magic performed on him. It brought back too many memories of Rowan singeing his eyebrows off and Reya giving him horns.

"Dammit, stand still for a minute," she snapped. And then he had no choice, as a strange light filled his vision and his limbs stopped obeying his mind's commands. Instead, everything was peace and floating and a comforting warmth that not only flooded his body, but also felt like a balm to his weary and tattered soul. A voice echoed faintly to him through a lovely, pleasurable haze.

"Don't you dare fall on me, you big lug."

Slowly, the light faded, though the warmth remained. When he came back to himself, so that he could see the little room and Poppy wringing her hands as though trying to cleanse them of some sticky, tough-to-remove substance, he felt better than he had in a long time.

"By the Goddess," he said, "you're amazing! I suppose I have to thank you again." A wild thought occurred to him, simple, but wondrous. Maybe he didn't need the dragon blood. Maybe if Poppy simply infused him with this strength-giving magic, it would be enough! It had never occurred to him that he needed to be healed, though he was certainly wounded. Could this be the answer?

The question was on the tip of his tongue, but it died in his throat at Poppy's solemn expression.

"Are you going to tell my sister?" she asked quietly.

He shook his head, not understanding. "Tell her what?"

"How bad it is."

He blinked, all of that wonderful warmth and all of the hope going cold in an instant.

"How bad is it?" he asked, knowing the answer just from the stricken look on her face.

"I can only do bodies, Bastian. Not souls. What's done is done, but she deserves to know what she's dealing with."

Meaning how little time she's going to have with you, Bastian thought. Poppy's words sent a chill all the way through him. But he'd known, at least intellectually, what was happening to him. He felt its effects every day. Still, it was one thing to deal with it yourself. It was quite another to have someone else confirm the severity.

A deep voice sliced neatly through his thoughts just then, bringing him back to the present.

"For the love of Drak, go. I've heard enough of your dulcet tones for one day. Any more and I swear I'll die in self-defense."

"You wish, Lucien," Bastian said, and headed out the door, Poppy calling after him.

"One more thing, Bastian."

"Yes?"

There was dark amusement in her voice when she replied. "Welcome to the family."

Chapter 8

"Cat."

"Catriona."

"*Cat.* Can you hear me?"

Cat kept her eyes firmly shut against the onslaught of familiar voices. Her head was throbbing dully, exactly the way it had been since she'd passed out, and her stomach was in knots. She wasn't unconscious any longer, or even asleep, though she really wished she were. Then she wouldn't have had to keep thinking about what she'd done. About how she'd trapped Bastian into an existence tied only to her, as though his existence wasn't screwed up enough.

But Duncan and Skye weren't giving up. And she couldn't play possum forever.

She opened her eyes to find herself in a low, circular chamber lit only by torches, a dim and quiet place that she hadn't seen before. But there was something familiar here, the thing she'd felt when she'd left on her run last night. Like a song she could only faintly hear but knew by heart. Bracing her hands against the cold stone floor upon which Duncan had settled her, Cat slowly raised herself to a sitting position and looked around in wonder.

She couldn't imagine where she was. It certainly didn't look like a room in *Iargail*. Then she saw it, jet black and inlaid with golden script, filling the air itself with a power that could be felt in every breath of air taken in this place. The only thing in the room besides her and her companions. In an instant, everything clicked into place.

"The Stone of Destiny," she breathed softly. Then she turned to look at her uncle, the man who must have carried her here and who was now crouched beside her with a worried look on his handsome, weathered face. "Why am I here?"

"You fainted. I wanted to get you somewhere quiet and out of sight of nosy relatives as quickly as I could. This was the first place that came to mind." He sighed and shook his head. "Skye tells me you didn't have anything to eat this morning. Never a good idea, especially when you're a bit lower in the, ah, blood department than usual." He looked away uncomfortably.

Cat looked at Skye, sitting cross-legged on the floor beside her. "Where's Poppy?"

"She ran to get Bastian." She raised an eyebrow at Duncan. "It was that, or someone else who shall not be named threatened to drag him here by his nether regions."

Cat gave her uncle a beleaguered look. "Oh, Uncle Duncan. That's... sweet... but it really isn't necessary." All she could think of was Bastian not being able to get out of bed yet, and the blowup of massive proportions that could result. She wanted to see him, yes. But minus any impending death threats. If only she'd remembered those bite marks... but how often did anyone bite her?

"Nonsense," Duncan said firmly. "You might not have known what you were doing, Cat, but Bastian certainly did. His own sister is married to a werewolf, for the love of God! And never mind what I said before,

Bastian's an honorable sort." He sighed. "If it weren't for him, Gabe wouldn't even be around."

"Really?" Cat asked, intrigued. Didn't that just go to show how little she knew about Bastian? He'd saved her cousin's life, and she was clueless about the whole thing. She knew nothing about him… *nothing*. And she'd gone and bitten him, ruining his already screwed-up life.

"Really," Duncan said. "But you're my niece, and he's damn well going to do right by you. I just want to make that clear. Then, I promise, lass, I'll butt out."

Somehow she doubted it, but it was touching that he was so protective. Her own father should have been acting this way, she thought. But she knew better than to wish for impossible things.

"Did anyone get Dad?" she asked dully. God knew what sort of reaction Freddie would have when he found out what she'd done. His furious eyes rose again in her memory, and she shuddered. When she looked at Duncan, though, he appeared to be sad and apologetic.

"Your sisters thought it might be best not to," he said softly, looking to Skye, who nodded. "I had hoped, when he called, that he'd changed." Duncan shook his head. "Foolish of me. Though I'm glad, so glad, you three have come. Better late than never."

"I don't know why he called you," Cat replied, feeling hot tears well in her eyes and blinking fiercely to keep them from falling. "We don't see him very often, you know. We didn't, after the divorce. And he never told us about you. Or really about anything."

"Aye," Duncan said, his jaw tightening. His eyes went far-off. "That's how I worried it would be. But you've done beautifully, lass. I just wish I'd known. He left, and I was angry for a very long time. I should've looked... kept track. My fault, that."

Finally, she asked the question to which she so desperately wanted to know the answer. "What happened between you two?" Cat asked softly.

"You know," Duncan said, tilting his head at her and looking pensive, "I never really understood. One day, everything was fine. The next, he was in the hall with his bags packed. Didn't want anything to do with what we were, he said. Spouted a lot of nonsense about what violent, horrible things we were, about how nothing but evil could come from the Stone. Hurt me. Hurt our Da, too. But who could stop him if he wanted to go? Said he wanted to be 'normal.' But we can only be what we are. I thought maybe that was why he'd come back."

"I always thought he hated being a werewolf," Cat said.

"He didn't, a long time ago. But he was always a skittish sort. I've often wondered, in the last couple of years, if he saw something," Duncan sighed. "Something to do with the Stone that set him off. Back then, we didn't know what it was capable of. And now... well, it's too late for what-ifs." He patted her knee. "You're here now. That's all that matters. And that you've found yourself a fine mate. Even if it was a bit unexpected and, ah, accidental."

Cat pushed thoughts of her father away for the time being. She wasn't sure whether it was better or worse that even his own brother didn't know why her dad had turned his back so completely, but there were other, more pressing concerns at hand.

"Uncle Duncan," Cat said softly, "I didn't exactly

ask if I could bite him. Bastian isn't responsible for me not knowing what I was doing. Really. So if he isn't interested in being my mate for life or whatever, don't decapitate him or anything. Okay? I'm a big girl. I'll deal with it."

"Didn't ask," Duncan repeated and then, shockingly, began to chuckle. Cat looked at Skye, wondering if she'd missed something, but Skye looked just as puzzled as she felt.

"Oh, forgive me, Catriona," he finally said, his laughter subsiding but the amusement still glittering in his eyes. "I keep forgetting that this is all new to you. But, ah, most werewolves don't... *ask*. It just isn't the way of things."

"Then what is the way of things? Ambushing people and forcing them into... into mate-hood, or whatever?" She grimaced. "Sorry, but that seems really unfair. Really *wrong*."

Duncan rolled his eyes heavenward. "That's all a bit dramatic, Cat. And inaccurate to boot."

"Enlighten me."

"Us," Skye corrected. "I don't want to be with someone who's eternally pissed off at me for chomping on him." She looked at Cat, wrinkling her nose. "Why'd you do it anyway, Cat? I've never felt like biting anybody but you and Poppy, and that wasn't for romantic reasons."

"I'd imagine she felt an overwhelming need to do it," Duncan replied. "Right from the first moment you saw him?" Cat stared at him, startled.

"That's exactly how I felt," she said softly.

"Ew," muttered Skye. Duncan laughed again.

"No, it's the way of things," he corrected her. "Our

kind knows our natural mates. Like a sixth sense. Drawn to them so strongly that the only choice we have is to get far away from them—or claim them with our bites."

"So they *don't* always want to be mated to us," Skye said triumphantly. But Duncan just shook his head.

"No, lass. That's the thing. Our mates are drawn to us as well, just as strongly. The bond is there from the beginning. But sometimes, in the case of humans, it's better to let them be. The blood bond turns them Wolf, but their bodies are often too fragile to take it." His eyes darkened. "My own sweet Laura was one. She did ask for the bite. And I resisted for years. Because I knew. But eventually, I gave in. And she was gone."

"Oh, Uncle Duncan," Cat murmured. "I'm so sorry. I didn't know."

"Pah," he said gruffly, waving his hand. "No need to be sorry. Love made both of us foolish, and we paid for it. Though she left me Gideon and Gabriel, and two finer sons I couldn't imagine. But what I'm saying is that Bastian isn't in any danger of dying from the bite. He's bound just as tightly to you as you are to him, and he no doubt felt just as you did beforehand. Otherwise he wouldn't have taken advantage of you so quickly," he added on a growl.

"I don't know how many times I have to say this," Cat started, "but he did *not* take advantage…"

Duncan cut her off before she could finish. "He's a good man, Cat, but a loner. His kind have to nibble on people every so often to keep their strength up, but not that often, and I've never seen him bring a soul back here. No, don't worry. You're different for him. Of course, you *are* a MacInnes." He patted her knee and got to his feet as footsteps sounded on the stairs far above, and Cat's heart fluttered despite herself.

"So quit your worrying. Everything will come out right. It's just…"

"The way of things," Cat finished for him, unable to help a small smile. "I think I got that part, at least."

"Good. And what's also the way of things is that I'll rip the limbs off anyone who hurts you, so get used to it. I've been driving my own sons mad for years, and I haven't tired of it yet." He dropped his voice to a conspiratorial whisper. "I may, in fact, be a bit of a pain in the arse, but don't tell anyone, eh?"

She burst into laughter. "Your secret's safe with us."

"Now then, come on, Skye. We'll leave you and Bastian be. Though I'll be having a private word with him first." Duncan disappeared through the doorway, rushing up to meet Bastian, and, Cat was unpleasantly sure, to accost him on his way out.

"Don't worry, Cat," Skye said, giving her a quick hug before getting to her feet and heading for the door herself. "It's got to get better from here."

"Why's that, again?"

Skye's smile was full of sympathy.

"Because it can't get much worse."

Unfortunately, Cat wasn't at all sure about that.

She didn't know what Duncan said to Bastian, but whatever it was, the man took his time.

Cat went from sitting to standing to pacing and finally ended up in front of the only other object in the room besides herself: the beautiful, frighteningly powerful *Lia*

Fáil. Its draw was magnetic, Cat thought. Just a hunk of black rock with some symbols carved into it, and yet the power it exuded was palpable as it swirled around her, whispering and cajoling. Singing, if only in her mind.

She wanted to feel it, to slide her hand over stone she was certain would be warm to the touch. To see how much those currents of power intensified when she was in direct contact with them. But something held her back, though whether it was fear or just respect she wasn't sure. In either case, her hand stayed suspended mere inches above the surface of the relic, which was so powerful that a saint had directed it to be guarded by a pack of werewolves, and a tribe of shape-shifting dragons had been willing to risk everything to have it. Then a voice, so familiar to her now, sounded from right behind her.

"It won't hurt you, you know. You can touch it."

Cat jumped and then spun around to find Bastian at her shoulder. She hadn't even heard him come in. Had she been that entranced by the Stone? Or was Bastian even quieter than the werewolves he lived among?

"God," she laughed breathlessly. "Scared me."

He stepped closer, just as overwhelming a presence as he had been the last time she'd seen him. It wasn't just his height, she thought, but the impression of great, restrained strength. In the shadowy half-light, he had all the mysterious, magnetic appeal of some dark god of night. When she didn't say anything, Bastian reached out, took her hand, and then brought it to the surface of the Stone. Cat's eyes widened at the energy that shimmered up her arm as soon as her hand connected with it. She didn't struggle, but just left her hand splayed beneath Bastian's, wishing the rest of her was touching him, too.

"I haven't been down here since I brought my sister to the MacInneses for protection," he murmured. "Seems like a long time ago now."

Cat turned to look at him and then swallowed hard as whatever she'd thought to say died in her throat. Bastian's closeness, and the sexual appeal that seemed to pour from him, was more overwhelming than she'd anticipated. It had been easier to deal with when she'd thought he was about to die. But to look at him now, one would never know what a state he'd been in the night before. His mouth hardened into a firm line as he studied her, and his eyes gleamed iridescent blue in the half-light of the chamber. It was, Cat thought, fighting a new wave of light-headedness that she was fairly sure had nothing to do with blood loss, less like being looked *at* and more like being looked *into*.

Even though she now understood what she'd done, the intimacy she felt with Bastian took her by surprise.

"How are you feeling?" he finally asked, the soft rasp of his voice making her shiver with pleasure.

"I was going to ask you the same thing," she replied. Bastian lifted one large, long-fingered hand to her cheek and smoothed away a strand of hair. Cat was chilled from the cool damp of the chamber, but his touch left a lingering warmth on her cheek. His eyes were tender and surprisingly full of concern. Whatever she'd expected to see—anger, revulsion, or just plain indifference—it wasn't there.

"I've had worse," Bastian said with a shrug. "Your uncle threatened to disembowel me as I was on my way in, and I was nearly decapitated by a flying tree right beforehand. For which, by the way, I am being held responsible. So I'm beginning to think it's going to be one of those days." His gaze, like a laser, focused intensely on her. "How about you?"

"Well," Cat said, trying to keep it light. She'd never had someone look at her that way, like her well-being was essential to their own. It was kind of awesome and… unnerving. "I'm fairly sure all of my long-lost relatives saw me take a header on the terrace. So that gets to be their first impression of me. Forever. And…" She paused, uncertain, and then figured what the hell. "I learned that sexy love bites can have long-term consequences." Cat studied his face, waiting for the first sign of disgust or displeasure. Instead, Bastian chuckled.

"It was definitely sexy," he agreed, and then slipped his hand beneath her chin and tipped her head to the side. His lips had curved into a faint smile, but his eyes were still serious. "All right, let me see it."

It took her several long, embarrassing seconds to figure out that Bastian was talking about the twin puncture wounds on her neck. Cat blushed, blaming her mind's triumphant plunge into the gutter on the fact that he'd used the word "sexy" in conjunction with her. Then she obligingly brushed her hair away from her neck, revealing the small marks.

She expected him to say something, or at least give some kind of "*Hmm*" or something. But when he remained silent, examining the wound, Cat fought the urge to squirm. She taught little kids. She much preferred noisy and easily readable reactions.

"I'll show you mine if you show me yours," she offered.

That earned her a soft snort, and his eyes, when he raised them to hers, were full of the humor she'd hoped to see.

"You'll be happy to know that's a universally recognized bargain." Bastian smirked at her. But when he returned his attention to her neck, he ran his thumb over the wounds, his frown returning. "I can see I might have gotten a little carried away. I'm sorry if it's sore. And I'm especially sorry it caused what happened this morning."

Cat gave a short, disbelieving laugh. *He* was sorry? And she had been sure she'd cornered the market on getting carried away.

"I'm fine. Now come on. A deal's a deal," Cat said, flustered, and motioned to his neck. Obligingly, Bastian pulled off the T-shirt he was wearing before she had a chance to brace herself.

Cat sucked in a breath at the sight of him, the ripple of taut muscle as he moved to discard the shirt, the trail of blond hair that disappeared intriguingly beneath the waistband of his jeans. She had to force herself to concentrate on the matter at hand when all she wanted to do was feel his warm skin beneath her hands again. Her awareness of his heat, his scent, and the very nearness of him was suddenly painful. Her pupils dilated, and her breathing slowed.

Then she caught sight of the bruised, reddish flesh at the base of his neck, the instantly recognizable pattern that could only have been made by a mouthful of sharp teeth. And the emotion that flooded her, far from being ashamed or remorseful, was immediate and overwhelming: it was triumph.

Shocked at the ferocity of her reaction, Cat only barely managed to hold back a pleased growl. Instead she cleared her throat and moved in to examine her mark more closely, wondering if it was as uncomfortable as it looked. It was certainly larger and more swollen than what Bastian had left her with.

"Does it hurt?" she asked, and saw Bastian tense as her breath touched his skin. His scent changed subtly, becoming stronger and more inviting. It was arousal, she knew. And it satisfied her on that primal level only he seemed to bring out in her.

"It's fine," Bastian said, his voice now slightly strained. "Aches a little, but I'm sure it'll pass. I, ah, don't have a lot of experience in the area of werewolf bites."

She drew back to look at his expression and was treated to a sweet, boyish smile that affected more than just her ridiculously overactive hormones. She no longer saw a beautiful, tortured soul as different from her as day from night. All she saw was a man with amusement dancing in his bright blue eyes.

Make that *her* man.

The instinct took over before Cat really knew what she was doing. She lowered her mouth to the wound and gave it a long, slow lick. Cat closed her eyes, hit by a wave of pleasure at the faintly sweet taste of him. Bastian exhaled shakily, and she felt him bring his hands to her back. It was a gentle touch, as though he was holding something particularly delicate. It was also an unspoken request for her to continue.

Cat gave the wound another stroke of her tongue for good measure, and her eyes widened when she noticed that much of the redness was now gone, the puncture wounds faded so that they were barely visible. A faint scar would remain, though. Somehow, she was sure of it. A reminder that he belonged to her.

And she to him.

She raised her head to look at him, dizzy from the opposing, simultaneous sensations of knowing Bastian both as well as she knew herself and at the same time, not at all. And dizzy because he was just a breath away.

"I think," Cat murmured, "that I am in very serious trouble here."

Bastian sighed, sounding helplessly exasperated at the same time that his eyes went to blue fire.

"You and me both," he ground out with a rueful shake of his head, then dragged her against him to claim her mouth in a long, slow kiss that ignited a burn at the very core of her.

The kiss sang through her blood, everything within her surging upward with savage joy. Cat could feel Bastian trying to keep his control, but it only inflamed her; she wanted him to lose himself in her the way she seemed destined to lose herself in him. His hand slid to the back of her neck, trying to hold her still as he tasted her with languid, sensual strokes. In return, she growled low in her throat and pressed against the length of him, nipping when he tried to be gentle, demanding more when he wanted to hold back. And slowly, surely, she felt that tightly held control begin to give way.

Bastian's breath began to quicken, keeping time with her own as his kisses turned hard and urgent. His hands, large yet surprisingly gentle, cruised roughly over her back, skimming down her waist and cupping her backside before resuming their exploration of her. It was as though he wanted to have his hands on all of her at once.

Cat knew how he felt, raking her nails down his back and digging into his hips. She couldn't seem to get enough of him. And she loved the way he responded to her, matching her passion even as it escalated. However reserved Bastian might try to be, in this, his reactions were beautifully honest.

Abruptly, he pulled back, tearing his mouth from hers with a gasp like a drowning man finally breaking the surface and looking as shaken as she was. Cat clung to him, knowing her legs would never hold her if she tried to stand on them now. Fortunately, Bastian didn't seem inclined to let her go, leaning down to touch his forehead to hers, eyes closed. They remained that way for a time, wrapped in each other's arms, every breath taken in perfect time.

"I don't know what to do," he finally said softly, "about this."

Cat looked at him, enjoying the way the torchlight illuminated his skin. She felt a little strange, almost as though she was having an out-of-body experience. It took her a moment to realize, with a small jolt, what she felt: she had always carried around more than her share of worry and stress, laundry lists of all the things she needed to do and people she needed to take care of playing on a constant loop inside her head. But here with Bastian, that inner storm had fallen silent to be replaced by something recognizable though mostly unfamiliar: contentment. And odder still, peace.

The feeling was utterly at odds with her suspicion

that she might incur bodily harm from being with him, but there it was, and she couldn't shake it.

"Which part in particular are you worried about?" asked Cat, offering a small smile even though she wasn't really joking.

Bastian's laugh was a short, sharp bark of sound, but genuine. "Do you have an hour?"

"Can't you summarize?" Cat returned, eyebrows raised. "I've got some concerns, too, and I'd like time to compare notes."

He chuckled again, a throaty sound that warmed her and sent heat coiling in her belly. She liked making him laugh. He didn't seem to do it nearly often enough.

Bastian opened his mouth to answer, but no words came out as the light abruptly left his eyes. Cat waited, confused, but the silence only continued. Like an animal scenting danger, he went stock-still, his eyes darting around the room. And then Cat began to feel it again, that unnerving prickle at the back of her neck that she was coming to understand was her natural reaction to danger, *true* danger, the likes of which she'd been lucky enough never to encounter in her normal life.

"We need to go," Bastian said suddenly. In movements so rapid they were nothing but a blur, he pulled away, put his shirt back on, and grabbed her hand to lead her toward the stairs.

Fear, cold and clammy, crawled up Cat's spine as she silently followed his lead. She knew it was the *thing*, whatever it was that had attacked him in the woods. She just didn't know why.

But the explanations could wait until they got the hell out of there. All that mattered, as she remembered the crushing, soul-deep pain from the night before, was that it wasn't an experience she cared to repeat.

Together, she just a step behind him and keeping her hand in his, Cat and Bastian flew up the long and endlessly curving stone steps toward the surface. She was suddenly thankful for her natural speed—no human could have matched Bastian's pace—but still, Cat was pushing herself, going faster than she'd known she was capable of.

Yes, she was terrified. But it was the sound, straight out of a horror movie, that kept her going despite the burn in her leg muscles. Behind them, she swore she could hear the quickening footfalls of someone or something else. Something that followed them and was gaining. Despite the burning torches set into the wall as they climbed, Cat was somehow certain that if she looked behind her, all she would see would be impenetrable blackness crawling the steps just behind them.

"Don't look back," Bastian instructed as though he knew what she was thinking. He didn't even sound winded, though their speed was now so great that everything passed in a rush. Cat concentrated on her feet, praying that she wouldn't catch a toe on one of the steps and crash.

"Hurry," she managed to gasp, her lungs feeling ready to burst.

"Almost there," Bastian replied, never turning. They rounded the final corner and came into the bright square of sunlight cast by the entrance, and the warmth and light that bathed Cat felt like heaven itself. Behind her, just as the brightness enveloped them, a rush of air at her back felt like the brush of fingers, grasping for purchase and just barely missing, but leaving the skin it had touched ice cold.

Then they were out, staggering up into the ruins of the old MacInnes chapel where the roof had long ago given way to a perfect view of the Scottish sky. Cat made sure she was well clear of the darkened hole from which they'd just emerged and then placed her hands on her knees and hunched over to drink in deep, shuddering breaths. Fresh air and sunlight had never tasted so sweet. She felt his hand on her back, keeping them connected and bolstering her until she could breathe easily again. Cat straightened, looking around and blinking in the light. Up here everything was beautiful and relatively normal. The encounter with a horrifying creature of darkness almost seemed like a figment of her imagination.

Almost.

As the hidden door slid shut behind them, a deep, wet-sounding snarl came from just inside the corridor.

"You can run now if you want to," Bastian said, his broad shoulders seeming to slump slightly in resignation as he looked away, toward the sealed entrance. "In fact, you probably should."

Maybe she should, Cat thought. But she'd seen so much that didn't make sense the night before. There had been a rush of images when she'd bitten him, flashes of things in Bastian's past that had made her feel close to him, and many that had saddened or frightened her without her knowing quite why. His days had been full of beauty and fascinating things. But his nights...

That was what she wanted to understand. There was something about Bastian that seemed very much alone. And despite her conviction that something was very wrong with him, there was no way she could let him be alone anymore. They were connected now, had been connected, Cat knew, even before she had given him that fateful bite. They were in this together. For her, it was that simple.

Or horrifically complicated. But either way…

Cat shook her head, closing the distance between them. "Nope. I don't scare that easily. Besides, shouldn't you be the one running? I took away your choice, Bastian. I didn't know I was doing it, but that doesn't change it."

His relief, as he realized she wasn't going to bolt, was palpable and became her own. He wasn't upset she'd bitten him. More, he didn't want her to go, even though he'd given her the option. Where they went from here, Cat had no idea. But it was a much better place to start than she'd thought.

Well, minus the evil lurking somewhere right beneath them. That, she could have done without.

"Catriona," Bastian said, his voice a sensual rasp. "It was fated. I felt it too. You don't need to worry about that." One corner of his mouth lifted in a half smile. "I just wasn't expecting you."

When the skit popped into her head, she couldn't resist. "Oh, well, you know. I'm like the Spanish Inquisition that way."

When he raised his eyebrows, Cat heaved an exaggerated sigh. "Monty Python reference. Didn't you live in America for a year? This is Pop Culture 101 stuff, Bastian."

He smirked down at her. "I lived with vampires. They liked strip clubs and horror movies. I think I can recite every line from *Underworld*, but those are about the limits of my knowledge." His look turned serious. "Things with me are… complicated, Cat. I don't want you to get hurt."

Remembering last night, she said softly, "I think it might be a little late for that."

He gave her a long look, and she knew he was remembering the same thing. Finally he nodded.

"I think you're right. So." He blew out a breath, a sign of the tension Cat knew they both felt.

"So," Cat repeated. And suddenly, once again, it was awkward. What did they do now? Date? Move in together? Ride off into the sunset on a white horse? Part of her, the part that was still roughly seven years old and had compelled her to buy every single Disney princess movie on DVD, liked the sound of that last option. Even though, from what she'd seen, they'd have some nasty creature slithering along behind them to spoil the honeymoon.

White horses, fairy tales, nightmarish creatures… suddenly, Cat knew exactly what she was dealing with. But this was no frightening Brothers Grimm concoction. This was reality. Her own weird, warped, befouled-by-rotten-luck reality. Which meant there were no guarantees of a happily-ever-after in lieu of a thrashing by giant trolls or magical dismemberment, or both.

"Shit," she said, looking at a man who could have easily been mistaken for a handsome prince and feeling a little sick as the truth hit her. "You're cursed, aren't you?"

Bastian looked stunned. He opened his mouth to answer, but no intelligible words came out. It was all the confirmation Cat needed.

"A curse. Great," she said, her sensitive ears picking up a distinctive clomping sound that was becoming very familiar to her. "I'm going to want to know exactly what we're dealing with, and soon, but Duncan's headed this way, so just answer one question, okay?"

Bastian nodded. Then he frowned. "You've got better ears than I do."

She had to smile. "Obviously. My uncle sounds like an oncoming freight train. Which he also sometimes acts like. Anyway, my question is this, and no bullshit when you answer: Is there any hope for *lifting* this curse?"

Not far away, a chorus of wild whoops and cheers went up from where the MacInnes Pack had just begun to celebrate. There was the sound of drums, the wild trill of a flute. Cat wished that they were there, instead of having to discuss life and death. Because she had no doubt that's what this was. Cat felt Bastian's heart beating steadily inside his chest where their bodies touched, and sighed. If the curse could be lifted, they had a chance. If it couldn't... did they at least have some time?

Stupid damn Shadow From the Black Lagoon, she thought ruefully. *God, what a mess.*

"There's hope, Cat." Bastian lifted a hand to her cheek and stroked a finger down it, watching its path with naked wonder. *How long have you been alone?* she thought, something strange and beautiful and somehow right welling up inside of her with that one gentle touch.

"In fact, I've got more hope today than I have had for a very long time."

She needed to know more, so much more. But for now, that statement and the honesty she saw on Bastian's face were enough to keep her going. If there was a way out of the trouble Bastian was in, she knew she could help him find it. Her sisters might tease her for having a bullet-pointed plan of attack for every situation, but that had always proved the perfect counterbalance to her predisposition for getting herself in trouble. She could help him. Cat knew she could. She'd finally found her mate.

And after everything she'd been through to get to this point, there was no way in hell that she was going to let him die on her now.

"Okay," she said with a small nod. "I can work with that."

Bastian's eyes crinkled at the corners, and he smiled even as he shook his head.

"You're a wonder, Cat MacInnes," Bastian said. "If this doesn't faze you, I think anything else I tell you is going to seem anticlimactic."

"You don't know that. But I am pretty awesome," Cat agreed, keeping her fingers interlaced with his. "Though I must admit, I'm not *completely* perfect."

He raised his eyebrows, blue eyes glittering. "No? Do tell."

"You're not supposed to ask. It's supposed to stay mysterious," she protested. Unfortunately, he didn't look at all deterred.

"No secrets," Bastian said. "I've got enough of them already."

And how exactly was she supposed to argue with that?

"Well," Cat said slowly, wondering exactly which of her less fabulous traits she could safely tell him this early on without sending him running. "For starters, I'm terrified of spiders; my housekeeping has been rated 'borderline slob' by my lovely sisters; and I seem to be only attracted to men who are trouble."

"Ah. For that last bit," Bastian said, pulling her closer, "I do believe we may just be a good match, given the chance."

Given the chance. She could only hope, Cat thought, heart fluttering wildly as Bastian lowered his mouth to hers. She let him brush his lips against hers once, then again, feeling the delicious heat that only he seemed to be able to produce in her shimmering from her mouth all the way down to her toes. She was just beginning to consider crawling up the front of him when a gruff brogue sounded, close enough to make her jump.

Oops.

Bastian's kiss had completely drowned out all awareness of a certain freight train.

"All right, you two," Duncan said, and though he was frowning, Cat could see any anger about the situation had entirely evaporated. Her uncle approved of the match. That was something. How she was going to explain all this to her father was another question entirely, but Cat pushed it from her mind. She had enough to think about right now.

"If everything is hearts and flowers here again, I've got some issues that are more important than you two snogging in public. There's a damned free-for-all over Harriet's roasted turkey legs, and the MacDonald contingent is trying to steal kegs and hide them in their camper. Not to mention that Alaric MacInnes and his crew have moved from caber practice to weight throwing and knocked three people out cold so far. I've had a word with him," Duncan said, a satisfied gleam coming into his eye, and Cat realized there were a few spatters of blood on his white shirt. "But the fun's just begun. Damned gathering's always like herding cats." He snorted, and then zeroed in on Bastian. He crooked his finger. "Come along, my young apprentice. Duty awaits."

The old Alpha laughed at Bastian's pained expression and then turned his attention to Cat. "You, too, young lady. You said you'd help. And since Poppy is nowhere to be found, and I think your sister Skye was convinced by a bunch of troublemakers to sample some of our fine Scotch whiskey, I'm needing it."

"Oh, God," muttered Cat as Duncan turned and strode off, remembering the last time Skye had been convinced to let her hair down. She might look like a conservative grad student, but add alcohol, and the girls from *Coyote Ugly* had nothing on Skye MacInnes.

"You heard him," Bastian said, starting to tug her along with a resigned look on his face, and she knew there was no way she was getting out of this one. "Duty awaits."

"Okay," Cat grumbled. "But if the music from *Braveheart* starts playing, I'm getting the hell out before I'm overrun by a bunch of drunken werewolves in kilts."

To her surprise, Bastian snorted with laughter.

"That reference, I got," he said when she gave him a curious look. "We rented a lot of movies back in Reno. The vampires were all about the end."

"Naturally," Cat said, rolling her eyes. "Gross."

And with a deep breath, Cat followed him into battle.

Chapter 9

IN THE DEAD OF NIGHT, ON A ROLL OF THUNDER beneath brilliant stars, he came.

The moon was sinking low in the Highland sky, and the howls of even the most dedicated revelers had long since faded, replaced by nothing but the whispering wind and the occasional call of an owl. But that was fine. That was best.

What Jagrin sought did not sleep.

Traveling to the Earthly realm had not been easy. Even now, Jagrin knew he must hurry. The draught he had taken would allow him to stay only so long before he was transported back to Coracin, so time was of the essence. It was just as well. He had no desire to linger in the lair of hated enemies.

He raised his head to scent the air in the dark of the woods where he walked and curled his lip in distaste. All here was fresh and alive and rather unbearably *green*. He wanted his desert, all stunted and sleeping. He wanted death.

Jagrin stood at the edge of the trees that ringed a large and impressive property, a manor house that might once have been a castle. A sea of tents began several yards from him and continued right up to the house. Within them, Jagrin knew, slept hordes of detested *arukhin*. He could sense them, smell them, and hear their steady breathing as they slumbered.

He had not expected so many. Under other circumstances, he would have taken great pleasure in destroying as many as he could. But the *arukhin*, as wretched as they were, were not his concern tonight.

Jagrin took the path into the woods, treading so silently that no branch or leaf crunched beneath his booted feet as he went. It was better here, he thought. Dark and shadowy, though again, he wished it were not so lush. He walked a way and then stopped in an area of deep darkness.

"*Narial*," he growled, quietly but in a voice that still carried, "come to me. I command you."

At first, there was nothing. Just a lingering silence. Jagrin waited, perfectly still. He could feel it out there, malignant energy watching and waiting in the night. And after a few moments, the waiting paid off.

"*Who calls me?*"

The voice was gravelly and garbled, sounding as though it had been dragged through thick and viscous mud. But a voice it unquestionably was.

Jagrin squinted through the dark, but even his sharp eyes could not make out a single shape or form. "I am Jagrin, highly placed in the court of the *daemon* king. He has sent me to you. Show yourself."

There was a wet chuckle. "*I will show myself when I choose, daemon. I owe allegiance to none but the king who bound me to the* Athin. *And he is long dead, I'm sure.*"

"You're wrong, creature. Cadmus still reigns," Jagrin growled. "And he wonders at your inability to fulfill your mission."

That did it. Jagrin fought to suppress his smirk as a

pool of blackness slunk from the trees to a spot directly in front of him and then rose from the ground to congeal into a shape that suggested a man. But this figure was faceless, save for the burning red eyes that were now fixed on him.

Jagrin's smirk faltered. The malice oozing from the shadow was far more unnerving than he had anticipated.

"*I,*" gurgled the narial, "*have feasted on the souls of the High Mages of the* Athin *for five generations. I have savored their torment and torn every shred of happiness and pleasure from them until they were begging me for release. I was not sent to them to make their deaths easy, daemon. And I have fulfilled that obligation.*" The shadow slid closer, towering over Jagrin, threatening.

Jagrin swallowed hard. By *Narr*, but he hated the soul eaters! He was glad that his own soul was far too black to draw the creatures' interest.

"Fair enough," Jagrin said, his voice sounding wretchedly thin to his own ears. "And... how does your current victim suit you?"

"*Very well,*" the *narial* replied, the red eyes going to slits. "*Why do you care, daemon? Cadmus has never sent anyone to check on me in all this time, which is the way I prefer it. Especially since I intend to return to the Blighted Kingdom before long.*"

"Oh? He is near death, then?" Cadmus was bound to be disappointed if that were the case.

"*Hardly,*" was the answer, sounding darkly amused. "*He fights me at every turn.*" There was a foul chuckle. "*He has even taken a mate, though he was warned. I believe I will have them both, at the end. Which will be soon... I find I miss the caverns of my people, all the lovely despair of the desert. Again, I ask you,* daemon*: Why do you want to know?"*

"I come on behalf of Cadmus. He has a final command for you before you are released from this service."

The *narial* snarled, sweeping to within inches of Jagrin's face. "*I have done what he commanded. I will be released once the* Athin *is dead. It is enough. If he wants more, let him come himself so we can... discuss it.*" It paused. "*Or perhaps you would like to act on his behalf in this matter as well.*"

Something in the creature's tone made Jagrin wonder just how much control Cadmus actually had over it. That was something he would tuck away to consider later. For now, he needed to get through this meeting with his skin on. Which meant doing something he had perfected over the years.

Groveling.

"I beg your pardon," Jagrin said, sweeping into a graceful bow. "I have no choice but to do as I'm ordered. Cadmus is a powerful king, as you know. I have enough healthy respect for the power of your kind that I would not have chosen this task, believe me."

"*Hmm,*" was the only noise the creature made. But it didn't advance any further upon him, so Jagrin continued.

"The king commands you," Jagrin said, subtly emphasizing *commands*, "not to finish the Dyim Bastian *an* Morgaine, no matter how he begs, or how close he is to dying. His death is not for you. Cadmus wishes it to belong to him."

The black mass that was the soul eater did not

react well to that news. It swelled in size, the swirling darkness that composed it becoming tempestuous. Sparks of red began to flicker in its depths.

Interesting, thought Jagrin, even as he fought not to recoil.

"*WHAT*?" it demanded, its voice like a thousand terrible voices joined into one. The force of its anger sent the trees rustling and Jagrin's tunic rippling against his legs. "*All these years, doing as I was bidden, tormenting the enemies of your king as no one else could have, and he seeks to deny me the pleasure of ending this final life? Of stealing the brightest light the* Athin *ever produced?*" Jagrin took a step back, the malevolent power of the *narial* stunning him. This was not a creature inferior to the *daemon*, he realized. And his kind had been fools to believe it so.

"*The work has pleased me*," the shadow growled, "*and I have fed well for many years now. But this* Athin, *this final one, is special. His pain is like nothing I have ever experienced. His power, his will to live, makes it so much more potent. This new love will only make it more so. I will have him,* daemon—*make no mistake. I will not be denied.*"

Jagrin felt icy cold sweat trickle down his back. "I only deliver a message from the king. I'll tell him about your… reluctance… and I'm sure he'll want to discuss it with you himself. Maybe if you left the mate for Cadmus to torture…"

"*Their souls are mine,* daemon," the shadow said. Then its tone turned thoughtful, calculating. "*Though Cadmus is welcome to try and take them. He will not succeed. But he can try.*"

The words seemed to hang in the air between them, echoing into silence: *He can try... he can try...*

Jagrin looked into the abyss that was the *narial*, the simple cadence ringing in his ears. And an idea, so simple, so risky, and so potentially transformative, flickered into being in the darkest depths of his soul. It was madness to think that it might work. But he knew he would not be able to let it go.

"When will you take them?" Jagrin asked, his fear leaving him to be replaced by terrible, growing excitement. "How long before the *Athin* are truly no more?"

The *narial* was silent for a moment, the burning eyes regarding him with something that felt almost like understanding. When it answered, its voice was again measured.

"*Days. A week or two, at most. I grow weary of waiting, here in this place so full of light. It will be the greatest feast of my existence. A banquet fit for a king.*" It chuckled again, that wet, gurgling sound bubbling up from its depths. The voice turned sly, teasing. "*Or is it to be the other way around, daemon? I can smell your fear, your excitement. I know your thoughts. What prize will I have, hmm?*"

"Nonsense," hissed Jagrin, jarred by the shadow's perceptiveness. "You know nothing of me. And you're a fool to refuse the king's command. He will come for you."

He could hear the smile in the *narial*'s voice. "*I look forward to it.*"

In an instant the shadow thinned and elongated, becoming a column of black smoke as it skimmed quickly over the ground and back into the forest.

"You'll be destroyed," Jagrin called after it.

"*We will see*," it replied, its voice drifting on the wind, barely audible as it disappeared.

Jagrin watched the creature vanish, until nothing was left but trees and silvery moonlight. He shook his head, wondering at the audacity of the shadow creature. Only a fool would deny Cadmus what he wanted. And yet…

There was possibility here, if only he was brave enough to grasp at it. Jagrin shifted, sending hot sparks of pain through his back where the whip had scored it. His lip curled at the memory of the humiliation of being lashed in front of the entire court as though he was no better than the half-mad *daemon* commoners who lived among the barren and shifting sands of the Blighted Kingdom.

The Earthly realm began to blur and ripple around him as his time there ended. The long gray tunic swirled around his legs, blown by the wind that would carry him back to Coracin and the impatient ruler who was about to be very disappointed, to say the least.

Which was fine, as long as he didn't take it out on the messenger.

He would consider his options, Jagrin decided, though he was probably mad to do so.

But it would be the ultimate madness not to think of himself, when all that stood between him and greatness was a little thing like death.

Even if it was the death of a king.

Chapter 10

THE FOLLOWING MORNING, CAT STOOD ON BASTIAN'S doorstep, fidgeting nervously and hoping she didn't *look* like she was fidgeting. It was eight, she saw, glancing at her small wristwatch again. Not too early, she hoped, especially since Bastian had slipped away from the festivities just as the sun was setting. He should be more rested than she was.

Not, Cat thought with a wince, *that his departure had been anything other than her own damn fault.*

At least dealing with her relatives hadn't been the struggle she'd been expecting after Duncan's complaints. In fact, entertaining them had been easy. Ill advised, Cat thought, but easy. *Managing* the newfound members of her family, on the other hand, had turned out to be downright impossible. Between the bawdy jokes, eating, drinking, dancing, drinking, random ripping off of clothing to shift into wolves, and even more drinking, all she could do was try to keep up with them.

Her lingering headache told her maybe she hadn't needed to try quite so hard in that area. But it had been fun to start getting to know her wild, hilarious, and possibly insane relatives. It hadn't even felt strange, at the end of the night, to crawl into bed as a Wolf. To have what she was be so accepted, to have Changing feel so natural, was something she'd longed for all her life.

The only thing missing from the celebration had been

Bastian. His absence had cast more of a shadow over her enjoyment than she'd expected. But then, she shouldn't have been too surprised, after what he'd told her when he'd managed to steal her away for a few minutes. Three days ago she had been just another elementary school teacher on vacation, albeit one with an interesting reaction to moonlight. Today, she was permanently bound to an otherworldly, blood-drinking sorcerer who had been pursued for most of his life by a soul-sucking shadow determined to destroy him. Oh, and her little sister was nursing an evil dragon shape-shifter back to health so he could be coerced into saving Bastian's life with his blood...

Thus far, it had been one hell of a vacation.

She was a little concerned about what could happen by the end of the gathering. A plague of locusts? An invasion by flesh-eating zombies? She shuddered and tried to push away the image of an army of the undead swarming the grounds. It wasn't going to get *that* bad.

She hoped.

Cat reached out to knock at the door, hesitated, and then pulled her hand back. How should she act when she saw him? Casual? Thrilled? Indifferent? They were mated now, something she still hadn't quite managed to wrap her brain around. And with the little time they'd spent together, she wasn't sure Bastian would welcome her tossing herself into his arms as soon as he opened the door. It seemed so... *needy*. And she'd always hated girls like that.

She sighed and ran a hand through her hair. It would have been nice if he'd stuck around a little longer so she could have tried to find some comfort level in interacting with him. As it was, her experiences with Bastian had been mainly about intense lust or abject terror, neither of which was a good indicator of how a "Hi, how are you" conversation would go with him. Considering how wild things had gotten at the gathering, she'd barely gotten to see him once Duncan had collared them.

At least he'd found her to say good night and to ask her to come by this morning, Cat thought. That was a good sign. They'd take a walk, he'd said, before the natives woke up and got restless again. He seemed to want to get to know her. Bastian hadn't pushed her away… yet. She supposed he was still trying to figure out what to do about their newly mated status, just as she was.

Well, in between thinking about getting naked with him. That was still a big barrier to rational thought.

"Quit being such an idiot," Cat grumbled to herself, smoothing her hands down her clothes one last time, pushing her hair back, and then dragging it forward over her shoulder again. She'd already spent way too much time deciding to wear a long, bohemian skirt and a spaghetti-strap tank top this morning, and she had been ready to tear her hair out in clumps before finally just leaving it to tumble around her shoulders.

She was a natural girl, always had been: jeans, long skirts, the earth mother to Poppy's naughty Goth and Skye's sexy librarian. She'd even gotten the compliment of being compared to Sandra Bullock more than once. In any case, her looks and style had never seemed to put guys off before. It was annoying to suddenly be worried about it with Bastian.

But this was a lot more important than getting

the average bar hunk to ask her to dinner. This was forever.

Cat groaned at her inability to lighten up and knocked at the door before she could think better of it.

When she heard the padding of approaching footsteps, Cat threw back her shoulders and plastered what she hoped was a relaxed smile on her face. But when the door opened slightly, it wasn't Bastian's face that peeked around the corner.

It was Poppy's.

Her sister's dark brows rose at the sight of her. "You okay? Why are you gritting your teeth at me?"

Cat rolled her eyes but ditched the smile. In truth, she was just as surprised to see Poppy as Poppy was to see her. "Why are you here so early? Bastian said you were working on Lucien, but I didn't know you'd moved in. I didn't see you at all last night."

Poppy smirked. "Yeah. I ran into Skye on my way to bed. She was feeling no pain… something about a keg stand?"

"Oh." Cat said a silent prayer of thanks that she'd dodged that particular bullet.

"And how you made Cousin Lucas play the 'Cha-Cha Slide' about ten times in a row."

Cat frowned at her. "It was only four. I think."

The smirk became a wide grin. "And how you demanded to be allowed to drive the MacDonalds' camper after line dancing on top of it."

Cat sighed. "They would have let me if I'd just pestered a little longer. And again, where were you?"

For a moment, Cat noticed, Poppy looked a little uncertain about how to answer the question. Finally, though, she just shrugged. "The crown prince seemed to want me to stick around for a while, and I wanted to see if the energy I gave him improved things at all. So I hung out longer than I meant to, and by the time he was asleep, I didn't really feel like doing much but going to bed. You know it takes a lot out of me."

"Yeah," Cat agreed. Poppy might only focus on healing for a few minutes at a time, but the concentration involved drained her of hours of energy. Once she'd heard how poor Lucien Andrakkar's health was, Cat hadn't been surprised that Poppy had volunteered her services. She might not like to show off, but Cat also wasn't dumb enough to think that her sister's patients had never reaped any benefits from Poppy's compulsion to heal and help.

"So… are you going to let me in, or do I have to crawl in a window?"

"Oh," said Poppy with a sheepish grin. "Oops. Come on. Bastian's in his bedroom." She waggled her eyebrows. "You're too late. I've ruined him for all other women."

Cat elbowed her in the ribs as she stepped in the door, smiling over her sister's *oof*.

The cottage was still neat as a pin, Cat saw, without much to indicate who, if anyone, was staying here. The only difference from the other night was that the mysterious bedroom door was now halfway open, while Bastian's was shut. She couldn't really see much but the edge of a bed and a pale, slim hand resting on the quilt, so she looked at Poppy.

"Is he any better?" she asked in a near whisper, not wanting to wake the dragon if he was asleep.

Poppy pursed her lips. "Actually, he's doing much better than I'd expected. Physically, at least. He came out of the dungeons with some really weird stuff in his blood, and I figured I would just end up making it worse, if anything. But he's responding to my energy, for whatever reason," she continued. Cat could have sworn her sister flushed lightly as she looked back at the bedroom door.

"I guess he isn't allergic to your cooties then," Cat replied, giving Poppy a more thorough look. She'd put on Cat's favorite pair of fitted denim crops and a baby-doll tee with a picture from the movie *The Last Unicorn* on it. Her curls were at least semitamed in a pony-tail and, something in the glow she had this morning, seemed decidedly suspicious. Or at least off... Cat couldn't honestly remember the last time she'd seen her sister in a purple shirt. Or any shirt that wasn't black, for that matter. It was a great color on her. But it was so... *happy*. Maybe it was just being limited to her sisters' suitcases.

Or maybe it was something else.

Before she could interrogate her about it, though, a deep, melodious, and thoroughly peevish voice floated from the room with the half-opened door. It was the same voice she'd heard the one night she'd been here, Cat realized. Except stronger and less sick sounding.

"Unless it's the great Drak himself, send whoever it is away. I need some water, and I think I may be hungry as well. Bring food, Healer."

Cat looked incredulously at her sister. "Don't tell me you're actually putting up with that."

"You know, I've told him to shove it up his ass

umpteen times by now," Poppy said with a graceful shrug and speaking loudly enough that her patient was sure to hear her. "But naturally, because he's a man, that's had the opposite effect on him. He's completely obsessed with me." Then she lowered her voice, leaning in closely to whisper, "Believe it or not, this is a big improvement. He could barely speak because he was so wrecked yesterday. Today he's weak, but a lot more obnoxious. From what Bastian said about Lucien, this is a good sign."

Cat looked at Poppy, her eyes bright and dancing with humor, and couldn't help but return her grin. Yeah, something interesting was going on here, all right. She'd seen this look before. But if nursing a potentially homicidal shape-shifter made Poppy feel happy and fulfilled, who was she to rain on her parade? Lucien's surly voice interrupted the amusement.

"*Healer*, I need water! Didn't you hear me? I need food. And it's freezing in here as well. Bring me an extra blanket. Are you coming?"

Poppy sighed and rolled her eyes. "What he means is that he needs attention."

Cat studied the long, pale fingers now tapping impatiently on the part of the quilt she could see through the doorway. "Uh, isn't this guy supposed to be some kind of terrifying dragon shifter?"

Poppy headed for the tiny kitchen. "He's also a man. The inner big baby has trumped the dragon because somebody doesn't feel good yet."

"I can hear you, you know," Lucien said irritably.

"You won't hear it when I poison your water," was the cheerful retort.

"I suppose you'll throw a party when I die, you wretched little creature."

"Yeah, that's the plan. Right after I toss your carcass in the front yard for everyone to point and laugh at as they come in. Stupid damn dragon."

"Mouthy *arukhin*."

Cat shook her head and headed for Bastian's room, sneaking a better look as she passed Lucien's door. She was curious about the legendarily nasty Lucien Andrakkar, a dragon shifter who had once tried to kill her cousin Gabriel and who was now trading barbs with her sister… and who sounded distinctly like he was enjoying it. She got a quick look at a sharp, strikingly handsome profile framed by shaggy black hair and a flash of eyes that looked to be faintly glowing violet. And yes, as she'd suspected, a smirk as the war of words continued.

"I didn't know you'd take all day, Healer. Did you find a bone and get distracted?"

"My name is Poppy, jackass."

"That's unfortunate."

"Drop dead, Lucien."

"I've tried that, but no one seems to want to let me."

Cat tuned them out as she turned the knob to Bastian's room, slipping inside quickly and shutting the door. The sudden silence was an instant relief. It was like stepping into a perfectly quiet bubble, the sounds of Bastian's houseguests cutting off midsentence the instant the door shut. He'd done something to the room, she guessed, to be able to sleep through the bickering. Must be a nice skill to have, she thought. And she certainly didn't blame him.

Cat breathed deeply, savoring the sudden peace. Then she looked around the small room, still devoid of any personal artifacts that would indicate who lived here.

That was, apart from the artifact sprawled on his stomach in the bed, only a sheet wrapped around his waist.

He looked as he had the first time she'd seen him, like an angel fallen to Earth. But at rest, the impression was even stronger. Cat stepped closer to the bed, eyes roving over skin that was bathed in light from the four lamps with which he'd surrounded the bed. Like a little boy warding off the monsters that came in the night, Cat thought sadly. Except Bastian's monster was real.

In sleep, Bastian's face was heartbreakingly beautiful, every care erased. His pale blond hair was tousled, his lips parted slightly as he breathed slowly and deeply. Every breath made the sculpted muscles of his back shift and flex slightly, and Cat stared, mesmerized. Then her eyes moved lower, to the backside that was covered by nothing but a thin sheet that left nothing to the imagination (thank God).

This was hers, Cat thought on a rush of longing so intense that it ached. She could barely believe that Bastian *an* Morgaine, for however long he drew breath, was hers. It was almost impossible to wrap her brain around.

Which didn't mean, Cat decided as her eyes did the full circuit of Bastian all over again, that there weren't other things to wrap herself around. Exasperated with herself, she gritted her teeth and forced herself to look away. He wasn't even *awake*, and he was making her think extremely naughty things.

She waited a few seconds for her subconscious to come up with a good reason why she shouldn't just jump on him, but in this case, as in many, no angel was sitting on one of her shoulders to counterbalance the devil. She only had two devils. And they tended to have interesting ideas when they got brainstorming.

A loud yawn from the bed snapped her back to reality in an instant and drew her attention to an entirely different problem.

Bastian was waking up. And she was standing in the middle of his bedroom, just staring at him. Like a goddamn *stalker*. Which matched up with the things she'd been thinking…

She watched with a strange combination of excitement and horror as Bastian's bright blue eyes opened.

And looked directly at her.

At first, he was sure he was still dreaming.

Bastian looked at the beautiful woman staring at him and blinked to see if she would simply disappear. When she didn't, and started to look like a startled deer that might bolt at any second, he knew she was real.

Cat.

He sighed softly. A night's sleep hadn't given him any more clarity about what to do where she was concerned. He'd dreamed of dancing with her, spinning in the lantern light of some unknown place where the darkness held no danger, only seductive promise. It was the first night free of nightmares he'd had in a long time.

And now she was here, looking like nothing less than a forest spirit, dark haired and golden eyed, her lithe form clad in the style that most suited her, simple and feminine. She would fit in well among his sisters, he realized, a creature of nature as they were. Just as she would fit well with him.

He'd always kept his heart to himself, knowing it was better for all concerned. But was it so selfish to want to know the woman who had become his mate? He remembered the way he'd been attacked the day Cat had arrived, in the shadow of the forest while the sun still shone, and knew it wasn't safe to want her so badly.

Bastian just didn't know how to stop.

"Good morning," he said softly, not moving. He didn't want her to run. That was something he was absolutely sure of.

"Um," she said, eyes wide. "Good morning. I… um… Poppy said you were in here. So I came in. And you were asleep." She paused and then crossed her arms defensively over her chest. "I wasn't staring at you or anything."

Bastian bit back a smile. Cat was a terrible liar. It was refreshing.

"I didn't say you were," he said easily. "I'm glad you woke me up. I don't usually oversleep, but it's been a problem recently."

She frowned, concern darkening her eyes. "Are you feeling okay?"

He nodded and yawned. "Just a little tired. It's nothing."

Nothing he wanted her to worry about, anyway. He felt lucky that after all these years, the worst effect he had, even now, was just being a little more tired than usual. His father seemed to have been right… the blood of his mother's people had protected him far more than even he had expected.

Still, he was no fool. The attacks had gotten far more violent, and the immediate aftermath was far worse than it ever had been before. The *narial* had grown tired of waiting for him to break. So it would break him.

Now he feared it would break Cat as well.

"Have you seen your sister this morning?" he asked, tucking one arm behind his head. He made no move to get up, since he wasn't sure how Cat would react to what he was wearing beneath the sheets. Which was exactly nothing.

"Poppy, you mean?" she asked, her eyes quickly flicking down the length of him before returning to his face. Looked like she'd already noticed he wasn't wearing anything beneath the covers. His cock hardened immediately in response. Bastian bit back a groan. This was never going to work, carrying on a conversation with her like this. All he could think of was how good it would feel to get his hands on her again. To make her wild for him again.

"Bastian?"

Oh, good. He'd been fixating. Bastian closed his eyes and tried to clear his head. "Yes?"

"You wanted to know about Poppy?"

"Yes." He tried to modulate his voice so it didn't sound as strained as he felt. "But more like how she's doing with my houseguest. I hope she went home and got some sleep last night... she was here later than he deserved."

He heard the smile in her voice and opened his eyes so he could see it. Her lips curved invitingly, and as she began to relax, her arms dropped to her sides, allowing him a better view of her long, slender waist. Fortunately, she seemed to have no idea what he was thinking about.

"She's also here earlier than he deserves. Poppy beat me here. You just seem to have the abuse blocked out," Cat said. He raised his eyebrows, surprised.

"It's a simple spell, to soundproof the room. I should have removed it, but they were arguing later than I felt like staying awake. Now I'm glad I left it on." He shook his head. "I can't imagine why Poppy would enjoy his company, but if she's already here, I can't think of another explanation."

"Don't try," Cat replied. "Whichever motive makes the least sense is usually Poppy's. So, um, did you want to go for that wa…" She trailed off as her eyes left his, drifting just low enough for her to get an eyeful of what her presence had done to him. "Oh. Ah. Walk. Or something."

Cat flushed a deep, appealing pink and found something interesting to study on the ceiling. One long, graceful hand moved to tuck her hair behind her ear, and the other arm wrapped itself around her waist again. She was obviously nervous and embarrassed. Bastian watched her, fascinated.

He'd had women throw themselves at him for much of his life. And for pleasure or for sustenance, or both, he had partaken often enough. But none of them had ever affected him the way Catriona MacInnes did. He knew that the mating bond was incredibly deep and unbreakable, once sealed. That he would feel drawn to her and compelled to be with her was natural. But there was more. He'd been given only tantalizing glimpses of Cat's past, and they weren't nearly enough. She was such an intriguing mixture of innocence and experience, sweetness and strength.

He hadn't been surprised to like who she was. He was surprised how quickly "like" was becoming something else.

"Something wrong?" he asked, unable to resist teasing her, daring her to say what she thought.

"No. Yes." She sighed loudly, and he grinned. Taking a chance, he focused his senses on her and was immediately rewarded with a double punch of heat in his lower belly as her scent, intoxicating as moonlight, enveloped him. He was glad that he could catch her emotions so easily, because now he knew he wasn't the only one who was aroused. Part of him was relieved.

The other part immediately began figuring out how to get her close enough to the bed to pull her in with him.

"You know," Cat said, her tone conversational even as her blush deepened, "I think I understand now why you kept telling me you couldn't talk to me when I was naked."

"Technically I'm wearing a sheet," he pointed out. "And you did come in here to wake me up. I'm not embarrassing you purposely."

"Oh, I'm not embarrassed," she said, and he thought he saw her jaw twitch slightly. "I'm trying to convince myself that I need to get to know you better before I jump you." Then her eyes met his, molten gold burning right through him. "How I feel about you... I know this is normal, I guess, for what I am, but it's all new to *me*. Everything is so strong, and it doesn't seem to make a lot of sense. I just want to make sure this is right. It feels too important to screw up… which I have a tendency to do. Does that sound stupid?"

"No," Bastian said slowly, focused completely on her, the invisible thread between them allowing him to feel her heartbeat accelerating right along with his. "It sounds about right. Except for one thing."

She took a small, tentative step toward him. "What's that?"

Bastian rose up on one elbow, willing her to close the rest of the distance between them. He wanted to claim her as his own, fully and completely. But the final decision needed to come from her. He would not push. But he would tell the truth.

"You, the part of you that recognized me as your mate… you already know me."

He watched her swallow hard. "Maybe that's true," Cat said softly. "Maybe that's why I'm already terrified of losing you. What happens to me if you never shake the curse? Is being with you this way just going to make it hurt that much worse if… if you…"

She couldn't seem to bring herself to say it, but it didn't matter. Bastian knew. And he didn't have a good answer for her.

"I don't know, Cat. It very well might. If you want to wait until something has given, one way or the other, I understand. I don't honestly know if it's better for me to watch over you or to be apart from you, or if it matters at all… this is new to me, too. I've never even come close to taking a mate."

Cat grimaced then, and it surprised him. "I have," she said.

"Hulking football type?" Bastian asked, remembering one particular player in the more recent memories of Cat he'd witnessed at their bonding. "Big mouth, new affection for silver bullets?" He paused, feeling a twinge of jealousy. "You were going to bite *him*?"

She wrinkled her nose at him, and her obvious disgust at the thought settled him back down. Whether it was right or not, he wanted to be the only one that both sides of her wanted, woman and Wolf.

"No, I didn't want to bite him. I was supposed to marry him, which I guess is not as big a deal around here." She laughed, but her expression changed and became softer, sadder.

"It's so strange. I want you so much more, and I don't even really know who you are."

Something twisted painfully deep inside of him at her words. He'd done it purposefully, of course, for many years: it had become second nature to hold himself apart. But just this once, however long he had with Cat, he didn't want it to be like that. Sometimes the thought that he might die without anyone ever really having known him terrified him.

And with that, he knew what to do.

"All right," he said with a nod.

"All right?" Cat asked, tilting her head. "Did we just decide something?"

So beautiful, he thought as he looked at her. And his, for the time being. So she deserved all he could give, however much or little that turned out to be.

"Give me a minute," he said, gesturing toward the door. "I think we need to go on that walk."

"Oh. Seriously?" Cat asked. And the Goddess

help him, she looked disappointed. It was enough to give any sane man pause. But Bastian steeled himself and nodded.

Cat was right. This was too important to screw up.

"Seriously," he said. "There's something I want to show you."

Chapter 11

POPPY CONCENTRATED, ABSORBING HERSELF COMPLETELY in the task at hand. Over the years, she had learned how to control the flow of the white light she carried inside herself passably well. But even a small thing like healing a cut or a scrape required her full, unwavering attention. Rooting out the insidious darkness that crawled through Lucien Andrakkar's veins was like hunting a ghost.

All sense of her body and her surroundings evaporated as power hummed from her through him. Then she *was* the power, cascading through a being whose essence glowed as violet as his eyes. There were areas of strength, pulsing strong and true. And then there were the dark places, smaller than before and weaker, but mobile. She needed to envelop the blights and destroy them. But first she had to give chase. The creeping rot that had infected Lucien was fast. But she, cruising to overtake it, was always faster.

On a burst of speed, she overtook the disease, her essence intensifying. There was a quick, terrifying sensation of senseless, violent hatred and the stench of decay. And then she felt the sharp, bright explosion within herself as all that she was overwhelmed the infection and destroyed it utterly. She and the power became separate again as her triumph shimmered through her body, along with the certainty that she'd won yet another round. Poppy, eyes still closed, grinned.

"Take that, you rotten little suckers."

Then his voice, in that dark and sonorous tone that did strange and unmentionably lovely things to her every time it sounded, brought her all the way back to the present. Poppy could admit to herself that she could be perfectly happy for weeks on end listening to Lucien Andrakkar read something as mundane as a take-out menu. His pissy insults, however, were wearing a little thin.

"It hurt that time, you know. And do you have to *talk* to whatever it is you're ridding me of?"

Poppy sighed and opened her eyes, looking straight into the violet gaze of the man whose attitude was rapidly becoming more of a pain than whatever plague she was trying to cure him of. Lucien looked back at her, his expression as irritable as usual.

"It's not like the alternative is that appealing, you know," she informed him, lifting her hands from his bare chest, which had warmed from her touch.

His response was simply to arch one ebony brow. She's gotten the impression already that Lucien wasn't all that invested in living, though his rapidly strengthening energy belied more of a will to live than he let on. She doubted she'd ever get him to admit it, though. Just like she doubted he was ever going to accept the fact that she actually had a name.

Sometimes it was funny. Right now, on the heels of something as intimate as sharing her energy with him, it was beyond annoying.

"How are you feeling, anyway?" she asked, trying to turn the subject from her perceived ineptitude, a favorite topic of his. "Better?"

His smile was as sexy as the devil himself's, which tended to be a warning sign.

As usual, she wasn't disappointed.

"Not as good as my captor and your sister, I'm sure, but I'm much better than I was yesterday."

Poppy felt her face redden, and the knowledge that he was purposely making her uncomfortable only intensified the blush. She didn't know where Cat and Bastian had gone (looking, she'd noticed, like they would rather be devouring one another than taking a damned nature walk, but what did she know?), and she didn't particularly care. Her sister needed someone like Bastian in her life. Well, minus the curse, but she was happy to try and help with that. Being with Bastian five minutes was enough to get the *I'm a good guy* vibe he gave off loud and clear.

Unlike some people. People with whom she certainly didn't want to dish about Cat's sex life.

Which Lucien, of course, knew.

The only thing that stopped her from clocking him was knowing how happy it would make him to get her to go ballistic.

"Glad to hear it," she muttered, busying herself rebuttoning the flannel shirt Bastian had found to keep the ornery dragon warm. Poppy frowned over the way he shivered at her touch. He still chilled much more easily than she'd like, but hopefully that would improve with time.

She just wished she knew how much time he was going to have.

"Why are you helping me, Healer?"

Poppy jerked her head up, startled by the question.

She waited a beat for the nasty comment that seemed to come free with every innocuous one, but this time Lucien was just... *looking* at her. He seemed genuinely perplexed. The problem was that Poppy had no idea how to answer him, because so was she. Why *was* she helping him, really? Not just using her gift on him, but playing nursemaid when no one had asked her to? She was all for coming to the aid of those in need. But Lucien was kind of an asshole. That wasn't something she was usually very forgiving about. And she wasn't just using her healing gift on him. She'd made him a PB & J earlier. With the crusts cut off.

It could mean nothing but trouble.

"Well," she said slowly, hoping something boring and believable would come to her, "you were dying. I thought I should do something about that." She looked down her nose at him and did her best to look withering, a look she'd been studying because Lucien wore it so often. "Despite your complaining, you know, you do look better. So something's working."

That was actually an understatement. It was also, Poppy realized, a lot of her problem. Lucien Andrakkar was, even beat-up and half-dead, the most gorgeous man she'd ever laid eyes on. His features were hawkish, striking in a face framed by tousled hair as black as jet. He was still too pale and too thin from the terrible things that had been done to him. But Poppy doubted he would ever stop looking dark and brooding, which was her Achilles' heel where men were concerned.

Fortunately she didn't like Lucien Andrakkar any better than he liked her. Looks only went so far.

Inexplicable lust went further, but she wasn't going to think about that right now.

The touch of his hand on her cheek shot that all to hell in a matter of seconds.

"Why is it that you're the only *arukhin* I've seen with hair like this?" Lucien asked, drawing a bright pink curl away from her face to examine it in the light. "It's such an unusual color."

"I, um," she said, flustered at the way her lower belly quivered from such a light touch. "I get it colored that way. It's really just boring brown. I'm boring enough," she joked, trying to brush off the queer sensation he provoked in her. It didn't work.

"No," he murmured, sliding the curl through his fingers before letting it fall back into place.

"No?" she asked numbly, watching those long, elegant fingers caress a single lock of her hair as though it was rarest silk and feeling as though that single moment lasted hours.

"You're not boring." His gaze was both intense and inscrutable, and Poppy, unnerved, had to look away when she answered him.

"Nah, just a stupid *arukhin* healer. But I'm good at fetching, so that's something." She shot a look back at him, daring him to agree with her. This whole exchange was completely out of character for him, and it was making her nervous. If she could get him to fight with her, sadly, that would be a lot more comfortable. As it was, she was starting to worry. Had the illness gone to his brain? Or maybe he was just dying, despite her best efforts, and had decided to get introspective. That couldn't be it, though. He was getting better; she could feel it every time she touched him.

Lucien didn't seem to be in the mood to oblige her, though. And that *was* normal for him.

"You didn't give me a good answer before. Why are you helping me? I'm hardly worth the effort. I'm not going to let that wretched Dyim bite me, and there isn't a tribe of Drakkyn in all of Coracin that would take me in right now. Not Mordred Andrakkar's son. They all think I'm as mad as he was." He thought a moment. "Actually, they more likely all think I'm dead. Which by rights I should be."

Something twisted painfully in Poppy's heart at the bland, matter-of-fact way Lucien stated such awful things. "You're not going to help Bastian?"

His violet eyes were cool. "No. Why should I reward him for dragging me here, for keeping me alive? I don't bear him any ill will for what happened with... before," he said, the first sign of any crack in his facade. "But I owe him nothing for prolonging my life. In fact, I see no reason he shouldn't be sorry he saved it."

Before. Poppy knew he was talking about the story her uncle had told them, about how he had thought himself in love with Bastian's sister Rowan and had hunted her across worlds. Except it turned out that his crazy father had set him up, trying to get Lucien to mate with his own half sister to create a more powerful next generation of their dying line. And then, though Lucien had run from the battle between his father and the Dyadd, who were backed by the MacInnes Pack, the *daemon* had gotten him.

He was right. Everyone thought he was dead. And, Poppy thought unhappily, no one was upset about it.

"You're not going to help him," Poppy said flatly. "Because he saved you."

Lucien stuck his nose in the air. He must have had lots of practice, Poppy thought, because it was extremely effective even from his sickbed. "Exactly."

Her eyes narrowed. "You do know he'll die without your help, right?"

Bastian shrugged. "He probably would have died anyway. The *narial* are some of the cruelest creatures in our realm. Even the dragons fear them, and we fear nothing. It was hopeless to begin with."

Poppy's mouth dropped open. The anger that rushed through her was a welcome return to form, and oh, did he deserve it. "That is the dumbest fucking thing I've ever heard!" she cried. "You can't just absolve yourself that way. You can help, and you don't want to. It's your right, I guess, but call it what it is."

Lucien snorted. "He's dying, Healer. You and your sister are setting yourselves up for disappointment." He turned his head away and closed his eyes. "Do yourself a favor and give up. Go have fun with the other furballs and leave me alone."

She bared her teeth at him. "Maybe I will, if you're that much of a lost cause."

He didn't bother to open his eyes. "I assure you, I am."

Poppy clenched her fists, and though she tried not to do it, a low growl escaped her. She had felt his energy strengthening; she'd helped it along. She absolutely refused to believe that he really cared so little about himself that it meant nothing to him. The disdain for the rest of the universe was probably real; that she could see. But actually wanting to die was a tough pill to swallow.

"There has to be something you give a damn about."

One eye opened slightly to regard her. "I told you

you're going to be disappointed. No, Healer. There is nothing left for me. My house has fallen from power. My line is at an end. And as a dragon, I am an utter disgrace. The truth is, there is nothing I have found worth living for."

It made her angry and broke her heart, both at the same time. That potent combination of feeling, along with a desperate need to prove he could feel something besides indifference, made her do what she did next.

Before she could talk herself out of it, Poppy did what she'd been wanting to do since Lucien had given her hell for knocking on the front door. She leaned down and pressed her lips against his in a hard, angry kiss. He stiffened immediately, and rather than being satisfied that she'd finally managed to offend the dragon, Poppy found herself hurt and infuriated. She pulled away and began to sit up, ready to tell him off for good.

Instead, before she knew what was happening, Lucien's hand shot out to grab her and drag her back. She barely had time for a gasp before his mouth was back on hers, but as the aggressor this time, hot, demanding, hard. There was nothing gentle about it as Lucien thrust his tongue against hers, leaving no doubts that however ill he might be, there was still a beast just beneath the surface… one she'd just succeeded in awakening. Poppy's coherent thought evaporated in a cloud of primal lust.

His hands tangled in her hair while she leaned into him, hardly caring how awkwardly she was half-sprawled across Lucien's chest while her feet were still on the floor. He seemed to be trying to scare her with his need, but Poppy's senses had awakened with brutal intensity. She matched his passionate assault with a bruising one of her own. The kiss was vicious and hungry, teeth scraping against skin. She felt as if her blood had turned to fire, and all she wanted was to crawl inside him.

For the first time, she was desired by a man who was as much animal as she.

It was painfully, violently arousing.

And yet as much as she wanted him, as close as she was to letting herself be overwhelmed by this unexpected torrent of desire, something pulled her back from the edge at the last minute. Poppy tore her mouth from his with a gasp, backing up so quickly that she slipped from Lucien's grasp before he could catch her. The chair where she'd been sitting toppled over as she knocked it with her hip.

They stared at one another, she with her back to the wall, he up on his elbows, the room dead silent but for the ragged sounds of their breathing. Poppy had no idea what to say. She'd kissed him more out of pique than anything, wanting to get a reaction out of him. Well, she had certainly gotten one. And if she'd been concerned that Lucien Andrakkar was truly unable to feel anything, that had been put to rest for good. His eyes glowed with fierce light, tangled locks of ebony hair hanging in his face as he watched her. He looked like a predator.

It made him that much more appealing.

But she wasn't about to crawl into that bed with him until some things changed drastically. And she had no problem saying what she thought. Even if that meant telling off a dragon. And even if that meant walking away as frustrated, sexually and otherwise, as she'd ever been.

Lucien's voice sounded hoarse when he spoke. "Get back over here, Healer. You started this."

Poppy took two slow steps toward him, noting how hungrily he watched the sway of her hips. Then she stopped, just out of arm's reach. "My name is *Poppy*, Lucien. And I'll be back when you decide whether *that's* worth sticking around for. Until then, cut your own damn crusts off your sandwiches. I may want to take a big bite out of your ass, but your attitude sucks."

And with that she strode from the room and out the door, leaving a stunned Lucien unable to do anything but watch her go.

"Where are we going again?"

"Come on. It's not far now."

Cat searched Bastian's face for some clue about what he was up to, but his mysterious smile gave away nothing. So, with a shrug and a sigh, she followed him as he took the lead, leaving the path to head off into the trees. It would have to be off the beaten path, Cat thought with a wince as a rock found its way between her shoe and the sole of her foot. Wherever they were heading, Bastian was impatient to get there.

In truth, so was she. She just hoped they were impatient for the same reason. Every time she thought about him staring at her from his bed, wearing nothing but that very thin sheet (and looking extremely happy to see her), she felt like she might spontaneously combust. Which would make her responsible for one hell of a forest fire. So she needed to behave.

She didn't understand why Bastian had decided

to behave. Back in the bedroom, he'd looked like he wanted to eat her alive.

Cat kicked at a stick in her path.

Damn it.

"Are you sure Poppy's okay with him all by herself?" Cat asked as she crunched along behind him, trying to occupy her overheated mind with worrying over her sister. It wasn't hard—Poppy and Lucien had still been bickering when they'd left.

"You don't think he'll just snap and... fry her, or something?"

Up ahead of her, Cat watched Bastian shake his head. "No way. I know she's small, but I'd put money on your sister any day of the week," he said. "I think the underappreciation is getting to her, so Lucien ought to be careful."

"Poor Poppy," Cat agreed, hoping her sister would come out to the gathering today and manage to blow off some steam, which she was sure to be full of. "She's done so much already, but I don't think his disposition is improving along with his health."

A wild hoot, followed by a burst of raucous laughter, sounded in the distance. Bastian stopped, looking off in the direction of the house. Cat used the opportunity to join him, but not before her toe found a rogue tree branch on the ground to snag. She stumbled quickly and then righted herself, hoping her near miss had passed unnoticed.

Of course, she had no such luck.

"I saw that."

Cat glared at the back of his head as she caught up to him. She didn't usually fall over her feet. Other things, sure, but not her own feet. Obviously, the sexual frustration was getting to her… and whose fault was that?

"Thanks for not mentioning it."

His raspy voice was laced with humor when he replied, "No problem."

There was another whoop, and someone began to play the bagpipes. Badly.

"Oh my God," Cat said, looking at her watch. "It's eight thirty in the morning, and they're at it again. I thought we had time!"

Bastian turned to look at her, his blue eyes bright with amusement. "We do. Unless you think we should join them?"

She blanched, and Bastian laughed.

"Uh, no. I don't seem to be able to keep up." She shook her head, looking in the direction of the house warily. "Nothing good can come of a repeat performance. One of my sisters can take a turn."

He raised his eyebrows. "Whatever you're talking about, I'm sorry I missed that part." He looked around them. "Almost there. Your foot okay?"

She pursed her lips at him. "Yeah. And once again, thanks for not mentioning it."

A quick flash of a grin, and Bastian was off again. Cat followed him, curiosity finally beginning to win out over frustration. He ducked beneath the branches of a tree, then turned and held out his hand to her. Charmed by the carelessly chivalrous gesture, Cat caught it and let him lead her down a small embankment to where a stream burbled merrily, splashing over rocks and shining in the sun. He stopped at the edge, pale blue eyes following the path of water that was much the same color.

"It's beautiful," Cat said, wondering why exactly he'd chosen to bring her here. The sound of the water was soothing, and the landscape as lovely as everything here in the Highlands. But she couldn't see anything that would have provoked the excitement that Bastian had shown. Still, she didn't doubt he had reason. There was, she was finding out, a great deal more to Bastian than met the eye.

The sunlight caught his hair, making it glow like pale fire, and his eyes glowed faintly as he turned to smile at her.

"It is beautiful," Bastian agreed. "But that isn't why I brought you down here."

She tilted her head at him, intrigued. "Then what is it?"

"You wanted to know about me. So I'm going to show you." He stepped back slightly from her and moved his hand, lifting it just a little, palm up, as though beckoning. And as Cat watched in amazement, the water responded. Tiny droplets of it leaped into the air, flashing in a shaft of sunlight to dance on the palm of Bastian's outstretched hand, each drop like a tiny jewel that worked its way into what became a shifting, glimmering orb.

She'd been amazed by what he'd done at the loch. But up close, "amazed" didn't even begin to cover it.

"Holy crap," Cat said, awed. She immediately winced at her own lack of eloquence. But Bastian grinned, and a gleam in his eye held all the excitement and pride of a child showing off a new trick.

"Not done yet. Watch this."

He brought the orb close to his lips and then blew.

And instead of warm breath, Cat could see a cloud of frigid air. The orb spun, shifted, lengthened, and changed. Until at last, Bastian held something she recognized. He held it out to her, but she hesitated, afraid she might break it.

"You won't hurt it," he assured her. Her eyes flickered to his, so terribly certain. So she did as he asked, gingerly reaching down to cup the perfect, glittering bloom he had formed for her. It looked like a rose made of diamonds, Cat thought. The drops that Bastian had fashioned it from weren't diamonds, though. He had turned them to ice.

It was cold in her hands as she took it, though, to her surprise, not so cold that it was uncomfortable to touch. "Oh my God," she breathed. "It's so beautiful! But... I'll melt it," she insisted, hating to think that such a thing was so impermanent.

"They last for a while," he insisted. "And I can always make another one."

"How? How can you do what you just did?"

"I'm Dyim," he said softly. "But I'm also *Athin*. My father's people were High Mages who could control water and lived in the ice and snow." Bastian quirked a half smile at her. "I managed to pick a couple of things up."

Cat held the fragile rose between them as they bent their heads over it, marveling at its perfection. Their faces reflected in each tiny surface, over and over again. A bird sang somewhere above them, the only thing that kept Cat from feeling entirely frozen in time.

"Do you like it?" he finally asked. Cat looked up at him and was surprised to see a hint of vulnerability in that crystalline blue gaze.

"Are you freaking kidding me?" she returned, surprised he even felt the need to ask. "You just made me a magic ice rose. I don't know about girls in Coracin, but where I come from, this constitutes a pretty kick-ass gift, Bastian."

The pleasure she saw on his face was worth its weight in gold.

"I haven't done that in forever," Bastian admitted, keeping his voice low and sounding as amazed as she felt.

"Why not?" she asked.

He leaned in closer, just a breath away. "Not enough pretty girls to give ice roses to."

She laughed breathlessly, enjoying this side of him.

"Bastian *an* Morgaine. Are you hitting on me?"

He twisted his lips into a sexy pout. "If you have to ask, I'm doing a pretty piss-poor job."

"It isn't that," Cat assured him, craning her neck to look at the forest around them. "It's just that every time you and I get close to each other, all hell seems to break loose. I'm waiting for something horrible to crawl out from under a rock and start wreaking havoc."

"You'll notice," Bastian replied, "that I picked a very sunny spot this time. I'd be happy if the *narial* slithered out here."

Cat watched him carefully, not wanting to throw a wet blanket on their first official date by talking about his impending doom, but he didn't seem to mind.

"So that's why you sleep with all the lamps in the house?" Cat asked. "Does artificial light work, too?"

"Sunlight is the only thing that can destroy it," he returned, very matter-of-fact. "But any sort of light seems to make it difficult for the shadow to materialize. It doesn't like light, period. Among other things."

They were both silent for a moment, and Cat pretended to examine the ice rose further, though her mind had drifted elsewhere. She knew what Bastian meant: the *narial* despised anything that wasn't about darkness or pain. It got its power from eradicating the beautiful and strong in those it afflicted. Guilt pricked at her again… all she had done was to give the shadow another reason to strike at Bastian.

It hated her. Which meant Bastian felt… well, something strong, anyway.

She wished she could be happier about it.

"So? What else?" she asked, turning the subject away for now. The sun was shining, and they were alone. There were countless better things to dwell on.

"What else what?" He looked back at her, all innocence.

Cat narrowed her eyes at him in mock irritation. "You're holding out on me, Bastian. I'll remind you that I can probably beat you up when I've got my fur on."

He grinned. "You wish." Then he looked over her head. "Hey, what's that?"

She fell for it hook, line, and sinker. "What…"

The moment she turned her head, he grabbed her wrist and jerked her forward with a wicked chuckle, the motion so fast she didn't have time to do more than gasp. The ice blossom fell from her hands as a flash of white light enveloped them both. She bumped against his chest and felt his arms come protectively around her. Then she blinked, and the blinding light was gone. Cat froze, trying to figure out what had just happened. She didn't feel any different. She looked up, and Bastian was still there, smiling down at her. Everything else, however…

"You did ask what else," he reminded her, his amused voice rumbling through his chest and against hers.

"*Oh.*" It was all she could manage at first. Cat looked slowly around her, utterly stunned. Only a second ago she'd been in a Highland forest. Now, she didn't know *where* she was.

"This was one of my favorite places to hide from my sisters as a child. I'm going to be insulted if you hate it," Bastian informed her, sounding amused as he watched her gape at their new surroundings. Cat wasn't ready to collect herself enough to say anything yet, though. All she wanted to do was stare. But she figured, considering her normally earthbound mere-mortal-ness, that she was entitled. So rather than answer, that's what she did, turning in the circle of his arms to gawk openly at a spectacle of nature like she'd never before encountered.

They stood on a small hill beneath an open and endless sky. That much, at least, was recognizable. But this was like a fairyland, the colors completely changed from what she would have expected. Long silver grass brushed their knees, rolling away from them into a landscape that was devoid of other people but dotted with massive trees. Those, she noted with wonder, had swirling, twisting trunks in a myriad of candy-shop colors and bushy tops that seemed to brush the aqua sky, which was lit by the twin orange suns that burned in it. None of this, however, was what ended up capturing Cat's undivided attention. It was what the air was full of, bouncing against one another in a bright and beautiful dance of color and light, filling it with a faint but unmistakable sound.

"Bubbles!" she cried delightedly, clapping her

hands together. She felt all of five years old again, full of wonder. "And they're..." She trailed off and turned her head to look at him, incredulous. "Singing bubbles? Seriously?"

"That's because they're alive," Bastian replied. "Took me poking one when I was about five to figure it out." He pulled her down to sit with him in the grass, which was whisper soft as it swayed around them in a gentle alien breeze.

"What happens when you poke them?" Cat asked, snuggling closer to him and watching in awe as an enormous purplish bubble drifted overhead, leaving in its wake a wordless melody that was one of the most beautiful things Cat had ever heard. "Don't they pop?"

"No. They poke back," Bastian replied, and then breathed deeply. She could feel her own tension leaving her as they sat. She could see why he'd once come here so often; this was the most relaxing place she'd ever been. The air around them was filled with music, each bubble resonating with notes that blended beautifully with the others, a constantly changing symphony.

"Incredible," said Cat. And it was. *He* was. She looked at him sitting there, quiet and unmistakably pleased with himself, and could hardly believe that one body could contain the ability to do the things he was showing her today. And it had brought him pleasure, she could see that. She was so glad she'd asked. And just as glad he'd been willing.

"Thanks. Once I discovered I could pop in and out of other places, other realms, I saw so many that I forgot a lot of them as soon as I was out of them. But this one stuck with me. Not to mention it was a great place to cool off after Rowan and I had gotten into it." His lips quirked as he remembered. "Which happened a lot."

Cat couldn't really imagine what it was like to have the usual sibling spats with a sister who could breathe fire... nor was she sure she wanted to. Poppy had been a biter, Skye more of a scratcher, and that had been enough. "Do you still come here often?"

"Oh, it must have been ten years at least, maybe more," he replied. "I'd almost forgotten about it, honestly. But when you asked... this was what came to mind." Bastian's eyes were closed, his head tipped back in pleasure.

She gave his hand a shy squeeze. "Thanks for bringing me here. It's beautiful. I didn't even know there were places like this outside of people's imaginations."

He opened his eyes to look at her. "Sure," he said. "If you know where to look. And, of course, if world-jumping is one of your special talents."

Cat shook her head. "Wild. I never thought being a werewolf would seem lowbrow."

Bastian cocked his head at her. "The *arukhin* are extremely powerful in their own right, you know."

Cat smiled ruefully. "Yeah, well. I'm lucky I can control the Change at all. The werewolf thing is just something we were left to deal with. But I'm a fairly quick study, thank God."

"Like me."

"Hmm?"

Bastian swept his hand around them. "I met my father all of once. I'm fairly sure he could do this, but none of the Dyadd can. Had to figure it out on my own. Wandering around, accidentally flipping into other

realms, or heading to one and winding up in another."
His eyes crinkled at the corners. "Only almost killed
myself once or twice."

She tipped her chin down. "You meet some less
benign bubbles somewhere?"

He chuckled. "Something like that. Except with fire
and man-eating spiders."

Cat cringed. "Okay, I'll take being inept at changing
skins, I guess." She shuddered, trying to block out the
images he'd just put in her head. Still, it was nice to talk
to someone else who'd had to fend for himself in the
supernatural powers department. She hadn't talked this
freely about her less human side to anyone but family
since, well... she'd tried with Todd, but he'd come
after her with holy water and skipped town with the
engagement ring he'd demanded back from her at stake-
point. Dumbass had mixed up his legendary creatures,
but she hadn't wanted the ring enough at that point to
enlighten him.

Bastian was quiet for a long time, pensively watching
the bright orbs that wafted to and fro in the otherworldly breeze. Finally, he said, "You'll be meeting my
family tonight."

"Yep." That was actually fairly high on her laundry list
of worries for today, though she didn't want to tell him she
was afraid of his sisters. She was a werewolf, for God's
sake. But trying to explain her relationship with Bastian
to a group of powerful demigoddesses was not something
she was interested in doing, especially since his favorite
sister was the ruling *Dyana*. Rowan *an* Morgaine was also
half-dragon and, according to everyone Cat had heard
speak of her, a force to be reckoned with in general.

He had kept his curse a secret for all these years to protect them, which she understood. But now it was her secret to keep as well. And having to lie to someone who could conceivably incinerate her was not something she really wanted to do.

"What are the rest of the Dyim like, anyway?" she asked, newly preoccupied with thoughts of having her ass summarily kicked by a horde of beautiful women. "Last night everyone seemed to be looking forward to them coming."

He smiled, and his voice was full of affection. "I'm not sure I should even try to describe them to you. I'll just tell you that I'm… atypical, I guess. I'm not much like them."

"And what is a Dyim that you aren't, exactly?"

His answer was simple and had her laughing out loud: "Fun."

"I'm sure you're fun," she said, hoping she sounded reassuring instead of doubtful. Sure, he wasn't Mr. Party or anything, but he had undeniably good reasons. And he couldn't always be serious. At least, she was fairly sure he couldn't.

"No," Bastian said, though he didn't look unhappy about it. "I've been known as the enforcer of no-fun for years among my sisters. Which saved a neck or two, but earned me no thanks, believe me."

Cat looked at him, a big, gorgeous man sitting contentedly beneath a sky filled with enormous musical bubbles, and felt the giggle bubbling up before she could stop it. His eyebrows went up at the sound, which only made her giggle harder.

"What?"

"Nothing. It's just… nothing."

His eyes narrowed, and a split second later Cat was flat on her back, sprawled beneath him and fully laughing now while Bastian grinned down at her.

"Confess. Or I have ways of making you talk."

"I'm scared, Bastian. Really," she managed when she could catch her breath.

"You should be. Now what's so funny?"

Cat grinned up at him. "I was just thinking that you might not be any fun, but you look surprisingly at home in the middle of a bunch of musical bubbles."

Bastian tipped his chin down at her. "Oh, come on, now…"

"It's okay. I think I like your girly side," Cat added, seeing the flash in his eyes that meant she was in for it. But in her opinion, he was due for some female teasing. Of that, at least, she was sure his sisters would approve. "Bubbles, music, pretty colors… any unicorns and rainbows around too?"

"I'll show you who's girly," he growled, his smile full of both warning and promise. Cat slid her knees up, wiggling against him suggestively. But when Bastian lowered his head for a kiss, she moved in a flash, slipping her feet quickly against his chest and kicking out on a burst of her Wolf strength. Bastian went flying, and she scrambled to her feet, laughing breathlessly as she began to run.

"You're going to have to catch me first!" she cried, hearing the grunt as Bastian hit the ground.

"Oh, you'd better run," he called back, gaining his feet quickly and beginning to swish through the long grass after her.

Cat did, with the full intention of eventually letting herself be caught. Once she'd let him know she was faster, of course. But as she dashed away from him, she caught the sound echoing through the alien sky and knew she would always remember it, no matter what happened. It was the sound of Bastian's laughter, full, hearty, and utterly carefree.

If nothing else, Cat thought, she could give him that. Because she loved him.

The realization hit her full in the chest, her heart swelling with the truth of it all at once. And in that instant, her feet tangled in one another and the truth knocked her, quite literally, off her feet.

She crashed to the ground with a yelp, but seconds later he'd caught her, rolling to absorb the impact. With his body pressed against hers, everything, from the airy song to the strange and beautiful surroundings, disappeared. She wanted him again.

She was beginning to understand that she *always* wanted him.

And this time, in the bright sunlight of another world, there was nothing to stop her from having him.

"Ready to surrender?" Bastian asked, fangs bared and a predatory gleam in his eye.

"You first," Cat replied.

Then she flipped him.

Bastian grunted as his back hit the ground, and Cat quickly seized the advantage, straddling his hips and pinning his arms. She surveyed the stunned expression on his face and grinned triumphantly.

"Don't look so surprised," she gloated. "You're the one who said my kind have great power of their own, remember?"

"I know. I'm trying to decide whether to let you stay there," he replied, his voice deepening. She felt him grow hard between her legs and shifted against him, trying to resituate herself. Her skirt was all caught up, and she'd initially thought to unbunch it. She did, but with the added bonus of now having no barrier against him but the silken scrap of material that was her underwear. The contact turned the core of her to liquid heat. Her breath caught, giving her away.

"If I didn't know better," Bastian said with a slow, seductive smile, "I would think you were going to try and take advantage of me."

Cat leaned down until she was only a breath away from his mouth and then stopped. "I'm not going to try. I *am* going to take advantage of you."

He glanced above them. "What will the bubbles think?"

"The bubbles are going to sing 'Sexual Healing' this morning," she replied, sliding her hands beneath his shirt to cruise over tightly corded muscle. She felt the muscles in his abdomen jump at her touch and felt herself tighten in response.

Bastian pulsed between her legs where she cradled him, and unable to help herself, Cat rubbed against him, closing her eyes with pleasure. Bastian slid his hands to her hips, urging her against him. Cat let out a shuddering breath at the heat coiling through her.

"Let me see you," Bastian rasped, his breathing beginning to quicken. He lifted his hands from beneath hers and rose up just enough to slide her tank top off. She didn't miss the glare he gave her favorite bra.

"Don't rip it," she warned him.

"I won't," he said, dragging her down for a long, hot

kiss. She barely heard the snap as the plastic clasp at the front of the bra was broken neatly in two. It slid off and she tossed it into the grass, thinking that a busted bra was a small price to pay for making love with Bastian in this strange, beautiful place. His hands went to her breasts, his rough palms turning her nipples into tight little buds as he toyed with them.

Cat leaned into his touch and watched him as she began to rock her hips against him rhythmically. It was a little thrill when his brilliant blue eyes begin to go hazy with pleasure. He arched into her, and Cat gasped, her head going back as sensation spiraled through her. She'd never had anyone bring her this close so fast. It was as though every place Bastian touched her became hypersensitized. And that was with clothes on.

"Your turn," Cat breathed, tugging at Bastian's shirt. With a lazy grin he pulled it off for her, leaving Cat to salivate over the broad, muscular expanse. She raked her nails lightly down his stomach, making him shiver beneath her.

"Your turn again." She grinned, starting to unbutton his jeans.

"Then let's trade," Bastian growled, and in a split second she found herself beneath him.

Apparently, Bastian had had enough of playing.

He crushed his mouth against hers, his hot tongue plundering her mouth as skin met skin. Cat moaned at the delicious friction of her breasts against the dusting of springy blond hair on his chest. He forced himself hard against her, the tip of his cock straining against his jeans, rubbing hard against her. Cat nipped at his lips, teasing and biting, as she slipped her hands back down to his fly and continued to unbutton it. In a few quick motions the hard length of him sprang into her hand, with nary a bit of cotton to impede it. He really had just pulled on his jeans, Cat thought.

Thank God.

Bastian groaned softly as she began to stroke him—long, languorous motions designed to drive him as slowly mad as he was making her.

"Wait," he hissed, rising quickly to his knees and pulling off her skirt with one impatient jerk. Cat watched, awed, as Bastian discarded his jeans as well. There wasn't an inch of him that didn't look sculpted from marble, from his broad shoulders to his slim hips to the cock standing erect between his legs. She swallowed hard. It was going to be an interesting fit.

Breathing hard, Bastian tore off her thong as though it was made of tissue paper.

"What exactly do you have against my underwear?" Cat laughed.

"Nothing," Bastian replied, reaching for her with a wicked grin. "I just don't think you should ever wear any."

With one quick thrust, he was buried in her to the hilt.

Cat cried out as she clenched around him, her orgasm rocketing through her. Bastian made a noise, a primal, guttural sound that only took her higher, spinning out waves of pure ecstasy. He had stretched her tight until she throbbed around him, fitting him perfectly. He began to thrust into her then, well-muscled hips pulsing against her in slow, deliberate rhythm.

She arched into him, bringing her legs up around him, wanting him deeper, though it didn't seem possible, and harder though she wondered whether it would break her apart.

"Gods," he groaned as she dug her nails into his ass, beginning to pump harder. And still he watched her, his eyes never leaving her as she began to climb once again. Every thrust sent shock waves through the tight bud of her sex, winding her tighter and priming her for some shattering release.

"Come for me," Bastian panted, pausing to brand her with a hot, open-mouthed kiss. "I want to watch you. So beautiful… Cat…"

She wanted to watch him too, to watch those glowing eyes go blind as he lost himself. His reactions were so honest, every expression of pleasure fueling her own. And yet she knew he was holding back, giving to her just a little more than he gave himself. But she didn't just want most of him. For however long she had him, she wanted all.

"Then let go," she demanded, her voice barely more than a ragged whisper. Her nails hooked into claws and raked over skin as her body continued to coil, getting ready to come apart. She needed him as woman and Wolf, and the wilder, the better.

Bastian's head whipped back in response, his fangs bared as he gave a hoarse cry. He slammed into her now, and Cat hung on, losing herself to sensation as he rode her. She could hear nothing, see nothing but him. He filled her vision completely, her icy god, turning her molten with heat.

And then she was coming apart, the slow implosion of her orgasm radiating outward from her core and sending pleasure all the way to her fingertips. There was a bright burst of light at the height of her climax, and just before it consumed her completely, she could see Bastian be claimed by his own. He pumped into her once, twice, and gave a sharp shout as he poured himself into her.

At Bastian's cry, Cat gave herself over to the pleasure completely. Her body bowed against him, and she screamed one word: his name.

They lay curled into one another for some time afterward, quiet as their hearts slowed their frantic pace and their breathing slowly resumed a normal rhythm. A faint breeze cooled their heated bodies, and the gentle music from the sky above soothed the frenetic energy of their coupling.

As they lay there, Cat pondered the truth, the thing that seemed to have filled up all the empty places inside of her before she'd even realized what was happening.

I love you, she thought wonderingly. *It's crazy and unexpected and probably nuts, but that doesn't change anything. I love you anyway.* It was so simple, so easy to accept. And yet something held her back from letting the words fall from her lips. Cat didn't know, despite everything, whether he would accept it. He was bound to her. He wanted her. But would he return her love? *Could* he?

So instead of saying anything more, Cat expressed herself the only other way she could. She turned to Bastian, savoring the way he looked at her, as though she were the only woman in the world, and she poured all her heart into a kiss, hoping that, on some level, he would understand.

Deep in the part of the forest where the sun could not reach, something roared in anger, in hunger… and waited for darkness to fall once more.

Chapter 12

CAT STOOD WITH HER SISTERS NEAR THE FRONT OF the crush of MacInneses who had gathered around the enormous bonfire. The moon was high, turning the landscape silver with its light, and though it wouldn't be truly full until two nights from now, Cat felt its power coursing through her veins. The mood among the pack was giddy, electric as they laughed and danced and brawled good-naturedly, all waiting for the same thing. Some had already Changed, Cat knew, as she could see the occasional Wolf gamboling through the crowd. The urge to do it herself was strong. But she wanted to wait until she saw the spectacle Duncan had promised.

The Dyadd was coming.

And strangely, Bastian was nowhere to be seen.

Cat turned to scan the crowd again, nervous. He'd been determined to be here. So why wasn't he? Her head kept trying to fill with visions of him lying broken and helpless, deep in the woods. What kept her from freaking out completely was the fact that if the *narial* attacked him, she was probably going to feel it.

So far, she felt fine. A little nauseated, but fine.

"This is so amazing," Skye said breathlessly, her gray eyes full of firelight. "Everyone talks about them like they're, well, some kind of goddesses. Which I guess they are. But still! And did you know that an *arukhin* tribe lives with them again? A few of them have even mated, and a bunch of little girls are coming… though I guess Harriet has already taken them to the house with a few other women to fuss over them, but we should see them tomorrow. And…"

"Wow, Skye, chill. You're thrilled. We know," Poppy grumbled.

Cat gave Poppy a sidelong glance, while Skye, her hurt feelings reflected in her expression, clammed up immediately. Her youngest sister was grouchier than usual tonight, but she didn't seem interested in explaining why. Cat had a bad feeling it had something to do with Lucien, but she'd discovered that subject was off-limits a little while ago. Not that it was going to prevent her from asking again, even if Poppy had nearly taken her head off just for asking a question with the word "Lucien" in it.

"What's that saying?" Cat asked quietly, so that no one but Poppy could hear. "Meddle not in the affairs of dragons, for thou art crunchy and taste good with ketchup?"

Poppy whirled on her so quickly that Cat nearly lost her balance, taking a quick step backward. "You know what? Bite me," Poppy snapped, and stormed off through the crowd, leaving her sisters watching open-mouthed.

"I should have known she'd turn this into Moodfest '09," Skye said, shaking her head. "What is *wrong* with her?"

Cat shrugged. "I don't know," she said, then lowered her voice. "I think working on you-know-who is affecting her brain."

"That's so *Harry Potter*." Skye grinned. "And it

would be the moody bad guy who Poppy would wind up involved with." Her smile faded a little. "Uh, you don't think she's actually interested in the moody…"

Cat hated to say it. But not saying it didn't make it any less true. "Yeah. I think maybe."

"Oh, for the love of…" Skye looked like she wanted to say more, but at that moment a high and beautiful ululating cry echoed over the crowd, which immediately grew hushed with anticipation. There was a single drumbeat and the jingle of bells.

"You girls will like this," said a gruff voice in her ear, and when Cat turned, Duncan was wedging himself in beside her, looking as excited as she'd seen him. "Put on a hell of a show when they came last year. They do like their entrances. And you'll get to meet my granddaughter!"

Cat had to smile. Duncan might be tough as nails as an Alpha, but he had a big streak of sweetness in there. And she'd just bet he was the spoiling kind of grandpa.

Duncan frowned. "Catriona, have you seen your father anywhere? I lost Fred earlier, and no one seems to have seen him. I want him to meet my sons."

Inwardly, Cat groaned. God only knew where her dad had run off to, but she certainly had no idea. He'd been conspicuously absent from the games today, though she supposed he might have just been avoiding her.

"No clue," was all she said. Her uncle looked disgruntled, but he at least accepted it.

"What about Bastian?" he asked, closer to her ear. "I thought I'd find him with you… you two haven't had a fight already, have you? I know he's an odd one, but you did pick him."

"He's around here somewhere," Cat said, forcing a smile. "Don't worry."

She was doing enough of that already.

Then the spectacle started in earnest, and she quit worrying about everything but watching what was unfolding in front of her.

The drum began a slow, steady *thump, thump, thump*. The cry sounded again, wild and musical, and then the flames of the bonfire shot at least twenty feet into the air, a towering blaze of light that had the crowd gasping in awe. The drumbeat grew quicker, and that was when the howling started.

It was soft as first, but then it rose steadily: scores of voices raised in Wolf song. Cat listened to the waves of the beautiful cries and felt the Wolf within her stir and respond until she wasn't sure she would be able to contain it. This, she realized, was what she'd been missing all of her life: the call of her pack. And though she had never heard it before, Cat knew it just the same. All around her, the MacInnes Pack joined in, heads tipping back to sing beneath the glowing moon. The cries were wild and somehow primitive. Some couldn't resist the urge to Change, and there were sounds of clothing tearing as flesh gave way to fur and fang.

Cat looked to her right and saw Duncan howling along with the rest. To her left was Skye, with a half smile and a shrug that plainly said, *Well, what the hell?* She couldn't have agreed more. So Cat threw her head back and let it come, her own howl rippling from her throat to mingle with the others and echo into the night sky. She heard Skye's delighted laugh beside her, right before she joined in as well. It was amazing and humbling to be a part of this. These were her people, her pack. Tonight, for once, Cat felt that she belonged.

The tower of flames spit a shower of sparks, and then, in a rush, dozens of werewolves poured straight from the heart of the blaze. A great cry of welcoming went up as the pack welcomed their own, Wolves of all colors and shapes, black and gray, white and red, loping forth and barking with joy. They raced from the fire into the crowd, greeting and being greeted, family returning home. Cat smiled, enjoying the warmth of the reunion even if she didn't know a soul. But soon enough the Wolves had all come through, and all eyes were on the bonfire again.

The wild trill of a pipe echoed hauntingly through the night air. And then all Cat could do was stare as, one by one, the most beautiful women she'd ever laid eyes on danced from the fire to the infectious rhythm of drums. No two looked alike, though they were all dressed in long, shimmering skirts that split into multiple panels of diaphanous material when they spun and glittering, midriff-bearing tops in every color of the rainbow. There were so many of them, each prompting cries of welcome from the pack as she emerged and joined the rest to dance with wild and joyous abandon.

At last, after the emergence of a dark-haired beauty dressed all in gold, the flames shot higher still, and the cries and howls grew almost deafening. Wolf and Dyim danced together, celebrating the night. Then the fire went from red to a cool, shimmering blue, and from it stepped a man and a woman. Cat breathed out in awe. She'd never seen such a pair.

He was tall and broad shouldered, with tousled brown

hair that grazed his cheekbones. Golden-green eyes glowed brightly in a face that was devilishly handsome, with a strong nose and lips that were already curved into a playful half smile. He was dressed simply in a belted forest green tunic, dark leggings, and leather boots that came to the knee, an outfit that did nothing to disguise his imposing physique. Utterly gorgeous and unmistakably Duncan's son, Cat decided. And beside him could be none other than Bastian's sister Rowan, the *Dyana an Morgaine* herself.

"Can I be her when I grow up?" Skye whispered in her ear. Cat had to agree. Rowan moved with the grace of a dancer, her long, slim body and perfect curves draped in raiment of crimson and gold. Her hair was an even more vibrant red than the fire, falling in a shining wave to well past her shoulders. Skin the color of porcelain made her eyes, a brilliant jade green, stand out even more in a face marked by sharp features that were somehow feline in their elegance.

Cat had never felt more intimidated in her entire life.

And oh, God, Rowan was heading straight for them.

As the music continued, and the Dyadd and pack converged to do what they did best, which was apparently party until their brains went to mush, Rowan and Gabriel made a beeline for Duncan, who was still right beside her.

"Gabe! Rowan! Come here, let's have a look at you!" Duncan was so excited he was almost beside himself, Cat saw, with a grin a mile wide and his arms outstretched to pull his daughter-in-law into a crushing hug. Cat stepped back to give them room, wondering whether a woman that beautiful might not get upset that her fabulous outfit was being wrinkled all to hell. She was pleasantly surprised, though, when Rowan laughed and hugged Duncan right back.

"Ah, I've missed you two! You need to visit more often!" he proclaimed loudly, lifting Rowan off her feet and swinging her around.

"Hey! We saw you two weeks ago," Rowan protested, her laughter an appealingly husky roll. "And we can't seem to get Malcolm to leave since Ani came. It's almost like having you there, except bossier, if that's at all possible."

"Yeah, Dad, do you think you could take Mal back? I didn't think he was part of your baby gift," Gabriel agreed.

In response, Duncan released Rowan and grabbed his son, slamming him on the back a couple of times and then stepping back to beam at them both. "Oh, you know Malcolm. He only wants to help."

Cat bit back a smile at the look, equal parts amusement and exasperation, that Rowan and Gabriel shared at that. Duncan, however, had other things on his mind.

"Where is my sweet girl, anyway? Don't tell me you've put her to bed?"

"Aniela is either asleep or tearing what's left of Mal's hair out up at the house," Gabriel said with a grin. "Count your blessings, Dad, because you'll get her full force tomorrow. The kid is already a force of nature, and she's only two months old." He raised an eyebrow at his wife. "Wonder where she got that from?"

"She's highly advanced. Highly advanced children are always busier," Rowan replied, accepting Gabriel's arm around her and snuggling into her husband's side. "I openly admit she got that from me."

"That's not all she got from you."

When Rowan stuck her tongue out at her husband in response, Cat looked at Skye and shared a puzzled look with her sister. It was probably unfair, but she hadn't expected people so beautiful to be so nice or so seemingly normal. Rowan and Gabriel looked to be both. Cat stepped back, intending to slink away and let Duncan have his time with his family, but he seemed to sense it before she could really make her move.

"Gabe, Rowan, I'd like you to meet Catriona and Skye MacInnes," Duncan said, one meaty paw shooting out to grasp her before she could get far enough away. Cat, in turn, grabbed Skye, who had gotten slightly further in her escape and was almost out of arm's reach. She didn't care about the dirty look Skye gave her, either. If it was time to meet the otherworldly relatives, she was *not* doing it alone.

Cat could see understanding dawn on Gabriel's face, right before he shared a look with his wife that confirmed it. "Are you Freddie's girls?" he asked, and Cat could see that she wasn't at all what he'd been expecting. But then, it was possible everyone had just assumed her father was some kind of Elephant Man, wandering around with a bag on his head and producing horrifying offspring.

"We are. I'm Cat. This is Skye," Cat said, sticking out her hand. But instead of getting a cordial handshake, Gabriel surprised her by giving a delighted laugh and picking her up to give her what was apparently the Patented MacInnes Bear Hug.

"This is great!" he said with a dazzling smile. "I

didn't even know you existed, you know, until a few days ago! First cousins, and I had no idea!"

"Nice to... nice to... meet..." Cat gasped out a few words, but Gabriel was squeezing her tight enough to cut off her air supply. Rowan, thankfully, came to her rescue.

"I think you'd better put her down, babe, or you'll be minus one of your shiny new first cousins."

"Er, oops. Sorry," Gabriel said, instantly releasing her and putting her down. "Great to meet you, though."

He then proceeded to scoop up a rapidly retreating Skye and give her the same treatment. Rowan put her hand over her eyes and shook her head, which made Cat laugh once she caught her breath.

"Sorry," Rowan said to her. "He's like a big puppy sometimes."

Cat watched him deposit a breathless Skye back on her feet and smiled. "I may be his cousin, but I have to say... there are worse things than being loved on by a guy like that."

Rowan flashed a grin that reminded her, with a funny little pang, of Bastian. "Oh, you won't hear me complaining," she said. "Nice to meet you. Love your outfit."

Cat looked disbelievingly at her. "Thanks. But seriously? I was about to say the same thing. Do you wear that stuff all the time?"

"Yeah. And it's okay. But believe me, I didn't realize how much I would miss jeans," Rowan sighed.

"So Cat," Gabriel interjected, moving back to his wife's side, "where's your dad? I'd like to meet my uncle and see if he's as much of a pain in the ass as his brother is." Duncan growled and gave him a good-natured punch that Cat was sure would have sent a normal person flying. And she just stood there, wishing she had a better answer.

"I haven't seen him today, actually," she said. "I'm sure he's around here somewhere, though."

"What about my brother?" Rowan asked, frowning as she stood on tiptoe and searched the crowd for him. "Have you seen Bastian, Duncan? He's not still hiding in that cottage, is he? I was sure he'd be right here." Her disappointment was palpable, and Cat could see that Bastian's affection for this sister in particular was quite mutual.

Duncan shot Cat a very amused, very obvious look, and she felt herself redden as all eyes turned to her. This was exactly what she'd been worried about.

"Oh," Duncan drawled, "He hasn't hidden the *entire* time, has he, Catriona? Did he mention whether he'd be joining us this evening?"

Cat fought back a cringe as both Rowan's and Gabriel's eyebrows shot up so far they nearly touched their hairlines.

"No," Cat stammered. "Um, I mean, yes, he said he'd be here. I dunno. Sometime." She glared at Duncan. "Thanks for asking."

Gabriel gave her a more thorough look this time and appeared to approve of what he saw. "Don't tell me you've managed to attract the resident hermit's attention, Cat! I'd say I didn't believe it, except that the MacInneses are so damned good-looking." His grin was wicked. "There's just no resisting us."

He seemed fine, but Rowan, Cat saw with a sinking

feeling, only watched her with an inscrutable expression and an intensity she found unnerving. She'd gotten used to it from Bastian, but his sister was another kettle of fish altogether. Did this mean it was okay? Not okay? Was she just pondering what to eat for dinner? She fought the urge to go hide under a rock until Rowan figured it out.

And of course, her uncle had to compound the problem by agreeing wholeheartedly with his son.

"Aye, we are irresistible, and it seems Catriona's no exception. But I won't say any more," he added with a wink at her. "I'm sure they'll tell you how things are with them when they're ready."

Cat fought a sudden, violent urge to knock the man senseless. He might as well have just put out a sign that read "Welcome home! Cat bit your brother!" and been done with it. She gritted her teeth and held her tongue, mainly because she was worried that whatever would come out if she didn't would be bad even by Lucien Andrakkar standards.

"Hey!" cried Skye, pointing into the crowd. "I think I see Gideon and Carly!"

Duncan followed Skye's finger, and his face lit up once more. "So you do! Gid, over here!" He waved his arms in the air, and Cat mouthed a thank-you at her sister. She knew a diversionary tactic when she saw one. It was one of the many wonderful things about Skye. She might be quiet, but she could always pull off a rescue when needed.

"We promised Poppy we'd meet her, but we'll see you all in a little while," Cat rushed out, grabbing Skye's hand and backing quickly away. "Nice to meet you. See you later, Uncle Duncan!"

"Hey, find Bastian while you're at it, will you? He'd better be drunk in a corner somewhere, or he's got an ass-kicking coming to him," Gabriel called to her, then looked in the same direction as his father. "Gid! What's happened to you? Having a sympathetic pregnancy, are you?"

Another voice, deep and with a growling brogue laced with amusement, answered. "Gabe, the only fat thing around here is your mouth, as usual. But if you'd like a closer look, I can give you a lip to match."

Rowan caught her eye just then, but before she could say a thing, she was sidetracked. Carly MacInnes, a beautiful little blonde whom Cat had met earlier in the day, bounded out of nowhere and squealed happily. Rowan seemed just as pleased, enveloping Carly in a big hug and then launching into excited, rapid-fire chatter while rubbing the barely visible curve of her friend's belly. Cat got a quick look at yet another tall, gorgeous MacInnes male approaching, this one dark and delectably brooding with an intriguing scar across one eye, before she turned and vanished into the dancing, partying masses with Skye.

She'd met Gideon earlier, too. Or rather, she'd watched as he'd kicked the collective asses of all involved at the caber toss. He seemed very friendly, if a little intimidating. But she wasn't in the mood to be social just now. Being presented as Bastian's hook-up, minus Bastian, sucked the big one. She didn't know why he hadn't come, instead of leaving her at the mercy of Duncan's well-intentioned but big mouth. But as hurt and anger flared, Cat decided she was damn well going to find out.

"Where are you going?" Skye asked as Cat broke away from her, starting to push through the crowd.

"Where do you think?" Cat asked.

"You know," Skye grumbled, just loud enough so Cat could hear it over the din as she stormed away, "you and Poppy are making me really glad I'm related to all of the other men here."

"You make it so easy."

The voice, thick and turgid, seemed to bubble up from the very soil. Bastian stopped in the middle of the path, lit by a patch of moonlight, and turned his head slowly to look at what he'd hoped had been a creation of his overstressed mind. But it was there, not far beyond the edge of the path: a patch of blackness that stood like a man, a faceless figure with red eyes that regarded him from beneath a large tree.

Damn.

He'd known there was no way it would last. All afternoon he'd battled a sense of rising dread. He'd been too happy. He would have to pay. It was part of the twisted cycle of his life, as familiar to him by now as breathing.

Resigned, Bastian responded. "That's insulting. I've fought you every step of the way. I'm not ready to quit now."

"You have a strange way of driving me off, sorcerer. I almost think you enjoy paying for your foolishness. My hunger grows stronger by the day... and I will make of your soul a grand feast very, very soon." Then, almost to itself, it snarled, *"No matter the whims of those insolent* daemon. *You are mine."*

It was as though someone had driven a spear of ice directly through his heart.

"What insolent *daemon*?"

There was a burbling chuckle. "*Ahhh, I can almost taste your fear, boy. Just like the night we met, yes? Your father was so unsatisfying to finish, already so broken. But not you. No, you and I will finish what was started so long ago in grand fashion. You are strong yet, if flagging. Cadmus would never appreciate your end as I will. He cares only for his ridiculous vendetta over lost, repulsive love. What a waste of hatred. But do not worry... I've already warned him to stay away. I've taken many lives for him because it pleased me. But the* daemon *must learn that they are not the masters of the shadows, as they think they are.*"

Bastian stayed silent, reeling. He had feared being discovered by the *daemon*, but he'd never really believed they would find him. No one had seen him retrieve the dragon. But then, it sounded as though this had less to do with Lucien than with the heart of the curse, and ending what had begun so long ago.

His heart began to pound in his chest, and the world tilted in his vision as a wave of dizziness threatened to take him down. He had kept the *narial* to himself all this time. But how could he protect everyone he cared about from the king of the most feared tribe in all of Coracin? What would happen if they came here, to the heart of the *arukhin*, and at the time of the gathering when even the Dyadd had converged upon this place? There could easily be a bloodbath, Bastian realized. The enmity between Cadmus's people and those who were at *Iargail* ran deep. And the *daemon* were the cruelest of the Drakkyn... their creativity where torment was concerned was legendary.

His own, Bastian realized, had already begun.

The delighted croon of the *narial* snapped him out of his increasingly dark thoughts.

"*Ah, now you begin to realize what you have done. So painful, isn't it, to know that you may have doomed them all? Especially the woman… perhaps I will take her too. Nothing prevents me, and she will be so full of anguish when she realizes the part she has played in your death.*"

"Shut up, creature," Bastian hissed. "You are the one killing me. She has nothing to do with that. I'd think you'd be proud to claim the credit."

The laughter was self-satisfied, full of black amusement. "*Didn't your father tell you that love would destroy you? Foolish Dyim, mating is a sharing of the soul. And you had little enough to spare.*" It laughed again, a thick, noxious sound. "*Now she carries a piece of you within her. I will have that too… and it will destroy her. She will long for death, no longer whole. You really should have listened. Fortunately for me, they never do.*"

"Liar. You only want a little more pain to enjoy the next time you swoop in to take what isn't yours," Bastian snarled, even as the ground seemed to crumble away beneath him. He didn't want to believe it. But something in what the shadow said rang hideously true. It was why Cat had been hurt that first night without the *narial* ever touching her. The part of his soul that had bonded to hers in mating died a little with every attack. And now, so would she.

The horror of it was suffocating.

The black shape shifted beneath the tree, and Bastian could see that it was becoming bored with taunting him. For now, at least.

"How tedious you are. I never lie. I don't have to bother. But if that's how you want to look at it, be my guest."

"If I gave myself to you," Bastian said hoarsely, desperation overriding his common sense. "If I agreed not to fight you… Is there any way you can make it so she won't be hurt?"

"But what a loss that would be for me, Bastian an Morgaine. Your love is so great that you burn with it. I can feel it, smell it, taste it, even when I must rest far away in the depths of this wretched wood. So I will take it from you, take it to a dark place and consume it whole. I will rip it from your soul and leave you with nothing but tatters, and then you will come to me, embrace me, beg for the death that only I can give you. She will, too, you know… when you are gone. You are bound too tightly to sever. Such a pity."

In all his life, he had never heard that hideous voice sound so pleased.

"I never said I loved her," Bastian protested, knowing how weak it sounded.

"As though your words mean anything to me," growled the *narial*.

Bastian swayed on his feet, overcome with sudden nausea, darkness encroaching on his vision. Everything he felt, the shadow knew. Denying it was useless.

By the Goddess above, he did love her.

It should have been a wondrous revelation. Instead, all he felt was a terrible, aching pain. Luck, though whether good or ill he couldn't really say, had delivered him his true mate. And years of emotional starvation had led him to be careless. He would have to warn her. He needed to get to Lucien, to beg, if need be…

The *narial* purred with delight. "*Ah, more of that lovely fear. Please, continue to fret about the inevitable. I deeply enjoy it.*"

Bastian steeled himself, took a deep breath, and started forward again, determined to get to the gathering. He wasn't far. He could see the glow of the lights ahead and hear the music of the Dyadd. Maybe if he could get close enough...

"Bastian!"

He heard her call him, and his heart sank. She sounded angry... and he supposed she would be. He was very late. Even later, in fact, because Lucien had been in a much fouler mood than usual this evening and determined to pick a fight. The Goddess only knew what Cat's introduction to his family had been like.

There was a wet chuckle. "*How convenient.*"

"Cat!" Bastian shouted, not caring whether anyone else heard him. "Go back!"

"Bastian?" Uncertainty. Not good enough.

"*Perhaps I should go say hello...*"

"Catriona!" he thundered, but he could already see the shadow slithering quickly off to make good on its threat. He had to do something, couldn't let this happen...

He flexed his power as easily as he flexed his hand, letting her face fill his mind and then letting go, like a bowman who had notched an arrow and then pulled the bowstring tight, the target firmly in his sights.

In a flash he had her in his arms. Another flash, and he had his father's staff in hand. He had never attempted to flip so quickly in succession, but he found himself gliding through space as smoothly as if it were through water.

On a fresh burst of light, they appeared before Poppy, perched on a large boulder near the edge of the crowd and sulking. Her eyes widened. And in the distance, there was the sound of the shadow, furious, rushing as quickly as it could to locate them.

"Stay with Lucien tonight," he instructed her. "I'll need to talk to you in the morning. Don't worry about your sister… she's with me."

"I…" Poppy began, but she was gone, the world bursting again as Bastian, Cat tucked close against him, her face buried in his chest to guard against the intense light, appeared before Rowan, in the middle of the group of those he wished to protect most.

"Damn it, Bastian. Way to blind us all," growled Gabriel, his arm thrown up to shield his eyes.

Rowan, however, as radiant as the flame that was her gift, immediately knew something was wrong. He knew she would. He also knew he could make her understand the important things quickly, and that she wouldn't panic. Not yet, anyway.

"Bastian," she said, her husky voice full of concern. "What is it?"

"A *narial*. No one else needs to worry. But I have to get out of here for the night."

"A what?" Gideon asked, frowning at Rowan. "What's he talking about?"

Rowan held up a hand to him, a silent gesture to wait. "Where?"

"*Etrais Athinia*, on the Northern plains."

"The ice kingdom," she murmured, more to herself than anyone. Bastian knew she would mull the choice over later. Then the jade green eyes were back on him.

"Be back at the house in the morning. *Early.* You're going to explain."

He smirked at her tone, so imperious, and eerily reminiscent of their mother. "Of course." He glanced down at Cat and then back at those who surrounded the two of them. "I'm taking Cat with me. Don't worry."

At that, Rowan rolled her eyes, and he could see both fear and irritation in them. And love. That was the most important thing.

"Yeah, right. Just come back early, or I'm using the Stone to come after you."

He gave a quick nod. "Morning."

And in one final burst of brilliant white light, he and Cat left the Highlands behind them, and entered the cold and silent land of his ancestors in the frozen reaches of Coracin.

Cat clung to Bastian's shirt, eyes shut tight, unsure when it was all right to look. There had been so much light and motion that she felt as though she'd stayed on an amusement park ride for way too long, and at this point, she wasn't moving an inch until someone told her the ride had stopped.

"Cat."

Her name rumbled against her ear through his chest.

"You can look. We're here."

Slowly, gingerly, Cat raised her head to look up at the man who had brought her here. Bastian's light blue eyes looked back at her, glowing bright with concern. All around them was darkness, but for a faint light emanating from the strange staff Bastian had grabbed from the little cottage in the wood. And, Cat realized with a shiver, it was very cold.

"Where is *here*, exactly?" she asked, reluctant to step away from his heat. She was shaking as much from terror as cold, she knew, and heat wouldn't help that. But it couldn't hurt, either.

"I'll show you," Bastian said, releasing her from his arms and stepping away. He took a few steps in the unfamiliar space, and then, all of a sudden, the room was lit as bright as day with beautiful, shimmering light.

Cat gasped as she finally saw where they were.

"This is *Etrais Athinia*, the seat of the *Athin* ice mages on the Northern plains of Coracin. It was my father's home, and all his line before him, before the *daemon* king wiped them out with his curse."

Bastian's voice echoed in the massive chamber as she looked around in wonder. It was a castle; that she could tell right away. But it was like nothing she'd ever seen. The walls, the pillars, and the archways were all made of glittering white stone, giving the impression that she was standing in a room carved from the snow itself. The floor was of a white stone polished to such a high sheen that it could have been ice. There was color, though. Instead of the tapestries she usually envisioned for a castle, intricate murals were painted along the wall. In them, from where she and Bastian stood at the head of the enormous hall, Cat could make out strange creatures gamboling through arctic-looking landscapes, sometimes joined by richly dressed lords and ladies (and sometimes *hunted* by the lords and ladies).

Lush fur rugs were scattered about the floor, and there was ornately carved furniture as well, chairs and tables, lounges and benches, all created from what looked like marble in pale shades that Cat thought of as Nordic. Plump cushions invited relaxation, and the entire effect of the room was of comfortable opulence.

She loved it. But there was another aspect to this place as well, one she wasn't as eager to share. It was a little too quiet here. She knew that this place had once been full of people, full of sound and movement. Now it was still, more like a museum than a home. And a little too much like a tomb for her taste.

Cat placed her hand on the chair beside her, and when she looked, she discovered with surprise that it was a rose-colored throne. Beside it, where Bastian now stood, was an even larger throne as white as the walls. His staff, the end of it sunken into the floor beside the throne, was giving off the brilliant light that had brought them out of darkness.

"I know it's a little creepy," Bastian said, watching her reactions closely. "It took some getting used to, when I first started coming here. But nothing here can hurt you. It's just… empty."

"Yeah," Cat replied, listening to her voice echo off the walls of the room. "Empty. I think 'desolate' might be a better description, but your call."

"It was the best place I could think of to come for the night."

Cat sighed, seeing the apology in his expression. "I guess this means I can't yell at you for not showing up tonight." She lifted her hands to begin massaging her temples, feeling the beginnings of a headache. "What happened, Bastian? You might as well tell me. I'm sure it's bad, or we wouldn't be here."

"It threatened to go after you. I couldn't let that happen."

The chill that plunged down Cat's spine this time had nothing to do with the air. Bastian seemed to sense it. He started back toward her, but then he stopped, as though he'd thought better of it. He looked, Cat thought, as strong as he always did. But for the first time, real fatigue showed in his face. It was unnerving; she hadn't even considered the possibility that she might lose him. Not really. Theoretical possibilities were one thing, but Bastian in person was so alive. He looked invincible.

She could see with her own eyes that he wasn't, and that was a sucker punch she didn't need. Not right now. Not tonight.

"Are you okay?" she asked, worry for him overriding everything else. "You don't look right."

His short, bitter laugh surprised her, and not in a good way.

"No, I don't suppose I would. I should have known better, Cat. I really should have."

"Being out tonight might not have been the best idea," Cat agreed, thinking he was lamenting ever having left the cottage this evening. But he shook his head, a look she'd never seen before in his eyes.

"No. I mean I should have known better the night I bit you. I knew that if there was ever a woman I should stay away from, it was you."

Cat blinked. The words cut her so deeply she thought she might bleed from them. It was strange, she thought, that a man she had known three days could hurt her more than her ex-fiancé, whom she'd known for three years, had ever been able to. But she wouldn't show him. There was a reason for this. And she'd be damned if she didn't get to the bottom of it.

"Well, you *didn't* stay away from me," she said, keeping her tone even, though it was hard. "It's a shame you're sorry about that. But I can't be."

Anger flashed in his eyes. "You wouldn't say that if you knew what it meant to be with me," he snapped, white teeth flashing in the light. "You would have been better off if you'd never met me."

Cat gritted her teeth in frustration. "What is this 'woulda, coulda, shoulda' bullshit, Bastian? It's a little late for that. But it would have been nice if you'd brought up this stuff before we, you know, screwed each other's brains out."

He winced as though she'd struck him, and Cat felt a rush of satisfaction. She didn't want to fight with him. But that didn't mean she wouldn't if he kept this up.

"Don't call it that."

Cat's temper flared. She was on a long fuse, generally. But he was hurting her purposely. "What should I call it, Bastian? Screwing? Fucking? If you're that sorry about it, then I'm sure as hell not going to call it making love!"

"I do love you! And you know what you get for the honor? You get to have it kill you!" he bellowed, his voice breaking with the force as the hall thundered with it.

"What?"

Her voice was intended to sound normal, but the word barely came out in a whisper.

"It's going to kill you," Bastian repeated, his voice only slightly below a shout. "That foul creature, the thing that wiped out an entire side of my family, is now very interested in destroying you. Or rather, the piece of my soul that belongs to you now that we're bound together."

"I meant the other part," she said.

Bastian looked at her, aghast. "You don't care that my love for you is probably going to wind up fatal for both of us?"

Cat closed the distance between them with just a few steps, sliding her arms around his waist and leaning into his heat, his strength. "Of course I care," Cat said softly. "I'm freaking terrified, Bastian. But I also just heard you tell me you love me for the first time. That's amazing enough to cancel out the awful, just for this second. Okay? The *narial* isn't here right now. You are. And I know you're not going to lose, Bastian. You'll find a way. I have faith in you."

"You're going to have to forgive me if I tell you you're insane," Bastian replied hoarsely. "I'm a second-rate sorcerer, Cat. I'm untrained. My entire life rests in the hands of a sickly dragon shifter who hates my guts. And no matter what I do, I can't seem to get my life back." His eyes were broken when they looked into hers. "You shouldn't want my love."

"And yet here I am, an equally untrained werewolf, wanting it," she said. "Sounds like a match to me. You're going to find out I'm stubborn, Bastian."

He exhaled through his nose, exasperated. "I may have noticed some of that already."

"Good. Then it won't surprise you that I love you too, despite the fact that we had the equivalent of a quickie Vegas wedding just a couple of days ago. But I can't seem to help myself, so I've quit trying."

Bastian frowned then, and Cat could see she was getting him back. The anger, at least, was gone.

"A lot of Drakkyn relationships happen quickly," he said. "You just think it's strange because you were raised with humans. Mates know one another and accept that as natural."

Cat smiled gently. "Are you finished being angry that you love me?"

"I'm not angry about that. I'm angry that I'm too inept to free myself, and you, from what is probably going to happen. My life is not worth yours, Cat." He closed his eyes and rested his forehead against hers. "I am sorry I shouted it at you, though."

"It's okay. I'll take it."

Cat stayed still and quiet for a time, mulling over what Bastian had said. She was scared. The mere thought of what the *narial* had inflicted on her through Bastian was enough to send her into a cold sweat. But she saw no point in throwing herself on the floor and gnashing her teeth over it. Nothing had happened yet. She was still very much alive, as was the man in her arms. And tomorrow, things were going to change in their favor, to her way of thinking.

"What are you thinking about?" he asked, his breath warming her face.

"I'm thinking your sisters look as if they could kick some serious ass," Cat admitted. "You're going to have to tell them tomorrow."

"I am," he agreed.

"And they're going to want to help," Cat continued.

"There's nothing they can do about the curse," Bastian said. "No, I can see you clenching your jaw, and stop. My sisters are incredibly talented women, but this is beyond them. They may have to help in other ways, though. Because tonight, I was told that the king of the *daemon* is also quite interested in my whereabouts."

"Oh," said Cat, still basking in the lovely afterglow of his declaration. It provided a welcome, if temporary, shield against any more fear. God knew she'd already felt enough of that tonight. And here, alone with Bastian, there were better things to think about.

"Now do you see why it would have been better for you to stay away from me?" Bastian asked, his voice soft now, but no less urgent.

"Hmm," Cat replied, rising up on her toes. If he wouldn't listen to reason, then she was just going to have to show instead of tell. Slowly, deliberately, she pressed her mouth against his. At first, his lips were stiff and immovable. But she was patient; Bastian was coiled so tightly at this point that she wouldn't have been surprised to feel him vibrating. Little by little, his lips softened, accepting her gentle overtures, until she'd engaged him in a long, thorough kiss that went a long way toward warming Cat up.

"What was that for?" Bastian asked, his voice thick.

"I was experimenting," Cat said. "And I am now completely positive that I much prefer being close to you than staying away."

That earned her a rueful chuckle.

"I'm not going to get you to regret me, am I?" he asked.

"Do you really want me to regret you?" she countered, cocking her head at him.

He looked at her for a long time, and the tenderness in

his gaze was almost her undoing. Why was she destined to do every damn thing the hard way? But Bastian was worth it, worth every terrifying subterranean creature and flesh-eating *daemon*. Even though she still really, *really* wished that those things were not involved.

"No," Bastian finally said. "I would never want you to regret me." He reached for a lock of her hair and rubbed it with his fingers, toying with the silken softness of the strands. "I'll do my best, Cat. I would like nothing more than to be a proper mate to you and to spend the rest of my waking hours making you crazy." He grinned, and it took the wind out of her.

"Good crazy or bad crazy? I need to prepare," Cat asked.

"Probably both," Bastian replied, and then dipped his head to nibble at her ear.

"Thanks for the warning, then," Cat laughed softly, tilting her head to give him better access. It was sweet at first, undemanding. But as always when Bastian touched her, need quickly sparked to life, and she wanted more.

She turned her head to claim his mouth again, opening her mouth for him and growling as the kiss turned hot and erotic. His hands began to cruise over her back and then up to knead her breasts. His touch was almost rough, and Cat could feel how tenuous his control was.

She urged him on, wanting it this way, needing to feel all his tension, all his frustration. She would match them with her own and then push him until everything vanished but the two of them. Because tonight, for all she knew, could be the last night they had together. She didn't want him to be careful; she wanted to feel *alive*.

"Cat," Bastian breathed, dropping his mouth to her neck, scraping his fangs across tender skin, and making her gasp.

"On the floor. Furs. Something," Cat hissed as she wound her fingers in his hair and he pulled her hips tightly against him.

"As you wish," Bastian growled with a flash of a smile. He scooped her into his arms and carried her from the dais, setting her down for a moment as he assembled a pile of sinfully soft fur rugs. Cat watched him as he lifted and tugged, pushed and pulled, licking her lips at the way his muscles flexed with every movement.

It took him almost no time to finish. When he was done, he stripped off his clothing, throwing it off to the side, and sank to the makeshift bed. Cat let her eyes devour him as she removed her own things, still wondering how she'd ended up with a guy who was a damn sight better looking than any centerfold she'd ever seen. And this particular dream guy watched her remove every bit of fabric as though each new expanse of skin she revealed was nothing less than the most decadent, delicious dessert he could imagine.

No matter what else happened, Cat decided, she was lucky.

Bastian sprawled before her, wearing nothing but his gleaming skin, and crooked his finger with a wicked curve of his lips.

Lucky, lucky, lucky.

Her heart beating wildly, Cat tossed her new, unbroken bra to the floor and moved to join him.

❖ ❖ ❖

Bastian watched Cat approach, letting his eyes roam over every inch of tawny skin. He didn't want to think tonight. He'd had enough of fear and guilt to last a lifetime. All he wanted to do, Bastian thought as Cat knelt before him, was feel. To forget everything but the woman he had found to be as much goddess as the ones who had once ruled his world.

Bastian rose on his knees to face her and lifted a hand to cup one perfect breast. He heard Cat's breath catch as he toyed with the pink bud of her nipple until it was a hard little pebble beneath his thumb. She pressed into him, her eyelids dropping to half-mast in pleasure.

He leaned in to claim her lips in a long, lingering kiss, letting his exploration be exquisitely thorough. Cat gave a soft moan as he deepened his tender assault, his tongue mating with hers in bold, increasingly demanding strokes. Her hands slid up his chest, while he let his own hand drop from her breast to skim down the long, flat expanse of her stomach. Her breathing quickened as he moved his hand lower, and this time there was nothing soft about her moan when he parted the dark curls between her legs to stroke the tight bud of her sex, which was already slick with moisture.

Cat pressed her hips into his touch, beginning to move restlessly against him as he stroked her. Bastian broke the kiss to watch her climb, feeling her hands tighten on his shoulders and the sharp points of her claws prick against his skin. Her breathing began to come in ragged pants, matching his own.

"Bastian," she gasped, making it sound more like a demand than an endearment. And if there was any question about what she wanted, Cat left no doubt when she suddenly shifted position, shoved him back, and threw her leg over him.

She looked beautiful, he thought, half-feral and all-powerful, with her dark hair tumbling wild over her bare shoulders and her eyes on fire. Everything in him rose in response to it, feeding off the wild energy they were creating together. And though before he met Cat he had never had the luxury of joining sex with play, with her the temptation to do so was irresistible.

"Oh no, you don't." He laughed breathlessly, stopping her when he felt her positioning him between her legs.

She bared her teeth at him. "Oh yes, I do," she growled. But before she could sink down on him, Bastian caught one of her legs with his own and flipped her so she was pinned beneath him. Cat snapped at him only half in jest, her incisors as deadly sharp as his own were now, and growled.

"I want you."

Bastian grinned, baring his fangs at her. "Not yet," he said.

He lowered his head to her collarbone, tracing a path over it with his tongue, before moving over the curve of her breast. He caught her gaze, burning gold, for just a moment before taking her nipple into his mouth and beginning to suckle in long, hard pulls.

Cat made a soft noise in the back of her throat and arched into him, tangling her fingers in his hair. Her heart pounded wildly against his mouth as he moved downward, exploring the hollow of her navel and the jut of her hip bone.

At last, he moved between her legs, parting her silky curls with his fingers and taking the sweet little nub into his mouth.

Cat cried out and bucked beneath him as he licked her, trying to drive her past reason with his mouth. He kissed the insides of her thighs and grazed his teeth across sensitive skin, but he always returned his eager lips and tongue to her where she pulsed and throbbed. He flicked his tongue rapidly against her when he felt her tensing, sensing that she was close to going over the edge.

Then at the last second, Bastian withdrew, rising to flip Cat quickly to her stomach despite her single, furious protestation. He needed to be in her.

Now.

Cat snarled, her entire body vibrating beneath Bastian's. Of all the times to decide to play with her, Bastian had chosen one of the most frustrating ones. Though she supposed that was the point. And he was going to find himself bitten all over again if he didn't...

She felt him grab her hips, and with one hard thrust he had filled her, stretching her tight around him so that the tiniest move sent shock waves through her. Her thought evaporated into the ether, unfinished, as pleasure claimed her for its own.

Cat moaned as Bastian pounded into her, driving her senseless with need as she knelt in front of him. She pressed back against every wild thrust, losing herself to the overwhelming sensation of having him so deeply inside her. His hips slammed against her, beating a primal rhythm as Cat began to come undone. Bastian sank into her, each stroke seeming to go deeper, coiling something inside her tighter and tighter until Cat found herself quivering around him, a heartbeat away from the fall.

She wanted his teeth in her again.

And as he always did, Bastian seemed to know.

With a final hard thrust, Bastian drove into her all the way to the hilt and sank his teeth into the side of her neck. He bucked against her with a guttural groan, riding the crest of his own wave as Cat's orgasm tore through her with a vengeance. She whipped her head back, pleasure and pain mingling to send her to a dizzying climax that seemed to go on endlessly as he pulsed deep within her.

Bastian collapsed beside her and then gathered her to his chest and buried his face in her hair. Cat tucked her head against his shoulder, sighing contentedly. She felt boneless, every inch of her wonderfully used and exhausted. All the stress, all the worry, all the anger of the last few days had left her to be replaced by the warm glow of being held by Bastian.

"Wow," she sighed softly, unable to think of any other word that described what he'd just done to her. She snuggled even closer to his heat, drowsiness settling over her.

"Wow," he agreed, his voice already drowsy.

"I love you, Bastian," she sighed, hoping that the moment would extend and last just a little while longer.

"And I love you, Catriona," Bastian replied, nuzzling against her and inhaling deeply. "With all I have."

Curled together, safe in the glow, they drifted off to sleep.

Chapter 13

POPPY WOUND THROUGH THE JOYFUL CELEBRATION alone, wishing she could just relax and enjoy it. She'd actually planned on doing just that, once she'd finished a healthy round of sulking. Then she'd gotten the spooktacular visit from Bastian and Cat, and now she didn't know what the hell to do. It would have been nice if she'd had a little more information about what was going on. It was hard to tell: Bastian always looked deadly serious, and Cat had been stuck to the front of him like Velcro. Not that she blamed her sister; he was completely hot. But she was not really in the mood to baby-sit Lucien just because *some* people decided they wanted a passionate night away from Satan's Lizard.

Then again, something could have been really wrong. In that case, it would have been nice if someone had, you know, mentioned it. But again, she got told to baby-sit, end of story.

She knew she was probably being bitchy. Just like she knew she'd get over it at some point and go cross swords with Lucien Andrakkar once again. Maybe his mood would have improved, she thought, trying to kindle a little hope inside. Maybe he'd be waiting at the door for her wearing nothing and brandishing a can of whipped cream.

Maybe she should get real.

Poppy heaved an intentionally dramatic sigh and kept

walking, managing to smile and wave at the people who greeted her. Apparently, the mad-at-the-world portion of events was over for the evening. At some point she was going to have to hunt down Skye and apologize. Raining all over her sister's parade hadn't really been necessary.

She didn't have a destination in mind, but as the crowd thinned and then disappeared altogether, Poppy realized that she wasn't far from the chapel ruins, beneath which the Stone of Destiny rested.

That was as good a destination as any, she figured. She didn't know how to go down below (nor was she sure she wanted to all by herself), but the area was at least quiet enough for her to cool off the rest of the way and to hear herself think. The MacInnes Pack was great, but man, were its members loud.

"Aren't I supposed to be having fun?" she muttered to herself as she approached the crumbling stone structure.

Poppy inhaled deeply, scenting ocean and heather, and tried to let the singular perfume of the Highlands soothe her. All of the wonder and excitement of this place seemed to have fallen away to be replaced by a sense of growing despair. How had she let herself get so twisted up over a bad-tempered nonhuman who turned into a dragon? Just how had she figured that was going to work out, exactly? She'd wasted her entire day, in freaking *Scotland*, brooding over a kiss. A single, lousy, hot, intense, mind-bending kiss.

"I suck," she said flatly.

Poppy jerked sharply to a halt a few hundred feet from the ruins, eyes scanning the darkness. There was no one to be seen. But her ears, even more sensitive than usual because of the impending full moon, were full of whispered conversation.

And one of the voices, she realized, was her father's.

"I can't remember," he was moaning, a pleading note in his voice that she'd never heard before.

"You'd better remember quickly, Wolf," said a deep, gravelly voice that Poppy didn't recognize. "We didn't come all this way to play with your kind."

"We may have to make good on our threats after all," said another, this one a strangely serpentine *hiss*. "Shall we start with the littlest one, Wolf? Will hurting her help your memory? She'd make a wonderful meal."

Poppy's blood ran cold.

They're talking about me.

"I can think of better things to do with her," interjected the other stranger with a nasty chuckle.

There was a frightened whimper from her father. "Not my Poppy. Not my girls… please, you promised…"

Who was threatening him? What the hell was going on? She scented the air instinctively, tipping her head back to try and glean what information she could. At first, she could only smell her dad and the overpowering, metallic tang of his fear. But there was something else, something strangely familiar. A little like incense. A little like…

But that wasn't possible, Poppy thought as everything suddenly clicked into place. It wouldn't make any sense. And yet the longer the conversation went on, the harder it was to deny. Her father was talking to dragons. And it sounded like he knew them.

"We promised not to hurt your daughters as long as you helped us use the Stone, *arukhin*. Just as we promised to rip them apart in front of you if you did not. You've been full of excuses the last two nights running, and now tonight you profess not to even remember how to open the chamber? Pathetic. And more than worthy of punishment."

"I told you, when you first came to me months ago, that it had been a long time since I'd done this. I'll ask Duncan. He'll help me remember, I swear it. There's just so much going on here, and I don't want him to suspect! Please, I just need a little more time…"

"Silence!" The one with the gravelly voice snapped angrily, followed by a long-suffering sigh. Poppy's first thought was that it sounded bogus. Her next thought was that it sounded a lot like what she'd just been doing, and she flushed, embarrassed.

"And to think that remembering all of Velorian's boring old stories seemed like a boon. The little *arukhin* shifter who used to come through the magical Stone to play with him, until the day he decided to show his furry friend the fun a dragon can have with trespassers. What a blessing from the Drak himself to learn that the tales were true!"

Then the voice went flat, dangerous. "I assumed you were a coward, MacInnes, when we learned you'd tucked your tail between your legs and run away just because your childhood friend made a snack of a few worthless villagers in your presence. Cowards can be useful, and simple threats managed to get you back to your ancestral home, didn't they? And to all of your mangy relations? You should thank us for pushing you, really. But if we had had any idea what a sniveling, weakling, worthless *arukhin* you were, we would have chosen another.

"Every day here, in this sea of our enemies, brings us closer to discovery. And you want us to wait again? To *wait*? We've been two long years in this realm, stranded and forgotten. Our king is dead. The dragons have all given us up for dead by now, no doubt, when we are two of the greatest warriors of our tribe!"

"I don't understand why you don't just go to Duncan," Poppy heard her father whimper. He sounded so afraid that her stomach clenched miserably. She wanted to go flying out and save him. But these were dragons, all right. And they sounded ten times as ornery as Lucien. To rescue her dad, she was going to have to live, so barreling into the situation was out of the question.

"If you just explain how you were left behind, I'm sure he'll help you get back," her father was pleading.

"Idiot." The other dragon shifter hissed. "He has all the power of the arukhin to command. Do you really think, after all you have told us has happened, that he'll be so accommodating with a pair of dragons? No, better to use you, his weakling brother. You may have no honor, but you do have the key to the Stone. So figure it out, damn you, or your pretty young one will pay for it!"

Poppy began to shake. She could hardly believe it. Her father had once been friends with a dragon? He'd known, then, about the Drakkyn, about the *arukhin*, about the Stone's true nature. And it had freaked him out so badly that he'd turned his back on *everything*. Poppy understood how seeing someone he'd obviously been close to behave so violently would have been a horrible shock. Had he begun to look at his own animal urges through that prism, she wondered? Had the Wolf that each of them kept inside frightened him so badly?

It must have. And that explained everything. She already knew, after watching the couples here, that he could never have bitten her mother. They were too comfortable being apart. He'd been trying, she now understood, to be human. To just be normal and human. Maybe he'd married a witch to try and negate the werewolf thing… who knew? But if he had, it hadn't worked.

In any case, he had screwed up royally with his hybrid werewolf-witch children. "Wait," her father suddenly said. "Wait, I think I remember… it may be…"

Poppy didn't want to wait to find out whether these dragons were bluffing about hurting her as an incentive. It was time to get Uncle Duncan. She was ashamed she couldn't do more herself. She was well aware of her limitations. She might be a werewolf, but she hadn't been trained to fight flying serpents. And dying wasn't going to help anyone.

Duncan was the Alpha. Duncan was her father's brother. He would fix this.

Then a large, rough hand covered her mouth, too quickly for even the hint of a scream to escape.

"I thought I smelled you, pretty," that low, gravelly voice breathed in her ear. "You should be more careful. I've been watching you for quite a while now. The old man may be a waste of fur. But his daughters look and smell far too good to be ignored."

Bastian broke the surface of sleep with a shuddering breath, arching off the soft pile of furs they'd used for a bed as his lungs filled with cleansing air. In his dreams, he'd been drowning, caught in thick and relentless blackness that oozed into his lungs no matter how he struggled to get away. He'd begun to question whether he shouldn't just give up and let the blackness consume him. But then, like a flash of light, he'd been hit with a wave of sensory impressions not his own, so intense that it had dragged him from the depths.

The chamber. Scent of incense. The Stone alight, ringing with song. A doorway into the Black Mountains. Wide and frightened golden eyes.

Screaming.

Bastian sat up quickly, waking the woman who had been sleeping curled beside him.

"Bastian? What's wrong?" Cat asked, her voice thick with exhaustion. He immediately regretted having woken her, seeing how dull fatigue had made her normally bright eyes. He wasn't even sure what sense to make of what he'd seen. The vision had left as abruptly as it had come, with nothing remaining but the certainty that something had just gone terribly wrong out in the night.

Something to do with dragons in the chamber of the *Lia Fáil*.

"We have to go," he said. That was all he knew for certain.

"But… it isn't light yet," Cat said, gesturing to the two stained-glass windows behind the throne dais. There was nothing beyond them but blackness. Bastian concentrated, trying to glean anything else he could from what he remembered. Suddenly, he had a glimpse of curly hair, shot through with pink.

"It's Poppy," he said. "I don't think she ever made

it to Lucien. She's in trouble." He paused. "And I think she's with your father."

He saw Cat's sleepiness vanish as quickly as if he had snapped his fingers.

"Let's go," she said. The two of them dressed quickly, and Bastian gently lifted the staff from where it jutted upright from the floor.

The lights went out.

Cat took his hand.

"We'll need everyone," Bastian said, hoping he wasn't too late. "They're at the Stone."

Cat gave her uncle a world of credit.

He and the others had been just heading back to the manor house to turn in when she and Bastian returned. The Alpha hadn't even batted an eye at Bastian's calm insistence that Poppy and Freddie were in danger. He just accepted it as truth, as did the others.

And just as quickly, he went into battle mode.

"I see," was all Duncan said. He looked at his sons. "Follow me. Don't say anything."

A ginger-haired man Cat hadn't seen before, lean and wiry with sharp eyes, walked over to join them.

"Malcolm," Duncan instructed him. "You stay behind. Wait for my signal."

"Uninvited guests?" Malcolm asked, his tone deceptively casual. This was Duncan's trusted lieutenant, his second-in-command, Cat remembered. And though at first glance he looked a bit like a distinguished professor, the gleam in his eyes marked him to be as much a warrior as her uncle.

"Two, we think. Of the scaly variety," Duncan replied and then shot a look at Rowan. "No offense, my dear."

"None taken," Rowan replied, and a flare of fire in her eyes transformed her instantly in Cat's mind from gilded princess to warrior queen. "Let's go."

Despite the danger that Cat knew threatened her father and sister, she felt a rush of relief as their small party, minus Malcolm and the pregnant Carly, set out for the chapel. These people had fought dragons before. They would know what to do. Bastian moved to confer with Gabriel and Gideon, while she stayed close by her uncle, speaking in hushed tones as they pulled away from the gathering.

"He's acted strangely for weeks, Uncle Duncan," Cat said. "I don't understand why they're here or how they even found him, but this probably explains why Dad's been behaving oddly."

Duncan's jaw was set, his face grim. "Never underestimate a dragon with time on his hands," he growled. "Not that lot, particularly."

"These must be the scouts that Mordred Andrakkar sent and then abandoned," Rowan interjected, gliding alongside them. She was bathed, as they all were, in a bright nimbus of light that emanated from Bastian's staff. In its glow, any shadows around them were banished. Cat wished, futilely, that it was so easy to banish every evil they might encounter.

She had a bad feeling that she hadn't even seen the half of it yet.

"I remember Lucien arguing with his father about it, when I was captured last year," Rowan continued. "He was angry at how Mordred had been sending warriors here without being able to get them back, trying to use them as scouts to find your weaknesses."

"And they're still here? We *are* good," Gabriel opined with a satisfied smirk.

"As long as this isn't Lucien himself," Duncan said flatly, "we'll try to make this quick and clean. That one I'd rip limb from limb slowly, and enjoy it."

Cat looked away, her stomach knotting at his words. What would he do, she wondered, if he knew just how close Lucien actually was? She glanced at Bastian, but his face was inscrutable. He no longer looked tired or vulnerable, Cat noted. Right now, Bastian was all warrior.

She felt a hand reach out and squeeze hers. When she looked up, it was Rowan, concern clouding her exquisite features. "It's going to be all right," she whispered. Cat could only nod, the words catching in her throat. She could only think about Poppy and getting to her before something terrible happened. She couldn't fathom what dragons would want with her sister—or her father, for that matter. Judging by the reactions of the others, though, it couldn't be good.

Gideon and Gabriel stalked alongside one another, silent and dangerous predators even in their human forms. The closer they got to the ruins, the more Gideon's face darkened.

Finally he stopped, staring. "Shit," he snarled. "They've definitely gone below." And indeed, Cat could see the faint and flickering glow in the darkness from the opened stairway.

Gabriel looked sharply at his father, gold-green eyes alight in the darkness. "Do we go in as human or Wolf?" he asked.

"Stay in this form for now," Duncan said without hesitation. "I don't want to provoke them if they're willing to let Fred and Poppy go. We'll see what we've got when we get down there."

Suddenly, like a bolt of lightning, energy surged through Cat, white light filling her head and flowing through her veins. She gasped, and at the same moment, a song echoed faintly to her, resonating in every cell in her body. It was haunting and ethereal, silvery as the moon itself, and Cat knew it without ever having heard it. This was the song of the *Lia Fáil*, the Stone of Destiny, which legend said sang at every full moon… and, Cat remembered with a prick of fear, when the gateway it controlled was opened.

"*Ama Dyana*, we're going to be too late," hissed Rowan, taking off at a speed that rendered her little more than a flash. Her brother went next, and the rest of them followed at runs that were only slightly slower. Cat found herself behind Gabriel as they spiraled down, endlessly down the stairs to the chamber. However long the stairs had seemed when Cat was fleeing the *narial*, they seemed even longer now, and she could hear nothing over the intensifying song of the Stone.

Finally, they emerged into the chamber, which was blazing with light. Time seemed to slow; for Cat, it was like watching something happening underwater. Each movement, every look, seemed drawn out and exaggerated. And she was powerless to stop it.

The Stone had awakened, the inscriptions on it glowing like golden fire burning beneath its obsidian surface. They were there, just as Bastian had said: the four of them, gathered around it in wonder as her father placed his hands on top of it. He looked haggard and terrified, and yet the minute his hands connected with the Stone, his eyes lit as brightly as the inscriptions, glowing with otherworldly power. She heard a shout. Duncan, she thought, yelling his brother's name. The two men on either side of her father looked up, imposing, menacing figures with their long, dark hair tied back, violet eyes narrowed in warning. One, Cat saw, gripped her father by the shoulder. The other had Poppy.

Oh God, Poppy... no...

Their eyes connected in that instant, and Cat saw nothing but the frightened little girl she'd once let into her bed in the dark of night, the child whose fears she'd soothed and whose dreams she'd tended. Crushed against her captor, Poppy looked almost childlike. She also looked more frightened than Cat had ever seen her.

Time began to speed up again in a rush of noise and color, shouts and threats echoing off the walls of the chamber.

"Cat! Skye! Help me, please!" Poppy screamed, straining against the man who held her.

"Poppy!" Cat shrieked, looking frantically for a way to get to her without making it worse.

"Do it now, Wolf," snapped the taller of the two dragon shifters, the one who was digging his claws into her father's shoulder.

"Freddie, no, wait!" Duncan's command echoed off the walls of the chamber. But Cat could see, from the defeated look in her father's eyes, that it was too late. With one claw, he slashed his forearm so that blood spattered onto the surface of the Stone. When he spoke, his voice came out in a roar: the cry not of a man, but of a Wolf.

"Open!"

A shaft of light erupted from the top of the Stone, and the air in the chamber seemed to become electric, making every hair on Cat's body stand on end. Her hair blew back from her face on a burst of alien wind, rife with the scents of a desert night. And through the doorway that the light had created, Cat could begin to see a dusty landscape, mountains rising in the distance, bolts of lightning as violet as the dragons' eyes racing across a bruised night sky.

"Go! Just go, and leave us be!" Freddie yelled at the dragons.

It happened in an instant. The one holding him dug his claws deep into her father's shoulder, ignoring Freddie's scream of pain to pick him up with one hand and hurl him across the chamber. Her father flew through the air, slamming against the stone wall to crumple in a heap to the ground, where he lay very still. Poppy began to struggle wildly, but the dragon holding her only held her tighter, a triumphant smile hovering about his lips. With dawning horror, Cat understood: they had no intention of setting her sister free. And Poppy knew it, too.

"Dad! Oh my God, Dad… you bastards, let me go, let me go…"

"Poppy, no!" Cat screamed, rushing forward, no longer caring whether she got hurt. All she could see, all she could think of, was her sister.

"Cat, watch out!"

A bolt of icy white power sizzled through the air, aimed squarely at the other dragon's heart the instant he stepped clear of his companion and her sister. That single instant, however, was not enough. The dragons dodged Bastian's shot and leaped into the light, wings bursting from their backs just as they crossed the threshold of worlds. Their bodies grew scales and became enormous, changing form even as Poppy remained in their clutches. Cat had just a single glimpse of giant, winged beasts soaring away from them and into that lightning-filled sky before the doorway burst into millions of sparks that fell to scatter across the floor... and then vanished altogether.

The silence in the chamber was deafening.

They'd failed.

Her sister was gone.

Just then an earth-shattering roar sounded from somewhere above them, so full of rage and loss that Cat slammed her hands over her ears to try and block it out. Dust rained from the ceiling as the chamber shook, and then the figure of a man, somehow familiar looking, shot through the doorway. He moved with such speed that his black hair flew back from his forehead, and his eyes glowed with violet fire.

Cat's mouth dropped open as she finally realized who had come.

Lucien Andrakkar, barely recognizable as the sickly wraith who had been haunting Bastian's spare bedroom, stopped short in the middle of the chamber, watching in horror as the last of the tiny sparks scattered across the surface of the Stone and winked out.

Everything about him stood out in stark relief in the dim light of the chamber, Cat thought. His skin glowed with a vitality that hardly seemed possible, and she could see now what Poppy had seen in him. Even in borrowed clothes that hung on his still-thin frame, Lucien was a magnetic figure, dark and dangerous.

As Cat watched him realize who else was in the chamber, his bright violet eyes narrowed, and she decided that "dangerous" was the operative word at the moment. This was not going to be good.

"Shit," she heard Bastian mutter from directly behind her, drawing Lucien's attention.

"You'd better explain this to your furry friends before they attack me, or I'm going to start breathing fire indiscriminately," Lucien hissed at him, eyes still wild, over the growling that had suddenly begun to fill the air around them.

Inside, a single phrase played over and over in Cat's mind. *Ohmigod, ohmigod, ohmigod, ohmigod...* Her sister had just been abducted by dragons. She had no clue how to start bloodbath prevention right now.

"Get away from the Stone, damn you!" roared Duncan, eyes glowing yellow as he rushed toward Lucien.

"Duncan, wait!" she cried, feeling utterly helpless in the face of her uncle's rage. "It's not what you think!"

He seemed not to have heard her plea, or simply had not cared. Either way, Cat could see the old werewolf was seconds away from shredding his clothing and making the Change, which was going to make everything a thousand times worse. With all Duncan's instincts telling him to tear out Lucien's throat, it would be almost impossible to get through to him.

And Gideon and Gabriel were already circling, teeth bared, waiting for the word to become Wolves and defeat their hated enemy.

She could only think of one thing to do, and it wasn't going to make her very popular. It might, however, save the man who was probably her sister's best chance at rescue.

"Uncle Duncan, no!" Cat cried again, leaping to stand between Lucien and the other Wolves, arms outstretched. "You can't kill Lucien!"

"She's right. Please, hear me out. There's an explanation for this." Bastian joined her, taking up the dragon's other flank. Then she felt someone press against her back: Skye. Two allies, Cat thought, looking at the blazing, angry eyes of the others. Well, that was better than nothing. And she did have both a sorcerer and a dragon. She might not die… that quickly.

"Lucien isn't here to hurt anyone. He doesn't want a fight." Cat tried to lower her voice to a nonhysterical level and looked to Lucien, wanting him to confirm his good intentions to the group.

The dragon's answering shrug was no help.

Cat clenched her fists and tried to restrain herself from pummeling her sister's would-be savior. Duncan was no longer growling, but Cat couldn't quite bring herself to be happy about it. Instead, he looked like someone had struck him. His eyes moved from Cat to Bastian to Skye, and then to Lucien, and back again. His snarl faded to be replaced by a look of utter disbelief.

"How," he asked softly, looking at Cat, "do you know the first damned thing about Lucien Andrakkar, may I ask?"

Cat swallowed hard at the accusation in his eyes, which until now had always been kindly when they looked at her. Duncan was a long-awaited connection between her human life and her werewolf one, more fatherly than her own father. And he thought she had betrayed him.

What was worse, she thought that, in some small way, she might have.

"I met him yesterday," Cat said, keeping her eyes locked with Duncan's, willing him silently to keep an open mind. "At Bastian's cottage."

"Bastian's…" Duncan's eyes flicked to Bastian, and she could see the stunned anger beginning to rear its head. "You… you've been harboring this creature? Here?" His voice began to rise. "*On my land?*"

Gideon and Gabriel continued to circle, growling menacingly as they stared at Lucien.

"What did you do, dragon? Put some damned spell on him?" snarled Gideon. "Is that how you weaseled your way back in here?"

"Yes," hissed Lucien, baring teeth that had grown long and deadly sharp. "Obviously, all I ever thought of doing during the year I spent in the dungeons of the Blighted Kingdom was coming to this paradise of the *arukhin*, alone, during a yearly gathering. It seemed like a marvelous idea."

"Bull," snapped Gabriel. "You struck a deal with those disgusting *daemon* and they let you out. You probably weren't even in there a day, were you?"

Lucien's response was to snap angrily at the brothers, and Bastian noted with alarm that his hands were now covered in glistening black scales and sporting long, hooked claws.

"I have to go get her," Lucien growled at Bastian, his eyes barely leaving the MacInnes brothers as they waited for an opportunity to attack. "Open the damned door for me, Dyim. You know it's my right."

"I don't think I can listen to this," Duncan said, his voice gone cold. "Whatever he promised you, I can't believe you went for it, Bastian. I trusted you. I thought of you as a friend, lad. And to repay me, you bring the creature here who tried to kill my son, who tried to enslave your sister. Nothing excuses that. Nothing." His eyes swept the four of them, Cat still acting as a barrier, Skye hovering protectively behind. At a loss, Duncan shook his head in disgust.

"Go ahead and open the door, Bastian," the Alpha said with a defeated wave of his hand. "Take your bloody dragon friend with you, too. I want you all out. I don't give a damn where you go. Just get out."

Cat took a step toward him, hating to see him like this. It would be fine, if he would just listen. But his gaze was shuttered, and it seemed unlikely that she would get through.

"Uncle Duncan," she said softly, pleading.

"Catriona," he returned. "Your father already broke my heart. Wasn't that enough?"

Before Cat could protest, another voice spoke up, husky and commanding, to draw everyone's attention.

"My brother is an honorable man, Duncan. He would never do anything to hurt your people. I suggest you listen to him before you jump to any conclusions."

Rowan stepped forward, one arm around Cat's father, whom she had obviously been supporting. She looked like a goddess dropped to Earth. She also looked willing to give them the benefit of the doubt, and Cat felt a dizzying wave of relief. As she watched, Rowan arched one flame-red brow at her brother.

"This had better be good," she said.

"No honorable man would bring *that*," Duncan snapped, flinging out his arm to point at a still-agitated Lucien, "to MacInnes land. How can you even say that, Rowan? You, of all people, should understand how I feel about this!"

Freddie, looking dull-eyed and shaken, had tears rolling down his white face and seemed oblivious to everything else that was going on. "My fault," he murmured. "She's gone, my little girl, all my fault…"

"*Fools!*" Lucien snapped, and Cat's stomach dropped when she saw how close he looked to losing it completely. "Do you know what they'll do to her, given enough time? She'll be a pretty plaything for one of them, I imagine. Until he breaks her. Think of me what you like, I'm the only one who can get into that castle without inciting a riot. I'll bring her back. But your delaying is killing her, and *I must go now*!"

"Please. You probably organized it," Gabriel snapped. "You couldn't have my wife, so you found someone else to steal, right? If we let you go, we'll never see you again."

Lucien drew himself up proudly, and again Cat was struck by just how much good Poppy had done him in the short time she'd been working on him. Maybe he was not quite his former self… but that might be a good thing. His voice, rich and sonorous, was outraged.

"I would never harm Poppy MacInnes," he said angrily. "Never. I've paid dearly for my misdeeds, Wolf. If you don't believe it, I suggest you try even an hour in the dungeons beneath the Blighted Kingdom. They would break you long before they were through."

"Then what the hell are you doing here, dragon?" Gideon asked, his voice still little more than the guttural growl of an animal preparing to fight. "What could you possibly want in a place where you couldn't be more unwanted?"

Lucien turned his head to look directly at Bastian, and while Cat saw no real malice, she could also see that Lucien had no intention of sacrificing his own hide to cover for her mate.

"I suggest you ask the sorcerer here what *he* could possibly want with a dragon. I didn't ask to be rescued from the dungeons, any more than I asked to be brought here. But then, he's brought more to your woods than just a detestable, *unwanted* serpent. Isn't that right, Bastian? You may want to clear that up, before someone finds your body floating in a stream."

"It's the *narial*, isn't it?" asked Rowan softly, and the stricken look in her eyes indicated that she understood the seriousness of what Bastian was dealing with. "A curse?"

Bastian nodded.

"Oh, Bastian," she sighed. "Why didn't you tell me? I might have helped."

"I'm afraid only Lucien can help," Bastian said, and Cat could have sworn she heard Gabriel mutter something that sounded like *God help us*. Bastian, however, ignored it.

"And is he going to do the right thing, or what we'd all expect of him?" Duncan interjected. He was still glaring at Lucien, and the simple question sounded uncannily like a threat.

"I haven't quite decided yet," Lucien answered

him with a faint sneer. "A bit torn, as you might imagine."

"Let him go get Poppy," Bastian said quickly when Duncan started to look like he might murder Lucien on the spot. "I'll explain everything, but Lucien isn't at fault. I brought him out of the Blighted Kingdom for my own admittedly selfish reasons. Whether he helps me is his decision. Poppy has been… he and Poppy have been…" He looked to the dragon, obviously at a loss as to why exactly Lucien was so insistent he save the girl.

Lucien looked away and said nothing.

"I don't think it's such a hot idea. Even if we believe him, how do we know he'll bring her back?" asked Gabriel.

Gideon eyed Lucien warily. "Well… he's the right species, I suppose. Maybe if he goes with us, he'll be some help."

"*He* is not very fond of being talked about as though he is not there," Lucien snapped, smoke beginning to coil lazily out of his nose.

Duncan looked horrified. "You're all bloody insane, trusting an Andrakkar to do anything!"

Lucien glowered at the brothers, ignoring Duncan. "I'll need someone to come who can reopen the doorway, but when it comes to the castle, I go in alone. Do you have any idea how asinine it would be for you to walk into *Drak'ra Tesh*? I don't care how strong you think you are. Two *arukhin* versus hundreds of dragons equals the end of your existence. I'm going. If I don't return, assume I'm dead. You're just going to have to accept it."

Skye summed up the general feeling with her next, simple question.

"But… *why?*"

Lucien's frown grew deeper. "Poppy was able to cure the illness that infected me during the time I was in the Blighted Kingdom. I owe her my life. Saving hers in my duty and my right. She's too delicate to be where she is going. She will end up… at least damaged, and that's not acceptable." He glared at Duncan. "Not when I could be saving her as we speak."

Cat raised her eyebrows. "You actually care that my sister doesn't have her spirit broken?"

Lucien dodged the question neatly. "Your sister has a big mouth," he replied flatly. "I don't want to see *that* broken." He turned and looked at Duncan and his sons in turn. "I don't know how to operate the Stone. Which of you will take me? I don't give a damn who it is, but hurry up."

Cat knew that everyone could hear the tenderness in his voice when Lucien spoke of her sister. She hoped that was enough to convince them. Because the clock was ticking.

Duncan, of course, glared stubbornly at him. "Rowan can go get Poppy. She's a dragon."

Lucien sighed harshly, smoke once again coiling up from his mouth and nose. "If you knew how few female dragons are left, and in what condition most of those are, you would understand what a terrible idea that is. I'm the only one who can do this, old man."

"I know how to use it. I'll take him."

All eyes turned toward Rowan in shock. After all that had happened between them, there was no reason why Rowan should ever want to be alone with Lucien. But Bastian's sister appeared to have made up her mind. And the stubborn expression on her face said it all. Even

Bastian didn't love the idea, Cat realized. She felt him come up behind her, pulling her back against his chest and rubbing her arm absently. The tension poured from him in palpable waves. Cat leaned into him, glad for the support. She hoped she was some comfort to him, as his quiet, steady presence was to her.

Gabriel was outraged. "You can't take him to the chamber! Don't you remember what happened the last time you went anywhere alone with him?"

Rowan looked blandly at him. "Yeah, well, that was before we knew he was my brother." She looked at Lucien. "You do understand that I will rip your weakling ass limb from limb if you so much as brush against me wrong, right? Because that would be incest, which is a thousand times worse. And it was bad to begin with."

Lucien had the audacity to look faintly amused. His violet eyes glittered. "I would expect no less."

She turned back to her husband, satisfied. "See?" she said. "All is well. Now let's get going. The Goddess knows what she's been through already."

Gabriel stepped forward so that he was almost nose to nose with the dragon shifter. "I'm coming too. And if you try a single damned thing…"

"Yes, I know. A painful death," Lucien finished for him impatiently. "I've been close to that once. It's not something I care to relive. In fact, I would prefer it if you'd come, Gabriel. There are…" He trailed off for a moment, for once seeming at a loss for words. "… things I think I need to say. In case I'm simply torn apart, which is always possible."

That was enough to surprise Gabriel into acquiescence.

With a graceful wave of her hand, Rowan made the

doorway appear once again. She led the way in, followed by Lucien and finally Gabriel, none giving so much as a backward glance before the column of light collapsed once again, leaving those who remained to look uncertainly at one another.

Cat was suddenly more tired than she had ever been in her life.

"All right," Duncan said. "I don't even want to think about what I just let happen."

"Are you okay?" Bastian asked her softly. "He'll get her, you know. I think he's in love with her." He smiled then. "That presents its own set of problems, but Poppy can figure it out."

"Let's get out of here," Gideon said. "Hanging around in here isn't going to do a thing, and Carly and Mal will be waiting."

Cat watched Skye try to guide their father across the floor, but he was crying quietly again, and she was having little success. She gave Bastian's hand a squeeze and then went to drape her father's other arm around her shoulder. Skye looked at her gratefully.

"You two must hate me," Freddie said haltingly. "I thought I could protect you if I kept you with me. Fat lot of good that did." He shook his head. "I don't know what to think anymore. But if that mouthy dragon hurts her, I'll kill him myself."

"We love you, Dad. It's going to be all right," Cat said, and found that she meant it. He was a deeply flawed man, but all she had to do was look at him to know he cared.

"Poppy will be back soon," Skye added.

"So," Duncan said as they made their way back up

the stairs, guided by the bright light of Bastian's staff. "Are you really cursed, lad?"

"Let's go back to the house, and I'll tell you everything," Bastian said. "More, I'll bet, than you want to know."

"I'll be the judge of that," Duncan grunted. Then his tone lightened just a little. "It's better than I thought it was, actually."

"What's that?" Cat heard Bastian ask.

"You being cursed. I had some ideas about what was wrong with you, but that wasn't even on my list."

Bastian frowned back at her uncle. "What did you think was wrong with me?"

Duncan grinned. "Well, lad. I'd pretty much decided you were just a regular old pervert."

Cat tipped her head back. It felt good to laugh again.

Lucien Andrakkar stood in the land on the other side of the Gateway Stone, watching slashes of violet lightning flickering in the sky. On either side of him were the two people he'd thought he'd be least likely to ever see again after that disastrous night in the Dyadd camp. The night he had decided that giving what was left of his worthless life to the *daemon* was better than causing more pain for the woman who turned out to be his sister.

He had never questioned his rationale, even in his darkest moments. And now, it truly seemed that the Drak himself had had a hand in his fate. The cold and wretched last son of the House of Andrakkar was capable of feeling real love after all. That it was for a mouthy slip of an *arukhin* woman seemed somehow fitting.

That he would have to run a gauntlet of fire to claim her was just the way his life seemed to work.

"So," said Rowan, tucking one side of her brilliant red hair behind her ear, "the plan is for Gabriel and me to wait here in the circle of stones. If you're not back by morning, we head back here to figure out a double rescue mission."

"If I'm not back in a few hours, I'm dead. It would still be a single rescue mission," Lucien informed her, folding his arms across his chest.

She frowned at him. "That's upbeat."

"Realism doesn't tend to be. Try to think of that scenario as simplifying matters, and maybe it'll be more palatable."

Rowan gave him a baleful look, but she didn't pursue the subject further. Lucien still found it surreal that he and this beautiful creature shared Mordred Andrakkar for a father. After watching the man all his life, Lucien had decided that the old dragon didn't produce anything that wasn't stunted or twisted, himself included. But Rowan *an* Morgaine was vibrant, passionate, and powerful. If there had been any good in Mordred, she had gotten it. It was his greatest shame that he had hunted her so and that he had nearly condemned her to the same life of misery that he'd lived.

He had not loved her. He knew that now. He'd simply felt their blood connection and been drawn to her, lost in frozen darkness and transfixed by her bright and shimmering light. Whether it was too late for Rowan to accept him as a brother, Lucien didn't know. But there was still something he needed to say.

"Lucien? You set?" Rowan asked.

"Not quite," he said, eliciting curious looks from both of his companions. His stomach knotted painfully. This was a dark day for him. He'd already made his peace with Bastian. He'd been taking care of that when he'd suddenly been rocked with the knowledge that Poppy had gone. It had been so strange to feel what she was feeling and see what she was seeing. Strange and then horrible, because he'd known he would never get to her in time.

At least he had been closer than if he had stayed at the cottage. And Bastian would discover soon enough that his misguided mercy had been repaid. The Drak forgive him, but he had come to sort of *like* the obstinate Dyim. This, however, was decidedly more difficult. He was unaccustomed to apologizing to anyone. However, should he be killed, which was more of a possibility than he'd let on, he wanted to ascend to the Higher Kingdom with as clean a conscience as possible. Granted, his would still be more dingy gray than lily white, but it was the best he could do on such short notice.

He cleared his throat. "I… don't have anything to say that would be sufficient, considering I nearly killed one of you and abducted the other," he began, frowning as he tried to think of a way to apologize that didn't sound weak and ridiculous. He was a dragon, damn it! Dragons were not remorseful creatures.

"Don't forget leaving me at the mercy of a *daemon* who had every intention of using me for some sick experiments," added Gabriel.

Lucien glared at him. "Yes. And that."

"And chasing Rowan for so long that she barely had any strength left. Oh, and threatening to kill her brother so she'd give herself to you."

Gabriel looked obnoxiously amused. Lucien gritted his teeth and waited a beat. When no more addenda seemed forthcoming, he said, "Are you quite finished?"

"No." Gabriel grinned, and Lucien felt the tips of his wings poised to burst through his skin. It was everything he could do to restrain himself from shifting. But somehow, he managed to cling to the sure knowledge that Poppy would not appreciate it if he ate one of her cousins out of spite.

Rowan finally ended it, giving her husband a dirty look before turning her attention back to Lucien and taking one of his hands in both of hers. He jumped a little at the unexpected touch. Her hands were soft and warm, alive with currents of power that, while different, were as strong as the ones he had felt whenever Poppy touched him.

"Go on, Lucien," she encouraged, her emerald eyes bright with understanding.

Was there more? Damn, he'd hoped the obvious intention would be enough. Lucien took a deep breath and tried to come up with the actual apology part of the apology. "Um, yes, anyway... I just wanted to make sure you understood that... er, that is to say, I would certainly never again... ah..."

Rowan squeezed his hand. "Okay, Lucien. You're sorry. Got it."

Lucien blew out a breath, relieved. "Yes. That."

She gave him a slow, beautiful smile. Her husband, on the other hand, snorted and glowered at him.

"It's not like that makes up for it, you know."

He found himself wishing there were some way to not want to rip off one of Gabriel's limbs and beat him with it every time the Wolf opened his mouth. But perhaps that would come in time. And, Lucien reminded himself, he did deserve it. Mostly. Not that it was at all necessary for Gabriel to shove his nose in it quite so much.

"Actually," Lucien replied silkily, "I believe I'd made up for everything I've done after the first forty-eight hours or so of torture at the hands of the *daemon*. Torture which, I will remind you, could easily have befallen you had events unfolded somewhat differently."

He waited for the sarcastic retort, but instead Gabriel just looked at him with his head tilted, considering. Finally, he murmured, "So you did do it on purpose. You attacked Jagrin knowing that he would take you instead of me if you did. I always wondered."

Lucien shifted uncomfortably. He'd thought of this particular *arukhin* as an enemy for so long. He wasn't at all certain how things would be when they were no longer enemies, even if they never became friends. With any luck, future steps in that direction wouldn't be quite so awkward as these first ones.

"Well. It seemed like the right thing to do, considering," was all Lucien said.

Gabriel looked at him a moment longer and then gave a curt nod, as though deciding something. "Right, then," he said. Then, before Lucien knew what he was doing, Gabriel grabbed him in a one-armed bear hug and smacked his back heartily with his free arm.

"What in the name of the Drak are you doing?" Lucien hissed, leaping out of reach and brushing at his arms as though they'd just caught fire.

"Forgiving you," Gabriel replied, chuckling. "Might as well, seeing that you're Rowan's brother. Which makes us family," he added, his grin widening.

"Oh. Well… thank you," muttered Lucien, maintaining his distance and eyeing him warily. He wasn't at all sure he was ready to be included in the list of Rowan's family if it involved hugging the MacInnes brothers in any way, shape, or form.

Rowan simply rolled her eyes. "Okay, hang on, new best friends… just let me make sure I can get this doorway open quickly if I have to." She inhaled deeply and exhaled, and a shimmering orb flickered to life in their midst, suspended only slightly above the ground in the middle of the circle of stones in which they stood.

"Open," she breathed, and in a graceful swirl of light, the doorway materialized. Lucien watched it, amazed. He could see why his father had wanted this sort of power: the power of the Stone. It would be a handy tool with which to conquer entire worlds with a formidable dragon army. Access to unreachable realms with a single touch. If one was inclined to conquest, this was a treasure worth killing for.

He didn't realize that Rowan was watching the way he stared at the doorway she'd created until she spoke, softly and near his ear.

"Tempted?" she asked.

He turned and looked at her, at the face of a goddess and eyes glowing green in the half-light. His sister, he thought, marveling at the fact that he still had one tiny piece of family left. She was obviously a treasured friend and ally to those she trusted. He had been none of those things, a function of what he was and the way he'd been raised. But still, he thought there might be much he could learn from her, given the benefit of the doubt and a chance.

She wondered if he was tempted to take up his father's mantle and rejoin the bloody quest to possess the Gateway Stone. Perhaps he would have been, if he'd been at all interested in challenging the current ruler of the dragons to reclaim his place among them. But those days had long passed.

All he could think of was the way he'd felt the first time the little Wolf with the ridiculously pink hair had placed her hands on him. And even if Poppy rejected him, he could not go back to what he was. Because now he understood what it was to find a mate, to feel that rush of connection, of intoxicating otherness blended with comforting familiarity. All the hollow victories he'd chased had only fostered further isolation and pain. But being with Poppy, even just being near her, was like coming home.

So he shook his head at Rowan and said, "There are prizes greater than this."

She raised her eyebrows at him. "Oh, really?"

He smirked. "It's amazing what a year of whippings does for your perspective, you know."

"He's become a zen dragon," Gabriel interjected. "Someone should write a book."

Lucien managed a soft laugh this time at the well-intentioned tweak. He was all for sarcasm and thought he could probably learn to at least tolerate Gabriel MacInnes's version.

As long as the man kept his paws off him. He was going to have to firmly draw the line at any hugging. Well, from the MacInnes males, at any rate.

"I'm ready to go," Lucien said, and with another wave of Rowan's hand, the orb was no more. He turned around and drank in his first look at his homeland in more than a year, the beautiful bruised sky shot through with the lightning he'd always loved to watch chase itself, even as a young boy. It was home. But he dreaded finding whatever awaited him there. He would have to fight for Poppy. And though he was almost completely well, there were no guarantees. Dragons fought dirty.

But then, Lucien thought with a smirk, so did he.

Bastian...

Bastian stirred in deep, contented sleep. A voice, strangely familiar, had drifted through his dreams, calling him. Some part of him wondered whether it was real or imagined, but when it did not come again, Bastian drifted back down into comfortable darkness.

He'd talked for a very long time, longer than he'd imagined he would. At the end of it all, he'd been gratified to find that Duncan and Gideon were not only supportive, they wondered what had taken him so long to come out with it.

When Duncan had begun to talk with Freddie, however, that was by rights a private thing. He and Cat had retired to the bedroom to try to rest and wait for news. It was a mark of all the stress and lack of sleep that Cat had fallen asleep almost as soon as she'd hit the pillow, and he not long after. But he knew, somehow, that Lucien would not fail. He would return with Poppy. And then, he was increasingly certain, Lucien would give him the help he sought.

It was a wonder that tomorrow at this time he might finally be free. That he and Cat could start to plan their future in earnest. The Goddess had finally seen fit to grant him peace. He could feel it.

And so he slept, and slept well.

Bastian.

That voice again. His eyelids fluttered at the sound of his name and of the voice, so familiar, though he couldn't quite place it. Familiar, and very, very cold.

Baaaaaassssstiannnn...

It echoed, as though from far away, drifting into his happy dreams and dragging him up from the peaceful depths, where he rested with his arms around the woman he loved.

"Enough sleep, sorcerer. It's time for us to go."

His eyes flew open then, sleep vanishing in an instant at the sight of the bloodless face hovering over his own, wearing a smile that would never inspire anything but madness.

"Jagrin," he said hoarsely.

"Surprise," Jagrin said, reaching for him.

And as the warmth of Cat's bedroom dissolved into the endless darkness beneath the Blighted Kingdom, Bastian knew his worst nightmares had just become reality. Worst, because this wasn't just his nightmare anymore.

Cat was still in his arms.

Chapter 14

Drak'ra Tesh, the Black Mountains of Coracin

"I say we make her a slave."

"Over my dead body, Tynan. The girl is mine. There is no *we*. And the only serving she will be doing is in my bed."

"I did all the work with the old Wolf. I got us home. That's far more consequential than what you did, just hanging about, keeping her all to yourself!"

"Tynan, Dex, enough! Two years away, and now you've been back ten minutes and my head is splitting with your incessant bickering over an inconsequential female *arukhin*! Perhaps we should all share her and be done with it."

Poppy sat stiffly on the stone steps in the great hall of the dragon castle deep within the mountain, alternately glaring at the overbearing assholes who were now wailing like preschoolers at the prospect of having to share her and tugging at the heavy manacle that had been fastened around her ankle. She felt decidedly Princess Leia-ish, though thankfully without the space bikini. She had also swung from being terrified to being furious more times than she could count and had finally settled somewhere in between.

Had she ever really wished for a dragon to sweep her off her feet? Because having it happen in the most literal sense had been far less appealing than the fantasy.

The dragon men might be handsome, but she had no illusions about their rugged exteriors hiding hearts of gold. These two, in particular, were all muscle and no substance, from what she'd figured out. And they were fully prepared to have an epic fight for the honor of screwing her brains out.

It might have been flattering, if they hadn't also tried to kill her father and then abducted her.

Poppy gave the manacle one more vicious tug, wincing at the way it bit into her leg. They'd locked her up after the shorter one, Dex, had tried to plant one on her and she'd kneed him in the groin. It had been a satisfying, if short-lived, victory.

"If you two persist in this, I'm going to order you to fight to the death so that both of you shut up. As that will only make one person here happy, and as that person is not me, considering the mess and the loss of an able-bodied young dragon, I suggest you come up with viable alternatives."

The dragon king, whose name Poppy was fairly sure was Kassius, looked thoroughly annoyed with her would-be keepers. She watched him glower at them, impressed with the smoke that poured more thickly from his nose and mouth the angrier he got. He was a little older, with gray at his temples and a short-clipped beard, and attractive in the dark way that all of his kind seemed to be. Nothing like Lucien, though.

Lucien. God, she had to stop this. She was in mortal peril—or at least in danger of finding herself attached to the dragon equivalent of the dumb jocks she'd studiously avoided in high school. And to mentally escape from the fear? She was picturing yet another dragon flying in on ebony wings to rescue her. There was no doubt in her mind that someone would come for her. There was also no doubt in her mind that it would not be Lucien Andrakkar. After all, he hadn't exactly come running after her once she'd kissed him.

Not that he could probably run yet. But still. There were phones. He could hobble. Something.

God, she was an idiot. He was just like these Neanderthals. Except smarter. And funny, in a super-sarcastic sort of way. And much, much better looking.

She shifted position on the steps, wiggling her foot because it had fallen asleep. Unfortunately, the clanking of the chain against the stone floor drew the attention of everyone in the vicinity. And with so many violet eyes staring daggers at her, she really couldn't be snotty about making the noise.

She felt her inner pendulum inching back toward "terror" and swallowed hard. She knew that the MacInneses and the Dyadd had fought off a few dragons and even managed to kill the former king, Lucien's father. But she only remembered them talking about four or five. Not a few hundred. And even though the ones hanging around in this impossibly big, Gothic-looking stone hall inside the mountain were mostly older, knowing that they all turned into fire-breathing serpents was enough to make her very worried about the chances of any rescue.

"Perhaps we should let the *arukhin* decide. She'll be more willing if she gets to choose, and I'll suffer less of a headache," said Kassius, considering her with eyes totally devoid of sympathy. "What say you, Wolf? Will you choose a master and be done with it?"

Poppy's eyes widened, and she looked between the two warriors who were staring at her expectantly. That had ended way more abruptly than she'd figured. Now she was going to have to stall, and she had no idea how to do it.

"Um, what happens if I say no? Just out of curiosity?" she asked.

Kassius's mouth thinned in displeasure. "Then I become unhappy and decide on an alternative."

"Such as?"

"We lost the *arukhin* slave that Mordred procured, because that one was released upon the old king's death. He was an excellent drudge, dragging things to and fro, fetching, serving as a moving target for flame-throwing practice... we even gave him a cozy bed of rags in the kitchens near the garbage chute. He wasn't allowed to shift from his Wolf form ever again, of course. But you might be, if the mood took one of our men, in addition to your other duties. You are, after all, quite lovely just as you are." His voice had gone quickly from cool to menacing, and Poppy felt cold sweat break over her skin.

"Oh," she said, trying to sound less terrified than she felt, which was a low bar to set. She thought she succeeded admirably.

"Then we're quite clear?"

"On that, yes, definitely. And, um, thank you for being so... detailed," Poppy said, trying for a winning smile and winding up with what felt like a cringe. "But here's another question. What am I supposed to do with whoever I pick?"

At the wave of snickers that provoked, she frowned and added, "Besides the obvious."

Kassius looked at the ceiling as though praying for patience before returning his gaze to her. "You'll do what every dragon's wife does. Take care of your mate's every need and bear many strong children to further the line."

Wow, that sounds great.

"How many is many?" she asked, and this time there were groans from her informal audience.

Kassius glared at her this time, and his voice was not quite as detached and even as it had been. "As many as your body can handle before it breaks down and you die from the strain."

Her mouth fell open. "Is that *common*?" she cried, completely flabbergasted.

The king actually seemed pleased that he'd upset her. He shrugged, a small smile playing about the corners of his lips. "It happens. Now choose. We have far more important things to consider than your mating preference. If I didn't already have a mate, such as she is, I would take you and have these two imbeciles killed if they chose to complain. You are quite pretty, despite your inglorious heritage." His eyes swept her slowly, and Poppy suddenly felt in dire need of a shower. "But alas, Merta is still alive. So end this, and now."

Poppy looked at the two dragons who were so hot to get their claws on her and tried to imagine either one of them as an acceptable husband and father. The headache she got almost immediately was not a good sign. And a quick glance at the door showed her nothing but emptiness. No conquering werewolves. No supercharged sorceresses. Just an empty doorway. Which meant one thing.

She was screwed.

"Ah. Um," she said. She looked at her suitors again and weighed the relative merits. Dex had copped a couple of cheap feels when he'd walked her in here, which didn't thrill her. But Tynan had been the one to throw her dad at a stone wall as hard as he could. Not that Dex probably wouldn't have. And not that Tynan wouldn't have grabbed her butt if he'd been the one to lead her in.

They were both good-looking, she guessed. But Dex was shorter and stockier, with rippling muscles. Tynan was taller, a little leaner. A little more like...

"The woman is mine."

Poppy snapped her head around at the voice, deep and resonant, as it echoed through the great hall like a thunderclap. It sounded almost like Lucien, but so much stronger. And it couldn't be. He'd been in bed. He was probably still in bed. But the figure who now strode toward the dais where the king sat, and which she was chained to, was clad in jeans and a black T-shirt like an Earth guy, and he definitely was not one of her relatives. Ebony hair was tousled and pushed back from his face, and a pair of intense violet eyes looked at her with a hunger she'd only dreamed of having directed at her.

Oh my God... he actually came for me.

Lucien strode into the hall like a king, moving with all the dangerous grace of a jungle cat. He might be clad in Earth clothes, but he might as well have been wearing the dark-colored, cassocklike clothing of his own kind. He was obviously all dragon. And though Poppy could hardly believe it, he appeared to be here for her. Alone.

She fervently hoped his outward confidence was justified.

"For the love of the Drak," said Kassius, peering at the approaching figure. "Is that Lucien Andrakkar?"

"It is," said Lucien, stopping in front of the dais and sweeping into an elegant bow. He gave her the barest flicker of a glance before returning his attention to the king, but Poppy didn't mind. She'd seen his concern. He'd wanted to make sure she hadn't been hurt. She smiled and then covered her mouth to hide it. That was just what she needed: a big, stupid smile to piss off the men who were collectively deciding her fate. But she couldn't help it. He'd come for her. *He'd come for her!* That had to mean something… didn't it? Well, unless he'd been asked because he actually was a dragon. Or someone had threatened to toss him back to the *daemon* unless he didn't. Or any one of another million things that she decided not to think about for the sake of her own sanity and reasonably fragile ego.

The great hall filled with echoing murmurs at Lucien's announcement. Some of the milling dragons appearing pleased, some interested, and some slightly hostile. She had to remind herself that until a little over a year ago, Lucien had been the heir to the throne. But he was the last of the House of Andrakkar, and when Mordred had been killed and Lucien vanished, the other Houses had battled until another strong dragon was selected to fill the void.

"Lucien," said the king, obviously surprised and somewhat less than happy, though he kept his smile fixed firmly in place. "Where have you been hiding? We thought you dead!"

"I was captured by the *daemon* the night of my father's death," Lucien replied. "I only recently escaped."

Poppy saw the way Kassius flinched at the mere mention of the word *daemon*.

"Foul creatures, the *daemon*," he said, curling his lip. "That business ended with your father, Lucien. We no longer instigate contact with that tribe. And we certainly don't do business with them."

Lucien's lips curved up in a self-deprecating smile that Poppy found devastatingly sexy. "As you might imagine after looking at me, I couldn't agree with that decision more."

There was a ripple of laughter from the assembled crowd, and even Kassius smiled, though Tynan and Dex eyed him warily.

"Indeed," Kassius said. "So what can I do for you, Lucien? Have you come to rejoin the tribe? Your chamber is just as it was. Well, it will be, after you fight Rejinn for it. I don't think he's touched too much."

"No," Lucien said. "I'm not entirely sure I'll be rejoining the tribe."

This was as much news to Poppy as to everyone else, but she kept it to herself.

"Have you come to challenge me, then?" asked Kassius, his expression darkening. "I'll give you a fight to the death, and it'll be yours, boy, if that's what you want."

Lucien gave a heavy sigh at the unprovoked belligerence. "No, Kassius. The House of Arinmar is under no threat from me. The honor to lead is yours by right."

"But then… surely you haven't come all this way just for this little slip of a thing, have you?" Kassius asked, looking puzzled. "I understood when it was a demigoddess, Lucien. But this is just a little *arukhin*. A plaything. I doubt she'll last a month here, and certainly not through birthing one of our children. Hardly worth your trouble."

Poppy glared up at Kassius, but he seemed not to notice. "I'm not a *dog*, you know," she grumbled. Lucien's gaze flickered to her again, and she read the message in his expression loud and clear: *Shut up.*

"Just the same," Lucien said smoothly, "she is my woman, and I've come to collect her. She was rather abruptly taken away by some of your warriors who didn't bother to ask if she was available."

My woman. Poppy wished she had a tape recorder. Then she could have the quote for always, even if he was just saying it to spring her. Not that it looked like it was working.

Tynan looked Lucien over without disguising his disdain. "You were there, with all of those wretched Wolves? *That* is what you choose over the glory of living with your own kind at *Drak'ra Tesh*?"

Lucien shrugged. "It's a long story, but yes. Why, Tynan? You almost sound like you miss me." He smirked, and Tynan reddened, baring his teeth.

"No one misses your father, that much is certain. And in any case, you have no claim on this girl. She is unmated. Your scent would be much stronger on her if she really belonged to you. So I'm taking her."

"Damn you, Tynan, it is not your right…" Dex began, only to be interrupted by Kassius, who now looked as though he was being entertained. Poppy groaned inwardly. She didn't know anything about the ruling dragon, but she knew that nothing good was going to come of this.

"Dragons, dragons, please," Kassius chuckled,

motioning them to settle down. "I believe," he said, addressing everyone in the hall, "that we will have a fight for tonight's entertainment!"

A cheer went up, and Poppy watched Lucien go a lot paler. And so he should have; he was far from fixed, and they both knew it. Still, he stood his ground, standing regally and a little arrogantly, with his arms crossed over his chest as he regarded his competition.

"Fine. Which of them shall I fight to win the lady back?" he asked.

Kassius grinned, and it was not, Poppy thought, a very nice grin. More like a biting grin.

"Why, if she is that important to you, I believe you're going to have to fight both of them. And once they kill you, they can fight one another for the privilege." He waved his hand dismissively. "I'm done listening to them whining about it."

Lucien looked insulted. "What do you mean, *when* they kill me?"

"Please, boy. Look at you, fresh from the *daemon* dungeons… I don't even want to know how you made it out, by the way… too thin and too pale, and I'm sure weak as a kitten to boot. Now look at Tynan and Dex, and tell me what you see."

Poppy watched Lucien manage to look down his nose at the competition before answering. She didn't blame him. This Kassius was a real asshole. She just hoped he wasn't right as well.

"Hmm. I see men with cold and empty beds in their futures," Lucien said. Dex and Tynan snarled, but Kassius shook his head, laughing.

"You really should come back, my boy, if you don't

die. I don't remember you being quite so amusing." He looked at the three of them and then at Poppy. "Well, are any of them fighting with your favor, or are you just going to sit there and mutter and sulk through it?"

"Are you going to unchain me?" she asked irritably.

"No."

"Then I'm probably going to mutter and sulk regardless," Poppy said. "But I do have a favorite." She thought a moment, remembering all of the times she'd watched *A Knight's Tale*. "Um, what, do you want me to give one of them a handkerchief or something? I might have a wadded-up tissue."

"How about your shirt?" asked Dex.

"Keep dreaming," Poppy replied, thinking about the three times that he'd already managed to brush a hand against her chest.

"Whatever you like," Kassius said, leaning back in his massive stone throne with a grin. He looked like all he needed was a supersize soda and some popcorn, thought Poppy. She supposed this could be considered a great night out in the pre–motion picture world. At least maybe she could get her hands on Lucien for a moment before he got ripped to shreds.

And all at once, she knew what she had to do.

"Lucien Andrakkar," Poppy said, standing up to address him. She cocked her hip and crooked a finger at him. "C'mere. Front and center."

Dex and Tynan hissed at him as he passed, but he didn't even look at them. Lucien locked eyes with her and didn't look away. He stopped when he was only a foot from her, his eyes sweeping her from head to toe, drinking her in.

"Question. Does this mean you like me?" Poppy asked, keeping her voice quiet enough that only Lucien could hear.

He tilted his head down to give her a look. "You're not very good at playing the maiden in distress, you know. Aren't you the least bit worried that a raggedy dragon might have some trouble taking down two hale and healthy warriors at the same time?"

She grinned. "Nope. Know why?"

He shook his head, bemused despite his obvious concern. "I can honestly say I have no idea."

Poppy grabbed the front of his T-shirt, dragged him forward, and poured as much of her white light as she could muster into a kiss. She heard him suck in a breath as the energy surged through him and then felt his arms come around her to crush her against him and lift her off her feet until the manacle bit angrily into her ankle. Forgetting where they were, caught up in the power of the connection, Poppy opened her mouth for him, deepening the kiss even as the energy she was giving began to fade, spent. Then abruptly, Lucien tore his mouth away, breathing harshly. She worried for a split second that it hadn't worked. But then he raised his eyes to hers, and they were a blaze of violet.

"I never tried it that way before," Poppy whispered to him.

"This is the second time you've left me hanging," Lucien returned, a dark promise in his gaze. Poppy couldn't have welcomed it more.

"You win this, and the third time will be the charm," she said with a smile.

She swore that his look could have melted her into a puddle right there on the floor.

"Well, I guess there isn't any question of preference." Kassius snorted as Lucien's opponents snapped angrily at him. They didn't seem to see the difference, but Poppy could. Lucien was fairly pulsing with strength now. She couldn't wait to see what he did with it. As long as he was winning, maybe this *would* be entertaining. She just hoped it didn't take too long.

"Clear the floor!" shouted Kassius, and the already sparse crowd of dragons scattered to the perimeter of the hall. "Dragons at the ready!" The three men walked to the center of the floor, standing some distance apart from one another.

"Begin!" bellowed Kassius, leaning forward excitedly to watch the fight. Sadly for him, Lucien must have been in the same frame of mind as Poppy, because it didn't take long.

Dex and Tynan began to shift, but Lucien practically burst into a dragon, one skin turning to another so seamlessly that he'd shifted and slammed Dex in the neck with his tail before Dex had even grown his. The stockier mostly dragon went flying and landed some distance away on the ground, coughing. Poppy thought he sounded like he was about to cough up the world's largest hairball, but he didn't look mortally wounded.

Next came Tynan. Lucien reared up in his hind legs, truly magnificent with his shimmering black scales, enormous wings outstretched, and burning violet eyes. Oh, and the fire coming out of his mouth, Poppy thought, awed. The fire breathing was pretty freaking cool.

Tynan, who had become a rust-colored dragon,

started to sit up as well, but in the blink of an eye Lucien had slammed him down, knocked him in the jaw, and then kicked him for good measure. When Lucien roared, Tynan scrambled away, morphing back into a man as he ran.

"It's just a girl!" he wailed. "I don't want to *die*, and he's going to kill me!"

Kassius stared after him, amazed, and then turned his gaze to the dragon that was Dex, still rolling around on the ground and making a terrible racket.

"Ah, well, Lucien," Kassius said, looking up as the black dragon approached the dais. "I guess I misjudged you. Are you sure you don't want to come back? The rebuilding will take time, but we need young warriors if we are to reverse our decline."

The dragon arched its long neck and shrank down quickly to become Lucien again. He had some color in his cheeks now, Poppy saw, and seemed pleased with himself.

"No, Kassius, though I commend what you're doing. It's been needed for a long time. I'm afraid my father just wouldn't listen." He looked around at the sea of interested faces gathered in the hall. "This place is already much improved."

"Well, then," Kassius smiled, looking pleased. "Unlock the girl, Carik. Take her and go in peace, Lucien." Another dragon sprang forward to unlock the manacle, and Poppy sighed happily as her ankle was freed. "You'll be welcome in my ranks, if you ever do decide to return to us."

"I'm much obliged," Lucien replied, bowing a little to him.

"You're free to go as well, *arukhin*," Kassius said, turning to her. "I'm not sure about Lucien's taste, but I must at least commend you on yours. Hopefully it will be a while before he breaks you." He smiled, and she gathered this was supposed to be a nice sentiment.

Dragons were definitely one of the strangest groups she'd ever met, and that was saying something, considering some of the Goth clubs she'd frequented a couple of years ago.

"Uh, thanks," Poppy said, concentrating on her almost-freedom instead of snotty dragons. She rushed forward to take Lucien's hand, and the two of them walked out the massive double doors together. Behind them, in the rumble of voices, she could hear Kassius giving her jilted suitors an earful and suggesting that one of them might like to meet something called a Cave-Dwelling Gargathan in battle to make up for what he apparently considered, in words she didn't entirely understand, a piss-poor performance.

When the outside doors swung open, all they could see was the night, punctuated by the flickers of half-light that came and went with the lightning. The door shut behind them with a *boom*, and Poppy and Lucien were alone.

Really alone.

A hurricane of butterflies suddenly swirled into motion in Poppy's stomach. Lucien came toward her, a cold wind ruffling his hair. Poppy rubbed at her arms, the chill seeping in quickly.

"You were amazing in there," she told him, her teeth beginning to chatter.

"I think we both know why. Not that I wouldn't have

done that well in a different situation," Lucien added, making Poppy smile.

"Of course you would have," Poppy agreed, her heartbeat picking up as Lucien slid his arms around her. He touched her reverently, Poppy thought, as his hands slid up and down her back, and so gently. She snuggled into his embrace, blocking out the cold, and looked up at him.

Mine, she thought with a smile. Nothing said commitment like participation in a dragon grudge match.

"I think you won me," Poppy said.

"Have I? Hmm. I suppose I'll have to figure out what to do with you then. You don't really match the furniture in the cottage." He lowered his head to brush her lips with his, once, and again. Then he let out a bewildered laugh, shaking his head.

"I can't for the life of me figure out what you see in me."

Poppy smirked up at him. "You're pretty sexy. And I like projects. Teaching you how to deserve me will give me something to do."

He laughed then, a throaty rumble that Poppy knew she would keep with her always. It was, she realized, the first time she'd really heard him laugh. Then he stepped away from her, and she shivered in the cold.

"Come on. If I'm going to get you to myself someplace where we're not freezing our asses off, we'd better get you home. Rowan and Gabriel are waiting for us."

Poppy looked at him and then at the edge of the outcropping where they were standing. "Um. Stairs?"

But when she looked back up, Lucien had vanished, to

be replaced by a huge black dragon. And as she watched, it kneeled down and looked at her expectantly.

"You've gotta be kidding me," she said. But when he just kept staring, she knew. It was time for a dragon ride in the magic mountains.

She climbed on awkwardly, finding a spot between his wings where she was reasonably sure she wouldn't fall to a screaming death, and sighed. She was a werewolf. Her boyfriend was a dragon. And she was about to ride him off into the sunset.

"It's a good thing I know so many other weirdos to tell this stuff to," Poppy announced. "Because all of my normal friends would just think I was on drugs." She couldn't wait to tell Cat about this. And she knew, without even asking, that Lucien was going to help Bastian. For the first time, she really felt like things were going to turn out right. Strange, she decided as Lucien's massive wings began to flap, but right.

"Let's go, hot stuff," she said, eager to get back and begin. "Tally ho."

Chapter 15

CAT AWOKE WITH A COUGH, CHOKING ON·THE DRY and dusty air that she assumed was just a lingering part of her nightmare. She'd been trapped in a crypt, and someone had been trying to seal her sarcophagus shut with her inside. Just a stupid dream, she told herself as she began to wake. No reason to worry. She'd certainly had stranger ones, usually involving her wandering around in public in her underwear.

For now, all she wanted to do was wake the rest of the way up and snuggle.

Upon opening her eyes, she realized that wasn't going to happen. She was either not yet awake, or she was in a lot of trouble.

Her eyes flicked around a small cell with walls of brownish stone and a floor of sand. Heavy metal bars dropped from floor to ceiling to block the arched opening into some sort of passageway. She was lying on the floor, arranged with her hands folded across her chest. As though, she thought with a chill, she were already dead.

As her mind moved from sluggish half-sleep to fully awake, confusion blossomed into full-blown terror. Where was she? And where was Bastian? Cat rolled to her side gingerly, afraid of what else might be in the cell with her, buried in the sand. But there seemed to be nothing, just her and the far-off echoes of a snapping sound that was the cracking of a whip, she realized after a moment.

Whip. Desert.

Her eyes widened as she realized where she must be, though she couldn't understand how it had happened.

"Ah, I see you're up." The voice startled her, and she jumped a little before turning her head to see who had come to the bars of the cell. So this was a *daemon*, she thought. The sight of him made her slightly sick to her stomach; all she could think of were the *Hellraiser* movies. There was something very Pinhead-esque about this creature, with his white skin and bald head. That, and the hungry look in eyes as red as blood. He gave her what she assumed was meant to be a pleasant smile, but it was all she could do to smother her scream as she got a look at his mouthful of sharp teeth.

Cat swallowed hard. "I," she began, and then had to clear her throat. The dust and faintly acrid air here seemed to have gummed up her lungs. "Where am I?" she asked, getting unsteadily to her feet. Her head had begun to ache dully, a hangover without the alcohol that normally preceded it. Her bare feet sank a little into the sand, and she realized she was still nude, as she had been in bed with Bastian. Left utterly exposed in this terrible place.

The *daemon* watched her dispassionately. He seemed disinterested in her physically at least, Cat thought. A small blessing, though she still wished she could cover herself. Everything about this place made her skin crawl and made her want to hide.

"You are now a guest in my home," the *daemon* crooned. "I am Jagrin, the one who brought you here."

He paused, his expression all dark amusement. He was playing with her, Cat realized. Like an animal toying with its prey before killing it.

"Don't tell me you're displeased with the accommodations?"

"Just please tell me why I'm here," Cat replied, wrapping her arms protectively around herself. "Is Bastian here too? Where is he?" It was eerily quiet here, enough so that even the crackling of the torches that lit the corridor could be heard as loudly as though they were right beside her.

Jagrin tipped his head to one side as he peered in at her, a slim, willowy being dressed all in gray. He steepled his long white fingers and pressed them to his mouth while he considered her. Finally, he decided to answer.

"Your Bastian is here, yes. Though he's getting… special… treatment at the moment. You'll see him soon, never fear."

Her heart began to pound in her chest. There was no mistaking Jagrin's meaning: Bastian was being tortured. It was, according to him, all these creatures seemed to like to do. An image flashed in her mind of Lucien, still wan and ill months after he'd been rescued from this place, and she shivered, though the chamber was warm. Her mate was here, somewhere in this awful place. Being hurt. And there was nothing she could do to stop it.

"Oh dear, you do look distressed," Jagrin murmured with a small smile. "I can't think why. You should be happy he's getting what he deserves after dragging you, a poor innocent, into this. He's a thief, you know. He stole something very precious from us. It can't go unanswered."

"I saw what you did to Lucien," Cat said, thinking that she had never in her life felt such complete loathing for someone as she did right now. The *daemon* was enjoying this; there was no question. And she had a terrible feeling that this was mere child's play to him.

"Yes? Then you've seen some of my most impressive handiwork, if I do say so myself. The dragon's wounds are mainly my doing, and I felt that I achieved an entirely new level of pain for him. I used a layering technique with the instruments I used... would you like to hear about it?"

Cat's gorge rose so that she couldn't even speak. She just shook her head and tried to block out the images she was getting. Jagrin chuckled.

"No? How sad. I've begun the same system with our mutual friend. I thought you'd be interested."

She stared at him in horror. It was too much to hope that he was bluffing just to hurt her.

"Where is he?" she asked, her voice breaking a little. Hot tears, more from abject terror than sadness, stung her eyes. But she refused to let them fall, refused to give this monster the satisfaction.

He seemed to know anyway.

"Poor little *arukhin*," he sighed. "Such sadness for one so unworthy of it. Well, if it's any consolation, you'll be reunited soon. The king is quite anxious to meet both of you. Of course, it will be a while, yet. We must make certain that the Dyim isn't able to use his wretched ability to jump from place to place. Can't have him leaving." He grinned, a terrible thing full of biting teeth. "Bleeding them always does the trick, you know."

Cat heard a choking sound, rife with disgust and pain. It was a moment before she realized it was coming from her. Jagrin closed his eyes and purred with pleasure.

"Mmm, how exquisite. I wish I could stay and chat, but I must get back to your beloved. I'll be back to fetch you, though. In the meantime, take heart, and please, make yourself comfortable. Look here, I even thought to gather clothing for you from that cozy little nest where I found both of you. Every creature comfort, do you see?" Jagrin disappeared from sight for a moment and reappeared with her bright yellow tote, stuffed with a pair of jeans she'd left on the floor and some sort of wrinkled shirt. The sight of her silly summer purse, which she'd bought because it was so cheerful, gave her a terrible feeling in the pit of her stomach. Which, she was sure was at least half the point.

He touched the middle bar, murmuring something in an odd, guttural language, and all the bars vanished at once. Jagrin walked in, and Cat shrank away, unable to stop herself. He stopped, watching her with those piercing eyes, and his mouth twisted upward into a cruel little curve.

"Afraid, my pretty little pet? Perhaps you should be. The closer I get, after all, the better I can see all of that beautiful, soft skin. You really should cover it, if you want to keep wearing it in this place." The pointed tip of his tongue flicked out to wet his lips, and Cat held her breath. So that was why he'd brought clothes… not for her, but to stop himself from ruining whatever was planned for later. Cat wondered frantically whether she should shift into a Wolf now, or wait and see if he backed off. She worried that Changing would only instigate a fight she didn't want, but she also worried that not Changing could cost her life.

Jagrin seemed to snap back to himself then, his expression reverting to the smooth, inscrutable one he'd worn when he'd arrived. He dropped the bag in the middle of the small cell and then backed away into the corridor. Instantly, the bars reappeared. Cat didn't move a muscle and just stayed near the back wall, afraid to say anything that would prevent his going away.

"Well, this has been fascinating, my lady, but I really must get back to your mate. Imagine how surprised we all were to find that he'd finally attached himself to someone… a bit too late to really enjoy, mind you, but we're all quite looking forward to the entertainment the both of you will provide. Until then, rest assured that he isn't very far away." He paused, and the malicious gleam came back to his gaze. "You know, sound carries quite well in the dungeons. Let his cries be like sweet music to you."

With an elegant bow, the *daemon* swept away. All that was left in front of her was her sad little bag and the blank wall beyond her cage, adorned only with a single flickering torch. Her body felt mired in quicksand as she struggled to take in the reality of her situation. She was trapped in the dungeons of the *daemon*, all as part of Bastian's punishment. She had no doubt they would hurt her and probably kill her eventually. Just as they would kill Bastian. And no one knew where they were to even contemplate saving them.

She was on her own.

Cat staggered to the bars of the cage to look out, only to feel biting pain when she gripped them. With a hiss, she pulled her hands away and watched, horrified, as blood ran freely down her arms from the twin slices in her palms. She made a soft keening sound as she stumbled backward and sank to her knees. The wounds began to heal almost immediately, as they always did with her kind. Still, to be opened up that way was revolting. And, she expected, only a hint of what was to come. What Bastian was going through probably right at this moment...

The desire to make a connection with him was sudden and overwhelming. Cat breathed deeply and closed her eyes, letting instinct take over as her mind sought his. This was an ability she knew he possessed, but she saw no reason why, with the strength of their bond, she couldn't sense him in the same way.

Bastian, she thought. *Please... where are you?*

And suddenly he was there, the *click* of connection like a bright starburst in her head as her own sensory impressions were joined by his. Now the tears did come, burning paths down her cheeks as she sat, helpless, and felt her mate's pain.

Aching, bone-deep, mind-numbing pain. It came from everywhere and nowhere, wracking a body that felt stretched to the breaking point, as though one more slice, even a gentle touch, might shatter it into a million pieces. Cat collapsed in her own cell, immobilized on the floor as she took in all of what he was feeling and searched for the spark of the man she knew. The man she hoped was still in this horribly damaged shell.

There was the faintest flicker of recognition.

Catriona?

Cat gave a soft cry. He was still there, however frayed the tether holding soul to body had become.

Bastian! I'm here!

She sent it with all the force she could, wrapped in all the love she had for him, hoping it would soothe even an ounce of what he was feeling.

You need to get out, he sent back, and she could feel the love he had for her in return, along with a desperate and wordless longing for things that would never be. He was dying more quickly now, not just from the effects of many years of having the *narial* tear at his soul, but from physical wounds that were slowly ceasing to heal the way they normally would. He was fading. Cat sensed it as though his body were her own. And God, how it hurt.

Please hang on, she thought. *Please, I'll find a way... please just hang on...*

Cat, he returned, groggier now. *Love you. Always.*

Bastian? Bastian! But there was nothing, just the sound of footsteps in the corridor, the *whoosh* of the bars evaporating, and a voice she recognized at once. Jagrin had left her and gone directly to Bastian. And she knew with a sick certainty that he had not even begun to truly work on him. Not even close.

"Hope you had a pleasant rest, my friend. I've just been to see your sweetheart, and I promised her some music. So let's begin, shall we?"

The connection snapped like gossamer thread, instant and brutal. Cat lay on the floor, tears streaming down her face. And for the first time in her life, she felt truly hopeless.

Then, far off down the corridor, the screaming began.

She curled into a ball, put her hands over her ears, and began praying for a miracle.

"They're gone."

Rowan rushed down the stairs toward the group gathered below, all the bright pleasure at Lucien's success vanished as the sweet scent of decay continued to hang in the air around her, continuing its assault on her senses. It was a smell she would know anywhere, inspiring sick dread. She joined Gabriel at the bottom of the steps, brushing her hand down his arm and trying to absorb some of his strength as she turned to address the others. It had always been her way to deal with things head-on and push through the worry with action.

But when something was wrong with anyone close to her heart, it was a completely different story. And this was her brother, her only brother, who had saved her life not just when he'd brought her to Earth to escape the dragon attack on their camp, but when he'd delivered her into the arms of her mate.

Her strong, silent brother, who had borne more than she could ever have guessed for so long. He had finally found his happiness, only to have it ripped away from him.

It was time to repay her debt to him. She just had to figure out how before it was too late.

Gabriel nodded, his green hunter's eyes somber. He knew.

"I can smell them."

Poppy, for whom Rowan had felt immediate affection because she had the looks and demeanor of a mischievous fairy, stayed close to Lucien. Rowan sighed, hating that her happiness had been cut so abruptly short. Poppy and Lucien had obviously formed a bond, and she above all welcomed it. It was time to begin to heal the wounds between dragon and *arukhin* now that Mordred was gone, and she couldn't think of a more fitting way to begin. But that new joy would have to wait. Poppy looked nervously from face to face, leaving her arms around Lucien's waist, and scented the air.

"What *is* that smell?" she asked, wrinkling her nose. "It smells like… like a…"

"Like a corpse," Lucien finished for her, looking steadily at Rowan. "They must have discovered who got me out of the dungeons."

It was an odd adjustment, thinking of her wayward half brother as an ally. But if the last few hours had proven anything, it was that he was certainly that. If only he had decided to relent and help Bastian sooner… but he couldn't have known that the *daemon* would appear so suddenly to get involved. And blaming the dragon for taking time to act with integrity was pointless. That Lucien seemed to be able to now, after a lifetime of behaving otherwise, was a triumph.

But she could see from the look on his face that he felt responsible.

Poppy's golden eyes widened in understanding. She looked up at Lucien, shaking her head. "Not the *daemon*. Not the ones who hurt you so badly." Her eyes darted from Rowan to Gabriel to Duncan.

And finally to Freddie, who'd held on to Poppy for a very long time when she'd returned. Something fundamental had begun to heal between Duncan and his brother, and between Freddie and his daughters. Rowan could feel it. But for now, he just watched his youngest daughter with obvious concern.

"You don't know." Poppy stammered, "You don't know what they did to him… you have no idea how sick he was… the scars that are left are nothing compared to the wounds they gave him, and there are still plenty of those… oh, God, are you sure?"

Rowan sighed and nodded. "Yes. I would imagine they'd be pleased to have both Bastian and your sister. It would add to their enjoyment."

"I'm going," Freddie said.

"What the hell do you mean, Fred?" asked Duncan. "You can't just run off into the bowels of the Blighted Kingdom from here. You don't know how, for one thing. And for another, those creatures will eat you alive!"

"Bull," Freddie replied, fisting his hands on his hips. "I can take care of my own. I'll tear up any who get too close." He glared at each of them in turn. "It's time I took a little responsibility for something. That's my daughter. I haven't been around for much, but I can damn well start making up for it now."

Lucien gave him a withering look. "I doubt Cat will appreciate seeing your remains after the *daemon* have finished with you."

"Now listen, you," snapped Freddie, stalking over to get in the dragon's face. "Just because you've saved one of my daughters doesn't mean you can talk to me that way."

"I'm afraid Lucien is right," Rowan interjected, and Freddie turned his furious gaze on her. She raised her hands, urging him to wait. "Hear me out. It's admirable that you want to go get her, but you need to understand, Freddie. You have no idea what these creatures are capable of. Their bodies are relatively fragile, but the dark magic the *daemon* practice makes each one as formidable as a small army. If we were just dealing with a few, that would be one thing. But Cat and Bastian have been taken into the heart of the Blighted Kingdom." She sighed. "Even if we all got there while they were still alive, this is the dead of night. The *daemon* thrive in darkness. It would almost certainly be our deaths."

It hurt her even to say the words, though Rowan knew they were the truth. She felt Gabriel's arm come around her, and she leaned into him, grateful for the support. Helplessness infuriated her, and this was as helpless as she'd felt in a very long time.

"Bastian got Lucien out," Duncan pointed out, his normally ruddy face pale.

"Bastian had the useful advantage of being able to jump from place to place and world to world in the blink of an eye," Lucien replied. "I remember telling him we were never going to make it out." He gave a soft, sad laugh. "He thought it was funny. I soon learned why, but if he hadn't had his gift, I would have been right. The *daemon* are far too good at what they do. That being said… I'd like to try."

"No, Lucien," Poppy insisted, looking at him beseechingly. "You just fought a bunch of dragons! I'm not stupid, I know you're nowhere near 100 percent anyway. You think you can fight off that many *daemon* all by yourself?"

"Poppy," said Rowan quietly, "Lucien is the only one of us who has any knowledge of the layout of the dungeons, which is undoubtedly where they're being held, if…" *If they're still alive*, she thought, but didn't finish the sentence. Even thinking it was bad enough.

"I'm responsible for the shape your brother is in," Lucien said. "They wouldn't have been able to catch him if he'd been stronger… I should have given my blood to him directly, instead of just leaving it with Cat's things in her room. If I can get to him somehow, I can at least make up for that."

Rowan looked at him, startled. "You left *what* in Cat's things?"

Lucien looked away, flustered. She attributed it to a lingering discomfort with being caught doing good things, which she imagined would go in time. But this, if he'd done what she thought he did, surprised her deeply.

"Before we left. I went upstairs and left a small vial of my, ah… blood. With a note. I assumed Cat would find it if I tucked it into the bag that held some of her everyday things." He slid his violet gaze back to Rowan. "I wanted to be sure I did what I ought where your brother was concerned. Just in case I didn't return from the mountains."

"Couldn't you have just let him have a bite before we left?" asked Gabriel, frowning.

Lucien looked at the ceiling and muttered, "I felt that might be somewhat awkward."

Rowan managed a smile for Lucien, grappling with the sense of opportunities lost. "It's okay, Gabriel. I don't think Lucien wanted to be nice in public. Which doesn't diminish the gesture at all."

Poppy looked at Rowan. "Are you sure she didn't find it? And that Bastian didn't take it?"

"I'm sure, Poppy," Rowan replied, hating the way that deflated her. "Lucien is right. The *daemon* would never have managed to take Bastian at full strength. His abilities, believe me, are something to see. And he can fight as dirty as any *daemon*." She smiled wistfully. "I made sure I taught him well."

"Well," Poppy insisted, "I want to make sure." She pulled away from Lucien and looked up at him. "Where did you put the vial?"

It was lovely and unexpected, Rowan thought, to see the way her half brother looked at Poppy. Gone was the desperate misery she remembered, replaced with genuine care and concern. And love. She was so happy that he'd found his heart.

If only she could truly enjoy it... but she'd lost an important piece of her own.

"She'd scattered so many things around the room that I worried it would get lost, so I just slipped it into some gigantic, hideous yellow bag she had resting on the dresser. It looked well used and had some money in it, so I assumed it was somewhere she would look before long if I didn't return. Particularly because I put the note and vial right on the top. Otherwise, I planned to talk to Bastian about it tomorrow."

Poppy looked at him, disgruntled. "You could have cleared a space."

Lucien looked back, unfazed. "I didn't have an hour."

"Children," Rowan warned them. "Go ahead and look, Poppy, if you like. Just don't get your hopes up, okay?"

Poppy bounded away and up the stairs, leaving the rest of them in silence. Duncan rubbed the back of his neck with his hand, and Freddie stared into the distance, lost in thought.

"You're really going to send him back in there?" Gabriel murmured into her ear. "He'll never make it."

"I know," Rowan sighed, turning to drop her head against her husband's chest. Even now, more than a year after they'd met, she found no greater comfort than in his strong arms. He had given her love and a beautiful child who had eyes just like his, and had helped her make a home amid the beautiful whirlwind that was life with the Dyadd Morgaine. He would also, she knew, give her his unvarnished opinion, whether or not she liked what he had to say. She often didn't. But sometimes, he was right.

"What do we do?" Rowan asked. "I can't let anyone else go. It would be madness. Even an army of *arukhin* couldn't fight the entire *daemon* tribe at full power. And by tomorrow…" She trailed off. In her heart, she knew that tomorrow they would be dead anyway.

Gabriel wound her in his arms and rubbed a hand over her back. "I think you know there's nothing we can do."

An excited yelp sounded from the top of the stairs, drawing everyone's attention away from their own dark thoughts.

"It's gone!" Poppy cried, and then raced down the stairs, plowing into Lucien with a ferocious hug and nearly knocking him over. "You put it in the right place. It's gone. She took it!" She leaped onto Lucien, wrapped her legs around his waist, and gave him a noisy kiss.

"Um, Poppy," Rowan said, laughing despite herself at the scene, "you honestly think your sister took her purse with her to the dungeons of the Blighted Kingdom?"

"Yes," Poppy said firmly, pausing to give Lucien another, sweeter kiss for good measure. From the way his eyes heated to a blazing glow, Rowan didn't think he looked very interested in putting her down, but he didn't stop her from sliding back to the floor.

"Sweetheart, I want to hope as much as you do," said Freddie. "But why the bloody hell would Cat take her credit cards with her?"

"I don't know," replied Poppy, putting her hands on her hips. "But I do know that she drags that stupid thing all over the place. It's an eyesore. I checked in my bedroom and Skye's, too. Where is Skye, by the way?" she asked, turning to Duncan with a frown.

"She was helping Malcolm fuss with little Ani," Duncan replied. "She's quite good with her, as it turns out. And Ani was throwing one of those nighttime fits I hear she's famous for."

Rowan smiled at the mention of her baby, suddenly overwhelmed with the desire to see her and hold her. She'd been grateful for the baby-sitting tonight, but she didn't like to be away from Aniela for long. But this needed to be dealt with first. And despite her resolve not to, she felt a faint glimmer of hope that Poppy might be right.

"Still, all we can really do is wait, Poppy," Rowan said. "Though I honestly think that if Cat knew about the vial, she would be standing here with us now."

"Yeah, I know," Poppy replied. "Which is why I need Skye."

The only person who seemed to understand that statement was Freddie, and his response was a slow, brilliant smile that reminded Rowan very strongly of his brother.

"I'll go get her, my darling girl," he said, striding over to her to pick her up and spin her around. Poppy looked surprised, but Rowan could see that the affection was welcomed. Freddie gave her a kiss on the forehead. "I've been a terrible fool in my life," he said to her before he left, "and a worse one with you and your sisters. But that changes tonight. No matter what happens. All right?"

Poppy just nodded, earning her another brilliant smile from her father before he ran off toward the back stairs, which were closer to the nursery.

"I think that was actually my dad," she said wonderingly.

"Why do we need Skye?" asked Rowan, too curious to wait and see.

"Oh," replied Poppy, looking back at her, her sparkling eyes making her look like a naughty faerie more strongly than ever. "We might be second-rate Witches R Us, but this is right up her alley. She normally doesn't like to get into people's heads because she thinks it's rude, but... well, you'll see."

Rowan blew out a breath and nodded, her heart beginning to pick up its pace. She already saw.

She just hoped it worked.

Chapter 16

CAT DIDN'T KNOW HOW LONG SHE LAY CURLED ON the sandy floor. She'd finally fallen asleep out of self-defense sometime after the aria of Bastian's cries had ceased, though she'd drifted off with her hands still covering her ears, and she knew instinctively she hadn't been out more than a half hour or so.

The yellow tote still sat untouched in the middle of the floor. She hadn't been able to move while Bastian was being hurt, and now she no longer cared whether she got dressed. How could it matter? She'd sought him again with her mind after there had been silence for a short while, but she couldn't seem to reach him.

She was going to die in this place. Cat knew it now. And though giving up hope went against everything she was, that was exactly what she was now doing. Eventually, she supposed, Jagrin would return and drag her away for the same treatment as Bastian. Possibly in front of an audience, since he'd mentioned her as entertainment. She might get to see Bastian then, though she wasn't sure how she would handle the sort of shape he was bound to be in.

If he was still alive. Which she doubted. The creatures must have overestimated how much he could take in his already-weakened state.

Cat.

She blinked, frowning. Why was she imagining her

sister Skye's voice? For comfort, probably, but then again, she might already be losing any grasp on reality.

Cat, can you hear me? I know you think you're imagining it... knock it off. Are you there?

Her eyes widened. Cat sat up, curling her knees against her. Could it possibly be...

Skye? Is that you?

Cat sat perfectly still, afraid that it was all in her mind. She knew that Skye had psychic abilities, but she was very funny about using them. So funny, in fact, that Cat wasn't sure how much or what kind of abilities her sister had. All Skye ever said was that messing in people's heads was unpleasant, and finally, after years of bugging to no avail, Cat had let it be.

The next thought came through loud and clear, and Cat could actually feel her sister's joy.

Cat, you're alive!

Pretty much.

Bastian?

Not sure.

After that came a rapid-fire volley of thoughts that left Cat's mind reeling and gave her a healthy new respect for Skye's telepathic ability. Images and words blended together so seamlessly that she wasn't sure, in the end, whether Skye had been talking or just showing. But either way, the result was the same. And the final thoughts were ones that Cat returned wholeheartedly.

Love you. Be safe. Come home.

Cat could feel her go, though the scent of her lingered in the dusty little cell. It was exactly what she had needed to bolster her spirits. If Bastian had managed to hang on, they might make it out of here alive after all.

She rose slowly and went to her tote, almost afraid to find out if it were really there. What if Jagrin had found and removed it? What if it had fallen out? She gingerly pulled out her jeans, her shirt. And there, beneath them, was a rolled-up bit of parchment with something hard inside. She touched it wonderingly with shaking hands. *This is real*, she told herself. *This is really real*. And she really didn't have time to mess around.

She dressed quickly, pulling on the jeans and the oversize T-shirt she usually slept in. All the better for concealing one precious prize.

If she ever saw Lucien Andrakkar again, the man was getting a big kiss.

Cat unrolled the parchment and read the short note with a thin smile. Then she tucked the small, dark blue bottle in the back of her jeans and buried the note beneath the sand.

And waited.

"Get up, Dyim. It's time to go."

Bastian opened his eyes slowly, his sight taking time to adjust to the small cell. He lay sprawled on the floor, every cell in his body awakening with shrieks and groans. He gritted his teeth, not wanting to give Jagrin the satisfaction of hearing any more of his pain.

He felt a vicious kick to his side, which had already been laid open and had only begun to knit itself back together.

"Get *up*, I said. You and your lover are about to meet the king. As well as your ancestors in the Higher Kingdom, of course, but let's take it one step at a time, shall we? Of course, your wretched *narial* seems to have vanished with the breeze… but perhaps it will grace us with its presence as well. The more the merrier."

The surprise was dull and barely penetrated the shock his body was in. The *narial* had left him? Somehow, he couldn't bring himself to be pleased, though it was probably a small blessing. If it had been hovering, he doubted he would have been able to move at this point. Of course, Bastian wasn't at all sure he could move anyway.

"Up!"

Slowly, and with excruciating pain, he raised himself to a sitting position. Blood began to run freely down his chest again, his movement opening his wounds. But there was nothing to be done for it. Somehow, he got his feet underneath him, catching sight of the numerous spatters of red on the dingy brown walls. It was all his, he knew.

And the creature responsible stood right in front of him, looking deeply pleased with himself.

"Ah, there you are. And looking quite well, I must say," he said, and chuckled softly. "Come, Bastian *an* Morgaine. We need to fetch your ladylove, and then we'll be on our way to the great hall."

Jagrin turned and Bastian started moving, one foot in front of the other. His vision kept doubling, and his legs threatened to go out from beneath him numerous times. But he needed to see that Cat was all right. If it was the last thing he did, and it probably would be, he would make sure she got out of here safely. Her refused to accept that it wasn't possible.

Down the corridor they went, Jagrin leading with a

bounce in his step. It was the closest he had ever seen a
daemon to true happiness, which boded very ill for him.
Bastian shuffled behind, bleeding, unclothed, but determined not to fall. Just a short way down the corridor,
Jagrin stopped in front of a cell, waiting for him.

It was so close to his own. With a sick certainty,
Bastian knew that Cat had heard every moment of
his torture.

Jagrin made the bars disappear with a touch of
his hand and turned to look at Bastian expectantly.
"Come and see, Dyim. Your mate has even dressed for
the occasion!"

He made it to the entrance, forgetting about his own
appearance in his hunger to see her. But the look of
absolute horror on her face reminded him all too late.

She looked beautiful, the only beautiful thing that
had probably ever touched this place. Her long dark
hair fell around her shoulders, and her eyes, glowing
faintly in the dim light, were puffy from crying. He saw
her fingers twitch, knew she wanted to come to him, to
touch him. But neither of them moved, not wanting to
invite any further torment from Jagrin.

The *daemon* watched them with eager interest.

"By all means," he said. "Have your reunion. It will
make it so much sweeter when you're parted. Well,
when parts of you are parted." He laughed, amused at
his own joke.

Bastian took one step in, then two. Cat simply stood
there, waiting for him. He'd expected her to rush to him,
but when she didn't, he closed the gap between them
quickly, wondering whether Jagrin had wounded her in
some way he couldn't see.

"Cat," he said softly, taking her in his arms.

"I don't want to hurt you," she replied haltingly, her voice breaking a little.

"You're not," he assured her, inhaling the sweet scent of her and burying his face in the dark silk of her hair. "This feels wonderful."

He felt her relax into him, bringing her arms around him, though her hands shook and she let them touch him only gingerly. He was glad for it, if only because he didn't want her to feel all the bloody whip scores across his back. He gave Lucien Andrakkar immense credit. He had stood this sort of treatment almost daily for over a year. How anyone endured that without their minds breaking was beyond his comprehension.

Suddenly he felt her slide something between them, a small glass bottle that had been warmed by her skin. He looked at her, and her eyes were perfectly eloquent.

Act normal. Don't say anything.

"This is all very precious, but we need to go in a moment," Jagrin said, sounding bored. "Wrap it up, if you would."

Bastian was suddenly grateful his back was to the *daemon*. He didn't know what Cat had procured for him, but he had complete faith that it was something that would help, at least in the short-term. There was a small cork in the top of the bottle, which she popped out smoothly with the tip of her thumb, her movements so fluid that he was sure Jagrin could see nothing but the two of them still locked in their embrace.

"I'm so glad you're all right," she sighed, concealing the bottle in her hand and reaching up to stroke his face. She managed to tip the contents quickly down his throat and then return the bottle to wherever she'd hidden it beforehand.

The instant the coppery tang of the blood hit his tongue, he knew what she'd given him. He closed his eyes against the strange sensations that flooded him, of power and incredible heat, fire, and darkness. There was a faint whiff of incense, and Bastian felt all of his wounds dissolve in one final flash of pain, burning as they closed and knit together at once.

Somehow, the dragon had come through. And the Goddess was indeed watching over him.

Thank you, Lucien, he thought.

It took Jagrin a moment to notice that anything was odd, but when he did, his high-pitched shriek was a far cry from the pleasant, conversational tone he'd taken just minutes before.

"What are you doing? What has she given you? Get away from her, get aw…"

Bastian turned on him, feeling his body shimmering with power in a way he hadn't in a very long time. He hissed, baring his fangs, and hurled his magic from his hands. Jagrin screamed as the beams connected with him, smoke beginning to rise from his chest. He collapsed to his knees, spitting blood onto the floor.

He was about to finish him when Cat strode over and punched him in the head as hard as she could. Jagrin's head snapped backward, his eyes rolled back in his head, and he went the rest of the way down to sprawl on the floor, unconscious.

"I don't know about you, Jagrin," she said, "but I found that highly entertaining."

"Come on," Bastian said. "Take my hand."

"Are we going home now?" Cat asked.

But Bastian shook his head. "Not quite yet," he said. "I need to finish this. For good. But you'll need to Change. You'll be safer that way."

She raised her eyebrows. "So… you want me to bite ankles or something?"

"Anything you feel like doing," Bastian replied, glad that her sense of humor was still intact. "But you may feel somewhat different as a Wolf here. More powerful. That's what I've heard anyway. If you do, use it."

"Ah. You want me to go ballistic on the *daemon*," she said with a smile.

"There are two of us and hundreds of them," Bastian said. "Please, by all means, go ballistic."

"You know, I'm pretty nonviolent," Cat said. "But after what they did to you, and to Lucien… I'm so on it." After pressing a quick, hard kiss to his lips, Cat quickly shed her clothes and shifted in a matter of seconds from human to a sleek black Wolf, large enough that she came to mid thigh, but slim and built for speed.

Bastian took a deep breath. They had to win. There were no other options.

"Here we go," he murmured.

He went to one knee beside Cat, running a hand over the silken fur on her head, and in a quick flash, they stood in the great hall of the *daemon* king. Their sudden appearance drew surprised cries from the various *daemon* lords at court, and the occupants of the hall scattered as Bastian made his way toward the creature who sat on the throne.

Someone began to recite a spell, but Bastian pushed his hand in that direction. The offending *daemon* went flying, and Bastian smiled. He felt all of his latent ability unlocking within, all of the power accessible in a way it had never been. Everything, even abilities he hadn't known he possessed, was available with a thought.

Cat stalked at his side, baring her teeth at anyone who caught her eye and growling low in her throat.

"Stand aside, all of you," the king cried, rising from his throne with a hungry grin. "This battle, I believe, belongs to me!"

"Cadmus of the *daemon*!" Bastian bellowed, his voice resonating throughout the hall.

"Yes," hissed Cadmus, descending the steps to meet him in the large space that had cleared in the middle of the hall. "I know you, Bastian *an* Morgaine. You look much like the man who first bore my wrath, the wretched High Mage of the *Athin* who denied me my love. Now you are the last, and I will finish what I started."

"Wrong. Tonight you descend to the Lower Kingdom to burn for eternity," Bastian replied.

"We will see," snarled Cadmus. He spun and hurled barbed bolts of flame red from his hands. Bastian leaped out of the way, Cat leaping in the other direction, as the bolts hit the floor and burst into a tower of flame before vanishing.

Bastian hit the ground and rolled, flinging daggers of ice from where he landed before bouncing back to his feet. Cadmus deflected each one, hurling them back with amazing force. They shattered on the ground around Bastian, smoke hissing from them as they dissolved.

The battle was engaged, lightning bouncing from the walls of the chamber as he and the *daemon* each fought for the upper hand.

"Is this all you have for me, you fool?" asked Cadmus, laughing. "You should have let Jagrin kill you. It would have been less embarrassing." He hurled a volley of tiny, exploding balls of electricity at Bastian that burst far too close to him for comfort. Bastian returned fire, producing whirling, jagged discs from the air to throw back at him.

One sliced through the edge of Cadmus's sleeve, turning the fabric black with the creature's blood. He screamed his anger.

"First blood, *daemon*," Bastian growled. "That was for my father."

Cadmus's lips peeled back in a hideous snarl. "Your father was a fool, as was all his line before him! They deserved what they got! And you are no better, *boy*!"

A blast of air knocked Bastian off his feet, throwing him across the room to the approving hisses of the *daemon* court. He landed with a surprised grunt, the wind momentarily knocked out of him. He knew the next blow would be quick behind it, though, so Bastian rolled to the side and narrowly missed being beheaded by a curved blade of energy that burst into blue flame upon hitting the stone. He leaped back his feet, sweeping his arm so that a giant white arc of power flowed from him to rush across the room like a wave. It crashed into Cadmus, taking him down.

Bastian barely registered the strange cries and screams that began to echo around him, so intensely focused was he. Cadmus, however, took his focus off him for a split second, and his smooth face contorted into a mask of fury.

"No! *No!* Kill her. Destroy the bitch! *Don't let her near you!*"

Bastian didn't dare take his eyes from the king, but at the periphery of his vision, he saw a massive black shape, even larger than he remembered Cat being in her Wolf form, plowing through the crowd of *daemon* with a vengeance. The bodies of those unfortunate enough to be in her path were thrown into the air, shaken in jaws like a steel trap, and discarded. Several seemed to have been tossed purposely at the feet of the king.

Bastian bared his fangs with pleasure. She had left the battle with Cadmus to him, but Cat appeared to be coming into her own as a fighter. And not only was it keeping his back covered, it was distracting Cadmus, who was watching his court be single-handedly annihilated.

Cadmus glanced away again, and Bastian took the advantage. A razor-sharp blade of ice erupted from his hand as he flung it toward the *daemon* king. The creature's red eyes widened a split second before he was again thrown backward, a shower of black blood flying into the air on contact. The king was almost done. Almost. Cadmus had ruled for five hundred years for a reason.

Cadmus staggered back to his feet, black blood dribbling from the long gash in his neck. It was deep, Bastian knew. He hoped too deep to heal.

"Where is the *arukhin* bitch?" Cadmus hissed, looking around the room. "I will tear her legs off and feed them to my lords while you watch, Dyim. Are you so weak that you cannot fight for yourself? No matter. I will kill both of you. In the hundreds of years I have sat on this throne, there are no tricks I haven't seen. Enjoy what blood you have spilled, Bastian. You will never defeat me."

A strange vibration filled the air then, thrumming so

that it echoed off the walls and stirred even the ground beneath. It was a deeply unsettling noise, making Bastian's skin crawl. And it was somehow familiar.

"Sire!" Jagrin came running toward them, his face still spattered with his own blood, his tunic shredded across his chest to reveal burned flesh. But his eyes were alight with feverish joy.

He barely spared Bastian a glance as he rushed past, coming to a halt right at Cadmus's side. The thrumming continued and became a horrible, hungry moaning. In an instant, Bastian knew what it was.

"Catriona!" he roared, and she appeared like a ghost, peeling away from one of the pools of darkness by the wall where she had been waiting to make another strike and instead rushing to his side. The floor began to shake harder, and the remaining *daemon* shrank back, looking around uncertainly.

"Sire, it is the *narial*! It insists you have stolen its right to kill the Dyim!"

Cadmus looked at Jagrin, stunned. "It defies me? You told me it had returned to the pits… no *narial* has ever defied a *daemon*!"

"This one does," growled Jagrin, backing away with a terrible smile. "And I lied. Fear not, Cadmus. Your name will be revered for ages when I am king."

"You… you will never be king," spat Cadmus. "Filthy traitor, I would have raised you above all the other lords…"

"You will," replied Jagrin, "with your death."

Cadmus looked as though he wanted to say more, but then he caught sight of the inky pool of shadow slithering across the floor. The torches flickered, their flames burning very low so that the entire chamber was plunged into near darkness. The *daemon* looked truly ghoulish now, white faces stark in the absence of light. And amazingly, rather than looking afraid, Bastian saw that they looked interested and excited. They stirred and shifted as they watched the shadow approach Cadmus, an electric murmur running through the crowd.

The shadow rose from the ground to stand at a level with Cadmus. Its voice sounded dragged from the depths of the Earth. And even Cadmus shrank before it.

"*I warned your messenger what would happen if you denied me,*" it said.

"It is my right to kill him. The insult was against me, not you! I command you to step aside, shadow. The curse is at an end. You are free!"

The *narial* gave its vile, wet chuckle. "*I have always been free, Cadmus. The shadows do not serve you. Nor will we continue to give you the impression that we do. We tire of the* daemon *plague in our land.*"

"Your land? This is our land!" Cadmus roared. "You remain by our leave!"

"*Oh, I think not. Our kind has been here since before your gods and goddesses descended from the Higher Kingdom. We are eternal. And the desert has always been ours.*"

It reared up and, with a terrible sound like thousands of voices screaming in unison, coiled around Cadmus so that he disappeared into its blackness. For a moment, his scream rose above all the rest. Then, silence. The shadow shrank into something resembling the shape of a man again, and turned toward Bastian as Cadmus's lifeless body collapsed to the floor with a dull thud.

"*Now for you*," it said.

"Not this time," Bastian replied. He let the power well up within him, filling him, coursing through his veins, and pulsing outward to surround him in a nimbus of white fire.

The *narial* screamed its battle cry, and Bastian rushed into it headlong. The scream turned quickly from fury to agonizing pain as Bastian stood in the middle of its darkness, letting it catch fire around him. It went up in blue-white flames, burning so brightly that Bastian had to shut his eyes against the glare, before what had once been shadow fell to the ground around him as so much dust.

There was silence for a moment, none of the *daemon* making a sound. Bastian walked slowly back to Cat, feeling his glow beginning to fade. He was suddenly dizzy with relief and incredibly tired. All he wanted to do was go home and curl up with Cat. His future. The woman he could now make his wife.

"King!" cried Jagrin. "I am king! Bow before me, *daemon*!"

Cat padded forward to meet him halfway, ignoring the creatures that slowly began to congregate before the throne. On Earth, she had been magnificent. On Coracin, she fairly glowed with power, larger and more imposing than he had ever seen her. She had tapped into her power.

Bastian wanted to shout his thanks to the Higher Kingdoms. This was yet another way in which she had helped to save him. He swore he would never take such luck for granted.

Just as Cat reached him, the rumbling began again,

even louder and more violent this time. Tortured, hungry moans filled the air, the sound of hundreds, perhaps thousands, of *narial* arisen from the pits to reclaim their home. Bastian paused for just a moment to watch Jagrin's look of triumph turn to horror as he saw what was coming through the door, seeping through the walls, and rising from the floor itself.

"No! *No!*" he screeched. "This is *my* kingdom now, *mine!*"

"I think the *narial* disagree," Bastian said to Cat as he leaned down to put his hand on her fur. "Now let's go home."

And in a flash, they were there.

Bastian slept for the better part of a week, rising only occasionally to eat or go to the bathroom. He didn't return to the little cottage in the woods, preferring to stay in the manor house with his family close at hand, and Cat even closer.

They lounged in bed together early one morning, a week to the day after their harrowing adventure in the Blighted Kingdom, Cat curled up against him with her head on his chest while Bastian stroked her hair. It was, Cat had recently decided, one of her favorite places to be on Earth… or anywhere else, for that matter.

"What are you thinking about?" she asked with a yawn. She felt completely relaxed, with not an ounce of tension anywhere in her body. But, she thought with a lazy grin, that was one of the many benefits of being awakened by a guy like Bastian. It was impossible to be tense after being made love to three times in a row.

"Hmm? Oh, nothing," he murmured, his voice rumbling against her ear. "Well, nothing of much importance. Just this and that. The sort of home we'll build together. Buying a Harley. Getting you a proper ring."

Cat propped herself up to look at him, huffing a strand of hair out of her face and making him smile. He looked different, she thought. Lighter, somehow, as though the weight of the world had been lifted from his shoulders. His eyes had lost the sad, haunted look they had sometimes carried. And there was something more, something she couldn't quite put her finger on. Maybe, she thought, it was just that he was finally at peace and happy. But whatever it was, she was absolutely certain she was never going to get tired of looking at Bastian *an* Morgaine.

"A proper ring, huh?" she asked. "I think I like the sound of that."

"I thought you might," he replied, tucking an errant lock of hair behind her ear. "I know just the one I want to give you, too. It's one my mother often wore. I've just got to sneak off one of these days without you knowing." He chuckled.

"And thus, the surprise is ruined," groaned Cat. "Way to go." She smacked him in the chest.

"It's been hard to do anything secretly anyway, considering how much time you and I seem to spend up here." He chuckled, blocking her next shot.

Cat teased him with a mock frown. "You complaining?"

"Never. I'm glad you prefer me to jewelry."

She leaned down for a long, slow kiss that warmed her from the top of her head to the tips of her toes.

When she finally pulled back, his eyes were glowing the way that she loved. The way that meant he was going to demonstrate again why they hadn't been out of the bedroom much recently. Cat reached up to play with his hair, still mussed from sleep.

"I'm also cool with the Harley, as long as I get to ride on it. And sing bad songs from *Grease 2*."

He raised his eyebrows. "Do I need to know what this is?"

"You're going to find out. It's on my list of essentials for your education in Earthly pop culture."

Bastian frowned at her. "Hey, I know pop culture."

Cat snorted. "Just because you have now watched *Transformers* three times with Gabe and Gideon does not mean you know pop culture. It just means you like to watch giant robots blow things up, which is a universal guy thing anyway. Sorry."

"Ah. Well, I'm sure you'll set me straight," he chuckled.

"Yeah. You can head for Gideon's house when you need your explosion fix." She settled herself back against his chest with a sigh. "You're really sure you're on board with moving to the wilds of northern New York?"

"It sounds like a great idea to me. I could use a fresh start. And there's lots of snow for me to play with, apparently. Why, having second thoughts?" he asked, a hint of concern creeping into his voice. He'd broached the subject two nights ago after having a long, private talk with Gideon, who she was coming to like very much. He might look intimidating, but he was as prone to amusing jackassery as his brother, which suited her just fine.

His wife, Carly, ran a successful romance bookshop

in a little lakeside town called Kinnik's Harbor, while Gideon and a group of friends renovated old houses and sold them at a profit. He was nearly done with one just a few blocks from them and had asked Bastian if the two of them might be interested in it.

Cat was still surprised that they were. She'd thought of moving out of Southern California dozens of times, but it was familiar, and her sisters were there. Still, when Bastian had asked, it had seemed like just the right thing. Everything was changing, and for the better: Poppy and Lucien appeared to be madly in love, talking about staying in Scotland and possibly even building on the grounds of *Iargail*. She was fairly sure that Lucien was getting twisted pleasure out of the thought of haunting Duncan for an extended time. Duncan, for his part, was still weighing the benefits of having a resident guard dragon against the drawbacks of the constant presence of Lucien's mouth. Freddie was making noises about an extended vacation as well and driving his brother halfway insane with his newfound interest in all things MacInnes. Even Skye was different, if only in that she had finally begun to seem comfortable with who and what she was. There would be someone amazing for her, too, Cat thought. She was sure of it. Though if it turned out to be another dragon, she thought her uncle might have to go on blood pressure medication.

No, she was ready for an adventure. And she was ready to start the next chapter of her life with Bastian.

"I can't wait," Cat said, and meant it. "Even though I'm not exactly a snow bunny. I make no guarantees about my ability to walk on ice, in Wolf or human form, but I can't wait."

Bastian laughed. "I suppose I'll just have to wander around behind you and catch you when you fall down."

"Hmm. You're going to be awfully busy then," said Cat, nuzzling his chest and feeling her eyes begin to droop again. "Too bad. Carly says she'll pay you to stand in the window of her shop and bring in droves of salivating women. I was thinking you should consider it. But I like the idea of you chasing me around to drop a pillow under me every time I tip over even better."

"Ah, Carly. I think I respectfully declined that one. I understand that some of those women are noted ass-grabbers." He wrapped his arms around her and sighed contentedly. "I may work for Gideon. We'll see. After hordes of *daemon* and years of being cursed, I'm not too worried about the horrors of finding gainful employment."

They lay together for some time that way, drifting back toward sleep in one another's arms, until Cat drowsily asked a question she hadn't yet broached with him. She hadn't wanted Bastian to have to relive the horrors of the night in the dungeons, worried that even though he bore no outward scars from the experience, he might have inner wounds that needed time to heal. He was so strong, though, she had begun to doubt even that. And this, she felt she could ask.

"Do you think they're all gone? The *daemon*?"

He considered the question, stroking a hand absently down her back. Finally, he said, "I do wonder about that sometimes. I can't imagine there aren't a few, but who knows? And the *narial* are just as bad, in their way. But maybe they'll just sink back into their pits and enjoy the quiet, at least for a while. The important thing is that the *daemon* tribe as a force is gone. For a long time, and maybe forever. I think my father would be proud that I helped with that."

Cat shifted in his arms to pull him against her, still marveling at the way he felt like the other half of herself. He was handsome and strong and incredibly brave. But most of all, he was just Bastian. Her Bastian. They'd been given a chance, whether it was by God or Bastian's Goddess or Fate or sheer luck. And she intended to make the most of it.

"I know he'd be proud," she said, and then claimed his lips in a gentle kiss.

"I love you," she murmured against his lips.

"And I love you," he returned, repeating it with every touch of his mouth against hers.

"I love you. I love you. I love you."

And as they came together, bodies twining together until they were one, Cat wondered at the strange and beautiful twists that life could take. She'd been born with magic and gifted with incredible strength and extraordinary powers. But with Bastian, she finally understood that the strongest magic of all was also the simplest.

In the wild Scottish Highlands, with her love in her arms, Cat felt it strong and true.

It was the magic of the heart.

Acknowledgments

As always, this book could never have made it out of my imagination and into the world without the love, support, and encouragement of my family. From my overworked husband, who took on many extra hours of child-chasing duty, to my sweet kids, who kept a check on my progress and made me cards to celebrate the writing of those lovely words *The End*, I was constantly spurred to keep going, even on the toughest days when my fingers seemed stuck together and my brain was mush.

Thanks to my mom and dad, my grandparents, and my wonderful in-laws for still getting excited every time they see my books in a store and reminding me how amazing it is that I've made it this far. Many thanks to my fabulous agent, Kevan Lyon, my invaluable sounding board and font of all publishing knowledge, who has never steered me wrong. A thousand thank-yous to my editor, Deb Werksman, for the sharp eyes and excellent instincts that I, and my characters, depend on! Thanks to my author buddies—from my wonderful, crazy-talented critique partner Katey Coffing and our gang of Writers In Pajamas, to my funny and fabulous Sourcebooks Sisters—for your friendship.

Finally, my great and heartfelt thanks to all of my readers, for letting my characters into your hearts and, in many cases, taking the time to tell me that you enjoyed the journey. Spinning tales for a living has been a life-long dream of mine, and I'm honored beyond words to be sharing my stories with all of you.

For a look at how it all began, read
on for excerpts from

call of the highland moon

DARK HIGHLAND FIRE

Now available from Sourcebooks Casablanca

From

call of the highland moon

Gideon turned at the edge of the clearing and streaked swiftly off into the sheltering woods, melting noiselessly into the shadows and trees. He was miles from the inn at this point. It wasn't in his nature to shy from a fight, but Gideon instinctively understood his vulnerability in this situation. He was alone, in unfamiliar territory, facing at least two adversaries stalking him with the intent to kill. Best to draw them into the open, take the advantage. He would not take the blood of another Wolf if he had a choice. It was how he had been raised, how he had been trained. No, the most important thing now was to alert the Pack, to let them know what wheels had been set in motion. Gideon might be the biggest obstacle to a change in power, but he was not the only one.

Speed, stealth before strength.

Keep safe the Stone.

Protect the Pack.

He flew silently over the snow, sensing, rather than hearing, that he was being pursued. His nose told him that he wasn't far from civilization—only a mile or two. He pushed himself harder, though he was already moving at a speed that could only be called supernatural. The smell of humans grew stronger, and faint lights began to flicker through the trees in the distance. He was going to make it out.

Hurry home…

Hurry home…

The first blow forced the breath from his lungs, knocking his feet from under him in mid-lope with unexpected force. Gideon skidded a short ways on his side, then scrambled quickly to his feet. He whipped around to face his adversary, hackles raised, a vicious snarl tearing from his throat. The smaller, stockier gray wolf faced him, yellow eyes seeming to taunt him, growling low in response. Gideon narrowed his eyes, claws lengthening, digging into the snow. This was no Wolf he'd ever seen, but a Wolf just the same.

No, not the same, Gideon thought, bristling. There was something off, something not right about this creature. He was smaller, but somehow radiated the sort of power only seen in the purest bloodline, a supernatural strength that threatened violence in the smallest flicker of movement. Gideon sensed this, and the oddity of it had him struggling to maintain his focus. But what was worse, what roiled his insides and screamed at him to *retreat*, to *run*, was the smell. It poured off of the Gray, befouling the air of the forest, burning Gideon's nostrils. It seemed to radiate from within him, from the strange collar that glinted from around the beast's neck, stinking of some unfamiliar and horrifying madness. It was an assault to his senses such as he'd never endured before.

He was suddenly determined to eradicate it at the source.

Gideon's muscles tensed, ready to spring, to rip, to tear. Then, suddenly, the growling grew louder, and louder again as two more Wolves padded menacingly out of the darkness. Gideon stilled, drawing himself up, staring down his would-be attackers. These were unfamiliar Wolves as well, and again, not Pack. Weaker. And yet their scent marked them as not entirely unfamiliar, either.

It seemed that his cousin had decided to break more than one sacred rule.

And, as usual, he had sent others to do his dirty work.

The jagged scar that crossed Gideon's right eye twinged a bit at the memory of Malachi's *last* deception, the wound inflicted by a Pack male who had been poisoned with tales of Gideon wooing his mate. It had been a painful lesson, but Gideon had tried to be thankful that he had at least kept his eye in the learning of it.

First, no harm against thy brother Wolf.

He'd always thought that Malachi had merely intended him maimed, a crime bad enough. Now, in this circle of Wolves with malice hanging heavy in the air, he was no longer so sure. From the ravenous look in these new werewolves' eyes, maiming was kind compared to what they intended.

Traitors.

The Wolves began to circle him, teeth bared, eyes fixed upon Gideon. For his part, Gideon remained immobile, head high, letting his disdain for them show. In this form, he was magnificent, very obviously of the Alpha bloodline with his broad, powerful chest, long, muscular limbs, and more than that, the fact that he stood a head taller than the others. He was calm, focused. He had been trained to fight. It was in his blood. If he had no choice but to use that skill against his own kind, then so it was. These were not of his Pack, and they were no brother Wolves of his.

But he had never imagined that he would have to stand for his Pack, and for the Stone, so far from either one.

When it happened, it was fast. The Gray, who seemed to be the leader, uttered a short, sharp bark, and all three set upon Gideon at once. All the years of sparring with Duncan and his two lieutenants, Ian and Malcolm, came rushing back as he fought them off. Rolling, slashing at vulnerable flesh, sinking his fangs past fur and into skin. For a time, there seemed to be nothing to Gideon's world but a snarling, snapping mass of claws and teeth, shot through with bright flashes of pain and brief moments of triumph when he caused more than he had received. Impressions flickered, vanished, raced through Gideon's consciousness as he fought to stay alive.

Hind claws finding purchase in a soft underbelly. A shriek of pain at the snap of his teeth. Vicious, tearing pain across his shoulder. And always, through the haze of blood and pain, the mocking gleam of yellow eyes like, and so very unlike, his own.

At last, Gideon managed to throw one of them off balance long enough to sink his fangs into the ragged brown fur at its throat. With no regret, he tasted blood as he found the jugular. The world finally seemed to still and right itself as Gideon gave the limp carcass a final shake and then tossed it from his jaws to land at the feet of the Gray, whose bloodied, battered sides were heaving as much as Gideon's own.

Gideon snorted out a hot mist of breath in the frigid air, hunching for attack, ready to finish it. It appeared that this Wolf was no more invincible than any other, after all. They regarded one another for a moment that spun out into an eternity, the only sound the soft moan of the wind picking up as the first flakes of snow began to fall, in slow motion, through the canopy of trees from the endless blackness above.

The stillness was finally shattered when the Gray bared his teeth at Gideon, then limped slowly backward into the shadowy trees. In seconds, first he, then the angry violet glow of the chunk of stone dangling from his collar, disappeared from sight. His one remaining companion was decidedly worse off. Ginger fur matted with blood, it followed as quickly as it could, dragging a broken hind leg as it went. Gideon remained immobile as he watched them go, sensing their message as clearly as if it had been spoken aloud.

This isn't over.

No, Gideon though, curling his lip. It sure as hell wasn't. And damned if he was going to let them go without finishing it. But it wasn't until he took a step forward—and the trees in front of him blurred and swam—that he realized the extent of his own injuries. He might have given better than he got, but it had still been three sets of fangs and claws to his one, and all of those had done some damage despite his best efforts. As Gideon stood there, swaying slightly, he licked the foam from his muzzle and tasted blood. As dread formed a leaden ball in his stomach, he looked down only to see more blood dripping from his chest, his legs, and his underbelly, slowly turning the snow beneath him crimson.

Hell.

He took another tentative step forward, and his vision

rimmed with black. *A draw after all*, he thought ruefully. He'd lost too much blood. If it had been anything but other werewolves, he could have rested, assured that he'd heal quickly enough to stanch the lifeblood slowly exiting from his wounds. But it was different among his own kind. It was why they were forbidden from harming one another, why he still carried the scar of that surprising attack so many years ago when the rest of his body carried not a mark. Their healing powers worked much more slowly when the wounds were inflicted by one of their own, and sometimes, as in the case of Gideon's scar, not quite as well.

Or not at all.

Gideon knew that if he didn't want to die there in the snow, he was going to have to find help, and fast.

Keep safe the Stone.

Protect the Pack.

It took a Herculean effort to start forward, toward the lights in the distance. And as he half-walked, half-dragged himself in their direction, it became harder and harder to keep at bay the blackness that wanted to consume him.

Hurry home, the voice in his mind whispered, mocking his efforts.

Later, Gideon would think that he must have blacked out and somehow still kept moving. It seemed as though one moment he was still deep in the pine trees, and the very next, he was lurching through the tidy backyards of a small town, trying desperately to stay clear of the bright glow of windows, of barking dogs who smelled wounded animal and blood. He raised his head as much as he could and scented the air for what seemed like the hundredth time, confused in his weakened state.

He was unsure whether he should attempt a Change, whether he even had the strength to make it through one, unsure of where to look for help in this unfamiliar place. He whined softly, his once glossy black fur now clumped and matted, exhausted from making it even this far. Despite his best efforts, he was going to have to lie down; and out here, with the storm coming in, Gideon was fairly sure that once that happened, he wouldn't be getting back up.

Then, just as his legs began to buckle for the last time, Gideon caught the faintest scent of… *something*. It was barely there, carried on a breath of arctic wind, but it was compelling enough to bring the great head up again, his nose searching the air greedily for another trace of it. What was it? So familiar… like berries and cream, with a hint of vanilla… and perhaps a dash of spice, something almost exotic.

And just like that, Gideon's pain faded around him as he concentrated on that wonderful, delicious smell, a scent both familiar and unknown, yet holding some mysterious promise of coming home. Instinct took over—propelling him, driving him. He put one paw in front of another, then again, and then slowly, deliberately, he was moving again, the intense need to find out the source of the intoxicating aroma overriding his body's every command to shut down.

Left, through a darkened churchyard.

There, a hint of cinnamon!

Now right, down a wide alleyway.

So much stronger, and impossibly, irresistibly sweet!

At last, all reserves of strength drained, Gideon got as close as he could to the source: a small red door, on which hung a simple holly berry wreath, that led into an old brick building from the alley. The door filled his vision. Its cheery color was a beacon that seemed, at that moment, made solely for the purpose of leading him out of the cold. In his delirium, Gideon lost all sense of time and place, hanging onto the promise carried on a whiff of arctic breeze.

Home?

He paused there, on the soft rubber mat, and willed everything he had left into raising one shredded paw to scratch feebly at the door. Once. He heard a voice from within, but it stayed distant. Twice, and then once more Gideon scratched, now whining pitifully as he sank to the ground, defeated.

Guard... Protect... Home...

Gideon's mind struggled, but he felt unconsciousness barreling toward him like a freight train. In those seconds before the blackness claimed him, Gideon rolled his eyes heavenward and said a silent prayer for a mangy, flea-bitten cur such as himself to be taken Home.

God, however, apparently had His own ideas. At that moment the red door swung open, bathing Gideon's broken form in soft, warm light as a feminine gasp of shock reached his ears. Hope kindled in Gideon briefly before he finally floated away on a dark and distant sea. His last conscious impression was that of being wrapped, head to toe, in that no-longer-elusive scent, rich with caramel and cocoa and so, so many of his favorite things. He moaned again faintly, this time with pleasure.

A small, graceful hand touched the side of his face gently, light as the brush of a butterfly's wing.

"Oh, you poor thing," sighed a voice like music.

Gideon turned his muzzle into the hand, seeking comfort, and then he knew no more.

From

DARK HIGHLAND FIRE

"Hey babe, wake up. You're next."

"Shit," she muttered, using one of her favorite human curse words as a curvy brunette wearing nothing but a G-string brushed past her, jerking her instantly back to reality.

Memories of spiced summer air and forest drums vanished instantly, leaving her with nothing but stale cigarette smoke and the opening notes of Rob Zombie's "Living Dead Girl."

It was just another Saturday night in Reno. And like it or not, she was on.

Rowan stalked out onto the strobe-lit stage, mile-high stilettos clicking in time with the thudding beat of the music. Wild howls and catcalls erupted from the packed floor of the club at her entrance, the individual faces of the usual motley crew of patrons obscured somewhat by the haze of white pouring from the smoke machine. The fistfuls of green already waving in the air, however, were readily apparent. And that, she reminded herself, was all that truly mattered these days.

Survival.

Even if it involved red satin hot pants and corsets.

She prowled her way to one of the golden poles that flanked the stage and wrapped one long, shapely leg around it. Rowan coiled sinuously around it, arching so that the long red mane of her hair nearly brushed the floor. She spun, slid, gyrated to the music, expertly whipping the crowd into a boiling frenzy of lust. They hung on her every smoldering glance, shuddered each time she bared her fangs in a seductive snarl. Simple men, powerless before wicked beauty, nearly coming to blows in the crush to give her their money.

Rowan accepted it all with a boredom that was increasingly edged with despair.

It wasn't the work, really. Her kind had always reveled in the unusual beauty of their physical forms, wielding that power like a sword when need be. If these human men really wanted to throw precious money at her for doing nothing more than dancing around without any clothes on, drooling over a body that would bring them a universe of pain should they ever attempt to touch it... well, that was their stupidity, to her way of thinking. She felt no shame, though she was often annoyed. But the monotony of it, night after night in this dingy place, all the while not knowing if she would ever be able to return home or whether there was anything to return to, ate at her very soul. She worried that in time the fundamental decay would begin to show. But for now she could only wait, work. And worry.

In the meantime it was just unfortunate that she'd grown to hate this damned song so much. Rowan watched a big bald-headed man with numerous tattoos attempt to pound a scrawny youth into the ground to get nearer the stage and wished desperately that Zin, the manager, would let her switch to something she could lose herself in. As it was, the fights were the only things that kept her from falling asleep in mid-wiggle. But according to him, her Stripping Vampire routine had put his sleazy little dive on the map, and she was going to keep doing it until either the men tired of it or her legs fell off.

Since neither thing had happened yet, she was stuck being The Pretty Kitty's own Living Dead Girl. But that didn't mean she had to like it.

Just as Zin didn't like her conditions for continued employment, Rowan thought with a smirk as she worked the crowd. No lap dances. No private shows. In fact, no anything she didn't specifically feel like doing. She showed up, she did her thing, she went home, end of story. Lucky for her that was all it took to bring in more money than all the other dancers combined.

Lucky for him he had a blood-drinking demigoddess desperate enough to continue to do the job. Much to Rowan's chagrin, in this realm neither her considerable talent nor her legendary beauty was any match for having gone to the place humans called "college." And what would have been her preferred methods of getting what she needed had been flatly condemned by her brother as *way too conspicuous*, seeing as they tended to involve flaming infernos of destruction.

But she could dance. And she could remove her clothes.

And whether or not it had been the best decision, here she had been for the nine months since she and Bastian had fled the smoking ruins of the camp of their people, breaking through to this strange realm on a terrifying burst of magic she still didn't understand. Rowan could comprehend the blinding flash that had thrown them from their own realm of Coracin into Earth no better than she could the horrible fate that had befallen their people. All she knew was that it was undeserved. And that whatever fault there was lay with her.

The Dyadd Morgaine were Drakkyn sorceresses who took little for their own and wielded their power wisely, holding court beneath the endless canopy of their forests and accepting the offerings of those who revered them. They had done nothing but what the Goddess had asked of them, to look after the Orinn villagers who had no magic of their own to protect themselves, often from one another. Now her mother, sisters, aunts were gone, borne away on leathery wings of death or fled in terror to who-knew-where. All because they would belong to no man.

But in truth, because *she* had refused to belong to a hateful *one*.

Lucien Andrakkar. May the Goddess curse you wherever you walk.

Rowan shed her hot pants in a series of fluid movements, then spun across the stage in her matching G-string, trying to escape the sudden swell of revulsion and anger within her. She'd gotten good at blocking it out, the black rage at the Drakkyn shifter who, with his blind lust, had stolen everything from her. Still, it seeped through from time to time, threatening her hard-won control over her emotions.

Her life on what these humans called Earth had been a carefully cultivated façade of apathy. Fortunately, that seemed to suit the so-called *vampires* who had taken her and Bastian in just fine. The pain, the crushing grief from that night had been buried deep in a place she could not touch. If she did, Rowan feared that the one her mother had called *Little Flame* would consume herself and everything around her in the blaze of her own fury. Instead, she played along, dancing for the pleasure of the weak, turning a blind eye to the perverse appetites of the Earthly vampires, and praying to the Goddess Morgaine that she and Bastian would soon be returned to their own world.

Returned… and granted vengeance.

Unsettled, distracted, she allowed yet another sweaty admirer near enough to slip a twenty under the thin strap riding her hipbone. He let his chubby fingers linger over-long against the smooth skin of her thigh, giving a tentative stroke to what wasn't his to touch. Rowan whipped her head around in a flash of temper and hissed, baring razor-sharp incisors.

He loved it.

She meant it.

The offending fingers were removed, but by now Rowan recognized that the slight tremor in the man's hands had nothing to do with fear and everything to do with unmitigated lust. He would touch her again in a heartbeat given the chance. She knew it, and her mood shot straight to potentially violent. It was that more than anything, the utter lack of respect accorded her by the males of this realm, that had her once-famous temper on an increasingly short leash these days. Well, she grudgingly admitted, that and the fact that she was so blood-starved at this point that she probably couldn't blow a leaf across a street, much less defeat the army of winged reptiles who certainly awaited her return in her own realm. But either way, every night it got harder to let the little things go.

Just as it got harder not to simply give up and put the fangs everyone here assumed were fake to good use. Rowan took a great deal of pride in her discipline. But she was so *hungry*.

Again, she wished for the freedom dancing had once brought her. Back when she had moved to the wild music of pipes and drums beneath different stars, a different moon. When blood had been something given in homage, taken and offered with love and honor.

Not coerced or stolen, ripped from the necks of the deluded, frightened, or simply unwilling. She had not been able to take what was not freely given, though she had tried. But instead of the warm flow of life, all she'd been able to taste was sick, nauseating fear. Her refusal to drink for many months now infuriated Bastian, and though it was not his place to question her, she could understand. She saw it every time she looked in a mirror, her loss of strength from this slow starvation. Yet though she had lost almost everything, she still had both principle and pride.

She only hoped they would not end up being all she had left.

Rowan shook her head to clear it, hating herself for letting the same old things interfere while she was performing. She would be blank, uncaring. She would do what must be done until there was another option.

I will control my temper. I will not bite. I will not cause any of the nice people to burst into flames. I WILL control my temper...

Just then she caught a flash of something, a familiar

face materializing in the haze beyond the stage as it pushed through the crowd. She continued to move to the beat as she tried to get a better look, craning her neck as her long fingers began to work at the scarlet ribbon that held her corset together. The face vanished, then reappeared. Electric blue eyes caught her own, and held while the mouth frantically repeated the same words over and over again.

Rowan paused, letting the ribbon fall. *Bastian?* What was her brother doing here? He made a point of avoiding the club at all times, since the one time he'd taken her to work had nearly caused a riot among the other dancers. Rowan hated to admit it, but her brother was almost as pretty as she was. He might be odd in that he was the only male ever known to have been born into her tribe, but his looks held the same startling perfection as all Dyadd. Bastian's looks were ice to her fire. Just as his temperament was the still, deep pool to her raging tempest. Though none of her tribe would ever admit to being dependent on a man, Rowan knew that without Bastian's unwavering calm and reason to cling to, she would have been utterly lost these last months. He was all she had.

And the only thing that could have brought him here tonight had Rowan's stomach clenching with sick dread. She watched the words he formed once more, just to be certain.

Outside. Run. NOW.

Rowan gave a faint nod, feeling glued in place for precious seconds as Bastian struggled against the sea of people to get to her. When the crowd only shoved him back, he repeated himself even more emphatically, then shot a sharp glance at the front entrance. Her eyes went there as well, and the senses she'd had to suppress just to exist here unfurled like the petals of some dark flower. Suddenly she could feel the power gathering somewhere just beyond, out there in the night. She swallowed, hard, with a throat that had become as dry as sand. And despite the raucous noise in the club, the jeers now directed at her as the music continued, her ears picked up a sound that kicked her heart into such a quick beat it might have flown out of her chest.

Thunder. A storm. Oh, by the Goddess, no.

She snapped into action then, moving at a speed not remotely human. Rowan snatched up her discarded shorts and raced from the stage so quickly that for most, a blink found her vanished. It was bound to cause talk. It would possibly get her fired. And none of that mattered now, she thought as she burst through the back door of the club. After all these months of relative safety, she and Bastian had been found. The dragons had come for her once again.

But this time she had no idea where to run.

About the Author

Kendra Leigh Castle started out stealing her mother's romance novels and eventually progressed to writing her own. She brings her love of all things spooky and steamy to her writing and firmly believes that creatures of the night deserve happily-ever-afters, too. When not curled up with her laptop and yet another cup of coffee, Kendra keeps busy in Maryland with her husband, three children, and menagerie of high-maintenance pets. For news of upcoming novels, or just to drop her a note (she loves to hear from readers!), visit her online at www. kendraleighcastle.com.